55

D0210756

DATE DUE

A MURDER

OF PROMISE

Also by Robert Andrews

A Murder of Honor

The Towers

Death in a Promised Land

Last Spy Out

Center Game

A Marian Wood Book

Published by G. P. Putnam's Sons
a member of Penguin Putnam Inc.
New York

A MURDER
OF PROMISE

ROBERT + ANDREWS

A MURDER

This is a work of fiction. Names, characters, places, and incidents either are
the product of the author's imagination or are used fictitiously, and any
resemblance to actual persons, living or dead, business establishments,
events, or locales is entirely coincidental.

A Marian Wood Book
Published by G. P. Putnam's Sons
Publishers Since 1838
a member of
Penguin Putnam Inc.
375 Hudson Street
New York, NY 10014

Library of Congress Cataloging-in-Publication Data

Andrews, Robert, date.
A murder of promise / Robert Andrews.
p.   cm.
"A Marian Wood book."
ISBN 0-399-14832-9
1. Washington, D.C.—Fiction.   2. Police—Washington (D.C.)—
Fiction.   3. Washington (D.C.)—Fiction.   I. Title.
PS3551.N4524 M89   2002   2001031935
813'.54—dc21

Printed in the United States of America
1   3   5   7   9   10   8   6   4   2

This book is printed on acid-free paper. ∞

Book design by Judith Stagnitto Abbate

Thanks to four who made this book:
friend and former neighbor Roz Ridgway for the spark;
District of Columbia Metropolitan Police Department detective
    Michael Farish for his patient instruction;
Robin Rue of Writers House for her skillful and cheerful agenting;
and Marian Wood for her humor and support, and the magic of her
    pencil work.

For Boo, Julia, and Robert—
my pride and promise

Every life is a promise.

ANONYMOUS

A MURDER

OF PROMISE

✠ **M**onday morning, October 16, 2000. Lilith Hoagland burrowed deeper under the comforter to get away from Figaro, who was nuzzling her neck.

His tongue grazed her cheek.

She sat up.

"All right, damnit," she said.

Twenty minutes later, Figaro cocked his right leg, urinated on the Eislers' boxwood next door, scratched at the brick sidewalk, then leaned into his leash, eager for his morning walk.

Sunrise in the Georgetown enclave of Washington, D.C. Last night's front had brought an invigorating chill and the promise of a clear, blue autumn sky. Hoagland held Figaro's leash in one hand, and in the other an insulated coffee mug. She felt like a long walk. And Figaro, an English pug, hadn't seen his pal Blackberry, a Portuguese water dog, in some time. So, she decided, they would go to the park.

Figaro sniffed and peed his way up the hill toward R Street, while Hoagland sipped her coffee and enjoyed the early-morning luxury of thinking about nothing in particular. Suddenly, a violent tugging on the leash snapped Hoagland out of her reverie. The small dog had disappeared into a tall hedge.

"Come here." She yanked at the leash.

Figaro whined and struggled farther into the hedge.

A cat or a squirrel, Hoagland thought.

Until she saw the blood on Figaro's muzzle.

✝ Franklin Delano Kearney and Josephus Adams Phelps looked down at the dead woman. Ten yards away, the woman who'd found the body stood on the sidewalk with the two uniformed officers who'd secured the scene. Forty-five minutes earlier, just after daybreak, her dog had followed a blood trail to the base of a giant sycamore, at the edge of the small park.

"Used a big blade," José said. He pointed. "Look here."

Frank walked around to stand by José. He bent closer to look at the woman's right hand. A victim's hands frequently got cut up trying to fend off a knife assault. Bone-deep gashes had laid the palm open. The little finger was missing.

Frank stared at the body, ticking over cases in his mind. Like a roulette ball, the names dropped into place. *Coleman and Janowitz.*

"Coleman and Janowitz? Didn't they . . . ?"

"Greek in the Creek," José said.

"Boukedes . . . Sarah . . . no, Susan," Frank corrected himself. Coleman and Janowitz had gotten the case two months before. White female. Hacked to death in Rock Creek Park. Defensive wounds to both hands. He got a tightening in his throat.

"Wasn't she missing a finger?" he heard José asking. He pulled air deep into his lungs and tried to shut out everything but here and now. He looked at the dead woman's face.

"Sort of familiar."

"Don't see how you can tell," José said.

Twenty-five years ago, there hadn't been many white-black partners on the District force. When Frank and José teamed up, everybody called them Salt and Pepper. Today it was unremarkable, and besides, no one dared talk that way anymore. Both were tall men, over six feet. Frank's dark auburn hair had grayed along the temples and José's close-cut nappy curls had turned a rich silver. Otherwise, both looked pretty much like their academy graduation photos: Frank the lean cross-country runner, José the heavyweight boxer. Both now were the most senior homicide detectives in Washington, D.C.'s Metropolitan Police Department.

Frank squatted low, taking care to avoid the blood-splattered leaves. The victim lay partially over her purse. He lifted the body enough to free the purse. Snapping it open, he found a key ring: two Schlage house keys and Volvo car keys. Then a billfold: three twenties, a ten, a five, and several ones. Behind a plastic window in the billfold, a District driver's license.

He looked up at José. "Mary Keegan," he said.

A nod of recognition. "Oh."

Frank looked back at the dead woman and tried to find a resemblance to the face he remembered. A regular on the Sunday talk shows. One of the best of the *Washington Post's* legendary investigative reporters. Mary Keegan, the scourge of shady dealmakers in the White House and on Capitol Hill, winner of a Pulitzer for her exposés of government malfeasance and corporate corruption. Good-looking in an honest, straightforward way. High cheekbones, subtle makeup, ash-blond shoulder-length hair. Frank checked the date of birth. September 3, 1958. Forty-two years old. Moderately famous and probably moderately well-off. At least she had been. Now she was just dead.

"Sixteen seventy-three Thirty-second," he read the address off the license. He placed the address. East of Wisconsin Avenue—Georgetown's East Village. A block down from Dumbarton Oaks. Six, seven blocks from his home on Olive. He recalled seeing her occasionally, the inevitable crossings in a small town. Joking with Steve at Potomac

Wines and Spirits. Picking up dry-cleaning at Uptown Valet. Buying stamps at the post office. Walking on late-summer evenings.

"Stabbed her first near the sidewalk," Frank said, looking back to where the woman and her dog stood with the officers. "She got away . . ."

"She got here," José continued. "He catches up with her. Stabs her in the back. She turns . . ."

". . . and he finishes the job."

"Last night sometime."

Frank studied the ruined face, trying to imagine it without the gaping wound below the left eye, the slashed throat. Trying to see her as she'd been yesterday this time. Maybe at church. Or a Sunday brunch with friends. A drive in the country. But alive. No idea of what was to come. Who she'd meet here.

"You know how this's going to go, don't you?" José asked.

Frank nodded. Mary Keegan might not be a household name, but she was known by a lot of people who were.

Early in his career, Frank had learned that Washington politics, like an overhead fan, was always turning. He imagined the fan picking up speed. Who was it, he wondered, who'd come up with the image of crap hitting the fan?

"Emerson's going to shit a brick."

"No doubt." Frank got a sour taste on the flat of his tongue, as if he'd bitten a penny. What got him about a high-profile case wasn't the pressure—the incessant phone calls, starting with Randolph Emerson, Homicide commander, and running all the way up the so-called chain of command—it was the time you had to waste hand-holding, answering the calls, sending up reports you'd already sent up before. Time you could be spending doing the job you were paid for, the job you signed on to do. He stood up, took a deep breath, and let his eyes wander over the park, searching out a world where there wasn't a dead woman on the ground and leaves covered with her blood.

Half an hour later, Tony Upton, the medical examiner, arrived, at the same time as Renfro Calkins and his forensics team. An hour after that, Frank released the body to Upton. The two detectives waited until they were satisfied Forensics was on track, then walked to the curb where they'd parked the car.

"You want to walk?" Frank asked. "Only a couple of blocks."

"Couple of blocks?" José frowned. "We walk a couple over, we got to walk a couple back. Couple blocks here, couple blocks there—"

"—and they begin to add up to some real distance," Frank finished.

The two detectives walked down Q Street and crossed Wisconsin, where the morning traffic from the Maryland suburbs was already starting to clog the avenue.

"You still bringing him home tomorrow?" José asked.

"Yeah."

"How's he taking it, coming in to stay with you?"

"What do you think?"

"It's only for a little while."

"He suspects it's the first step to moving him into town."

"He's what . . . seventy-five? -six . . . ?"

"Seventy-eight."

José shook his head. "Not good, living out there by himself."

"Too old to be alone . . . stubborn man."

"Something about 'Like father, like son,' " José said.

"I think I've heard that."

"He looked good last month."

Last month had been a hundred years ago. Before the call at two in the morning. His father's voice, choking over words that wouldn't come out right.

"It was a warning. He might not be so lucky next time."

✝ Mary Keegan's home on 32nd Street and scores of others like it made Georgetown Georgetown: a two-story red-brick Federal town house, white ornamental detailing around windows with rippling glass panes that had looked out on cobblestone streets two hundred years before.

Georgetown's years as a major colonial port still shape the village's geography. Shops and businesses line M Street and run down to the waterfront. The residential area begins with modest row houses just above M. It crests on R Street with Montrose Park, Dumbarton Oaks estate, and the homes of Washington's power elite and the B-list pilot fish slipstreaming in their wake.

Frank lived just a block off M Street. Fifteen years ago, coming out of the divorce, he'd bought "as is" a crumbling little house on Olive Street. He'd stayed longer than he'd intended. He'd gotten attached to Georgetown. He felt more at home in the quirky, human-scale village than in downtown monumental Washington. Now the place on Olive had a dry basement, a sound roof, and fifteen years of sweat labor invested in plumbing, wiring, and plastering, not to mention refinishing floors, revamping AC and heating, and stripping layers of paint from wood paneling.

Now, as he stood in front of Mary Keegan's house, the brick walls glowed in the autumn sun's slanting light, and October's yellows and reds flared against a sky so blue it seemed to go into forever.

"Nice place," José said.

"Yeah."

"Washington does fall good," José said as they climbed the steps to the front door.

"Too bad it doesn't last longer." Frank rapped sharply with the heavy brass door knocker.

Down the street a painter rattled an extension ladder into place against a house front.

"Nothing going on inside," José said.

Frank knocked again, and waited.

After a moment, José shook his head. "Nobody home."

Both men snapped on latex gloves. Frank fished Mary Keegan's key from a Ziploc. The key turned smoothly as the heavy deadbolt fell back. Frank eased the door open. The two men stepped inside and stood motionless in the entryway, as if trying to get a sense of the house through the pores in their skin.

Frank identified the acid tang of tomato and under it the licorice of fennel and the solid blue-collar richness of garlic. Soft sounds of a flute solo came from somewhere in the depths of the house.

José touched Frank's shoulder. "Alarm," he said, nodding toward a keypad panel on the wall. A red light glowed steadily, accompanied by a low buzzing sound.

Frank flicked open his cell phone and dialed the security service number on the panel. The phone rang once, twice, three times.

"Somebody's still asleep," Frank said.

The red light now blinked angrily. Somewhere in the house above, a siren opened up with a howl. Finally, a dull voice answered. Frank gave the shut down code that the District-licensed commercial security companies supposedly recognized. The voice at the other end sounded confused and put Frank on hold. The siren now switched to a braying klaxon.

Through the open door, Frank watched a patrol car pull up to the curb, its light bar blazing blue and red. A woman darted from a home across the street to the car and pointed to Mary Keegan's house.

José, flashing his badge, met the uniformed officers at the door. At that moment the alarm shut off.

"Thank God," Frank said, looking over Jose's shoulder.

The woman who'd run out into the street stood on the sidewalk at the foot of the Keegan house steps, hands on hips. Slender, with short, well-cut gray hair. Camel-hair jacket, white silk blouse, red patterned silk scarf, dark gray flannel pants. Very neat. Very Georgetown. Mid-sixties, Frank guessed. She turned to leave. Frank edged past José and the uniformed cops.

"A minute, ma'am?" Frank called out.

"Me?"

Frank walked closer. He opened his badge case. "I'm Lieutenant Kearney, and this's my partner, Lieutenant Phelps."

"I've seen you," the woman said, looking at him as if trying to place him somewhere else.

"I live down on Olive, ma'am."

"They had a fire down there several weeks back."

"Two doors up."

"You have any damage?"

Frank shook his head. "Smell of smoke. Lucky, I guess. You live over there?" He pointed across the street to the white-brick duplex.

"Fifty years." She tilted her chin up. "Husband came here with Harry Truman."

Seventies, Frank thought, adjusting his estimate of her age.

She extended a delicate hand. A large diamond flared blue-white in the sun. "I'm Judith Barnes. Is there trouble?"

"We have an emergency involving Ms. Keegan," Frank said.

Barnes searched Frank's face. "She's in trouble."

"We need some information. Can we step inside?" Frank asked, nodding toward Mary Keegan's open door.

Barnes hesitated, then nodded. Frank stood aside. Judith Barnes entered the house and led the way into the living room. José closed the door and joined Frank and Barnes across the room.

Barnes looked around the room, started to sit, then changed her mind. She looked sternly at Frank and José.

Frank began. "Mrs.—"

"Just a damned minute, Officer." Barnes held up a hand. "*You* tell *me* just what's happened."

A moment's hesitation, then Frank said, "She's dead."

Barnes's hand flew to her throat.

"How?" she asked in a strangled voice.

"We can't say yet, ma'am."

"Murdered?" Barnes's eyes widened. "But it *was* murder?"

"It looks like it."

Barnes sagged into a chair, shut her eyes, and hugged herself. "Murder," she repeated in a disbelieving whisper. She silently shook her head, then looked up at Frank and José. "You need information," she said, her voice picking up strength.

"Did you see Ms. Keegan yesterday?" José asked.

"Yes. I'm the block's nosy old maid, gentlemen," Barnes said. "I see a lot."

"Tell us when you last saw Ms. Keegan yesterday," Frank said.

"When she came back from her run. She went out just after four in the afternoon. She came back around five."

"Her running," Frank asked, "a regular thing?"

"You could set your watch by her. She was a disciplined woman. If her alarm hadn't gone off, I would have come over this morning, anyway."

"Why?"

"It's Monday. She's usually up and out by now. But her car's still there." Barnes made a head motion toward the cars parked along the street.

José made a note. "She drove it yesterday?"

"Grocery shopping. Two, two-thirty. I'd just come back from a friend's. We waved to each other. Didn't say anything, though. I saw her through my kitchen window when she went out to run. As I said, that was just after four."

"Do you know of any relatives?" Frank asked.

"There's Damien, her brother. He lives in Boston."

"Parents?"

"Both dead."

"She was single?"

Barnes fell silent. As if hit by the second wave of realization of Mary Keegan's death.

"Married once," Barnes picked up. "I never met him. They lived up Wisconsin, near the cathedral. She bought this place after his death. That's when I met her, ten years ago."

"You've met the brother?"

"Oh, yes. Mary introduced us several years ago. A splendid young man. I have his phone number. When Mary travels, she leaves the key with me and asks that I call Damien if anything happens."

"Has anything ever happened?" José asked.

"Not until now."

"How about when Ms. Keegan was here? Anything unusual happen?"

Barnes frowned at Frank for a moment, then shook her head. "She was a good neighbor. No parties. Perhaps some people over for dinner occasionally. She wasn't terribly social. I saw the light on in her study"— Barnes pointed to the ceiling—"she worked late at night quite frequently. I've read all her articles, books. She wrote well. It's hard to find young people these days who can write a simple declarative sentence."

"Any regular visitors?" José asked.

"*Men,* you mean?"

"Men will do."

Barnes shook her head. "Nobody in particular. I mean, it wasn't as if there were a lot of . . . that there was *any* . . . promiscuity. She had some men friends." Barnes pursed her lips as if she'd stepped in something disagreeable and wanted to get away from it. "Mary Keegan was very much her own woman."

"You'd know," Frank asked, "if there was any one man in particular?"

"I'd *know,* Lieutenant. Despite our age differential, we had gotten quite close."

"Any recent men visitors?" José asked.

"Well . . ." Barnes seemed to be weighing her response. "Yes. One gentleman."

"Did you know him?"

"No."

"Did you and Ms. Keegan talk about him?" Frank asked.

"No."

Frank keyed in on Barnes's guarded tone. He glanced at José. José had picked up on it, too.

"What did he look like?" José asked.

Barnes hesitated. Her look said she realized she'd said too much and had been left with nowhere to go but forward.

"Ma'am," José said softly, "she's dead and we have to find who killed her."

Barnes drew herself up.

"He was black." She blurted, eyes straight ahead. Then she looked at José and blushed, raising a hand to her mouth. "I mean," she stammered, "African-American."

"A black male African-American," José said, keeping a straight face.

"Tall. Well dressed," Barnes added.

"How often did he come calling?"

Barnes mouth tightened. "I wouldn't describe it as 'calling.'"

"How often did you see him?" Frank asked.

"Several times."

"When was the last time you saw him?"

"Last month sometime."

"Any specific date stick in your mind?"

Barnes frowned in concentration, then shook her head. "I'm sorry . . ."

"Car?"

Barnes thought. "A Buick, I think. Gray. Very conservative."

"Did Ms. Keegan ever mention him?"

"No."

"You never asked her?"

Barnes frowned. "Of course not."

"Did she ever talk about enemies?"

"Enemies? That sounds rather melodramatic, Lieutenant."

"People difficulties, then."

"There were people who didn't like what she wrote. But they had only themselves to blame."

"How do you mean?"

"I mean that Mary Keegan discovered the truth and wrote about it. There are people in this town who have a congenital aversion to the truth."

José asked, "She ever mention any of them as problems?"

"No. None that I can recall. It was as if she kept those kinds of matters in another room. Another compartment. Separate from her personal life."

Frank glanced at the mantel clock. It was nine forty-five. It felt later. "You said you have Ms. Keegan's brother's phone number?"

Barnes stood. "I'll fetch it."

Frank and José walked her to the door and watched her cross the street. Frank turned and looked back into the house. He knew the layout. Not this particular house. But enough of ones like it. Straight back from the entry, the hallway would run toward a rear courtyard with living room, dining room, and kitchen off to the right. To Frank's immediate left the stairway to the second floor. Upstairs he'd find a bedroom at the back, looking down on the courtyard, a bathroom, and a second bedroom at the front, overlooking the street.

Frank glanced appreciatively around the orderly kitchen. Mary Keegan hadn't scrimped on the renovation. Sub-Zero fridge, Viking range, Miele dishwasher. A small fortune on English cabinets. Lustrous terra-cotta tile floors and creamy soapstone countertops. A small wine rack held a Merlot and a Shiraz that Frank recognized and several Chiantis he didn't.

Upstairs, the front bedroom had been turned into a study. Bookcases and cabinets built into three walls. A stereo was tuned to WGMS. Something by Bach replaced the flute solo they'd heard on entering. One of the Brandenburg concertos, Frank thought, but he wasn't sure which one. An easy chair with a floor lamp faced a small fireplace. A large antique walnut desk paired off with a credenza that ran under the windows. On the credenza, a computer. Keegan had left it on, and as Frank watched, a rendering of Monet's water lilies morphed into a scene of a town on a river. Frank nudged the mouse. The screensaver vanished, its place taken by several columns of numbers.

José glanced over Frank's shoulder. "Refugees," he read.

"Looks like a research paper of some kind," Frank said. Index cards had been neatly laid out on the credenza next to the computer keyboard. He glanced at the top card. "German," he said.

Frank turned away from the credenza. Mary Keegan had kept a neat desk. A brass banker's lamp, a leather-edged blotter, and an appointment calendar.

Only one entry for Sunday, the fifteenth. At seven P.M., a handwritten annotation, "1789."

"Seven o'clock last night," Frank read. "1789."

"Meaning?" José asked.

"Down on Thirty-sixth and Prospect, the restaurant."

"Walking distance."

And the park where Mary Keegan had been murdered lay halfway between her house and the restaurant.

A gleam of silver behind a stack of books caught Frank's eye. He held up an antique picture frame. Keegan stood beside a man. She wore a summer dress. She was smiling and looking at ease. For an instant, a screen flickered behind Frank's eyes, a TV clip—Keegan in talk-show banter, then the Keegan in the park. He switched focus to the man in the photo. He was dark-haired, ten, fifteen years older than Keegan. He had the fine bones of good breeding offset by a thickening along the jawline. Beneath the smile, Frank detected a world weariness; a man who'd seen a lot and wasn't eager to see more. In the background, the Eiffel Tower.

"That's her."

"Probably her husband," José said.

Frank put the picture back. He worked through the desk drawers. The expected home office supplies. In the large bottom drawer on the right side of the desk, file folders neatly tabbed with cryptic notations.

He walked around the room, scanning the books and mementos on the floor-to-ceiling shelves. Keegan had been a serious reader, he concluded. The Romans—Juvenal, Seneca, the Plinys Elder and Younger—nestled against Freud, Schopenhauer, Marx, and Engels. Two shelves filled with Churchill's works and a bronze bust of the bulldog prime minister. Government Printing Office collections of presidential papers, reports on world trade, United Nations references on population, food, and energy. Fiction, too. Her taste ran from Elmore Leonard through Cormac McCarthy to Thomas Hardy and Henry James.

By the window, a framed photograph caught Frank's eye. Richard Nixon stood in the Oval Office, handing a book to a young girl. Frank recognized the girl's smile. Nixon wore a shifty look, as if caught at the border of a forbidden act. Mary Keegan looked like she owned the office and Nixon was her visitor. The inscription across the photo was standard Washington boilerplate: a best regards, a signature, and a date: "June, 1971."

Frank looked out the window, down onto the street. A nanny pushed a stroller along the sidewalk. Where'd he been in '71? Returning to College Park, Maryland, a twenty-two-year-old sophomore. Coming back to UMD after a year in Vietnam and a year getting over Vietnam. And Mary Frances Keegan had been thirty miles away in the White House getting a book from Richard Nixon. And now she was dead and he was standing in her house looking out the window. On the opposite sidewalk, a big black Lab, strained at its leash, pulling its human, a slender, white-haired man, from tree to tree. Who owned who, Frank wondered.

Frank glanced at his watch. By now, Tony Upton would be checking the body into the morgue.

The thought came to him that, outside this house, people were going about their lives, lives shaped and influenced by their connection to Mary Keegan. Her brother. Friends and maybe lovers. And, despite what Judith Barnes thought, enemies: this was Washington and Mary Keegan hadn't been a person to spare the pen.

Tony would photograph the corpse, take DNA samples, and lift a set of prints. And then the woman who'd lived in this house yesterday would never return here but would be laid out on a tray and rolled into a locker in the body cooler.

And the word would spread of Mary Keegan's death. And Washington's network would buzz. And then the connections would bypass the void. And people would readjust their lives and move on. And leave Mary Keegan in a fast-receding past.

Down below, the street was empty. The nanny with her stroller and the Lab with his white-haired man had disappeared.

Suddenly, like a camera shutter closing and opening, Frank was no longer thinking about Mary Keegan. Now he was looking at a mental picture of the dark outlines of the killer. Like the silhouette target at a pistol range. He heard recorded voices. He turned around. José was making notes of calls left on the answering machine. He waited until José had finished.

José closed his notebook and put it in his pocket. "1789?"

"1789."

. . .

✛ Frank knocked on the locked door. He waited and knocked again.

"They keep pretty good hours," José said. "Maybe we ought to go into the restaurant business."

"Policing's safer," Frank said. He knocked again.

Finally a pale face materialized out of the dark interior of the restaurant and mouthed the word "closed." A small, stocky man in a shirt and tie shook his head and started to turn away.

Frank held up his badge.

✛ "Mary Keegan?" Marcel Dubois, 1789's manager, nodded. "She's a regular."

"Was she here last night?" Frank asked.

"I wasn't," Dubois said. "We can check the reservations." He led them back to the maître d's station and opened a leather-bound ledger.

"Around seven o'clock," José prompted.

"I hope there's no trouble," Dubois said, trolling while running his finger down the Sunday dinner page. He looked up, and when Frank and José didn't say anything, he turned his attention back to the reservations.

Dubois shook his head. "No reservation in Ms. Keegan's name." Before Frank could say anything, Dubois raised a manicured hand. "But . . . she is listed as an expected guest."

"Whose guest?" Frank asked.

"The Honorable David Trevor." Dubois said it with the lofty majesty of a DAR dowager. As if to make certain Frank and José appreciated the importance of David Trevor and the glory his presence reflected on his restaurant, Dubois added, "He is deputy secretary of state." And as if that weren't enough, "He is Madeleine Albright's deputy."

"Thank you for telling us who the Honorable David Trevor is, Mr. Dubois," Frank said dryly. "Now, can you tell me if he was here with Ms. Keegan?"

Dubois examined the ledger. "There's a line through his name. We do that to show that the guest arrived. He claimed his reservation shortly before seven." He bent closer to the book. "But there's no line through her name."

"Trevor," José said, "can you tell when he left?"

Dubois thought for a moment, then snapped his fingers. "Last night's checks are in the office."

Ten minutes later, Dubois handed Frank a restaurant check. Stapled to it, a credit card charge slip. David S. Trevor had been billed for a bottle of San Pellegrino and a glass of Chardonnay. He had paid with an American Express card, leaving a three-dollar tip on the twelve-dollar charge. The check had been closed out at 7:43 P.M.

✠ It struck Frank that standing outside 1789 was like standing outside an eighteenth-century tavern. But then, look across the Potomac at Rosslyn and the glass-and-aluminum towers of *USA Today* and you fast-forward a couple of centuries. He turned away from Rosslyn to José.

"If we want to cover our asses, we'll sit down with Randolph before we go talk with the Honorable David Trevor," Frank said.

"On the other hand," José said, "we drop that in Randolph's lap, we'll have to sit there while he agonizes about you and me pissing off the establishment. And we end up talking to the Honorable Mr. Trevor, anyway."

Frank nodded. "Yeah," he said. "Let's save poor Randolph the agony."

TWO

✠ Frank found a parking space behind the Federal Reserve building on C Street. As he locked the car, he surveyed the State Department headquarters. A graceless, pale, pinkish-gray granite shoebox a block long. Eight parallel rows of rectangular shutterless windows down the length of the building reminded Frank of one of those old computer punch cards. He'd seen better-looking prisons. Sometime back, he'd decided that if he ever got the choice of three buildings in the District he could demolish, State would be one of them, along with the Kennedy Center, and the FBI building.

Security check-in took fifteen minutes, interspersed with multiple phone calls and repeated examinations of credentials. After a dead space of another five minutes, a plainclothes security officer appeared, issued Frank and José visitor badges, and escorted them to the seventh floor.

They followed the security officer down a corridor to a uniformed guard at a desk beside a pair of massive doors. Their escort waved, electronics buzzed, and the doors opened.

"Treaty Room," said the escort.

It was an attractive room at odds with the sterile exterior of the building: large and richly detailed, gilt-framed portraits, colonial blue walls accented with moldings in white, all set off by exquisite parquet floors and museum-quality Federal-era antiques.

Frank recognized the room: the secretary of state would march down the carpeted corridor toward the gathered guns of the TV and print media, mount the podium emblazoned with the State Department's fierce crest, and do battle with smart-ass Washington reporters.

The small expedition traversed the Treaty Room and filed down the secretary of state's carpeted corridor. The escort officer angled to the right and opened the door to an executive suite. A handsome silver-haired woman sat at a delicate French period desk. She nodded to the escort officer, who led Frank and José to a cluster of stiff-backed Victorian chairs.

Frank thumbed through a *Foreign Affairs* issue. He tried to get interested in an article intriguingly titled "The One Percent Solution." Two paragraphs in, it became clear that the solution wasn't a solution, but a problem. The problem being that the State Department needed a bigger budget. It didn't sound to Frank like anything to stop the presses for. Every government organization always needed a bigger budget. Every year.

Trevor's assistant answered her phone, listened briefly, and hung up. "The secretary will see you now," she announced.

The escort officer put down his copy of *Newsweek* and walked Frank and José past Trevor's assistant down a short passageway. On one side, an elevator, on the other, a small breakfront chest in which a delicate porcelain tea service glowing under the light from skillfully hidden lamps. Ming dynasty, Frank guessed. At the end of the passageway, the escort officer knocked once and then opened the door. Frank and José entered. Their escort stayed outside, closing the door behind them.

Four windows lined the right side of the room, bookcases the left. In front of the windows, a large seating arrangement of chairs and small sofas. Burled walnut panels covered walls not taken up by bookcases and windows.

David Trevor sat at his desk at the end of the long office. He was on the phone. Seeing the two men enter, he raised his free hand in a "Just a moment" gesture, then pointed toward the chairs and sofas by the windows.

A large armchair, its back to the windows, looked as if it would be

Trevor's. So Frank took a facing chair, and José the one adjacent. Frank made out only bits and pieces of Trevor's conversation. Something to do with the fallout from a conference in Oklahoma. Or Okinawa. Trevor stayed on the phone. Just as Frank began to wonder if he and José shouldn't wait outside, Trevor hung up with an audible sigh and got up from his desk.

Frank's first impression of Trevor was of England and English breeding: double-breasted gray houndstooth-check suit, blue-and-white-striped shirt with a spread white collar and precisely knotted burgundy tie. Bankers' lace-up shoes polished to a modest sheen. Medium height and slender build, Trevor carried himself with the balanced assurance of a gymnast. He was bald. It fit him. Frank thought he would have looked odd with hair. Perfectly proportioned eyes, nose, mouth, and ears complemented a lean, smoothly oval face. The kind of face you saw in Schweppes ads, looking out from under a polo helmet.

Frank and José stood as Trevor approached. He offered his hand to Frank.

"I am David Trevor." Trevor had a clear tenor voice, one that would carry well singing in a choir or a bar.

Frank took the hand. The wiry strength surprised him. "Lieutenant Kearney."

Trevor nodded as if remembering Frank's name was important. He shook hands with José with the same intense concentration.

Frank reached for his badge and credentials. Trevor waved him off.

"I'm certain you've pulled those out enough, getting up here. How can I help you?"

"We're investigating the death of Mary Frances Keegan," Frank said. "We understand the two of you were to have dinner last night."

Trevor's composure shattered. He stood as if frozen, then, wordlessly, waved Frank and José to be seated. His knees appeared to buckle as he slumped into the chair Frank had guessed would be his. He sat, staring through Frank.

"Her body was found early this morning," Frank said.

"My God." Trevor ran a hand across his eyes. "What happened?"

"It appears she was stabbed to death," José said.

Trevor's energy drained. "Stabbed? I can't believe . . ." He shook his head in disbelief. "Last night . . . she never showed up." He looked from Frank to José. "We were to meet at 1789—"

"She was supposed to meet you there?" José asked.

"Yes. Walk down from her house."

"What time did you get to the restaurant?" Frank asked.

"A little before seven. It wasn't like her to be late. I waited for half an hour. Maybe a few minutes more. Then I left."

"You didn't call her from the restaurant?" José asked.

"No. Not right away. She lived close by. So I drove by her place. Rang the bell. Nothing. Then I drove back here. Around nine or so I called her and got her answering machine."

"You came here?" Frank asked. "Last night?"

Trevor gestured toward his desk. "Weekends are often the only time I can catch up on paperwork. This, unfortunately, is anything but a nine-to-five job."

"The dinner with Ms. Keegan . . . social?"

Trevor appeared not to hear. He stared into the distance as if trying to fit new puzzle pieces into an old and familiar picture.

"Yes and no," he said slowly. "You see, I've known . . . I *knew* Mary for twelve years. We met in Moscow when the *Post* sent her there in 1988. I was the embassy's political officer at the time. We got to be friends. But the relationship's always had a business side to it as well. Mary was a good conduit for information we wanted to make public. And now . . . now she was writing a book about my father and me."

"Charles Trevor," Frank said. Vague memories of John Kennedy and the men who came with him to Washington. A resignation some time later having to do with the war. "He's still alive?"

"Very much so, though that may surprise a lot of people," Trevor said. "But to Mary's book: she'd been working on it for about a year. We would meet occasionally for an interview or to discuss an issue that had arisen."

"The last time you saw her?"

"Here." Trevor pointed toward the chairs where Frank and José sat. "September. I can check the logs . . ."

"We can get the exact date later. How would you characterize her? Was she anxious? Frightened?"

Trevor stroked his chin. "Well, Mary was a writer . . ." he said, and let it hang there.

"And that means . . . ?" José asked.

"I haven't known a writer yet who wasn't a nail-biter," Trevor said with a sardonic smile. "I think you have to be that way before you can write. I don't suppose," he added patronizingly, "that you've read her."

"Just *A Door into Hell* and *The Fall*," Frank said.

"Oh," said Trevor, slightly taken aback, "then you know how meticulous she is—was."

"Do you know anybody she was afraid of?" José asked.

Trevor smiled sadly and shook his head. "I think she feared God . . . no one else. You read *A Door into Hell*," Trevor said to Frank, "you can imagine what she went through to get the material for that. She was a tough, tough lady."

"Did she ever say anything that would lead you to believe that she felt in danger?"

"No," Trevor said emphatically. "Absolutely not."

Frank glanced at José. José shook his head. Frank stood and handed Trevor his card. "Office and home phone numbers. If your assistant could get us the date and time of that last meeting . . . ?"

✠ In the car, José searched his notebook. He found the entry he wanted. "Matches what I got off her answering machine. Message: 'Hello, Mary. This is David. It's nine-fifteen. I guess we missed connections tonight. Please call when convenient.' "

"He leave a phone number?"

"No."

Frank started the car. "Want to grab something to eat?" he asked. "Or do we go make Randolph's day?"

José laughed an evil laugh.

. . .

✚ Randolph Emerson had the incredulous look of a man just told of the world's end.

"Mary Keegan's been murdered? And you're interviewing the *deputy secretary of state?*" Emerson rolled his eyes skyward.

"Cheer up," José said, "this's only Monday."

Emerson, commander of Homicide, stood behind his majestic desk, a massive glass slab supported by two black iron sawhorses. A nameplate in the shape of a billy club rested in a teak cradle, a suck-up gift from the warden at Lorton. Hitler were still alive today, he'd have a desk like that, Frank thought. Big enough to plan a campaign to conquer the world.

Frank used to hold Emerson in poisonous, spit-on-his-grave contempt. Randolph Emerson was a cop only because of the official job description. Emerson, Frank, and José had been in the same class at the academy. But while Frank and José had hit the streets, Emerson had found a desk, and behind a succession of bigger desks he made his career. Emerson kept his political fingertips sandpapered. He had an uncanny ability to grab credit and avoid blame. Couple those talents with an exquisite sense of when to kiss up and when to kick down, and it was no surprise that as the District's murder rate soared, Emerson still got promotion after promotion.

Then, ten or so years ago, Frank had an epiphany: *Every bureaucracy had a Randolph Emerson.* Bureaucracies couldn't function without the Emersons greasing the gears. Whatever would be happening on the outside, an Emerson would be hard at work inside, tightening this regulation, loosening that standard, hammering out new titles, and shuffling blocks around on organization charts. If this Randolph Emerson dropped off the face of the earth—fell into the District's Ultimate Pothole— there'd be another Randolph Emerson sitting behind the glass desk with the steel billy-club nameplate. And so, coming to terms with the inevitability of Emersons, Frank and José came to accept the Emerson they had on a "better the devil you know" basis.

"I *said*," Emerson repeated, "what are you doing, talking to someone like David Trevor?"

Frank raised his eyebrows. "Oh. You think we shouldn't talk to him?"

Emerson flung himself into his chair. Upholstered in black leather, it had an extraordinarily high back. It looked as if it'd come out of the command center of the starship *Enterprise*. He made a tent of his fingers. Frank knew from the practiced gesture Emerson was about to embark on his Washington 101 lecture.

"David Trevor is a *very* important person," Emerson intoned. "He is a very *powerful* person. We have enough problems . . . *challenges* . . . without the State Department or the White House coming down on us because we overstep our authority."

"I thought we had the authority to deal with homicide in the District, Randolph," Frank said. "Are you saying that the important and powerful should be excluded from a criminal investigation?"

"What I'm *say*ing is that we have to be *care*ful. And I'm saying that you and Phelps have earned a reputation for a certain . . . *direct* style. We will deal with homicide in the District. But we will break minimum china in doing so." Emerson paused. "Is that clear?" He fired a meaningful look at Frank. "Clear?" He shot another look at José.

Neither Frank nor José said anything.

"Okay," Emerson picked up, "we've got the Greek in the Creek and now the lady in the park. Both sliced. Both missing pinkies. Question"— he looked from Frank to José—"does that add up to a serial killer?"

Then, before either could say anything, Emerson held up a restraining hand. "Okay, so they're both missing pinkies in a knifing. But coincidence isn't proof. Where's the proof?"

José sighed wearily. "Media doesn't need proof."

"People are going to ask. We better have an answer," Frank added.

Frank caught José giving him the eye. José knew what was happening, too. Emerson's trouble sensor was giving him an internal five-alarm. Better to have a string of gang killings than have two women—two *white* women—getting carved up under apparently similar circumstances.

Emerson took that in. He tried again. "Are we certain it's Mary Keegan?"

"Prints match."

"You sure?"

Frank nodded and watched Emerson go off into his own world.

"Not good," Emerson said to himself. "Not good at all. The *Post* is going to go apeshit over this. One of their lead columnists . . ." He trailed off and swiveled his chair around to look out the window. A moment later, he swung back to face the two detectives.

"When's Upton doing the autopsy?"

"After we get an okay from next of kin" Frank said. "A brother in Boston."

"When's that?"

"Boston Homicide is sending two guys around. They'll call us when they get back."

"So maybe this afternoon?"

"Maybe."

Emerson stood up from behind his desk and reached for a file in his in basket—his signal that the meeting was over. At the same time he looked at Frank. "You call Upton. You tell him I want that autopsy done if he has to stay there all night. I'm going to have to hold a press conference tomorrow. One thing for certain," Emerson stared at Frank.

"What's that, Randolph?"

"We're going balls-out on this."

✠ There were Tijuana jail cells larger than Frank and José's office. Their window, however, had no bars and you could see, several blocks away, the tops of trees on the Mall. If you leaned one way, you got a glimpse of the red-brick towers of the Smithsonian Castle. Lean the other way, the Capitol.

Along one wall, unmatched bookcases held dog-eared volumes of District and federal statutes, two dictionaries, a thesaurus, telephone directories for the District and its Maryland and Virginia suburbs, two well-worn editions of Geberth's *Practical Homicide Investigation,* and an assortment of plaques, trophy cups, and embossed mugs, the residue of luncheons with long speeches by city officials, civic organizations, and law-enforcement associations.

Six four-drawer cabinets filled with old case files lined the opposite wall. Frank and José had kept the files despite admin's badgering to convert the musty coffee-stained reports to neutered entries in a computer registry. A coffeemaker shared the top of one of the file cabinets with a framed photograph of Ella Fitzgerald standing between Frank and José, her arms around their waists.

Two wooden chairs waited in a corner. Frank and José's desks were the only other furniture. These had been pushed together to face each other under the window.

What was left of the morning was spent on the Keegan paperwork. A break for lunch, then more paperwork, this time a massive questionnaire from Human Resources. Ten minutes into the questionnaire, José tossed his pencil down and tilted back in his chair.

"We aren't doing police work. We're killing forests. Nerds asking questions they already ought to have the answers to," he said in disgust. "They want to know my grade and salary and years of service, why don't they look in their own damn records? It's not like we just picked up a badge."

"Remember when it used to be called 'Personnel'?" Frank asked.

"Why you think they changed it?"

"Politically correct. 'Human Resources' sounds more warm . . . touchy-feely."

"Different logo but same clerks running the same store."

✛ Detective First Class Harrelson, Boston Homicide, called at seven that evening. Frank took the call. Harrelson had met with Mary Keegan's brother and got authorization for the autopsy. Harrelson's voice came across hollow and angry, and Frank knew how he felt.

Twenty minutes later, Frank looked through the glass panes set into the double doors leading into the white-tiled autopsy suite. Ten tables—slanted stainless-steel trays with plumbing and raised edges—filled the room. At the nearest table, Tony Upton adjusted an overhead microphone. At the body cooler along the wall, Upton's assistant—the diener—wrestled a body out of a roll-out drawer and onto a gurney. Both men wore hospital scrubs and plastic face shields.

José pressed a plate on the wall and the doors opened with a hydraulic sigh. Pushing through the double doors, Frank reflexively held his breath. He finally inhaled, trying to keep it shallow. It didn't help. The cold smells of death assaulted him, the stratospheric razor-keenness of alcohol, the heavier, putrid-sweet odor of formalin fighting its losing battle with human decay.

Upton looked toward Frank and José, the overhead lights making light bars across his plastic face shield. He gestured to a spot beside him. "Show time," he said.

Upton probed and measured each of twenty-six stab wounds, then methodically took apart Mary Keegan's body. Organs were weighed, dissected, and put into save jars. Keegan's corpse was sliced, peeled, sawed, and finally, two hours later, sewn up and rolled back into the cooler.

Clearing his throat, Upton addressed the overhead microphone.

"The cause of death was multiple stab wounds to the chest and throat. The mechanism of death was loss of blood." He paused dramatically for a beat and looked at Frank. "The manner of death was homicide," he said. His show over, Upton switched the microphone off.

"Lab reports next week on the organs." Upton snapped his latex gloves off and tossed them into the lidded container by the scrub sink. "You guys hungry?" He looked back and forth between Frank and José. "I'm going down to Kinney's for some ribs."

✠ Fifteen minutes later, Frank found a parking space, locked his car, and ran through the rain to a tall brownstone just off Pennsylvania Avenue on Capitol Hill. At the door, he pressed the buzzer.

"Yes?" the voice came through a squawk box by the door.

"It's me."

"Just a minute."

Frank turned and scanned the neighborhood. The streets and sidewalks were empty, rain-slicked and shining. A bright overhead light went on, and he turned toward the door at the sounds of locks opening and bolts sliding.

"Sorry about dinner," Frank said as the door opened.

Kate shrugged. "I had some homework to do. You hungry?"

"No. Coffee would be good, though."

Kate Dwyer, five-six, blond, and forty-eight, nodded and for a moment didn't say anything, just stood looking at Frank. She'd given him that same measuring look four years ago when they'd met, fighting over a taxi in the rain. She did it every time they met. Frank liked the look: a quarter-smile that played at the right corner of her mouth and a slight narrowing of the eyes. He'd asked her about it, later, when you could ask a woman about such things. She had laughed, saying something lawyerlike about due diligence. As he followed her down the hall to the kitchen, it struck him as it always did: she had a nice bottom. He'd read somewhere that all women hated themselves from behind. Maybe so, but hers fit well with her other nice parts.

By the time he'd finished his coffee, Frank had described the murder scene in the park, the Trevor interview, and the session with Emerson.

" 'Greek in the Creek'?" Kate frowned.

Frank shrugged. "A lot of guys do that. It's how they get by, day to day. They make up a goofy name for a crime so they don't have to deal with the victim's name. Last week, we had a drug dealer his buddies shot. They stuffed him in the trunk of his car. He became the 'Skunk in the Trunk.' Some guys would go nuts if they didn't make a sick joke of it."

"You don't."

"I would, if it'd help. It doesn't. I can't depersonalize." As he said it, he found himself half-thinking of it as an embarrassing affliction, like crooked teeth or bad breath. "I remember the name of my first victim. I remember his face. I think about him a lot."

She looked at him for a long time. For a moment, he worried that she'd reach out and put her hand over his and say something squishy. But he knew she wouldn't. She didn't, and that made him feel better.

Instead, after yet another beat or two, a smile played around the corners of her mouth and she said, " 'Balls-out'? What did he mean by the department's going balls-out?"

"Randolph's going to hold a press conference tomorrow. They're going to ask him what he's doing."

"Oh. Going—"

"Balls-out," Frank finished.

"The serial angle?"

"Randolph's got a point. Two women knifed doesn't mean Jack the Ripper or Hannibal Lecter."

"But the fingers . . . ?"

"I've seen hands hacked off."

"But—"

Frank nodded. "It's like Hoser says, the media doesn't need proof. A serial killer sells papers."

"Autopsy say anything about the knife?"

Frank shrugged. "It's not like a shooting. A stabbing, the best you can do—and Upton's good at stab wounds—best you can do is estimate shape of the blade and a minimum-maximum range on the size. Tony says both killings could have been done by the same knife. Or two very different knives."

Suddenly, from his jacket, Frank caught a faint trace of Formalin, and the odor brought back the scene in Upton's autopsy suite. He pushed his unfinished coffee away. "I'm tired as hell." He got up.

Kate came around the table and held him, resting her cheek on his shoulder.

"You want to stay?" she asked.

He felt her warm against him. He tightened his arm around her. "Yeah. But not tonight. There's too much of . . . *it* with me."

Kate gave him her measuring look again. "You're a good man, Frank Kearney."

Frank smiled back. "I try."

THREE

✠ **E**ntering the press room always made Frank think of climbing into a boxing ring. It wasn't the shape. The low-ceilinged room was long and narrow. What brought the boxing metaphor to mind was the way the police and media squared off against each other. The department spokesman came in from one end of the room. The reporters entered from the other. Both came for a fight. The reporters to rack up a gotcha or two on the department; the cops to pummel the media in the clinches. The place had a belligerent smell to it—equal parts sweat from close-quarters combat and decades of cigarette and cigar smoke that had saturated the room's pores before the Surgeon General declared war on tobacco.

"Sell-out crowd," José said behind him.

Frank took up a position with his back to the wall where he stood and surveyed the room. Directly to his front, a low stage with a scarred lectern. To his right, a ragged assortment of folding chairs, now almost filled with reporters. On his left, José, Tony Upton, and the door through which Randolph Emerson would materialize.

"Nothing like blood in the water to bring the sharks," José said.

Frank eyed the reporters. "And the weasels," he said, spotting Hugh Worsham.

Worsham made eye contact with Frank and nodded. Deadpan,

Frank looked away. Cameras this morning. Bad. Cameras meant lights. Lights meant squinting and sweating and looking shifty on the tube. The Supreme Court wouldn't let you use bright lights on the perps anymore. Sweating a confession was too unsportsmanlike. But nobody ever told that to the TV boys.

A public-affairs flunky shouted, "Commander Emerson," in a "Here comes the judge" voice. Emerson posed for a beat in the doorway, then bounded to the low stage with a palms-down patting motion with both hands, as if to let the reporters know they didn't have to rise.

None showed the slightest inclination to do so. The noisy conversations continued.

Emerson stood motionlessly for a moment, waiting for silence and for the reporters' attention to shift to him. But the hive kept buzzing. Emerson tapped the microphone with a fingernail. The loudspeakers clattered, then gave out a caterwauling screech. The reporters answered with curses. Frank saw a hand shoot up from the crowd to give Emerson the finger.

"I have a statement," Emerson said, "then I'll take questions."

Frank watched the reporters fall silent. Not a respectful silence, he thought. But the tensed waiting of a cat eyeing its prey.

Emerson adjusted his notes on the lectern and began.

"Yesterday morning just after daybreak, a citizen found the body of a woman in a park on Thirty-fifth Street, Northwest."

Frank noticed that none of the reporters were taking notes. They didn't have to—they'd already gotten bootleg copies of Emerson's statement from their sources in the department. The statement belonged to Emerson; the good part of the press conference—the questions—belonged to the reporters.

"The woman has been identified as Mary Frances Keegan. Our chief medical examiner has declared her death a homicide. Ms. Keegan suffered multiple injuries from a sharp instrument."

Emerson paused, then said in a tone he meant to sound heavy with emphasis, "The department is devoting full resources to this case. Around the clock." He paused again and thrust his chin out and up—a gesture Emerson had borrowed some years back from Bill Clinton in the belief that it conveyed tough-minded determination. After a second of this, he rapped the lectern with deadly intent: "Full resources"—*rap*—"around"—*rap*—"the"—*rap*—"clock"—*rap*.

Another chin thrust, then, "Questions?"

Reporters shouted to be recognized. They reminded Frank of grade-school kids wetting their pants to get teacher to call on them.

"He's going to pick Worsham," Frank heard José say under his breath.

Emerson held up both hands, palms out, then pointed into the mob.

"Hugh Worsham?"

Worsham stood to an accompaniment of groans and rolling of eyes. A television "personality," Worsham, with his wiffy hundred-dollar haircut and blue shirt with white collar and cuffs, stood out among the rumpled working print reporters like a groomed thoroughbred wolfhound in a kennel of mangy mongrel mutts.

"Hugh Worsham, Channel Six Investigative Reports." Worsham said in his sonorous voice as if he were on camera.

The mutts groaned.

"Two months ago, Susan Boukedes was stabbed to death in Rock Creek Park. That's just over a mile from where Mary Keegan was murdered. My question: Has it crossed your minds that we have a serial killer at work?"

Frank watched Emerson take a slow, deep breath. Knowing Emerson, Frank knew that he'd gone over hundreds of Q&A's preparing himself for this. It was what Emerson worked hardest at—what got him command of Homicide and the big desk—looking good while handling the tough questions.

"We are considering all plausible scenarios."

Worsham persisted. "Is this a serial killing?"

Emerson, after flashing a grimace of irritation, finally managed a friendly yet serious smile back at Worsham.

"Hugh," Emerson began patiently, "we're treating both cases as homicides."

"Susan Boukedes was missing a finger. How about Keegan?"

In unison, the mutts swiveled their heads from Worsham to Emerson. Frank cursed silently. Some details you tried to keep out of the press. But Worsham obviously had an inside source.

Emerson ignored the question, pausing to make bouncing, wholesale eye contact with reporters front and rear, right and left. "Someone killed Mary Keegan"—he shook his index finger—"and someone killed Susan Boukedes." Another shake of the finger. Yet another chin thrust. "We're going to pursue our leads and apprehend whoever killed these women, whether it be one or more persons."

Worsham remained standing. Frank heard whispered "Sit down's," but Worsham ignored them.

"What progress have you made in the Rock Creek killing?"

Emerson gave Worsham his "I regret I can't tell you, old buddy" look. "Hugh, it's against department policy to comment on certain aspects of active investigations." He shook his head as if siding with the reporters against the wrongheadedness of the invisible bureaucrats who had made the policy, then pointed to one of the print reporters.

"Weathers, *Baltimore Sun*," said a young red-haired man in a rumpled corduroy jacket. "When, approximately, was Ms. Keegan killed?"

Emerson considered the question for a moment. "Our best estimates . . . and I emphasize they *are* estimates . . . are that the death occurred early Sunday evening."

Weathers scribbled in his notebook, then got one more question in as his colleagues began yapping at him. "Was there any evidence . . . indication . . . that Ms. Keegan had been sexually assaulted?"

Silence dropped across the room like a sudden chill.

"It's against the policy—" Emerson began.

Weathers waved his closed notebook in surrender and sat down.

"One more," Emerson announced, and pointed to a young woman with dark hair. "Ms. Lewis."

"You said," Lewis consulted her notebook, "quote, 'The department is devoting full resources to this case. Around the clock.' Unquote." She looked up at Emerson.

"Yes?"

"Well," Lewis said, "is this case more important because of Ms. Keegan's connections?"

Emerson drew himself up indignantly. "This department considers the act of homicide as a threat to all people of the District," he said loftily. "The *act*, Ms. Lewis, concerns us first, not the victim's status."

✠ José and Frank worked their way through the knots of reporters outside the press room. Well down the corridor, José shook his head in wonder. "Emerson . . . man's unreal. 'The *act*, Ms. Lewis,' " he mimicked, " 'not the victim's status.' "

Frank shrugged. "All God's chilluns got a talent. With Randolph, it's sincerity. People trust sincerity. When you learn how to fake it like Randolph you got it made."

José belched. "You want to read files when you get back from the hospital?"

Frank couldn't think of an excuse not to. "Yeah," he said.

"Tell your dad hello."

✠ Leaving headquarters, Frank drove north on Massachusetts Avenue. He liked the drive. He found it easy to imagine the avenue the way it'd been a hundred years ago. Huge oaks and elegant mansions hinted of a more orderly time before the twentieth century's savagery made its way from battlefields and gas chambers to architects' drawing boards. He reflexively avoided the sight of the newly built Finnish embassy, a monstrosity that reminded him of barbed wire wrapped around a jumble of rusted bayonets.

Minutes later, Frank pulled into a parking space at Sibley Hospital. If you were the president or a member of Congress, the military doctors took care of you at Bethesda or Walter Reed. Less fortunate Washingtonians went to the Hospital Center, where the staff was highly skilled in treating gunshot wounds and other trauma. Moneyed Washington preferred Sibley—Club Sibley—conveniently located near the acres of elephantine mansions of Potomac, Great Falls, and McLean.

Frank pushed through the door to find his father standing by the window, gazing out. The older man leaned heavily on a cane, making him look stooped and tired.

"Planning an escape?"

His father turned slowly. He shuffled in small steps, as if he had to think through each motion. Tom Kearney stared at his son as if seeing him for the first time.

Inside Frank, a desperate voice shouted "No!" Before the stroke, before the cane, Tom Kearney would have moved on the balls of his feet with the casual grace of a much younger man.

As a boy, Frank had come upon a scrapbook in an attic trunk. He recalled his surprise when, opening the scrapbook, he saw himself in uniform. The photo, of course, was of his father, then a boy soldier of seventeen. Now he saw in his father what he, Frank Kearney, was to be in some certain tomorrow. *His is my future, and I am his past.*

"You're here more than that damnfool sawbones of mine."

Frank's darkness retreated. The face was lined and the speech slightly slurred, but the eyes of the young paratrooper still looked out at him.

"Don't you have a job?" his father asked. "Or have the good citizens of the District stopped slaughtering each other?"

"Yes, I have a job. No, they're still at it."

Tom Kearney dropped his mock judge's look. He read Frank's face for a moment, then motioned to a pair of armchairs. "Let's sit," he said, pulling the chairs closer together.

"You know Mary Keegan?" Frank asked.

Tom nodded.

"Somebody killed her."

"No!" Tom looked stunned, then shook his head. His eyes settled on Frank. "And you've got the case?"

"Yep."

His father settled back into his chair. "Tell me about it."

For the next ten minutes, Tom Kearney listened.

Frank finished, describing the press conference.

His father sat for a moment, thinking. "Press conference an hour ago?" he asked, mulling it over as if calculating the pace of the events the Keegan killing would produce. "Well, it's all around town by now. Washington sympathy has a shelf life of about a millisecond, then everybody's got a wet finger up to see which way the wind's blowing. There's going to be a squeeze on this one."

"Already started," Frank said. "Tell me about the Trevor family."

"They in this?"

"Mary Keegan was doing a book on Charles Trevor and his son."

"I don't know Charles Trevor personally. I mean, we've met several times over the years. Exchanged small talk. A lot of it about the war. He'd been in the Pacific. A Marine." Tom Kearney's eyes shifted toward his memories, then shifted back.

"But about Charles Trevor," he picked up. "To understand Charles Trevor, you have to realize there're two Washingtons," he began. "There's the official Washington, with its fat cats who've bought Cabinet jobs and plush ambassadorships at campaign fund-raisers. They're out to put another notch in their social résumés. Obsessed with titles. First to demand their perks. Last to do any real work.

"Then there's working Washington—people who know each other from way back. People who've paid their dues doing grubby jobs no one else would do. Jobs that had to be done. These are the people sprinkled throughout the bureaucracy who will work on Sunday or their son's birthday or over the long Labor Day weekend or when their daughter has her piano recital. These people know they're there for one reason—to help the man the American people elected president. Charles Trevor has always been that kind of man.

"Trevor and Kennedy—Jack Kennedy—were at Harvard together. Kennedy a year or so ahead of him. Apparently they got to know each other before the war. After the war, Kennedy came back to go into politics. Trevor came back to study law. He dropped out of law school for a year to manage Kennedy's congressional campaign. Got his law degree, started off with a Boston firm. Then went to New York. Made a bundle at Lehman Brothers . . . investment banking. Kennedy got to be president, asked Trevor to be his secretary of state."

"He had two sons. Joe and David."

"Joe was killed in Vietnam. Early in the war. Charles buried him at Arlington one morning and resigned that afternoon."

"David?"

Tom Kearney's eyebrows arched. "I was surprised to see Clinton pick him to be Albright's deputy."

"Why?"

"Oh, most of us Monday-morning quarterbacks saw David as bright enough. Good education, but something missing. Nowadays they call it fire in the belly. Some said that if he hadn't had a famous name, he'd have been lucky to be a GS-7 over at HHS."

"He's doing pretty well."

"I guess his slow start fooled a lot of people." Tom Kearney smiled. "Even us Monday morning quarterbacks can be wrong."

"But I hear your lab work looks good."

The sudden turn brought a frown. "Ought to," his father said. "Nothing wrong with me that taking twenty years off wouldn't cure."

"Doctor Laessig said they're letting you out tomorrow."

"Parole? Work release? Time off for good behavior?"

"I think she called it self-defense. I'll pick you up."

"I want to go home, Frank." Tom Kearney's voice had an uncharacteristic whining undertone to it.

Frank felt his chest constrict. "Dad, we've been through this. You have tests, therapy. It's more convenient for you to stay with me."

"I'll be a pain in the ass."

"No you won't. Just a week. Maybe two, Dad. Humor me."

His father retreated to a fall-back position. "I can get to your place on my own. I don't need you picking me up like some damn invalid."

Oh God, I hate this, I really do. "I know. But it's hospital rules," Frank said, trying not to sound overbearing or weepy.

"Covering their asses," Tom Kearney said, voice now crusty with disdain. "Probably push me out of here in a wheelchair."

"Blame lawyers and judges."

Tom Kearney laughed and the tension broke. He held a hand over his heart. "Touché."

"Pick you up tomorrow."

Tom nodded. "The defense rests." He reached out and pulled Frank into a bear hug. "I love you, son. But if I stay longer than a week, I *will* be a pain in the ass. I promise."

✝ "Damn, Hoser, you started without me," Frank said.

Over the top of his reading glasses, José looked up from an open folder. "Yeah, I knew you'd be real disappointed. But I couldn't resist." He pushed a stack of the Boukedes files over to Frank's desk. "Autopsy's not here. Everything else is."

Frank had always found picking through files a tough go—reading someone else's reporting, trying to inject touch, taste, smell, and sound into cliché-riddled cop prose. He didn't want to sit down just yet, so he pulled a quarter from his pocket.

"Flip to see who makes coffee?"

José shrugged. "You always win."

The coin arced in the air. "Call it."

"Tails."

"It's heads."

José shrugged again. "See?"

Frank pocketed the quarter. "I'll make it."

"But I lost."

"You got the files, I'll make the coffee."

✝ Two hours later, the Forensics fiber analysis of the Boukedes crime scene wasn't making any more sense on the fifth reading than it had on the first. Frank's phone rang. He answered, listened, then hung up and turned to José.

"Guy named Halligan's at the desk. Asking for us."

✠ The only civilian at the desk was a blond-haired man Frank judged to be in his mid-to-late thirties. Slender, tall, wearing an expensive but battered tan trench coat and carrying a canvas overnight bag.

"I'm Frank Kearney. My partner José Phelps," Frank said, offering his hand.

"Damien Halligan." Halligan shifted the overnight bag to his left hand. "I'm Mary Keegan's brother." The Irish accent was strong, like his handshake. Halligan had the light, balanced poise of a basketball or soccer player. "That one *e* or two?"

Frank took a second to register Halligan's question. "Two." He spelled his name as he handed Halligan a contact card.

Halligan studied the card, then looked up as if to fix Frank's face in his memory. The eyes were deep-water blue. "How'd she die?"

"We can talk in private here." Frank gestured toward the small conference room behind the desk sergeant.

✠ Frank opened with the same statement Randolph Emerson had used in the morning press conference, then added the details elicited by the reporters' questions.

Halligan, expressionless, listened intently. He said nothing until Frank finished, then, "So this woman in the park . . ."

"Boukedes," José supplied.

"The same person killed her, killed Mary?"

"*Might* have," said Frank.

"Might *not* have," said José.

Halligan's lips tightened. "Where do you come down?"

"No place," said Frank. "Yet."

Halligan persisted. "If you were a betting man?"

"I'm not," Frank said. "I go for sure things."

"And what's that? The sure thing?"

"Somebody killed your sister. And somebody killed Susan Boukedes."

Halligan leaned back in his chair and studied Frank. "That's *it*? That's the sure thing?"

"Right now it is," Frank said. "And we build on that. Now . . . mind if we ask some questions?"

"Ask."

"When did you last talk with your sister?"

"Last week. Wednesday night."

"She sound worried or concerned?"

Halligan shook his head. "The usual . . . her writing. Deadlines. Editors. That kind of worry."

José asked, "Anything about her safety?"

"No. Mary has been . . . was . . . in some pretty tight situations around the world. She didn't scare easily."

"She walked alone at dark," José said. "You find that unusual?"

Halligan shrugged. "She was with the *mujahidin* during the blood-iest of the Afghan War. And she covered the fighting in Beirut. Like I say, Mary didn't scare easily."

"Your sister's name, Keegan," Frank said.

"She was married to Joe Keegan."

"And?"

"He was killed in an automobile accident. They were vacationing in France. Eight, nine years ago." Halligan paused, then asked, "Where is she?"

"The medical examiner's," Frank said.

"The morgue, you mean." Halligan said it without emotion. "I want to see her."

"We have her prints and a DNA match," Frank said. "Perhaps you might want to wait . . . see her at the funeral home."

"I think now," Halligan said.

"She doesn't look—"

Halligan stood. He picked up his overnight bag and slung it over a shoulder. "Give me the address, I'll take a cab . . ."

Frank got up. "We'll take you."

✠ Tony Upton met them at the entrance and led the way back to the autopsy suite. Without a word, Upton unlatched the cooler drawer and rolled out Mary Keegan's body.

"I'll do it," Halligan said, as Upton started to unzip the body bag.

Upton stepped back, joining Frank and José.

Halligan worked the zipper down only as far as the top of his sister's breasts. Upton's cuts, the Y-shaped incisions running from each shoulder to the sternum had been sewn shut. The thick twine stitching always reminded Frank of the seams on a baseball. The killer's work, however, remained—the obscene opening of the slashed throat, the multiple stab wounds to the face, neck, and chest.

Frank watched Halligan, waiting for a reaction, anything—sadness, anger, revulsion. But there was nothing. Then Halligan leaned forward and with his thumbs rolled his sister's eyelids up. He bent over her, motionless, for several seconds, then straightened up and closed her eyes. He crossed himself, then zipped up the body bag.

Walking out to the car, Frank spoke first. "Mr. Halligan, your accent . . . County Down?"

Halligan looked surprised.

"Close. Armagh." He looked at Frank as if he realized he'd missed something the first time. "You know Ireland?"

Frank nodded. "Father born in Derry. I spent some time there."

"And when was that?"

"Most of 1969."

"When the bombing began."

Frank did the mental arithmetic. "You must have been a kid when the bombing started."

"Old enough to remember," Halligan said bitterly, "never old enough to forget." He opened the back door. "Mind dropping me at a subway?"

"You have a place to stay?"

"I have friends."

✠ José and Frank sat in the car and watched the lone figure of Damien Halligan disappear into the mist near the Union Station Metro stop.

"Well, what about that?" José asked.

"Hard case." Frank made a mental note to run a files check on Halligan.

José tugged reflectively at his earlobe. "What was that deal about the eyes?"

"Old wives' tale. The eyes of a murder victim carry a picture of the killer."

"Think Halligan saw anybody?"

"Don't know," Frank said. "But he was looking."

"Coleman and Janowitz said they'd be back by three."

Frank glanced at the dashboard clock. Three-forty. He looked toward where he'd last seen Halligan, then pulled away from the curb and headed back to headquarters.

FOUR

✝ **Y**ou guys ever on time?" Henry Coleman, elbows on the table, hunched protectively over coffee in a Styrofoam cup and doughnuts in a Dunkin' Donuts box. Frank noticed half the doughnuts were gone. Leon Janowitz, Coleman's new partner, sat beside him. Janowitz, head down in a file, lifted his eyes, scanned Frank and José, then dropped back into the file.

Coleman had earned his nickname "Cold Case." More than sixteen hundred homicides remained unsolved in Washington over the past ten years, and Frank was willing to bet a month's pay that Coleman had contributed more to those cold-case files than anyone else on the force. Coleman was the most incurious detective Frank had ever known. The great mystery was how he kept his job. Frank thought it was because Randolph Emerson believed that somebody had to anchor the bottom of the Bell curve, and Emerson wanted a somebody who never got into trouble.

Leon Janowitz was one of a long line of Coleman's partners. One good thing about Coleman—a tour as his partner tested a young cop's determination to be a detective. A year with Coleman, Janowitz would either move on or get out.

"Afternoon, Henry, Leon," Frank said.

Coleman frowned. "You guys are late."

José sat down across from Coleman, and without invitation, snagged a doughnut out of the box. "Yeah, aren't we."

Frank smiled and sat down. "Sorry to keep you waiting, Henry. I know how busy you are."

Janowitz followed the exchange, eyes tracing the invisible web between the three men. Neither Frank nor José seemed in a hurry to get started. The sound of rushing water came as someone upstairs flushed a toilet.

Coleman broke the silence. "Leave it to Emerson to fuck things up."

"How so?" Frank asked.

"This serial-killing talk. Emerson's got the heat on us."

"The papers are going to say what the papers are going to say, Henry. Hoser and I were at the press conference. Emerson did what he had to do."

"We didn't get the autopsy files, Henry," said José.

Coleman turned accusingly to his partner. "You got them, Leon?"

Janowitz shook his head. "I gave them back to you."

"We'll get them later," Frank said. He pointed to the files in front of Janowitz. "What we have is two homicides. Question—do we have two killers? Or one?"

José picked up. "We have two Caucasian females. Keegan was forty-two, Boukedes thirty-two. Both single. Both smart. Neither had any recent lifestyle changes—at least as far as the files show."

"Both women lived in Georgetown. Boukedes lived on Q Street near the bridge, Keegan on Thirty-second," Janowitz offered. He got a sidelong glance from Coleman. "Both lived, worked, and died within a two-mile circle of each other. Both were missing their little fingers."

"You guys look for Boukedes's finger?" Frank asked.

Coleman got a put-upon look. "Course we did. That area . . . woods, the creek . . . figured a rat or raccoon . . . hell, they even got foxes in the park."

"Boukedes financials?" José asked.

Janowitz leafed through his notes. "Salary income. Ninety thousand a year. Electronic deposit every two weeks. Paid-up mortgage and condo fees. Savings and checking, Riggs Bank. Top credit rating. No unusual spending or transfers."

"Friends? People at work?" Frank asked.

Coleman shrugged. "Nothing."

"What do you mean, 'Nothing'?" Frank asked.

"I mean we did our canvass and we got no pissed-off boyfriends. Or girlfriends, either. She showed up for work. No complaints from the embassy."

"Things are a little different now, Henry."

"How?"

"You said it, Henry—heat's on. With the Keegan killing," Frank said, "we have to look for possible connections between her and Boukedes."

Coleman stretched and yawned. "And end up doing a lot of work for nothing."

Janowitz searched the ceiling as if looking for a way out.

"I guess we ought to sit back," José said, "and wait for a snitch to bring us the goods."

Janowitz watched Coleman.

Coleman got up. "You need any help, you let me know."

"Sure, Henry," Frank said, "we'll let you know."

The door closed behind Coleman and Janowitz. José shook his head. "That Henry—he's the original Limp-Dick Tracy."

Frank glanced at his notes. "What say we talk to a Greek?"

✠ Theodore Pappas's title was Commercial Counselor. His offices next to the Greek embassy took up a four-story red-brick Federal townhouse on Massachusetts Avenue. Pappas sat at a large ornate Empire desk. Frank's first impression of the diplomat was a flashback to Omar Sharif in *Lawrence of Arabia*—tan, dark hair, chiseled features, and a mouth full of perfect teeth.

Frank introduced José and himself. Pappas ignored the detectives' credentials.

"Thank you for seeing us on short notice," Frank said.

Irritation pinched a small furrow between Pappas's eyebrows. "I spoke earlier to two other officers," he said.

Frank nodded. "Coleman and Janowitz."

"Yes."

"Some more questions have come up," Frank said.

Pappas threw up his hands in a gesture of surrender and stood, giving an irritated look at the stacks of paper on his desk. "If you work for the government," he sighed, "there're always more questions." He led the way to a circle of chairs facing a floor-to-ceiling window.

"Ms. Boukedes worked here eleven years," Frank said. "A long time for Washington."

"Our senior American employee."

"Is it common to hire an American to work for your government?"

"Oh yes. Just about every embassy in Washington either contracts with American consulting firms or hires Americans as direct employees. We were lucky to get Ms. Boukedes. She was unmatched in her job and spoke fluent Greek."

"How long did you know her?"

"Almost five years. She was working as a commerce analyst when I was posted here."

"What does a commerce analyst do?"

"She studied the American market, looking for opportunities for Greek businesses. She was also the focal point for American companies wanting information about Greece."

"She worked directly for you?"

Pappas hesitated. "Well, actually for my deputy."

"But you saw her frequently?"

"Well. Yes. On business."

"Socially?" José asked.

Pappas crossed a leg, taking care not to ruin his trouser crease. "She attended the usual embassy functions—receptions for other diplomats, national-day celebrations—that kind of thing."

"She have any boyfriends?" asked Frank.

"She brought men guests occasionally. I hadn't thought much about that . . . that part of her life. She was interested in men."

"Interested? What do you mean by that?"

"I mean I didn't notice her with a steady male friend."

"You would have noticed?" José asked.

"What do you mean?"

"I mean, if she did have somebody steady, you would have noticed."

Pappas frowned. "I suppose I would have, but then again perhaps I wouldn't." He tilted his chin up. "I don't make a practice of playing with hypotheticals, Lieutenant."

"What were her working hours?"

"Generally nine to five-thirty. There were times, of course, that required night work."

"Night work," José said. "Do you keep records of working hours?"

"Administration section does."

"Computer?"

Pappas cocked his head to stare at José. "Computers?" he asked. "What about them?"

"I meant," José explained, "that they probably keep a computer file of when people sign in early or leave late."

"Oh. Most likely. You might want to ask at the entry desk. Where you signed in."

"Ms. Boukedes's behavior the last several months before she was killed," Frank said, "anything unusual? Out of character?"

Pappas shook his head. "Nothing I noticed."

"Her work up to par?"

"I had no complaints."

"You said she brought friends to embassy events."

"Yes."

"Security would have records?"

"I assume so." Pappas shot out an arm and took a long look at his watch.

"We'd like to get a copy of security records on Ms. Boukedes," Frank said.

"The other detectives didn't . . ." Pappas trailed off.

"All the same," Frank said.

"I will talk to our security officer. I'm certain something can be arranged." Pappas checked his watch again. "I have to see the ambassador, gentlemen. If I'd known you were coming, I could have arranged more time. I can see you later, this evening, if you can wait . . ."

Frank glanced at José, who shook his head.

✠ Outside, homeward-bound traffic knotted Massachusetts Avenue just below Sheridan Circle. Leaving Pappas's office, Frank and José walked shoulder to shoulder half a block before José said, "Think all those Greeks are antsy like him?"

"Don't know, Hoser. You think he was antsy?"

"Yeah."

"About what?"

"Beats me," José said, pulling out the keys as he got to their car. "Something was crawling around in his underwear."

✠ Monty glared as Frank heaved the grocery bags onto the kitchen table.

"Don't look at me that way," Frank said to the cat. "Had to stop at Safeway. You want tuna tonight? Or tuna, or tuna?"

Monty's gray-blue eyes flickered as a cat-thought finished winding through his mind. He meowed once.

Frank shrugged. "Okay, tuna."

As he opened Monty's dinner, he turned on the kitchen TV. Tom Brokaw stood by a clip of the latest French strike—farmers dumping rotting cabbage in the Paris streets. Filling Monty's bowl, he switched channels.

"Here, Your Lordship." Frank set the bowl down by Monty's flap door.

Monty looked at Frank, then at the bowl. *Do you really expect me to eat that?* the big cat seemed to say. With cosmic indifference, he stood, arched his back, stretched his forepaws, then sprang lightly to the floor and picked his way over to examine Frank's offering.

Turning around, Frank caught Mary Keegan's face on the screen. Next to her, Susan Boukedes. He recognized Hugh Worsham's voice-over. He turned up the volume.

". . . despite the similarities in the murders, senior Washington police officials refuse to declare this the work of a serial killer."

Then a clip from the morning's press conference. Randolph Emerson shifted about behind the lectern, pale and sweaty under the klieg lights, waiting to take a question.

The camera turned to Hugh Worsham—handsome and assured. "Has it crossed your minds," Worsham said, "that we have a serial killer at work?"

Tonight, Worsham's voice sounded different. In the press room, he'd come across as neutrally reasonable. Now Worsham was authoritative and contemptuous, as if he were talking to the class dullard.

The camera switched to Emerson, squinty-eyed at the lectern. Frank waited for Emerson's answer, "We are considering all plausible scenarios." The answer had been edited out. Instead, Emerson stood mute, as if stonewalling.

The camera swung back to Worsham, who appeared to be waiting for an answer. Worsham demanded: "Is this a serial killing?"

Worsham came on camera live. He shook his head. "We never got an answer to that question."

For the first time in a long time, Frank felt sorry for Emerson. He aimed the remote at Worsham's forehead and squeezed an imaginary trigger. Worsham faded.

"Well," Frank said to Monty, "another example of why we ought to repeal the First Amendment."

Monty gave Frank a bored look, then nosed through his door and went out into the garden.

Frank put the groceries away, then opened a Rolling Rock. Carrying the bottle, he climbed the stairs to the small second-floor library to check his phone messages. His father had called just after four o'clock. He was, Tom Kearney said with a trace of sarcasm, "making it out over the wall" at Sibley the next afternoon at two. Kate called a few minutes later with an invitation to dinner tomorrow night for Frank and his father. The next message had come in fifteen minutes ago. It was from Damien Halligan.

✝ Half an hour later, Frank stood in front of Mary Keegan's house. Light shone through all the windows. He rapped twice with the heavy brass knocker. He heard the sound of footsteps and the door opened.

"Forgive the abrupt invitation," Damien Halligan said. "I didn't realize you lived so near until Judith Barnes told me." Halligan wore a dark green cashmere sweater and gray flannel slacks. He held a glass in his hand. Frank smelled the faint smoky odor of good whiskey.

Halligan motioned Frank in.

"You staying here?"

"No. Down at the Latham." Halligan started back toward the kitchen. "I came up this afternoon. To begin inventory."

Frank followed. "That's never easy."

"The things she collected over a lifetime." Halligan led Frank into the kitchen. "Her antiques. Books, paintings, records. A person's belongings, they add color . . . depth . . . to what they were. The person dies, belongings become just things again. Lonely pieces. No longer bound to each other. Pieces of what used to be. And what never will be." Halligan raised his glass. "Beer? Wine? Whiskey?"

"Beer."

Halligan opened the refrigerator and peered in. "Ah, yes," he said, reaching in and coming out with a Pilsner Urquell. He opened the bottle and found a mug in a cabinet. He watched as Frank poured. "I don't see how you Americans drink it so cold."

"An acquired taste."

From a half-empty bottle of Jameson on the counter, Halligan refilled his glass and raised it in a toast.

"Sláinte!"

"Fad saol agat," Frank answered.

Halligan smiled. "Good Gaelic."

Frank smiled back. "Hang out in enough pubs . . ."

Halligan studied Frank for a moment, then pointed with the glass. "I was upstairs . . . in Mary's study."

A well-banked fire cast a warm glow in the small room. The computer screensaver was doing Monet's water lilies. A battered leather briefcase lay open on the desk. On the floor nearby, a sturdy cardboard box, the kind lawyers use to store files.

Halligan motioned to two chairs in front of the fire.

"What'll you do with the house?" Frank asked.

Halligan looked around the room. Frank got the impression he was waiting for an answer to come to him from the bookcases that lined the walls. "No need to do anything right away," Halligan finally said. "Mortgage is paid off. I talked with Ms. Barnes today about keeping an eye on it if I close it up for six months, a year."

"There were just the two of you?"

"We were always there for each other."

"You stayed in Ireland."

"There was more for Mary here. Ireland's changing. But still . . . there was more for her here. More promise, she put it."

"But now you're in Boston?"

"Not permanently. I'm in the States working for an Irish firm."

"Oh?"

"Recruiting."

"For?"

"Technicians. Ireland has a surplus of writers and poets—and a shortage of engineers and computer programmers."

"Headhunter."

Halligan cocked his head as if he hadn't heard right. "What?"

"You're a headhunter. That's what we call you here."

He smiled. "Oh. Yes." The smile went away. Halligan leaned forward in his chair and stared at Frank. "I called you because I saw on television something that disturbed me greatly."

"Oh?" Frank said, knowing already what it was.

"The afternoon news. A press conference at police headquarters. A reporter . . . Worsham?"

"Hugh Worsham. I saw the later edition."

"This Commander Emerson—"

"My boss. Randolph Emerson."

"He as much as admitted you are looking for a serial killer. That surprised me. Did you find something since you and I talked?"

Frank shook his head. "No. What Randolph really said was left on the cutting-room floor."

"What do you mean?"

"Emerson said the same thing I told you—that we had two murders and we're going to catch whoever's involved, whether it's one or two or even more."

"He said that?"

"He said that."

Halligan frowned. "The reporter left a different impression."

"He meant to. He's got a reputation. Likes making news better than reporting it."

"So no serial killer?"

"Not yet."

Halligan took that in.

"How long have you been in police work?"

"Twenty-five years."

"A long time."

"Some ways. Other ways, it was like yesterday."

"You like your work."

The way Halligan said it, it wasn't a question, but Frank nodded, anyway. "Some days are better than other days. And once in a while, some days are very bad. The days like that, you hope you never see again. But I wouldn't be doing anything else."

"I did some reading at the library. There was an article about you and your partner. Complimentary."

"Oh that."

Two years before. A clown named Jimmy Foxworth had killed an old woman in a 7-Eleven. An eager reporter happened to be on the scene when Frank and José had closed in on Foxworth. There'd been color close-ups of cops in action—cars chased, doors kicked in, shots fired. Better than *NYPD Blue*.

"The article said you tilted at windmills."

"I think all it said was hard-headed."

"All the same. It's a compliment."

"You recruiting?"

"How do you mean?"

"I got the impression you're checking me off against a set of requirements."

"I just want to be certain my sister's killer doesn't . . . as you say, *walk*."

"Nobody can give you a guarantee. I won't."

"I don't want a guarantee."

"What do you want?"

"I want to know you'll follow this wherever it goes."

"You have some idea of where it might go?"

"If it's a serial killer and you stop him, that's as far as it goes."

"And if it isn't?"

"If it isn't," Halligan said, "then someone killed my sister for a reason other than she happened to be out walking that night."

"You think there might be reasons?"

"There could be."

"*Could* be? Like what?"

"Like telling a truth."

"Like what truth?"

Halligan looked steadily at Frank. "Someone might have to find out so someone could find the person who killed my sister."

"And the someone would be me."

"I would hope."

"You said earlier that your sister . . . that *Mary* . . . was working on a book."

"She described it as a generational biography."

Frank rolled the words around. *Generational biography*. Words like that could mean nothing or everything. Describe the commonplace or hide the terrible. *Executive action. Special operation. Final solution.*

"Was there a title?"

"*Fathers' Sons.* She mentioned it once. Sometime back. Doesn't say much, does it, Lieutenant? I mean, all us men are that."

"Where was she? In writing the book?"

"She finished the first draft two months ago."

"You read it?"

Halligan smiled. "Read Mary Keegan's first draft?" He shook his head. "Might as well try to steal the crown jewels. Mary had a rule: 'Nobody *ever* reads my first draft.' Her first draft was for her and her alone. That way, she felt she was writing without pretension, without witnesses, so she didn't have any compunction about strangling the baby in the crib, as she put it."

"She wasn't a subtle writer."

"You know her books?"

"A couple. And the newspaper stories."

"She was a straightforward woman." Halligan made it a pronouncement.

Frank glanced around the study. On the computer screen, the lilies had given way to the town on the river. "You've found the draft?"

Halligan shrugged. "I haven't been through all her files. And I'm certain there's something on the computer. That's where she wrote."

"We're building a timeline. For Mary. And for the Boukedes woman. Anything you find—schedules, calendars, appointments . . ."

"Certainly."

"Your sister had friends here . . . who would you say was closest to her?"

"Jessica Talbot." Halligan said it with a sharp edge. "Runs the foreign desk at the *Post.*"

"You sound like you don't care much for her."

"I don't."

"Any reason?"

"Abrasive bitch."

"I guess that's a reason. You've made arrangements? For—"

"I'll be taking Mary back to Armagh. To our family plot. Judith Barnes volunteered to sponsor a memorial service. For Mary's friends here."

"When?"

"Day after tomorrow. Holy Trinity. On Thirty-sixth Street. Eleven o'clock."

Frank stretched. "Thanks for the beer. It's been a long day." As he said it, he realized Halligan had the look of someone interrupted just as he were about to say something.

"Sorry." Frank extended a hand in a "Your turn" gesture.

Halligan started to speak, then shook his head. "You're right." He smiled. "It *has* been a long day."

As he left, Frank glanced across the street to Judith Barnes's house and to the shadow behind the curtains on the second floor.

FIVE

✠ The following morning, Frank called Jessica Talbot at the *Washington Post*. Her assistant put him on hold, but seconds later, Talbot came on the line.

You know Stoney's?

Frank did.

Stoney's at nine?

Stoney's at nine.

José came in as Frank was hanging up.

"Cold Case." He fell into his chair in a semicontrolled crash.

"You ever thought of a career at Ikea testing furniture?"

"Cold Case is trying to set a new record for slow," José said. "*Still* hasn't come up with the Boukedes file."

"Tony's got it in the computer. Ask him to run another copy."

José leaned back, stretched, and yawned. As long as he'd known him, it always impressed Frank just how big José was.

"I know," José said, coming forward to rest his elbows on his desk, "but asking for another copy . . . it makes us look sloppy."

"Well? You mean we aren't?"

José ignored the gibe: "And it takes the heat off Cold Case. He doesn't come up with it by lunch, I'll call Tony. You picking up your dad today?"

"Yeah. After lunch." Frank locked on José's eyes, so he could catch any reaction. "I had a beer with Damien Halligan last night."

José's eyes hooded under heavy lids, but he didn't say anything.

"He was up at his sister's," Frank continued. "He called. I went up and we talked. Worsham had gotten him spun up."

José got a disgusted look. "Join the club. I caught it on the late news." He paused. "You know, Frank, he's a weird guy."

"Worsham?"

"Him for sure. No. I mean Halligan. I woke up this morning, thinking about him looking into his sister's eyes." José opened his eyes wide and did a spidery finger air-dance with both hands up by his face. "Made me go, *Ooooohh.*"

Frank laughed. "Yeah. Cue up the *Twilight Zone* music. There's something about the guy."

"He a Forever?"

"Definitely a Forever." Over the years, Frank and José had identified three major categories of homicide victim's relatives—Forgetters, Forgivers, and Forevers. Forgetters put everything behind them and moved on. Forgivers shed tears for the killer as well as for the deceased. Forevers never forgot and damn sure never forgave.

"Anything new or different besides Worsham getting him agitated?"

"Memorial service tomorrow at eleven. Holy Trinity."

José made a note. "Where's the burial?"

"Ireland."

José looked up.

"Halligan's taking her back."

José shook his head. "Weird."

"You want to go with me to talk to Keegan's boss?"

José was already on the phone to Woody in Surveillance. "No. I'm going to stay here. Keep on Cold Case's ass."

✝ At 13th and L, Stoney's is several blocks from the *Washington Post* building on 15th Street. There's a Starbucks closer. But there's only one

Stoney's. The younger *Post* staffers go to Starbucks for latte, mocha, or cappuccino; the older ones to Stoney's for coffee or a Bloody Mary.

Frank got to Stoney's ten minutes early. A handful of customers sat at the bar. Frank chose a table at the back, ordered coffee, and opened the *Washington Times*. For once, the *Times* was in sync with the *Post*. The lead editorials of both papers fired broadsides at the District's crime rate. The *Post* demanded more cops on the street. The *Times* aimed at the District's lenient judges. As usual, Frank thought, each paper had it about half right.

"You Lieutenant Kearney?"

Frank looked up. Jessica Talbot's face matched her photos: round face and dark hair upswept into a halo. A mother's smile and a card-sharp's eyes. He had imagined her a tall woman. The woman standing at the table barely cleared five feet.

Frank showed his badge and credentials case. "Thanks for taking the time."

Talbot sat down. "Sorry to keep you waiting." Her voice was a mix of tobacco rasp and bourbon purr. "Goddamn office is a three-ring circus."

Stoney himself materialized. He put a mug of black coffee in front of Talbot and disappeared.

Talbot pulled a package of unfiltered Camels out of her purse. "Mind?" Even as she asked, she fired up a battered stainless-steel lighter.

Frank shook his head.

Talbot saw Frank watching. She held up the lighter. It had Air Force wings engraved on one side.

"Not very feminine, is it?"

Frank shrugged. "Never thought of Zippos having a gender."

Talbot lit the cigarette and inhaled deeply. "You and your partner were front page, January, February."

"Yes."

"The O'Brien murder."

"Yes."

"Something I wanted to ask you about that."

"Yes?"

"There was a political connection, wasn't there?"

Frank gave her an offhand smile. "In this town—"

"Yeah. I know." Talbot dismissed him with a wave of the hand with the cigarette. "In this town, everything's got a political connection." She sipped her coffee. Over the top of the mug she measured Frank with her cardsharp's eyes. She put the mug down. "So tell me, was there a connection?"

"Nothing that would have held up in court."

Talbot nodded knowingly. "Would it hold up on the front page?"

Frank shook his head. "Front page is your game."

"Not yours?"

"You trying to recruit me as a source?"

"You don't ask, you don't get."

"I've got enough work doing my own job, Ms. Talbot."

"Are you and your partner the guys they keep around to handle the dynamite?"

"This case's dynamite?" Frank asked innocently.

Talbot shook her head and gave Frank a cynical grin. "Come *on*, Lieutenant . . . you don't nail that bastard, our new mayor's going to get a ton of shit dumped on him. And you know where shit runs . . . downhill."

"The *Post* and the *Times* are already dumping. Some of your work?"

"What do you think?"

"Tell me about Mary Keegan."

Talbot pulled hard on her cigarette, then exhaled, sailing the smoke toward the ceiling. "She was my best friend," she said softly. "I met her in '82, when she came to town. After Afghanistan."

"She came to work for you then?"

"I couldn't get her on. She wanted the Middle East account. Management said women couldn't handle that beat. So she went to work for Mickey Gorton. Mickey's an old-line Scoop Jackson Democrat . . . puts out a monthly political magazine. He encouraged her to write her book about Afghanistan."

"*A Door into Hell*. The Pulitzer."

"Yeah." Talbot smiled cynically. "Once she got the Pulitzer, all of a sudden management decided she could handle the Middle East beat. I made her the offer. Mickey told her if she didn't take it, he'd fire her."

"This was . . . ?"

"January '85."

"You made a smart hire."

Talbot nodded. "Too many reporters share a common picture of how the world works. They see something new or confusing to them, they don't question their tribal wisdom. They just hammer the new stuff until it fits their picture. God knows," Talbot rasped, "they wouldn't want any of their colleagues laughing at them. Mary didn't give a big rat's ass. She wasn't afraid of facts."

"She married—"

"Joe Keegan. A lawyer. Classic attraction of opposites." Talbot paused for coffee and glanced around the shop. "She was the passionate one. He had the cool of a jewel thief. I thought it would be a shitty match." She took a last drag on the cigarette then stubbed it out. "I probably would have said the same thing about Romeo and Juliet."

"A good marriage."

"Good but short. They were in France and did a head-on with a truck near Grenoble. Joe died right away."

"And Mary Keegan?"

"Not a scratch. Got back here, dived into the bottle. Damn near drowned."

"This was . . . ?"

"February '88. The accident. Mary did the *Lost Weekend* bit for a couple of months. I dragged her out to Betty Ford, got her dried out, then sent her to the Moscow bureau in June. She stayed almost four years. Came back in January '92, a month after the commies threw in the towel."

"She wrote about that."

"*The Fall.* About how none of the twits in the Bush White House saw it coming. And didn't know what to do when it did."

"Must have added to the enemies list."

Talbot waved it off as if shooing away a gnat. "You aren't a journalist if you don't have enemies."

"Any that would kill her?"

She shook another cigarette from the pack and took her time tapping it on the tabletop, then lighting it.

"Oh, there're some who would have liked to see her dead. But," she said with contempt, "nobody with balls enough to do it. Mary's enemies were bloodthirsty, but they'd faint at the sight of blood."

"How's that?"

"Revenge is Washington's moral equivalent of war. The weapons are subtle—rumor, innuendo, leaks. My reporters don't have to beat the bushes—pardon the pun—we could fill up the *Post* every day with stuff that comes in over the transom. Remember Reagan's neutron bomb? Kills people but leaves buildings standing? Our Washington revenge bomb kills a person's reputation but leaves them walking around."

"The dead ones sometimes come back to life, don't they?"

"Yeah. Nixon was the great Lazarus act. But watch our boy Clinton. Or our recently departed mayor . . . we haven't seen the last of them."

"Any men in her life?"

"Sure. You men come in handy. You fill chairs at dinner parties. And you're useful when the hormones rage."

"Men, but no man."

Talbot nodded.

"She was working on a book."

"Yes."

"You have some idea of what it was about?"

Talbot hesitated. "About the sons of famous men."

Frank sensed a guarded note in Talbot's answer. Protecting a dead friend? Reluctant to talk to a stranger . . . and a cop at that? He figured her as hesitant, but not hostile. The little he'd heard of her over the years had been of a tough but fair professional. So maybe to get a little, he'd have to give a little.

"Yeah," he said, "I talked with David Trevor about it."

Talbot's face remained inscrutable. But behind her eyes, Frank caught a flicker of curiosity. She dropped her eyes to her coffee mug. She carefully nudged it as though it was critical that the heavy ceramic mug be placed just so before she started probing. A journalist's *feng shui*. She looked up at Frank.

"So," she asked, "your impression of the great man?"

"Hard to say."

"Oh?" Talbot arched her eyes dramatically. "I find it hard to believe . . . a professional investigator like you doesn't have an impression of the deputy secretary of state when you've grilled him in a murder case?"

"It wasn't a *grilling*," Frank said, not about to let her define the situation. "It was a conversation." He paused. "You're right. I usually meet people, talk with them, come away with a pretty definite impression. It may be totally wrong. I might have to adjust it later. But I have one." He shook his head. "Trevor . . ."

Talbot gave Frank a small welcoming smile, as if he'd passed an entrance-exam question and was now admitted to the club.

"Trevor," she finished for Frank, "is a lightweight."

"But he is where he is," Frank challenged, taking over as inquisitor.

"David Trevor is one of a Washington species," Talbot proclaimed, "men who make careers of being their fathers' sons."

"I always thought sons of legends had a hard time."

Talbot studied Frank, a small smile playing around the corners of her mouth. "You're being provocative."

Frank smiled. "Yes. Yes I am."

"What the hell." Talbot shrugged. Deciding to go the whole route, she leaned across the table. "Sons of legends don't have a hard time in this town. They always have that name as a safety net. They screw up . . . the establishment covers for them. Spins the disaster away."

"Where did David Trevor screw up?" Frank asked, thinking he'd caught Talbot short.

"He didn't," Talbot said, undaunted. "That's an alternative behavior pattern of fathers' sons . . . most of them don't have the initiative or ambition to do anything where they *could* screw up. They just sit in do-nothing positions with impressive titles. They go to receptions and conferences and write long inconsequential memos to each other."

"Did Mary Keegan write it that way in her book?"

"I haven't read any of the book. Mary was rabid about not showing early drafts. But I don't think so."

"Why?"

"She and I talked a lot about what she called the 'Famous-Man's-Son Syndrome.' She claimed that David Trevor was a late bloomer. I argued that he was just lucky. As my father used to say, 'Even a blind pig will occasionally find an acorn.' "

"What acorn did Trevor find?"

"Do you know George Kennan?"

Frank shook his head. "I'm afraid . . . ah . . . *Kennan?* A diplomat? I don't know . . ." He trailed off, feeling foolish.

Talbot nodded. "Kennan's in his nineties now. He's still up at Princeton, but it's been some time since he was a headliner.

"In 1947 Kennan returned from a tour at our embassy in Moscow. He wrote an anonymous article for *Foreign Affairs,* describing the Soviet Union as bent on worldwide domination.

"Fast-forward to 1989 . . . David Trevor writes an article for *Foreign Affairs.* That he wrote an article at all was a surprise. The bombshell that shook Foggy Bottom was that he bucked conventional wisdom and made a case that the Soviet Union was falling apart."

"A pretty good call."

"The foreign policy cognoscenti shit on both Kennan and Trevor—at first. Several months after Trevor publishes his article, the Berlin Wall comes down. Then it becomes apparent that Gorbachev can't hold the Soviet Union together."

"And it becomes apparent that David Trevor was one smart cookie along with George Kennan."

Talbot shrugged as if still baffled. "That was how Mary saw it."

"But you didn't?"

Talbot made another adjustment to her coffee mug, then looked up at him. "But I *still* don't."

Frank gave her a perplexed look.

Talbot shrugged. "Woman's intuition. The guy's a lightweight."

Some kind of sour grapes, Frank thought, remembering Damien Halligan's "abrasive bitch" assessment. Moving on, he asked, "Was she having any trouble with the book?"

"Every writer has troubles, Frank. The better the writer, the more shit they go through. They do it to themselves."

"How was she? The days before?"

"Absolutely bitchy."

"Was that normal?"

"No. I mean, I've seen her up and I've seen her down. So what I saw wasn't unusual."

"But it bothers you."

Talbot nodded. "I always knew what was behind her ups-and-downs. This time I didn't."

"Did you ask her?"

"No . . . yes."

For the first time, Frank saw her uncertain, indecisive.

Talbot must have read Frank's puzzlement on his face. "We could talk about anything, Mary and me. But this time around, when I started to, she just"—Talbot reached for a word—"put up a wall."

"Her mood—sad? angry?"

"Both. Add distant and bitter and you'd be close."

"When did you first notice?"

"Mid-August. I gave it a week. When it hadn't gone away by Labor Day weekend, that's when it seemed out of the ordinary."

"You think it had anything to do with the book?"

"I don't know." Talbot leaned across toward Frank. "Tell me, Lieutenant—what difference does it make?"

"What do you mean?"

"I mean, if some fucking nutso with a meat cleaver is doing in women, what did Mary's mood have to do with what happened to her?"

"I don't know."

Talbot persisted. "You don't know if we have a nutso? Or you don't know if Mary's mood had something to do with her getting killed?"

Frank picked up the check. "I don't know, Ms. Talbot . . . either . . . both."

Talbot put a hand on Frank's forearm. "One way or another, whichever it was, we're going to be on your ass, Lieutenant. Squeaking wheels get the grease. And I know how to make the wheels squeak." She smiled, reminding Frank of his third-grade teacher. Sister Agnes—quick with a smile, or a ruler across the knuckles. "Nothing personal, you understand."

Frank didn't smile back. "Yeah. Nothing personal."

SIX

✢ From the outside, the stone millhouse looked much the same as when it had been built in 1762. The ground floor had housed the mill, powered by a large waterwheel. The miller and his family had lived on the second and third floors.

Tom Kearney had meticulously restored the millhouse. Electricity and modern plumbing were present but unobtrusive. Structurally, the only major change had been converting the mill into a woodworking shop. But as with the rest of the building, his changes stayed true to the period. An eighteenth-century cabinetmaker would have been at home in Tom Kearney's shop. Overhead, a massive oak shaft from the water-wheel powered a web of pulleys and leather belts. The pulleys and belts ran a lathe, router, drill press, and several saws. Workbenches stretched along one wall. Storage bins for assorted hardwoods filled the opposite wall, and the air was thick with the spice of fresh-sawn wood.

A partially completed armoire waited on a work stand. One door had been hung, the other lay on a nearby bench. Frank ran a hand over one side. The walnut felt warm and smoothly inviting to his touch. The seams where the wood had been joined were invisible.

"I was going to have that finished by now," Tom Kearney said.

"It's a beautiful piece of work." Frank turned to his father. "You ever think you should have done this instead of running a courtroom?"

Tom shook his head. "I loved the law. I loved being a judge. I think I was a good one and I got a lot of satisfaction from the work I did. But one day, I looked at all the paper . . ." A wistful smile played on his father's lips. "Suddenly, I decided I wanted to make things that you can slap a hand on and say to yourself, 'That'll be here when I'm gone.'"

"You could have been doing this earlier."

"There's a certain age for doing cabinet work . . . a *right age*. Younger, I wouldn't have had the patience." His father looked lovingly at the armoire. His lips pressed together. "Much older, I wouldn't have had the time."

Frank knew his father was wondering if time had finally run out, and he felt a cold wind cut through him. For the first time, he saw his life without his father. Impulsively, he put his hand on his father's shoulder. "You'll be finishing that soon."

His father smoothed a hand over the deeply grained wood. "Yeah," he said without conviction. He took a last look at the armoire, then turned to Frank. "Let's go upstairs and I'll throw some things into a suitcase."

Using the cane, Tom Kearney slowly made his way up the narrow stairs to the third floor. There, his bedroom looked out on Waterford, a mile away down the valley. Phil Sheridan's troops had burned much of the village's commercial buildings during the Civil War, stunting its economic growth. After the war, the railroads bypassed the community, and paved roads didn't arrive until shortly before World War II. The proverbial blessing in disguise, Frank thought. The isolation saved Tom Kearney's mill and many of Waterford's buildings from suburban sprawl's invasion and the pretentious McMansions, the architectural felonies perpetrated by "modernization" and "developers."

"These are new." Framed photographs covering a wall drew Frank's attention.

Tom Kearney looked up from an open dresser drawer. "No. They're old."

"But new here. I haven't seen them before." Black-and-white photos. A young Tom Kearney in parachute and combat gear standing in front of a C-47 with a handful of other young paratroopers.

Tom walked over and stood next to Frank. "Parachute school, Fort Benning. This was just before our graduation jump." He caressed the rank of soldiers with his fingertip. "We stayed together through the war . . . those of us who made it through."

He gestured to the other pictures.

"I've had them stashed away all over the damn place. Boxes, footlockers. Never got around to framing them until now." He stood staring at a photo of another group of soldiers, this time in full battle dress, faces blackened. Standing in a crowded circle, Quonset huts dark in the background, a ramrod figure in the foreground, a general in neatly tailored short jacket, oblivious of the mud underfoot. The general stood with awe on his face, smiling at Tom Kearney, clasping the young soldier's shoulder.

Frank recognized the general. "Eisenhower."

"Evening of June 5, 1944. An hour after they took that picture," Tom said, voice catching, "we loaded up, we flew across the channel, and we jumped into France." He stood looking at the picture, and Frank knew he was hearing the roar of airplane engines.

"God, we were scared. We were all scared we'd die. But I think we were more scared that we'd fail."

"The last good war. You knew what you had to do."

"We had Franklin Roosevelt and Winston Churchill," Tom said. "You had Lyndon Johnson and Richard Nixon."

"If I'd gone to Canada, would you have supported me?"

Tom studied his son's face. "I never knew you thought about doing that."

Frank laughed. "I didn't, until I was in Vietnam." He looked back at other photographs on the wall. He pointed to one. His father and mother after their wedding, two days before Tom Kearney shipped off to North Africa. "She was a beautiful woman."

"Kind of woman you don't forget," Tom Kearney said.

"Because you can't?"

His father smiled. "Because you don't want to."

"You ever think of remarrying?"

Tom gazed at the photo, then at Frank. "She told me to, you know."

"When she was dying?"

"Yes. I never gave it any thought."

"It's been ten years."

Tom shook his head. "You get used to it."

"Being alone?"

"Being by yourself. There's a difference. Anyway"—Tom shook his head, as if wanting to go somewhere else—"it'd take a saint to put up with me, and there're damn few of those around." He motioned to a large walk-in closet. "One more thing and I'll be ready to go."

Frank walked over to the suitcase on the bed while his father disappeared into the closet. "You didn't pack much," he called out.

Tom came out of the closet leaning on an ornate cane. "Not planning on staying long."

"Where'd you get that?"

Tom held up the cane. "A souvenir. Belonged to an SS colonel. If I'm going to have to live in Georgetown, I'm damn sure not walking around with that scruffy thing they gave me at the hospital."

SEVEN

✠ Frank opened the office door. Leon Janowitz sat in a chair beside José's desk, opening a cardboard soup container. José was spreading mustard on a thick roast beef sandwich.

"Picnic?"

José waved his sandwich toward a brown bag on Frank's desk. "You got pastrami."

"Ruth still out of salami?"

"She gave you a quarter off. You get your dad settled?"

"If that's the word for it. He's not a happy camper."

José motioned to the young detective. "Leon here found the Boukedes autopsy files. I bought lunch to celebrate."

Janowitz smiled.

Frank sat down at his desk and began unwrapping his sandwich. The slender files lay beneath the soup container. "Thanks for letting us in on the case, Leon."

Janowitz got a bruised look. "Don't be pissed at me. Coleman stuck them in another case file. Took me two hours to find them."

"Maybe"—José waved a dill pickle spear—"I should give him José's first observation about being a cop?"

Frank bit into his sandwich. "Please do."

"Young Leon," José intoned, "José's first observation is that being a cop is like being Jesus."

"Being Jesus?" Janowitz frowned. "I wouldn't know."

José ignored him. "You can do miracles, but no matter how good you are, you're always going to piss somebody off."

Frank held out a hand. "Can we look at the file?"

Janowitz slid the file across to Frank's desk. Frank opened it to the photographs. A woman's naked cadaver lay face up on a stainless steel dissection table. Her head lay back at an improbable angle, an obscene grin beneath her chin where her throat had been slashed. Frank passed the photo to José.

"Wound patterns are different," Janowitz said. "If it was the same killer, wouldn't the patterns be more similar?"

Frank shook his head. "Not necessarily. If both women had been tied up, maybe. But both were fighting him off. He'd put the knife in where he could."

"He?"

"Yeah," said José. "Both victims were killed outside."

"So?"

"So," José said, "most women use a knife indoors. Kitchen, dining room, bedroom."

Janowitz looked at José for a beat, then when he was satisfied the older detective wasn't pulling his leg, he asked, "Now what?"

"You see this?" Frank asked, held up the lab work-up report across to Janowitz.

Janowitz shook his head.

Frank handed the three-page document to him. Janowitz ran a finger slowly down the first page. He stopped in the middle of the second and looked up at Frank with surprise. "No. I didn't."

"What is it?" José asked.

"Read it," Frank said.

Janowitz bent closer to the report, then read in a low voice: " 'Glycoprotein p-thirty test of vaginal swab indicates presence of semen. Sample analysis indicates sexual activity within two hours of death.' " He looked at Frank, then José, then back to Frank. "I didn't see this. I"—he searched for the words—"I fucked up."

"José's second observation?" Frank asked.

Downcast, Janowitz nodded.

"José's second observation," José said, "is that there's a lot of fine print in police work, and you got to read it all."

"What now?" Janowitz asked.

Frank reassembled the Boukedes file and handed it back to Janowitz. "We find the owner of that semen."

Janowitz took the file with both hands and held it across his chest. "And how do we do that?"

"We divide up the contacts you and Coleman canvassed. We go back and talk to them. We ask them different questions." Frank paused. "When can you give José and me a list?"

"Tomorrow?"

"Tomorrow—when?"

"Tomorrow afternoon?"

"How about tomorrow morning?"

"Okay, tomorrow morning."

Janowitz got up. He was at the door when José stopped him.

"Leon?"

"Yeah?"

"Where's her stuff?"

"Stuff?"

"Boukedes's belongings," José said.

"Condo on Q Street. Still there, I guess."

"All this time?"

"Probate. It was sealed, last time I checked."

"We better take another look," José said.

"I'll get the warrant," Janowitz said.

"Coleman let you off?"

"I don't think he'll miss me," the young detective said.

"Well, go ahead," Frank said, "and while you're at it, get Forensics to send Renfro Calkins."

"Get Forensics," Janowitz repeated.

"*Renfro Calkins* from Forensics," Frank emphasized, "don't let them give you anybody else."

"It'll take time."

"It'll take more time," José said, "the longer your young ass stands there."

Frank watched Janowitz leave, closing the door behind him. "Kid's got a case of the slows," he said.

"What're you hoping Renfro can find?"

Frank shrugged. "Anything, Hoser. Anything."

✠ WGMS was wrapping up a Beethoven sonata. The sonata wasn't helping with the traffic.

"Kate called this afternoon," Tom Kearney said.

A silver Lexus SUV from the next lane suddenly cut in front of Frank. "Idiot," he whispered. Wyoming plates. Mom and pop. Three kids in back. He finally turned to his father. "She want me?"

"No. Called to talk to me."

"Oh." Eyes back on the road. They were approaching the traffic knot at Pennsylvania and L. The Lexus had abruptly switched back to its former lane. Tourists and Washington's evening rush-hour traffic. A truly deadly combination.

"She wanted to know if I was getting settled. If I needed anything."

"And you said . . . ?"

"I said I was very comfortable."

Beethoven had given way to news-on-the-hour. Kosovo again.

"That all?"

"She wanted to know what I'd like for dinner tonight."

"Let me guess . . . meatloaf."

Tom Kearney nodded. "You find a woman who does meatloaf as good as that, you've found yourself a fine woman."

"The meatloaf standard for a happy marriage?"

"Good a measure as any." Tom said. "How'd things go this afternoon?"

"Oh." Frank paused, trying to find a word for the meeting with Janowitz. "Discouraging . . . no . . . disheartening." He described how the autopsy file had finally shown up and how, despite having the file for more than a month, Coleman and Janowitz had ignored it, missing the implications of the semen test.

"No semen in the Keegan autopsy?"

"No."

"Boukedes?"

"Semen sample positive, but no indication of violent sex."

"So if we have a serial killer, sex with his victim may not be part of his profile?"

"So far, if there is a serial killer, the only profile says Georgetown, knife, white female, outdoors after dark, missing little finger."

Up ahead at Constitution and 17th, the traffic thickened again. And WGMS had quit the news for a Vivaldi violin concerto.

"I'm hungry," said Tom Kearney.

"So am I."

✠ "Seconds?" Kate asked Tom Kearney.

It had been a family meal in Kate's kitchen. Dinner wreckage littered an antique harvest table: empty salad and dinner plates, a half-empty bottle of Merlot, and the heel of what had once been a large loaf of home-baked sourdough.

Tom Kearney held up his hands in surrender. "You're charitably unobservant. I've had seconds and thirds already. Any more, you'll have to roll me out of here."

Kate raised her glass. "To having you in town."

Tom frowned theatrically and thrust an accusing index finger at her. "Frank put you up to that."

"No—no, he didn't. But you can't blame him for worrying."

"I should move into the District so I can be *safe?*" The theatrical frown became an equally exaggerated look of amazement. "Hell, Kate,

I only had a small stroke." He turned to Frank. "How many times did I have to come to the emergency room because you'd been shot? Twice?"

Frank nodded.

Point made, Tom turned back to Kate, leaning forward on his elbows. "As long's we're talking about futures, how about you? My old firm just took in a government affairs specialist with nowhere near the résumé you have. Probably three times the salary and half the hours."

Kate swirled the wine in the bottom of her glass. Then she looked up at Frank, then to Tom. "Some days, I'd jump in a minute. Others . . ."

"What keeps you in a city job?" Tom asked.

"The same thing that sometimes makes me want to leave it . . . politics."

Tom cocked his head.

Kate got what Frank called her "earnest missionary" look, eyes looking to somewhere beyond and, in a way he couldn't describe, *into*.

"I like being where I can make a difference. Even a small difference. And I can—even in the district government. But it has a dark side, too . . . the corruption. In any government there's always an irreducible minimum of fraud and abuse. Sometimes I think that's the grease necessary to make the wheels turn. But when it gets too bad, the way it was in the District a few years ago, I'd like to fly off to someplace where everything's squeaky clean."

"Power corrupts," Frank said.

Tom shook his head. "Lord Acton was wrong. Power doesn't corrupt. Money doesn't, either—at least as long as you know who's taking what."

"Oh?" Frank sensed he was playing straight man.

"What does?" Kate asked.

"Pay the piper," Tom said, holding out his glass.

Kate filled it.

Tom took a sip and smacked his lips in satisfaction. "Ass kissing," he said in a dramatically reverent voice. He nodded as if in agreement with himself. "Ass kissing is the greatest threat to our democracy."

Silence.

Kate raised a skeptical eyebrow. "This will be interesting," she said. Frank nodded. "Original, anyway."

Kate tapped her spoon against her wineglass. "You have the floor," she said to Tom Kearney.

Tom got to his feet, one hand pushing against the edge of the table, the other using the cane. His manner was that of a judge instructing a jury. A jury of two.

"Lady and gentleman," he began, with a courtly bow to Kate, "Washington is a company town. That company's business is redistributing the nation's wealth. It takes in wealth by taxes and gives it back in the form of grants, entitlements, purchases, and outright pork barrel handouts. Like any business, the proprietors—Democrats and Republicans alike—the proprietors want their business to grow. So every year, government gets its hooks into more and more of what the average citizen makes and does." Tom paused. "Questions from the jury?"

Kate laughed and shook her head. "Carry on, Judge."

"So in this town," Tom continued, "two distinct classes of people have arisen: the wanters and the givers." Now playing an examiner, he pointed to Kate. "We call these distinct classes . . . ?"

Still laughing, Kate managed, "The ass-kissers and the ass-kissees?"

Tom gave her a thumbs-up. "Exactly! Now the kissers—you can also call them lobbyists—the kissers get better at it each year as the government business grows. And the kissees—our professional politicians—stay here for a career. And they get used to a life where everybody around them kisses their asses and tells them they are witty and charming and infinitely wise."

Frank raised a hand. "But there are elections—"

Tom dismissed him with a wave. "Incumbents run the show! They milk the ass-kissers for hundreds of millions in campaign funds. Few challengers can match that. In the last Congress, ninety-four percent of those who ran for reelection beat out their challengers. And even when these guys lose, they stay *here!*" Tom rapped the floor with his cane for emphasis. "They don't go home! Defeated ass-kissees become ass-kissers."

Kate parried. "But isn't all the ass kissing just an exercise in ego boosting?"

"Ah, Kate," Tom said. "Ego inflation's harmless—a misdemeanor at best. The felony—what hurts the country—is that all this ass kissing has led to a sense of entitlement. The kissee class believes they can do no wrong. They develop a religious certainty that anything they do is so marvelously virtuous that they have a permission slip to cut ethical and even criminal corners to achieve it. They come to believe they alone can bring about utopia, and that getting to utopia justifies any means."

Kate's smile slowly dissolved. What had started as a humorous after-dinner rant had run up on a hidden reef of hard truth.

As though sensing the show was over, Tom folded his napkin and put it on the table. "That's the sermon for the night. For a cup of coffee, I'll help with the dishes."

EIGHT

✠ **A**t quarter to eleven Thursday morning, Frank and José stood at the corner of 36th and O Streets, taking in the tangle of traffic in front of Holy Trinity Church. Sunlight danced on a parade of cars dropping off passengers into the apple-crisp autumn air. They clustered outside the church, as if reluctant to go in, talking and greeting newcomers with hugs, handshakes, and air-kisses.

"Looks more like a pregame crowd," José said.

Not right, Frank thought. It ought to rain on funerals. And mourners should stand in the rain as six grays pull a caisson with its flag-draped casket around a bend and out of sight into a dark forest.

Beat the drum slowly and play the pipes lowly.

He shook his head clear of the image.

"Woody?" he asked.

"Top floor, the school." José didn't look that way.

The school, a red-brick building, lay just past the church. Its upper-story windows offered a direct line of sight of street, sidewalk, and churchyard. No way you could get into the church without Woody's cameras catching you full face and profile.

"We got an appointment with the Thomas woman at two. Rutledge at four." José said.

Thomas? Rutledge? Carrie Thomas. Patrick Rutledge. Susan

Boukedes's friends and acquaintances. Retracing Coleman and Janowitz's initial canvass. Frank nodded toward the church. "Let's get a seat."

They found an empty pew toward the back. A crystal vase held a single rose, a drop of blood against the dark wood of the pulpit. Somewhere an organist played a Bach medley.

Black crepe bows marked the first two rows of pews for relatives and close friends. Frank recognized Mary Keegan's neighbor Judith Barnes, her head bent in close conversation with an older woman sitting next to her.

How many victim's funerals had he and José been to? There'd been . . . what? Average ten a year? Twelve? Okay, a compromise— 11.5. Times 25. That'd make 287. Two hundred eighty-seven *point* five, precisely. Stalin had said one death was a tragedy, a million a statistic. So you keep the point five because that way it's statistics, not tragedies. But faces kept intruding on the numbers. Hundreds of faces of the dead and hundreds more faces of the grieving. He felt someone sit down beside him. He realized it was his father, and the faces left.

Tom Kearney squeezed his son's arm.

"Looks like the A-list is here," he whispered.

Frank glanced back toward the door just as David Trevor came through. An attractive blond woman held his arm. His wife, Frank assumed. Flanking the blond, an older, taller man. Frank's first impression was of a soldier, a man used to command: erect, sharp, hawklike profile, snow white hair cut close on the sides with a black patch covering his left eye.

"Who's the older man?" Frank asked his father.

"Charles Trevor."

The Trevors chose seating across the aisle and several rows up. In the next few minutes, six senators, nine congressmen, and a Supreme Court justice filed past. He spotted Jessica Talbot just as she saw him. She rewarded him with a curt nod before moving on to find a seat in the front.

A short bit later, Damien Halligan entered, striding down the aisle alone, straight for the altar. When he got to the reserved front row,

Frank saw Halligan smile at Judith Barnes. Barnes stood and embraced Halligan.

"Who's that?" Tom Kearney asked.

"Mary Keegan's brother."

"And the woman?"

"Judith Barnes," Frank answered, "Mary Keegan's neighbor."

The church was almost filled and new arrivals had thinned to a trickle in the center aisle. The Bach medley faded. A few moments later, an elderly priest mounted the pulpit and stood motionlessly. The conversation buzz slowly died.

"Requiem aeternam dona eis, Domine . . ." the priest began the entrance antiphon. *Grant them eternal rest, O Lord . . .*

At that moment, José nudged him and dipped his head toward the aisle on the far left of the sanctuary.

A tall, erect black man in a conservative charcoal gray suit, his iron-gray hair clipped short and close to the skull, walked beside a petite black woman. He escorted her protectively, one hand cupping her elbow, the other placed lightly on her far shoulder.

Tom Kearney followed Frank's gaze.

"Isn't that Lamar Sheffield?" he whispered.

Frank nodded.

Frank followed Sheffield's progress down the aisle. The woman with Sheffield pointed to a pew. Sheffield smiled as if the woman had made a world-class choice.

"Almighty God, our Father . . ." The priest continued with the opening prayer.

The familiar ritual flowed around him, receding in the distance. Frank stared at Sheffield and flashed back twelve years.

August 20, 1988. Midnight in an Anacostia schoolyard. No gathering of the curious. Normally a raucous light and sound show, the surrounding street and sidewalks were dark and deserted as the backside of the moon. There was the stillness and the smell.

A subtle break in the service drew Frank's attention to the pulpit. Damien Halligan had taken the priest's place. Frank realized it was time for the first reading.

Halligan announced a passage from the Book of Job.

" 'Ah, would that these words of mine were written down,' " he read, " 'with iron chisel cut into the rock forever.' "

Halligan's anger flowed in his voice, deep and powerful like a subterranean river. The congregation, captured in a hypnotic trance, froze in place.

Halligan looked up from the pulpit, the only motion in the vast sanctuary. And it seemed to Frank that Halligan was looking directly at him.

"This I *know*," Halligan said to Frank, "my avenger lives . . . and he will take his stand on earth."

Halligan ended the verse with a finality, like closing the covers of a book.

Frank knew Halligan had said all he was going to say. But Halligan stood motionless, a magnet, holding the congregation in an invisible force field. Then he abruptly returned to his seat. One moment he was there. The next he wasn't. An almost unbearable stillness stretched across the sanctuary. Then a cough. A shuffled foot. And the stillness snapped and the congregation, released, came to life.

The priest stepped to the altar. As he did, the stop-motion image of the Anacostia schoolyard went to forward.

Three men facedown on the outdoor basketball court. Hands wired behind their backs. Blood pools, reddish black under the floodlights. Bits of bone and tissue. The smell of the blood acid and metallic and sticking in the back of your throat in the hot summer night.

Sheffield had put out the word. No crack, no smack. But the money had been too much for Mookie, Travis, and Snake. And now their brains mingled on the dirty concrete.

"It's over," Frank heard his father say. People filled the aisles and Sheffield was already at the exit. Finally outside with his father and José, he glimpsed Sheffield's back at a distance through the crowd clustered along the sidewalk. The tall man ushered the woman with him into a limo's backseat and followed her. Frank stood at the curb and watched the car disappear into the traffic.

José and his father joined him.

"Age suits Mr. Sheffield," Tom Kearney said, looking in the same direction as Frank. "He looks like Nelson Mandela."

"He isn't."

"I thought he'd still be in jail."

Frank shook his head.

"No, Dad. He got twenty, reduced to fifteen, and got out in eight."

"What's he doing now?"

"Word on the street, he's retired," José said. "Living off the interest."

"So what was he doing here?" Tom Kearney asked.

"Good question, Dad," Frank said. "A very good question."

"Good morning, Mr. Kearney, Mr. Phelps. Who's this you have in tow?"

Judith Barnes had suddenly materialized at Frank's side.

"My father, Thomas—"

"Tom," Tom Kearney said.

"Mrs. Barnes was a friend of Mary Keegan's."

"Judith." She extended her hand to Tom Kearney.

"A beautiful service," she said to Frank.

"Yes. There were a lot of people."

"All Mary's friends."

"Did you happen to notice the tall black man—"

"The one with the silver hair? *So* distinguished." Barnes fairly gushed.

"Like Nelson Mandela," José suggested.

Barnes's smile grew. "Yes. Yes, he did, didn't he?"

"Have you seen him before?" Frank asked.

Barnes thought, then shook her head. "No." She paused, then shook her head more emphatically. "No. Should I have?"

Frank shook his head. "Anyone want a ride?" he asked Judith Barnes and his father.

His father shook his head. "I'll walk home," he said, and turned back to Judith Barnes.

Frank and José made their way up the block toward their car.

"You think Sheffield was seeing her?" José asked.

"Crossed my mind. I mean, why was he there?"

José shrugged and glanced back at the thinning crowd. "Don't see the brother."

"I think he's still inside."

"Reading was short and sweet."

How had Halligan said it? "This I know, my avenger lives."

"Short," Frank said, "but not very sweet."

"The man's definitely a Forever. A weird Forever."

And the image flashed across Frank's mind . . . Damien Halligan, staring deep into his dead sister's eyes.

NINE

✝ Just before two, Frank and José filed through the serving line in the National Gallery of Art's coffee shop. Frank got a mug of coffee and José a double-scoop dish of vanilla.

Fifteen years before, Frank had stopped smoking. *Wednesday, May 8, 9:35 in the morning*. Whenever he got tempted to quit quitting, he'd visit the coffee shop, an easy walk from police headquarters. In the courtyard between the west and east buildings, a fountain splashes onto granite paving stones. Underground, the fountain run-off cascades against a glass wall in the coffee shop, creating an illusion of natural serenity even when the shop is crowded. Frank credited the coffee shop for helping him dump the habit and for introducing him to impressionist art.

At the cashier, José turned around. "Flip?"

"Yours is two-fifty," Frank protested, "mine's seventy-five cents."

"Yeah."

"Well?"

"But you always win."

"Okay," Frank said. José's quarter arced through the air. "Heads," he called.

José caught the quarter and slapped it onto the back of his left hand. He raised his right hand and peeked at the coin. "Damn," he breathed.

While José paid, Frank made for his favorite table, a place near the waterfall where he could watch both entrances.

"Sheffield was looking good." José put his ice cream down and pulled up a chair.

"All that clean living at Lorton," Frank said. He sipped his coffee and frowned. Institutional coffee was either one thing or another. At headquarters, the stuff could wake the dead; here the coffee needed a black cell transfusion.

"He was always a clean liver," José said. He dug his spoon into the ice cream. "Never smoked, never drank."

"Yeah, that Lamar was a regular saint."

José excavated another spoonful. He held the spoon out for Frank to see. "Why do they say vanilla when they mean plain?"

"What?"

"Somebody says plain, they compare it to vanilla."

"Beats me, Hoser."

José tasted the ice cream. "Vanilla's complex. It just looks simple."

"There's a message in there somewhere?"

José shrugged. "Just that if a place makes good vanilla, the rest of the ice cream's gonna be good, too."

A thin white woman in her thirties, attractive in a brown-haired, girl-next-door way, came toward them from the direction of the gift shop.

"I think that's her?" José asked.

The woman wore Nike running shoes with an expensively tailored dark green wool suit and a paisley blouse. Backpack slung over one shoulder, she carried a bottle of water. *Urban safari chic.*

"Yeah. Probably."

The woman came to their table. Frank and José stood.

"Ms. Thomas? Carrie Thomas?" Frank asked.

She nodded. "You are . . . ?"

"Frank Kearney."

"I'm José Phelps."

"José?"

José pulled out a chair for Thomas. "Short for Josephus."

Thomas eased the backpack to the floor by her chair then sat down.

Frank and José flashed their credentials. Thomas, like most civilians, gave them a perfunctory glance. Credentials might as well be a Buyer's Club card. Terry Quinn had once stuck Adolf Hitler's picture over his own and started a pool in Homicide. Guess how long it would be before anybody picked up on it and you take the pot. It took Randolph Emerson a Saturday-morning inspection two weeks later to notice. Terry won his own pool and donated the winnings to the relief fund. And four days later, Terry'd been killed in a dark parking garage.

"Where's Detective Coleman?"

"He's working another case," José said.

"It's gotten bigger, hasn't it?" Her voice had an apprehensive edge.

"Bigger?" Frank asked.

"Mary Keegan."

There was something familiar in the way Thomas said the name, so Frank asked, "You knew her?"

"We'd met."

"Oh?"

Thomas, picking up on Frank's interest, shook her head. "It was nothing. A book signing two years ago. I said I liked her writing. She said thank you."

"That was it?"

"That was it." Thomas got a sad, withdrawn look. "But when I read about her . . . what happened to her . . . I mean, she was a real person to me. Not just another name. Susan, then her."

Thomas paused, then leaned toward Frank and José as if she was about to share a secret. "Somehow you think that people that you *know*—they're *protected*—that something as awful as *that*—can't happen to them." She leaned even closer as if it was important that the two men hear her and understand her. "I'm not a coward. But I'm frightened."

"Ms. Thomas," José said, "you work at Commerce. What do you do there?"

It took a second for José's question to reach her. When it did, she seemed relieved.

"I'm a Mediterranean trade analyst."

"How'd you meet Susan Boukedes?"

"I explained that to Detective Coleman."

"Once more? For us?"

"It was two years ago. Two years ago last June. At a reception. It was one of those dreadful government things. Where you stand around with a bad drink, talking to people you'll never see again about stuff you don't care about. We—Susan and I—met at the bar. Both of us were bored witless. She said she was doing trade at the Greek embassy. I said that I'd just been promoted to the Mediterranean position. That I didn't know the Med very well. She offered to help. I liked her. There was something about her that was very likable. Anyway, we said we'd get together for lunch. A couple of weeks later, we did."

"So you knew her for a little over two years. Did you consider her a close friend?"

"We were close for knowing each other only two years."

"She ever describe anyone who might have been an enemy?"

"No. No one."

"How about Patrick Rutledge?" José asked.

"Every woman has an old boyfriend. Or two."

"How long ago did they break up?"

"Over a year ago."

"Who broke up with who?"

Thomas looked down at the tabletop. Finally she said, "She told me they decided to end it."

"Like it was mutual."

"Yes."

"Could it have been another man?" José asked.

"I asked. She said no."

"You sound uncertain."

"I guess I am . . . was."

"Why?"

Thomas shrugged. "Susan was the kind of woman who always had a man."

"You knew her only two years," Frank said.

Thomas gave Frank a "God help me" look. "Women just *know* about other women," she said, as if talking to a small child who'd asked how she knew the stove was hot.

Frank slogged on. "But you don't *know* if she did?"

"No."

"Don't you find that unusual? I mean, since you were so close and all?"

Thomas's mouth tightened. "There's a lot I find unusual, Lieutenant. For starters, that she was stabbed to death in Rock Creek two months ago, and you haven't found her killer yet, and now another woman's dead."

For a moment, a brittle silence, then the anger in her eyes dissolved into tears. "I'm sorry." She reached into her backpack and came up with a Kleenex.

"How would you characterize her state of mind before she was killed?" José asked.

"State of mind," Thomas, preoccupied, dabbed at her nose with the Kleenex. "She seemed . . . hemmed in."

"How so?" Frank asked.

"Apprehensive. Nervous. Whenever we went out, I had a hard time getting her attention. She was constantly . . . watching, looking for something, somebody."

"When did you first notice this?"

"Sometime this summer. I don't recall exactly."

"You talk to her about it?"

"I asked her if she was okay. Several times. She'd always answer, 'Fine, fine.' Either I was wrong or she didn't want to talk. I didn't ask again."

Thomas glanced at her watch. "I have to get back."

Frank handed her his card. "You'll leave here and remember something. Most people do." He pointed to the card. "You do, call. Anytime. Call."

She looked at the card, then slipped it in a pocket. She stood and shouldered the backpack. "He's out there, isn't he?" she said to Frank. "Planning the next one?" Reading the answer in Frank's eyes, she turned and left.

Frank watched her make her way out of the coffee shop, then turned to José. "We've got a few minutes," he said, "want to look at the Monets?"

✠ Rutledge Construction occupied a site at the northwest corner of 24th and Pennsylvania. Six months before, Frank recalled sadly, a large Victorian-era office building had defined that corner, an ornate extravaganza of dark red brick, crenellated towers, mansard roof, and verdigris copper guttering and downspouts. The old building had watched almost a hundred and fifty years of Washington pass its doors.

The wrecking ball had brought it all down in a morning. Now a ten-foot chain-link fence surrounded a large pit in which dozers, excavators, and graders noisily carved the earth for the foundation of a more energy-efficient, environmentally responsible building that would resemble a glass-and-steel cube.

The construction office, a large white mobile home, stood on creosoted timbers at the north end of the pit. Frank knocked, then opened the door.

Three men in hardhats and twill work clothes huddled around a long drafting table. On the table, coils of blueprints. Above the table, a large picture window looked out over the work site.

The three men looked up as Frank and José entered. One, the tallest of the three, a heavyset man, stepped forward.

"Help you?"

"Patrick Rutledge?" Frank asked.

"That's me," the man said.

Frank judged Rutledge to be in his late thirties. Blue eyes. Slightly over six feet. No gut to speak of.

Frank and José flashed their badges. "Kearney and Phelps," Frank said.

Rutledge turned to his two companions and angled his head toward the door. The two men rolled up the blueprints and left.

"Okay," Rutledge said, "what now?" He made no move to shake hands.

"Some follow-up questions about the Susan Boukedes killing," Frank said.

"Yeah?"

"You want to stand or sit?" Frank asked.

Rutledge didn't say anything but turned and walked over to a cluster of folding metal chairs near a bank of file cabinets.

Frank felt a rising irritation with Rutledge's short manner. "You told detectives Coleman and Janowitz that you and Susan Boukedes had been going together for two years."

"Yes."

"Was it an exclusive relationship? For both of you?"

"Not at first."

"When did it become one?"

"Didn't take long."

"Can you be more specific?"

"Why?"

Slow down, Frank told himself, slow down. "Because it might be important."

"How?"

Frank tamped down his rising irritation. "You have a problem, Mr. Rutledge?"

"Yeah, I got a problem," Rutledge came back. "I got a problem laying my life out for a couple a strangers."

Frank felt his gut tighten. "Susan Boukedes doesn't have any problems anymore," he said. "You want to help us? Or you want to screw around with us? We can talk here, or we can go downtown."

Rutledge took his hardhat off and ran his fingers through his dark hair. He shrugged and dropped the hardhat on the floor beside his chair.

"We met March '97," he said. The edge in his voice disappeared, and in its place a flat, toneless sadness. "She and I . . . we . . ."—he searched somewhere over Frank's head—"we fit together like we'd known each other all our lives. By June it was a one-and-one thing."

"Until?"

"Until April last year."

"She told Carrie Thomas the breakup was mutual."

"Mutual?" Rutledge winced. "*She* broke it off. One minute, everything was great, the next, I get a phone call. 'I don't want to see you anymore.' That's all she said. All she said after two years." He shook his head at the memory. "A fucking phone call," he said to himself.

"Piss you off?" José asked.

"What do you think?" Rutledge leaned forward, elbows on his knees. He raised his big hands palm up, as if in supplication. "I can understand some woman . . . all of a sudden looking at me and deciding that's it. But I'm an engineer." Rutledge glanced toward the window and his construction site. "If something goes wrong, something breaks, I want to know why."

"And she didn't tell you why?"

Rutledge shook his head. "And I'll never know."

Frank mentally reviewed Coleman's canvassing notes.

"You were home the night she was killed," he said.

"That's right."

"Alone."

"Alone." Rutledge's voice was calm.

"After you broke up," José said, "you ever see her again?"

"No."

"You said you want to know why something goes wrong," José said. "You didn't go by where she lived? Her office?"

"I told you I wanted to know," Rutledge replied. "Susan would have told me if she'd wanted to. She didn't tell me because she didn't want to. I wasn't about to go hanging around pissing and moaning. I'm a lot of things. But I'm not a whiner."

"You got any guesses as to why?"

"Well," Rutledge said with a trace of bitterness, "I don't think she was going off to be a nun."

"You think there was another man?"

"Yeah. That's what I think."

"But," José persisted, "you don't know."

Rutledge gave José a weary look. "There's lots of things I *don't* know. And there's lots of things I wouldn't give a shit *to* know. And that's one of them."

"It bothered you then, but now you don't care?"

"Sure, it bothered me. It bothered me for a long while. But a long while isn't forever. I *can* put things behind me."

"Where were you last Sunday?" Frank asked. "From six in the evening on?"

"Home."

"You with anybody?"

"No. Should I have been?"

✛ Frank got home after dark. Down the hallway, his father sat at the kitchen table. He heard the sound of another man's voice. His father waved him on back.

"We have a visitor," Tom Kearney said as Frank came into the kitchen.

Lamar Sheffield wore the same dark suit he'd worn at Mary Keegan's service. And his father had been right. Sheffield did look like Mandela. Some of it was the straight backbone of a man who'd never learned to bow. And some was the rich silver hair. Most of all, Frank decided, it was the serene confidence in his eyes. A look like that came from knowing you'd faced your worst fears and learned to live with them. Both men had been drinking coffee.

Sheffield rolled an open hand toward Tom Kearney.

"Your father," he said, "is a very hospitable gentleman."

Tom Kearney got up. He acknowledged the compliment with a small bow.

"I'm a very *curious* gentleman," he said. "But now it's bedtime for Bonzo. The sadists have me on the treadmill tomorrow morning early."

Frank watched his father walk toward the stairs. Then he sat in his father's chair.

"Second time today you surprised me, Mr. Sheffield."

Sheffield adjusted his coffee cup in its saucer.

"You and José are working the Mary Keegan case."

"Why were you at the service? Why are you here?"

"I want to help if I can."

"Why?"

"I knew her. She was a good person. And"—Sheffield paused—"I knew you'd connect me sooner or later with Ms. Keegan's last days. So I decided to get this part of it over with."

"How would I have connected you?"

"Through the book."

"Book?"

"Why, the one she was writing."

"Look, Mr. Sheffield, you came here on your own. I guess it was to tell me something. I have to drag it out of you?"

Sheffield raised both hands in surrender. Frank noticed a gold Masonic ring on his right hand, a wedding band on his left.

"Talking to police doesn't come easy, Lieutenant. Some habits are hard to break," Sheffield said. "Ms. Keegan came to me last summer . . . a year ago this past June. She said she wanted to do a book. A book about fathers and sons. And she wanted to write about John and me."

"She tell you what the book was about? I mean, any more than it was fathers and sons?"

"She didn't talk about it. She interviewed John and me. Sometimes together. Most times separately."

"John . . . he's the real estate John Sheffield? The one doing the condos?"

Sheffield's chin lifted.

"The same."

"When'd you see her last?"

"Early this month."

Sheffield reached into an inner pocket and came out with a leather-bound appointment book. He leafed through it.

"Tuesday, October tenth. My office."

Five days before . . . before . . .

"And before that?"

Sheffield worked back through the book, stopped at a page.

"August sixteen this year. A Wednesday. We usually talked once a month. But she was gone a lot of September."

"You know where?"

"She didn't say. I didn't ask."

"What was the last meeting like?"

Sheffield closed the appointment book and put it away. He tugged at his lapels to straighten his suit jacket.

"Unhappy," he said.

"How?"

The old man smiled sadly, shaking his head. "I really can't remember. The interview started off on a sour note, then just got worse. At one point, I had trouble with my memory, and Ms. Keegan got wound up. Really wound up."

"Was that unusual?"

"The year-plus I knew her, she was steady. Professional."

"What happened that day?"

"Well, Lieutenant, like I say, I had a memory problem. She got vexed. That's the word, *vexed*. I just smiled. And kept smiling. We talked. My memory got better. Then she said she was sorry. I said that's all right."

"And that was that?"

"That was that," Sheffield said. He tilted his head back slightly and gave Frank a measuring look. "They say you're looking for a serial killer."

"What do you say?"

Sheffield thought about that.

"Not taking anything away from you folks in blue," he began slowly, "but you have to admit, you close most of your cases with snitches. You got a serial killer, you got a loner."

"But you think you can help."

"I didn't say I *could* help," Sheffield said. "I said I *would* help. There's a difference."

"A big one."

Sheffield gathered himself up. As he stood, he buttoned his suit jacket.

"I wanted you to know you could call on me," he said. "Too many good people getting killed."

"I never thought killing bothered you."

"What bothered me was some people, the only answer was killing them."

"And you made the decision."

"*They* decided. They had a choice. They made the wrong choice."

"Do what you said or don't do what you said. That was their choice."

"We were in a business. I was the boss."

"No more."

"No more," Sheffield said. The way he said it, he was relieved and oddly sad at the same time. "I'm retired"—he flashed a smile heavy with irony—"I'm retired and now the streets are safer, aren't they, Lieutenant?"

"You and I have been here before," Frank said.

"Yes, we have. A long time ago. And we can't go back, can we, Lieutenant?"

Frank walked Sheffield to the front door. Frank reached around and opened it. Across the street, a car's interior lights went on as its driver got out and opened the back door.

Sheffield stepped out onto the stoop, turned, and offered Frank his hand.

"I still think that if you and I had reached an accommodation, the District might have been a better place today."

Frank took Sheffield's hand.

"Maybe better," Frank said. "But not good enough."

Sheffield studied Frank.

"Still an idealist."

"Still a cop."

Sheffield started down the steps, then stopped and turned back toward Frank.

"Thank you for your hospitality, Lieutenant. And tell your father good night for me. I'd had a lawyer like him defending me, you'd never have sent me to Lorton."

"You'd had a lawyer like him," Frank said, "you'd have had me between a rock and a hard place."

Sheffield laughed. "I think you like rocks and hard places, Lieutenant. Good night."

✠ The next morning, Frank dialed Jessica Talbot's direct line. He got the answering machine. He left a message asking her to call, then took the coffeemaker to the men's room, rinsed out yesterday's grounds, and filled it with fresh water. When he got back, José was hanging up his jacket.

"Damn car," José muttered.

"You stop buying those antiques," Frank said, "you stop buying somebody else's troubles." José had talked Frank into car hunting last year, and they'd found a '65 Mustang at a garage in Olney. Dark green with tan top and tan leather upholstery.

"It's a classic," José said, "all it needs is a generator overhaul."

"*Today,* all it needs . . ." Frank amended.

Going on the offensive, José pointed to the glass coffee container. "You clean that thing too much," José said, "coffee loses its character."

Frank peered into the container. "Yeah, but it was getting sort of green and there were little crawly things I couldn't identify. By the way," he said, "Lamar Sheffield was waiting for me when I got home last night."

"In the bushes?"

"Sitting at the kitchen table with my dad. Two old guys drinking coffee and talking like they've known each other all their lives."

"He didn't come to talk with your daddy."

"Mary Keegan was putting him in a book."

"Woman had a lot of irons in the fire. The Honorable David Trevor and his Honorable daddy. Now Lamar. This one gonna be called 'Crooks I Have Known'?"

"I think the Trevors and the Sheffields were in the same book."

"Helluva combination."

"Sheffield said she'd been interviewing him and his boy."

"He have any idea who did her?"

"No. He offered to help."

"Help? How? Why?"

"Nothing specific. But I got the feeling the offer had something personal behind it."

"How?"

"The way he talked about it . . . like he saw what Keegan was doing and the book was some kind of redemption."

"Re*demp*tion?"

"Just a guess, Hoser." He shrugged it off. "Just a guess."

José was still looking at him with a mixed expression of amusement and cynicism when the phone rang. Relieved, Frank picked it up.

Jessica Talbot's voice came over the phone like sandpaper. "You found Mary's killer and that's why you called me."

"No. Because I need a confirmation."

"Oh?"

"Her book—*Fathers' Sons*—who else besides the Trevors?"

"Ah," Talbot hesitated, then, slowly, "Lamar Sheffield and his son, the real estate guy."

"That's it? Four guys?"

"Four lifetimes, Lieutenant. More than enough for one book," Talbot said. "Now can I ask you a question?"

"Sure."

"Why're you asking? Something up? You going to arrest Lamar Sheffield or something?"

"Nobody's being arrested, Ms. Talbot," Frank said carefully. "I'm asking because it's just part of the background."

"My bullshit detector just went off, Lieutenant. Talk off the record?"

"No."

"How about background?" Talbot's tone grew more insistent.

A real nutcracker, Frank was thinking.

"No."

"Well, *shit*."

Do not gratuitously piss off anybody who owns a printing press, Terry Quinn once said. "There's nothing to talk about," Frank said, trying to sound cooperative without coming across like a suck-up. "Like I said, this's just part of the picture I'm putting together."

Listening to Frank's side of the conversation, José rolled his eyes toward the ceiling.

"Bullshit detector's still buzzing, Lieutenant." But Talbot's voice seemed a degree less abrasive.

"This's Washington, Ms. Talbot. Like pollen, there's always an irreducible minimum of bullshit in the air."

Talbot laughed and hung up.

"Pollen and bullshit," José bantered as Frank put the phone back in its cradle. "I gotta remember that."

"Do that, Hoser, and you'll go a long way." Frank got up and stretched. "Coffee ought to be ready." He had José's mug in hand when Leon Janowitz came in, waving an envelope.

"I got the warrant."

"Good," José said. "Warrant for what?"

Janowitz looked injured. "For the Boukedes place."

"That's half of it," Frank said. "How about Calkins?"

"Got him, too," Janowitz said, now smiling.

"What time?"

"Ten."

Frank checked his watch and stood. "We have half an hour."

"Where're you going?" José asked.

"See Eleanor about some people."

✠ Frank took the stairs to the third floor. Down the hall, past Randolph Emerson's office, he came to a door marked RECORDS AND

MODUS OPERANDI. A cipher lock keypad had been set into the door-jamb and beneath it a small plaque said RESTRICTED ACCESS. Frank keyed in his five-digit PIN. A relay clacked. He pushed the door open and entered.

A half-dozen men and women in civilian clothes sat at metal desks, each with a computer terminal. Frank made his way to a desk in the far corner. Eleanor had worked from the same desk when Frank first came on the force. The computer and the Internet had taken the place of stacks of newspapers, magazines, and scissors and tape, but Eleanor's job remained the same. If there was anything she didn't know about crime in the District of Columbia, it was in her files. And if it wasn't in her files, she knew where to find it.

Fingers flying across the keyboard, Eleanor didn't look up from her screen. "I'm working on it, Frank."

"What's 'it'?"

"The life and times of Jack the Ripper," she said, still locked onto the monitor.

"Maybe later," Frank said. "How about life and times of Charles Trevor and his son David?"

Eleanor dropped her hands into her lap and looked up at Frank, rimless glasses flashing in the overhead lights.

"*The* Charles Trevor, *the* David Trevor?"

"Yeah," Frank nodded. Then he added, "And whatever you can get on John Sheffield."

"Any relation to Lamar?"

"Son."

She scribbled on a yellow sticky and stuck it on her monitor screen. "Encyclopedia? Book? Dissertation?"

"One or two pages," Frank said. "Two at the most."

"Encyclopedia's easy. Two pages are hard."

"That's why I come to you."

Eleanor frowned. "You never give up on the charm."

"Hey, I try to read more than a couple pages, my lips get tired."

"When?"

"This afternoon?"

"The Trevors—they're part of this?"

"Maybe."

"Big time, small time, or just medium?"

Frank rolled a hand, palm up, palm down. "Maybe."

"Something like this, you have a lot of maybes."

"Something like this, everything's a maybe. This afternoon?"

Eleanor nodded. "This afternoon."

"One or two pages?"

"One or two pages."

✠ Just before ten, Frank, José, and Leon Janowitz stood on the Q Street bridge, looking south. Below, down a steep embankment, traffic streamed steadily on the Rock Creek Parkway. Rock Creek proper, a broad, clear stream, ran beside the parkway, and on the other side of the creek, a paved running path.

Leaning over the railing, Janowitz pointed to underbrush at the base of a bridge support. "Guy working on the bridge found her down there."

"So she wasn't *in* the creek," Frank said.

"I figure she was coming back from Dupont Circle." Janowitz's hand traced a path off to the left, where a sidewalk ran along the top of the embankment. "He knocks her off the sidewalk. Drags her into the underbrush. Anybody walking up top"—he shrugged—"wouldn't see a thing."

Janowitz gave Frank and José time to scope in the scene, then pointed to a sprawling five-story brick building just off the west end of the bridge. "Her condo's over there."

✠ A short entry led to a surprisingly large living room with glass sliding doors opening onto a balcony that overlooked the P Street bridge to the south. Two doors off the entry—one to a storage closet, the other into a smallish galley kitchen.

Susan Boukedes's taste ran to traditional. The walls had been painted a light chocolate with cream-colored crown moldings. The principal piece of furniture was a long couch in beige velour. Two Queen Anne chairs upholstered in a conservative floral print faced the sofa across a coffee table.

The doorbell chimed. José opened the door to Renfro Calkins and two of his evidence specialists with their equipment suitcases. The three newcomers paused in the doorway, taking in the place.

The chocolate-and-cream motif carried down the hallway to the bedroom. It had been furnished with an eclectic mix of flea-market scrounging and downscale antique hunting. A canopy bed, mismatched bedside tables, painted wood chests of drawers, a platform rocker.

Janowitz started for the bed.

"What're you doing?" José asked.

"Pull the sheets."

"Renfro'll get them."

Janowitz stood at the bed with an uncomprehending look on his face.

"You strip a bed the wrong way, you might lose something," José explained. "A hair. Flake of skin. Fiber from somebody's clothes. You strip that bed"—he pointed and shook his finger for emphasis—"and Renfro's gonna be certain you lost something."

"But—"

"But you'll be able to ride his lower lip for the rest of the day, he catches you stripping that bed," José said.

"Why don't you see how he's doing in the living room?" Frank suggested to Janowitz.

For the next twenty minutes, he and José searched nightstands, dresser drawers, and two closets.

"Well," said José, looking around the room to see if he'd missed anything, "no sign anybody's been here except her."

Frank stepped into the bathroom. To his right, a glass-enclosed shower. Toilet, bidet, and a tub for two on the left. To his front, a long tile counter with two side-by-side sinks beneath a wall-to-wall mirrored medicine cabinet. He opened one door. Cosmetics, hair stuff, lotions.

A woman's medicine cabinet always made him feel he was in a foreign country. Behind the adjacent mirrored door, stuff for the inside woman: aspirin, a box of tampons, dental floss, mouthwash, contact lens solutions and cleaners, and nasal spray. A separate shelf for the prescription drugs: Susan Boukedes had a cholesterol problem, a minor asthmatic condition, and—

"What's that?" José asked.

Frank tossed a plastic container to José.

José pulled a pair of reading glasses from his jacket and read the label. "Refilled a week before she was killed." He scribbled the prescription number in his notebook and tossed the container back to Frank.

First, the autopsy semen swab and now a current prescription for birth control pills. "Looks like she had a man on a regular basis," he said.

"Best kind to have," José said. "Other bedroom?"

Susan Boukedes hadn't used the second bedroom as a bedroom. At one end of the room a StairMaster and a stationary bike waited like a pair of patient draft animals. A white towel hung over the bike's handlebars. Frank touched the towel, as if it might connect him with Susan Boukedes. He felt only the towel's rough texture through his latex gloves.

"Frank?"

The other end of the room had been fitted out as a home office. José stood in front of a computer set up on an old-fashioned rolltop desk. Nearby, sectional bookcases bulged with large black three-ring binders. Frank opened one—Commerce Department trade abstracts, licensing regulations from State, Pentagon bulletins on foreign military sales. Replacing the binder, he picked up the telephone. No dial tone.

Frank scanned the room for another moment.

"Let's find Renfro," he said.

✠ Renfro Calkins took in the room with quick, skirting movements of his hazel cat eyes. Calkins was a wiry, humorless man in his late forties with a blue-black skin. His hobby was collecting small things—stamps, shell casings, thimbles. And each small thing he collected told a story about a previous owner.

"What do you want to know?" he asked Frank.

"I want to know everything she did with this computer. Programs, files, e-mail, calendars. Everything."

"I can do that."

"I know, Renfro. That's why I asked."

On the sidewalk outside the Boukedes house, Frank and José leaned up against their car, thinking about what next.

"She had the prescription filled at the CVS on Dupont Circle," José said.

✠ Frank remembered when a Peoples drugstore had been on that corner. For generations, an old-line Washington business with a solid blue-collar name. Then CVS bought out Peoples. The chain had also bought the old Biograph theater on M Street. And the movie house on MacArthur Boulevard. They were putting a damn CVS on damn near every damn block in the damn District.

And he still didn't know what the letters stood for. It was like some monster was eating up entire neighborhoods. Whenever he thought about it too much it made him, like a kid, want to stay in bed and pull the covers up over his head.

The store was nearly empty. Back at the prescription counter, a lone pharmacist intently studied something on her computer screen. Unhappy with what it told her, she impatiently rapped on the keyboard. Frank and José stood quietly for a moment. The pharmacist kept working.

José tapped the glass partition with his badge. The pharmacist turned. Her annoyed scowl vanished when she saw José's badge. He passed his notebook through the partition.

"You refilled that prescription," José said, tracing the prescription number with his index finger. "When was it first filled?"

Frank nudged José. "See you outside."

Standing outside and looking over Dupont Circle, Frank found Patrick Rutledge's number in his notebook.

Rutledge answered on the second ring. Frank heard the sound of heavy earthmovers in the background. Frank identified himself.

"Yes?" Rutledge's tone was guarded.

"A follow-up about you and Susan Boukedes," Frank began, already feeling foolish for what he was going to ask next.

"Okay?"

"You were sexually intimate?" Frank asked.

"We went together two years."

"Yes or no?"

Rutledge laughed. "We fucked. I guess that counts, doesn't it?"

"What birth control did the two of you use?"

"Aw . . ."

Frank waited for Rutledge to answer.

"Didn't have to," Rutledge said finally.

"How do you mean?"

"I was married before. Two kids. Got myself a vasectomy."

Phone dead space.

"What next?" Rutledge asked. "You want to come over and check my balls?"

Frank hung up. "Prick," he muttered to himself.

José stood beside him. He had an amused grin.

"You two had a good-buddy conversation?"

Frank told José about the vasectomy as they walked down P Street.

"That tells us something."

"What?"

José arced a thumb over his shoulder, back into the CVS. "Boukedes got her initial prescription filled a month before she broke it off with Rutledge. Got it refilled every three months since. Clockwork."

"And that tells us . . . ?"

"She was fucking a married guy, Frank."

"Walk me through it."

"Okay. All of a sudden she breaks it off with the engineer. Doesn't tell him why, doesn't tell her best friend."

"And that means . . . ?"

"Means she met a guy. He was married. They had a quickie. Decided they wanted more. She goes on the pill. He was the guy she had sex with the night she was killed."

"Gut feeling?"

"Pretty good gut," José said, slapping his belly.

At the corner of Hopkins and P Street Frank pointed to a Thai restaurant. "Lunch? Something spicy for your gut? Then we talk to the neighbors?"

✠ Frank and José spent the afternoon in a neighborhood canvass. From the Ace Hardware to the Brickskeller, a lot of people knew Susan Boukedes. And a lot of those remembered her with Patrick Rutledge. But no one had seen her with another man since Rutledge stopped coming around. At Susan Boukedes's building, they found Janowitz's car and Calkins's van gone. Boukedes's front door had been locked and sealed.

"I think that's it for the day," José said. "I gotta pick up my car."

"I'll drop you," said Frank. "You need a loan? Maybe a second mortgage?"

✠ Back at the office, Frank found Eleanor's report waiting. Dialing the number Eleanor had provided for Charles Trevor, he got Trevor's assistant. A brief explanation, and he had an appointment with Trevor for ten the next morning.

He read the report again, then tilted back in his chair, and gazed out the window. The sun's last light had turned the Smithsonian castle a reddish orange, and a velvet autumn night had begun to settle over the trees on the Mall, several blocks away. He picked up his phone and dialed Kate's office.

His mood dropped as the phone rang three, four, five times. He was about to hang up when she answered. His delight in hearing her left him momentarily tongue-tied.

"Hello?" Kate repeated.

"It's me," Frank got out. "I was thinking about you."

"Good, I hope."

"Don't want to say over a government phone. How about over dinner?"

ELEVEN

✠ **F**rank got to Sam & Harry's just before eight. Michael, one of the two owners, met him at the door. Together the men walked back to Frank's customary table. There they spent a few minutes talking about the restaurant business, new additions to the wine list, and the Redskins season, already a disaster. After Michael left, Frank sat for a moment, scanning the nearly full restaurant, then took Eleanor's report from his jacket.

Eleanor had laid out the lives of the Trevors and the Sheffields in four chronologies. He hadn't started to read, when he felt a hand on his shoulder.

"Rule one. We leave the office at the office."

Kate wore a dark green knit suit with an antique gold pin Frank had gotten her when they were in Spain two years before.

He stood and kissed her. The pin and a faint tendril of Kate's perfume reminded him of sun and wine and an impossibly blue Andalusian sky. "Sometimes I'd like to leave the office, period."

"Ah, yes. The little house in the hills above Granada," Kate said, reading his mind, but not really, since it was something they'd talked about off and on ever since Spain. "No TV, radio, or newspapers, and in two weeks we'd drive each other absolutely wall-banging batshit."

"Who said women were romantics?" Frank asked. "Besides, I'm wall-banging batshit now and I haven't even left the District."

"Not going well?"

"I've got a feeling it's going to be messy."

"I thought your dad might be here."

Frank shook his head. "He said he had plans."

He motioned to the waiter standing by their table. "Drink?"

"Yes, but let's order. I'm hungry."

"The usual?"

Kate nodded and Frank ordered: a gin-tonic for Kate, martini for himself. A shared house salad, two New York strip steaks, both medium-rare, one baked potato, one mashed, a '97 Summers Merlot.

"What kind of plans?"

"Who?"

"Your dad—what kind of plans?"

"Fathers don't have to explain," Frank said. "Anyway, I wanted you to myself."

"Greedy boy."

"I am, I am."

The drinks came, big, strong, and cold. Frank savored the icy gin as it exploded silent and warm on the way to his stomach.

Kate pointed to Eleanor's report, still sitting by Frank's elbow. "Catching up on your reading?"

"Adding more pieces to the puzzle."

She scanned the introduction.

"Subjects of the book Mary Keegan was working on when she was killed."

Kate smiled, half amusement, half curiosity. "The Trevors and the Sheffields?"

"Fathers and their sons."

"Strange subject."

"How?"

"A book about *men?* Fathers and sons? All you read about is mothers and daughters, women and girls," Kate said. "And a *woman?*—

writing a book about fathers and sons?" She paused a beat, thinking about it. She laughed softly. "Probably would have been a best-seller."

Kate handed the report back to Frank. "But anything to do with her murder?"

"I don't know. Somebody kills somebody, it's like you've got an ocean of facts in front of you. Some have a bearing on the case, others don't. And we have to dip through that ocean with a teaspoon."

Frank saw their waiter approaching, balancing the serving tray overhead, weaving easily between the tables and crowds of customers.

Kate put her drink aside to make room for the salad. "And what are you going to do with those?" she asked, pointing to the Trevor and Sheffield bios.

"Start dipping." He put the report in his inside jacket pocket.

The steaks came as they were finishing their salad. The sommelier materialized at the same time, their wine cradled in the crook of his arm. The steaks were crusty, pink, and juicy, and the wine smooth, leaving a taste of spice and plum on the tongue.

Later, the steaks gone and the wine nearly so, Frank sat back in his chair. The lights were lower and the early hubbub of the restaurant had softened to a pleasant drone. Close your eyes just a bit and look around Sam & Harry's at the glass and the brass and the dark wood paneling and you could have been in Washington's gaslight days, a world alien to instant communications and unaccustomed to instant gratification. Maybe not a better world, Frank thought, but one that ticked over at a reasonable pace.

"You look content."

"There's something you get from a good steak that makes it worth the cholesterol," Frank said. "Add to it a bottle of good wine and a beautiful woman, and you begin to think that all that stuff at the office is unreal."

Under the table, he felt the top of Kate's foot nudge his calf.

"If you're calling me beautiful," she said, "I'll take that anytime, even if I do come after beef and wine."

Frank saw their waiter walking toward them.

"You want dessert? Coffee?"

"No." Frank felt her foot caressing his leg. "I want to go home. Do you want to go with me?"

"Yes," he said. And he did.

✚ "What time is it?" Kate murmured.

Frank rolled closer and kissed her throat.

"A little after two."

"Thought it'd be later."

"How late?"

"Maybe," she said, "a thousand years later."

She was silent for a long time, and Frank felt the pulse in her neck beating slowly and evenly against his lips.

"Tell me here's real," she whispered.

"It's real."

"And out there's unreal."

"It's unreal."

"That's good," Kate said, drifting off to sleep again.

TWELVE

✠ **W**hen Frank opened the office door, José was sitting at his desk, frowning at a booklet and penciling in spaces on an answer form.

"Bastards," José whispered to himself.

"You still screwing around with that?" Frank asked.

José took off his reading glasses. "I started thinking: I pitch this thing, then I can't bitch about the crap that comes out of personnel. Next time I'd go in, they look at me all innocent-like and say, 'Why Mr. Phelps, you didn't respond to our human resources questionnaire.' So I'm going to finish it, take it down there. Make sure they got it."

"Odds are, Hoser, even if you fill that out, they're gonna ignore it anyway."

Frank handed José the bios on the Trevors and Sheffields. "I called Charles Trevor's secretary last night. We're on to see him at ten."

Mug in hand, José got up and walked past Frank to the coffee-maker. "You'll have to go alone. I got a meeting with George Dalakas at ten-thirty."

"Dalakas?"

"Admin officer over at the Greek embassy. Thought I'd look at a few records."

"Checking on antsy Greeks?"

José filled his mug, wrinkling his nose over the coffee. "Damn stuff's burnt."

He turned to Frank. "Yeah. Something there." He looked into the coffee as if deliberating its fate, then shrugged and took the mug to his desk where for the next several minutes he read Eleanor's bios.

"Charles Trevor," José said, handing Trevor's bio back to Frank, "looks like he used to be the go-to man."

Frank went over the terse paragraphs. Trevor, born in 1920 and orphaned by a fire at three, had been taken in by his aunt in Glouces-ter, Massachusetts. A star athlete in high school, he had worked two years after graduation as a hand on a fishing trawler to save up for tuition at Harvard. Then came World War II and Trevor joined the Marines.

He made the big ones, Frank thought. A Marine Corps hat trick—Guadalcanal, Tarawa, Iwo Jima. On Iwo Jima, he dashed across a shot-to-hell clearing to ram a demolition charge through the firing slit of a Japanese machine-gun position. He won the Navy Cross, a third Purple Heart, and lost his left eye.

Then back to Harvard. This time, law school, paid for by his VA disability and the GI Bill. A renewal of the prewar friendship with another vet, former Navy lieutenant John Kennedy. After law school, marriage and a practice in Boston, with time out to manage Jack Kennedy's second congressional campaign in 1948. Then on to New York, the world of high finance at Lehman Brothers, and building the Trevor fortune.

Jack Kennedy called again. Again Charles Trevor dashed through gunfire. This time he rescued a faltering campaign in New York and delivered its forty-five electoral votes. And after Kennedy summoned Americans to ask what they could do for their country, he asked Trevor to come to Washington to be secretary of state.

Somewhere along the way, at some indefinable point in his rising trajectory in Kennedy's New Frontier, Charles Trevor had become an American grandee. A man—*a name*—sought after by the social elites of Washington, New York, and Los Angeles. A confidant of Wall Street and the Federal Reserve Board. A guarantor of a full house at Council on Foreign Relations dinners.

Frank's phone rang. Renfro Calkins from Forensics was on the other end.

"The Boukedes computer, Frank." Calkins sounded disappointed. "We have a problem."

"We? Problem?"

"I can access part of her files. Word processing, spread sheets, calendars, correspondence."

"Yes?"

"There's something I can't get to."

"Why?"

"A large segment of the hard drive is password protected, Frank. We've got some pretty good computer guys, but we could run into trouble getting around the password barrier. It could be rigged so we break through using a random password generator, everything inside melts down."

"It's a question of talent, Renfro?"

An injured silence.

"It's a question of budget, Frank. I can't hire what we need."

"I know somebody, Renfro. You okay with that?"

"I can't pay him."

"You won't need to. Play it right, he'll pay you."

Frank left early for his appointment with Charles Trevor. Stopping in Friendship Heights, he entered a walk-up apartment building and, on the second floor, knocked on a door. From somewhere down the poorly lit corridor came the peppery smell of chorizo and the sound of a woman scolding a crying child in Spanish.

He started to knock again.

The door opened. Bottle-bottom glasses, thin goatee, ratty ponytail. Hunter Elliott, a stick figure in jeans and plaid flannel shirt, stood in the doorway.

"Frank."

The astringent odor of electronics overcame the chorizo. Behind Elliott, a living room that resembled the East Coast branch of Microsoft. Racks of black boxes, flat-panel displays, and keyboards filled every inch of wall space. In the background, a slow, mournful orchestral piece played over unseen speakers, and a soprano sang in a language Frank guessed was Polish.

"Good morning, Hunter. Like I said on the phone, we have a computer problem."

Elliott nodded eagerly. "Is it big and bad?"

"Yes. Yes, it is."

Elliott smiled. "Come in. Come in."

✠ Leaving Elliott's apartment, Frank drove south on Connecticut, turned left on Tilden, and crossed Rock Creek Park north of where Susan Boukedes had been murdered. The directions he'd gotten from Trevor's assistant took him to Park Road, a wooded lane along the ridge overlooking the park. He pulled in at a fieldstone gateway. A squawk box stood on a cast-iron pillar. He rolled down his window and pressed the button on the box. A disembodied voice answered. Frank identified himself. The box didn't answer, but the high steel gate swung smoothly open.

The drive climbed the ridge, making several turns through a thick grove of oaks. Like curtains opening on a stage, the oaks parted dramatically to a table-flat expanse of lawn. Stage right, a butter-colored limestone mansion, complete with a turreted tower and leaded glass windows.

The graveled drive turned left then circled back to the right, bringing Frank to the front of the house. Off to the left of the house, a low limestone balustrade edged an elevated terrace. An old but highly polished Lincoln waited in a widened portion where the drive intersected the walkway to the house.

Frank pulled in on the far side of the Lincoln and got out. With the house at his back, he took in the panorama that the builder had meant to capture. The lush green lawn fanned out right and left, sloping down toward monumental Washington, a miniature city laid out in intricate detail like the display in a Fabergé egg. Put a flock of dark-faced Romanov sheep on the lawn, Frank was thinking, and you've got a Loire Valley château.

Charles Trevor's assistant, a slender, dark-haired woman, met Frank at the door. She introduced herself as Louise Stokes, examined his credentials carefully, then led him to the library.

The desk dominated the large room. Fully ten feet wide, Frank guessed, slate inlaid top and intricately carved oak. Two Morris chairs in rich maroon leather faced the desk. Behind the desk, French doors led out onto the terrace he had seen driving in. Crafted bookcases covered the walls from floor to the twelve-foot ceiling. Two fireplaces with carved marble surrounds accented the long interior wall. Between them stood an antique library table with six straight-back chairs. One of the chairs was pushed away from the table and cocked at an angle. On the table in front of the chair, open folders of clippings, a yellow legal pad, and a pewter cup with pencils.

"He'll be with you in just a moment," Stokes said. "Have a seat." She motioned toward the Morris chairs.

Frank turned down her offer of coffee or tea. She smiled and left. He walked slowly around the room, taking in the contents of the bookcases. Charles Trevor's taste in fiction ran to the international: Kafka and Dostoyevsky shared shelves with Hemingway and Rushdie. Foreign policy leaned toward the Anglo-Americans: Churchill, Eden, and Thatcher; Acheson, Marshall, and Kissinger.

Framed photographs randomly interrupted the rows of books. They weren't the meet-and-greet photos that adorned ego-walls in government offices and K Street lobbyist suites. These were amateur snapshots of generations of kids and dogs and bikes and families at the beach or a mountain lake. People playing, eating, laughing, singing.

"Good morning, Lieutenant." It was a voice accustomed to command. A smooth baritone ribbed with steel.

Startled, Frank turned. The instant impression of Charles Trevor was old-guard New England WASP: black eye-patch punctuating the long narrow face, square chin. Blue blazer, charcoal flannel trousers, cordovan tasseled loafers, and a repp tie worn with a white button-down-collar oxford shirt. A man who would still play hard on the tennis or squash court—flat belly, soldier-straight backbone, strong grip of hands tempered by decades of summers spent sailing.

"Good morning, Mr. Secretary."

At that, Trevor flashed a broad smile. "Mr. Secretary," he echoed, as if rolling it over for the sound of it. "You know your ancient history." He smiled again, then, suddenly, more seriously: "Louise said you were here about Mary Keegan."

"Yes, sir. And Susan Boukedes."

"Boukedes?"

"She worked for the Greek embassy . . ."

Trevor's chin raised in comprehension. "Oh . . . yes. Horrible." He motioned toward the two Morris chairs. "God, how could such things happen?" He stopped by one of the chairs. "I knew Mary, of course, and this other poor woman . . . murdered just over yonder." Trevor gestured sadly out toward the park for a moment then sat down.

He crossed a leg and looked at Frank with a steady, open gaze.

"What can I do?"

"Did you know Ms. Boukedes?"

"No."

"Well, then," Frank said, "you can help me fill in blanks about Ms. Keegan."

"A magnificent young woman." Trevor's voice carried a tone of affection and remorse. "A woman of great promise."

"When did you meet her?"

"The summer of 1982," Trevor said. He paused for a moment and looked out the French doors. He nodded, as if confirming to himself a date. "Yes. June. Pakistan."

"June '82. Pakistan," Frank said, "now *that* leads to a couple of questions."

Trevor laughed softly. "It was a good time for me, Lieutenant, an old wheel-horse recalled from the pasture to take on a piece of meaningful work. That summer, the Afghan resistance was on its last legs. Soviet helicopters were decimating the *mujahidin*. The president asked me to see if we could help out.

"Ms. Keegan was a correspondent for Agence France-Presse. She had been in Afghanistan for some time—about a year as I recall—she had some very good sources. She found out what we were up to and asked me for an interview. There was nothing I could tell her, of course."

"Stinger missiles?"

Trevor rewarded Frank with a nod and a smile and a look that said he'd made a subtle calibration to his initial measurement. Trevor neither denied nor confirmed Frank's guess, thereby confirming it.

"Ms. Keegan got the story and came back to me. She had all the details—our safe houses in Peshawar, logistics routes, training camps. I asked her to hold off publishing until we could get the resistance trained and equipped."

Trevor paused and got a pensive look. "She did. And because she did, we surprised the Soviets. We drove the Red Army from Afghanistan, and, I'm convinced, set in motion the forces that brought down Lenin's little house of cards."

"And so the Soviet Union fell apart because of Mary Keegan?" Frank asked it impulsively, intending it as light irony. Immediately he regretted the flippant tone, but Trevor smiled broadly.

"In every chain of events and actions, Lieutenant, there are any number of places where the king's messenger can fail for want of a horseshoe nail. The weather at Normandy, Jeb Stuart at Gettysburg. In Afghanistan, we might have found another way to twist the bear's tail if Mary had published that story, but she didn't, and we didn't have to."

"And your contact with her after that?"

Trevor smiled ruefully. "Washington's blessing is that you get to meet interesting people; Washington's curse is that you have to spend most of your time with the dull ones.

"I didn't see Mary for several years." Trevor continued. "I returned to the banking business. She came back to the States. Won the Pulitzer.

I sent her a congratulatory note, she phoned me; we had lunch and a good conversation. Several years later, I went to her wedding. I think that was 1986." Trevor paused, then nodded. "Yes, 1986. It was the next year that she published her biography of Eleanor Roosevelt. I hosted a book party for her here. I've seen few people with such a future ahead of them. Few who were genuinely good and honestly talented."

Trevor paused. When he picked up, he did so more slowly, a man less certain of his new footing.

"Then the accident . . . her husband's death. It devastated her. Some wrote her off—the ones who didn't know her. Her editor at the *Post* . . ." he reached for the name.

"Jessica Talbot," Frank said.

"Yes. Talbot." Trevor picked up speed again. "Did the right thing. Shipped Mary out to Moscow. Mary was a trooper. The kind to march toward the sound of the guns."

"So she and your son were there at the same time."

"Yes. They had met here in Washington while he was at Foggy Bottom. David got posted to Moscow as our embassy's political officer. He arrived there several months after Mary did in 1988. After the wheels fell off Moscow's little red wagon," Trevor continued, "she came back to Washington. She wrote several very good books. She and I usually managed to get together for lunch several times a year. Then, last year, she asked for my help with her new book. April, May, I think. I agreed. Thereafter, we met frequently.

"Louise has my calendar. Do you want . . . ?" Trevor looked inquiringly at Frank.

Frank shook his head. "Perhaps later. When did you last see her?"

"At lunch, here. It was a Friday in late September."

"How would you characterize her mood?"

Trevor thought for a moment. "Distracted," he said. He thought about it, and nodded, as if satisfied with the word. "Distracted," he repeated.

"We had found it most useful to divide our meetings into two parts. At the start, she'd go over notes from earlier meetings. We'd resolve any discrepancies—dates, places, people, that sort of thing. That done, we'd plow new ground. Ordinarily, she'd have a well-organized list of questions. I tweaked her once. Said she could have starred in the Inquisition. She was a digger . . ."

Trevor stopped. A flush came to his cheeks. "I've wandered off course, Lieutenant . . ."

"She was distracted at your last meeting."

"Ah." Trevor nodded. "Yes. Well-organized questions—we would march through them. Some I could answer right away, others I'd note to research and answer by mail or the next time we met. But at our last meeting, the September meeting, she didn't go back to the questions I owed her. And the questions she asked, the new ones, well, I felt I could have given her the most outrageous answers and she wouldn't have picked up on it."

"What were you supposed to be talking about in the meeting?" Frank asked.

"The political relationships between Moscow and Washington in the last days before the Communists lost power." Trevor nodded. "As I said, she seemed only partially here."

"Did you ever get to read any of her book?"

"No. I never asked. She never volunteered. I had the impression she held her work quite closely."

"Can you imagine anything related to the book that could have gotten her killed?"

The older man shook his head sadly. "I don't know what was in the book, but I can't think of anything David and I said that could cause anyone grief." Trevor slumped back in his chair, closed his good eye, and massaged the eyelid with thumb and forefinger.

Frank shut his notebook. "I've taken enough of your time."

Trevor dropped his hand and opened his eye wide. "Are you sure?"

Frank got up.

"For now. Thanks."

Trevor got up, pushing himself out of his chair with obvious effort.

"I'll walk you out."

Frank started to protest but held it. As the two men walked toward the library door, a framed photograph on a low side table caught Frank's eye. An earlier version of Charles Trevor stood by a helicopter. In the background, more helicopters, trucks, tents, sandbagged hootches, and coils of razor wire—the architectural elements of the American firebase in Vietnam. Trevor looked very much out of place, wearing a wrinkled seersucker suit and standing beside a tall young soldier in combat fatigues. On the boy's face, a man's confident grin.

Frank recognized the shoulder patch. "First Cav," he said, mostly to himself.

"My son."

Silence . . . and more silence.

Frank gave Trevor a sidelong glance. The older man was staring at the photograph, lost back in the day when he'd stood by his son.

"That was my son Joe. That was the last day I saw him," Trevor finally said.

Another awkward silence, then Trevor took Frank's elbow and walked with him to the front door.

Frank stepped outside and turned to thank Trevor.

Before Frank could say anything, Trevor said, "You were there, too—Vietnam."

"Yes, sir, '68 through '69. First Infantry Division."

"The Big Red One," Trevor said. "Officer?"

"Grunt. Squad leader."

Trevor's face softened. "Tell me, how do you think about it now—thirty years later?"

Thirty years? All that was thirty years ago?

Memory's images warred with the calendar's realities.

Hot and dry. Wet and cold.

Fear. Anger.

Beautiful, deadly countryside.

Faces . . . faces alive, faces dead, faces alive but about to be dead.

Crackling AK-47 rounds. Ramp of the Freedom Bird at Tan Son Nhut.

With a start, Frank came back to now. He realized Charles Trevor was looking at him with an expression that was at once curious and, at the same time, knowing.

"It used to make me angry," Frank said slowly, putting it together carefully. "It made me angry a lot. I still get angry." He paused, then faster, as if gathering emotional momentum, "But not as often. Not as much. Mainly, when I think about it now, it makes me sad, thinking about how the wrong guys won."

Weariness gathered in every line of Trevor's face. "And who let the wrong guys win?" he asked in a near whisper, a man who knew he had to ask the question, knowing at the same time he didn't want to hear the answer.

Frank glanced out across the lawn. Far away, the Lincoln Memorial and the Washington Monument and the Capitol dome gleamed pure and white, unsullied in the late morning's sun. He turned back to Trevor.

"You were here where those decisions were made, sir. You'd know that better than me." Frank said it not unkindly. "I'll tell you this: My squad didn't let them win."

THIRTEEN

✠ Frank stopped his car outside the gate to Charles Trevor's home. The dash clock said it was almost noon. He dialed José's cell phone. José answered on the second ring. He was at the Greek embassy. He guessed he'd be there another two, three hours. In the rearview mirror, Frank watched the gate close.

It took him ten minutes to get to the embassy and another fifteen to find a parking place where he wouldn't have to put a department permit on the dash. The permit kept the meter maids away. But it attracted assholes with a tire-iron or a couple of bricks and nothing to do but cruise around smashing windshields and sideview mirrors.

He met José in a foyer as big as a skating rink, all columns and marble inlaid floor. With him a short, black-haired man in a neat dark suit, white shirt, and paisley tie. José and the man were talking animatedly with their hands as if they were old pals.

"This's George Dalakas," José said.

Frank offered his hand.

Dalakas took the hand and smiled, showing small even teeth. "Mr. Phelps and I have found we have similar interests." Dalakas smiled some more.

"George has a '54 T-bird," José said. "And he knows his computers. He's been very helpful."

George. Frank recognized José's look—like Monty cornering a mouse. *Hoser, you smooth talker, you.*

"Sorry to be late," Frank said. "Where are we?"

"We've just had coffee," Dalakas said. "Would you—"

Frank waved him off.

"Well then," Dalakas said, businesslike and precise, but friendly. "Shall we continue?" He gestured down a hallway.

Their footsteps echoed off the polished marble floor. Frank marveled at George Dalakas's bureaucratic empire. The administrative section offices occupied both sides of the long corridor that formed the embassy's backbone.

"George is in charge of security," José said, "as well as care and feeding of the staff."

"And everything else the diplomats find insufficiently diplomatic," Dalakas said. He said it jokingly, but Frank thought he detected a sharp edge just below the surface.

Wherever he was on the embassy pecking order, Dalakas hadn't been shorted on real estate. His elegantly furnished corner office looked out on Massachusetts Avenue and Sheridan Circle.

"We were working here," Dalakas said, walking to a Louis IV table where two chairs centered on a stack of files and computer printouts. He pulled up a third chair for Frank.

"George pulled up a printout of staff log-in and log-out times," José explained. He pushed a legal pad over to Frank. On it, José had sketched a rough matrix.

Frank saw that the matrix was four weeks of a work-week calendar: Monday through Friday. The calendar covered July 10 through August 7, the day Susan Boukedes had been murdered.

"Logged out four in the afternoon," Frank read. He turned to Dalakas. "That normal?"

Dalakas paused. "Senior staff pretty much set their own hours. As long as they get their work done. And Ms. Boukedes was one of our most highly rated local employees."

Frank worked backward. Susan Boukedes had taken off at four every Monday in the four-week period. "Can we look at her time sheet for the past year?" he asked Dalakas.

"Now, *that* will take some time," Dalakas said, clearly unhappy with the prospect. "The way our computer is programmed, we will have to go over each day's master log and find Ms. Boukedes entries among the others."

José gave him a big smile and squeezed his shoulder. "We appreciate the cooperation, George," he said. "Where do we start?"

✝ "I'm gonna see numbers in my sleep tonight." José, eyes closed, slouched in the passenger seat, head back against the headrest.

Frank started the car. Years ago, he'd given up trying to apply any logic to the District's traffic. The only predictability was the unpredictability. Pick your route and pray. This afternoon he decided to gamble on a straight shot down Mass Avenue around Dupont, Scott, and Thomas circles, jink a right, then a left around Mount Vernon Place, then drop down 7th Street to headquarters on D Street.

He knew how José felt: the last hour with the mountain of printouts, his eyes felt as though somebody had gone over them with steel wool. They had a better picture of Susan Boukedes's last year at work—and more questions.

At Dupont Circle, a standoff between a forty-foot Metrobus nose to nose with a VW Beetle snarled traffic. The bus trying to get into the circle from P Street, the Beetle trying to leave the circle at 19th. Both drivers had apparently taken their blockhead pills that morning and neither would let the other pass.

Frank found a Maalox tablet in his jacket pocket. Susan Boukedes's early afternoon log-outs and long lunch hours had begun picking up about the time she'd broken up with Patrick Rutledge. What was that old song? "Afternoon Delight"? Another dot to put somewhere on the blank page and hope that if you collect enough dots and connect them right, you'll come up with something that makes sense. But it was already a very big page and there were damn few dots.

"You see Hunter?"

"He's going to call Renfro."

"How about Trevor? He do anything for us?" José asked.

Up ahead, traffic shifted enough for the Beetle to slip past the bus accompanied by blaring horns and extended middle fingers.

"Remember," Frank said, "how Jessica Talbot said she thought Keegan was off her feed the month before she was killed?"

"Yeah?"

"Keegan and Trevor had lunch the week before she was killed. He described her as distracted, unfocused. Something bothering her."

"No idea what?"

Frank shook his head. *Take Connecticut, then a left on K?* He gave that up and decided to stay on the circle and get off at Mass Avenue.

"Unusual," José said.

"How?"

"We got two worried women. But neither tell their closest friends what they're worried about. Don't hear of that, much." José paused a beat to look down Connecticut. "No traffic down there," he said.

Frank cut a glance. No traffic, but it was too late to turn off.

"Trevor able to name anybody who'd want Keegan dead?" José asked.

"No," Frank said, "and no connection to Boukedes."

"What was he like?"

Frank sifted through his impressions. "Smart," he said finally. "Rich. Connected to just about everybody who's walked through the White House in the past forty, fifty years. And a very sad man."

"Sad."

"Worst kind."

"What's that?"

"Kind that comes from regrets."

"He told you all that?"

"Not in so many words."

"Unh-huh."

Frank didn't have to look. That patronizing tone in José's voice was always accompanied by theatrical eye-rolling. "A feeling I got," Frank said, slightly pissed. "Body language. A feeling . . ." he finished lamely.

"You head-shrinking without a license," José kidded.

Frank ignored him. "More I look at this, the more I think Mary Keegan had a good book going. Fathers and sons. A lot of ground to plow there."

"Yeah, and a big audience. Every son has one. A father."

"Profound, Hoser. Can I quote you on that?"

José's cell phone burred.

"Feel free," he said, answering the phone. "Yeah?" he asked his caller. A moment, then: "That's good, Leon. Real good. First thing tomorrow morning." He clicked his phone off.

"Timeline inputs on Boukedes," José explained. "Janowitz's starting to get some traction."

No traffic at all around Thomas Circle. *Figure.*

"We ever that young?" Frank asked.

"Sometimes it doesn't seem like it. Other times it does."

"Same thing hit me with Trevor. Asked me what I thought about Vietnam thirty years later. My first reaction was, *Thirty years later?* Hell, it was just yesterday. And then I realize . . . it wasn't just yesterday. It *was* thirty years ago. But part of me still doesn't want to believe it because the picture's still so sharp, so bright . . ."

José sighed. "Yeah," he said wistfully, "the stuff that stays with you."

Both men were silent for several blocks. Just before Frank turned down 7th, José asked, "Boukedes and Keegan . . . what the hell was it that was bugging them?"

"We find that out, Hoser, it'll put a lot more dots on the paper."

Headquarters garage was just a couple of blocks away when the radio squawked. Commander Emerson requesting the presence of Lieutenants Kearney and Phelps. ASAP.

. . .

✠ Randolph Emerson's assistant waved Frank and José into Emerson's office. Emerson was at his desk, head down, signing papers, a bureaucratic little Dutch boy, furiously plugging leaks in the organizational dike.

"Charles Trevor," Randolph Emerson said without looking up from his signing, "how'd it go?"

Frank caught a sidelong glance from José. Both men stood silently. Frank watched the top of Emerson's head. Emerson shuffled through another document before he realized he hadn't been answered. He looked up with an impatient frown.

"Charles Trevor?"

"Yes, Randolph?" Frank answered.

"I asked how it went."

"No connection with Susan Boukedes. He confirmed that something was bothering Mary Keegan the week before she was killed. Nothing else new."

"It went well, though?"

"You asking was the great man irritated at having to talk to the police?"

Emerson's eyes hooded, and Frank imagined a cobra's forked tongue flicking angrily across the thin bloodless lips.

"Charles Trevor," Emerson said in a near whisper as if speaking to a dull child, "is a very important person. He is a very *powerful* person. And his *son* is—"

José cut him off. "We've heard this number before, Randolph."

Emerson tensed, pursing his lips in prim disapproval. He laced his fingers together in his lap.

"You want us to get your clearance before we interview?" Frank asked.

Signaling dismissal, Emerson reached for his pen with one hand, with the other for the next document in the stack on his desk. "I'm *saying*, I want this case closed as much as anyone. *That's* what I'm saying."

. . .

✠ " 'I'm *saying*, I want this case closed as much as anyone. *That's* what I'm saying,' " José mimicked in the hallway.

"What he's really saying is he wants to be head of Homicide but he doesn't want to deal with homicides. Just in-boxes and out-boxes." José punched Frank's biceps. "What do *you* say, Detective Lieutenant Kearney?"

Emerson had been so *Emerson* and José had been so Emerson that Frank couldn't help laughing.

"What *I* say, Detective Lieutenant Phelps, is my pop and I are going to eat some food we didn't have to cook, off plates we don't have to wash."

✠ Just past seven, Frank and his father walked to Café Milano on Prospect Street. Washington's European émigrés wouldn't begin showing up until after nine, and so the major activity in the restaurant was at the bar, where the last of the hard-core after-work drinkers were hanging out.

Tom Kearney studied the menu, then decided on a simple green salad and veal Milanese. Frank ordered an antipasto of grilled calamari, a cavatelli with sausage, and a '98 Mondavi Barbera.

An hour later, Frank's father sat back, looked approvingly at his empty plate, and reached for his wine. "That's almost worth coming into town for."

"How about the pleasure of staying with me?" Frank asked.

"Very definitely worth it, if I didn't have to put up with the doctors."

"Tests show anything?"

"They reveal a crotchety old man." He sipped his wine. Frank noticed the hand was steady and there was no dribbling at the lip.

His father put the wineglass down and gave him a severe look. "Well? I pass muster?"

Frank flushed at being caught. "The vision?"

"They say I've got a minor depth-perception problem."

His father had probably added the "minor." Frank made a mental note to check.

"Temporary?"

"They're not going to go out on a limb with something definite like that, especially to a lawyer. They're doctors. They're more afraid of getting sued than having a patient die."

"Okay," said Frank, "is it fixable?"

"They gave me a prescription for glasses. I took it down this afternoon." Tom Kearney reached over and filled Frank's glass. "You saw Charles Trevor today?"

"Yes. Yes, I did."

"Sounds like you aren't sure."

Frank thought about it. "I guess you're right. I'm not sure."

His father sat waiting.

"José kidded me today, about being a shrink," Frank began. "I've made mistakes reading people. But I never had a hard time doing the reading before."

"No handle on Trevor?"

"I think he's the second deepest man I've ever run into."

"The first?"

"I'm looking at him."

"It's called a father's edge," Tom Kearney smiled, obviously pleased. "What struck you about Trevor?"

"Something he said," Frank stopped. "No," he corrected himself, "it was the *way* he said it. I asked him how he happened to be in Pakistan when he met Mary Keegan. He said something like, "The president asked me to help out." Just like that. As if the president calls everybody and asks for a little help now and then. I wonder if it was just a sophisticated name-dropping technique."

"I don't think so." Tom Kearney shook his head. "Trevor wasn't dropping names. He's an old-school Democrat, but he's always been welcome at the White House—whoever's there."

"Do you think he wanted his son to carry on the family tradition?"

The place was starting to fill up: sleekly dressed men with tall women in short skirts. Frank lifted the wine bottle. His father held a hand flat over his glass. Frank emptied the bottle into his.

"Would you have wanted me to be a lawyer?" he asked.

"Follow in my illustrious footsteps?"

"I could have gone on to law school, joined the firm, maybe later become a judge."

Frank watched his father take that on. He'd started out kidding, but once he said it, he realized he cared about the answer.

"Kearney and Kearney," his father said reflectively. "Has a sound ring to it. Any father with an ounce of pride would warm to the thought of working with his son. But I wouldn't have done it."

"Why?" Frank asked, feeling a twinge of disappointment.

"I'd have worried that you were either sacrificing your independence for what you imagined would please me, or that you were reluctant to go out on your own. Either way, it'd mean that I'd been a failure." Tom Kearney let that sink in, then said, "But you're missing an element in the Trevor family makeup."

"What's that?"

Tom Kearney gazed off, trying to capture the passions of politics a generation ago. He smiled ironically. "We Americans fought against a British king, but I suspect we secretly miss the pomp and circumstance of a royal family. There's a powerful cultural yearning in this country for a political dynasty. When Nixon took over the White House, there was a lot of serious talk in the Democratic party about Charles Trevor as nominee for president. A bright, self-made man with two sons . . ." Tom Kearney shook his head. "David Trevor may not have had any choice but to be his father's son."

FOURTEEN

✦ Standing with one elbow resting on a filing cabinet, Frank looked at the first viewfoil Janowitz projected on the office wall. Plaster patches dimpled the images of three credit cards.

"Visa, MasterCard, and Discover," Janowitz ticked off. "She kept them paid off. Day she died, she owed less than a thousand, total."

"She got all three in June?" José asked. He sat at his desk, both hands around a mug of coffee.

At first, Frank didn't see where José was going. Then he realized that all three cards had the same expiration date—June 2002.

"She asked for new cards in June from all three companies," Janowitz said. "She told Visa and Discover credit managers that she'd lost her cards. MasterCard didn't keep a record as to why a new account was opened, but the most likely cause is loss or theft of the card."

"She report any theft?" Frank asked.

"No record she reported a theft or loss of property," Janowitz said. "Something else: earlier, in April, she changed her phone numbers and her Internet account. Phone company said she complained that someone had hacked into her computer."

"Did Ma Bell confirm it," Frank asked, "the hacking?"

"They couldn't. Not right away. I asked them to go back."

"How long will it take?"

"They don't know."

"You get anything else?" José asked.

Janowitz took the first viewfoil off the projector and put on another. "Susan Boukedes's last day. Logged in at the embassy at eight thirty-six in the morning of August 7. At four in the afternoon, she checked out of the embassy computer net. Forty-five minutes later, from her apartment, she called BeDuCi and got a reservation for two at eight. Two to four hours later, according to the ME's estimate, she died down near the creek."

"Anybody at BeDuCi remember her?" José asked.

Janowitz shook his head. "I found the waiter who had her table. Showed him her picture. Nothing. I said she might have been in there with a man. He said a lot of women come in with men. A smart-ass."

José's phone rang. He answered and listened.

"Upton," he said, hanging up, "he's got Susan Boukedes's little finger."

✠ Tony Upton held the finger in a pair of forceps. "It's hers," he said. "DNA . . . fingerprint . . . no doubt. It's hers."

He offered the forceps, grips-first to Frank. "It tested positive for sodium carbonate."

Frank took the forceps and turned the finger under Upton's examining lamp with its built-in magnifying glass. If it hadn't been for the fingernail, he thought, it could pass for a small dried-up sausage. He passed the forceps to José.

"Sodium carbonate?" he asked Upton.

Upton took the forceps from José, dropped the finger in a plastic evidence bag, and handed the bag to José. "Common name, natron. A desiccant," the medical examiner explained. "Takes the moisture out of human tissue. The Egyptians used it for embalming."

"Mummification? How long would that take?" Frank asked.

Upton thought for a moment. "Temperature and humidity are the major drivers," he said, "but normal indoor conditions this time of year, changing the sodium carbonate frequently? . . . a week, ten days."

"Where'd you get it?" José asked.

"One of Dayhuff's killers brought it in. They found it in a crack house on Kentucky Avenue. Almost spitting distance of the Capitol."

✠ "Yeah," Dayhuff said, "found it in the kitchen." Hal Dayhuff was a collection of muscles topped off by a precision-ground flat-top hair-cut. Behind him, on the firing line, his SWAT team shredded paper sil-houette targets in a roar of gunfire from a variety of pistols, shotguns, and submachine guns.

"Just a minute." Dayhuff turned away from Frank, José, and Janowitz and picked up a bullhorn. He gave a cease-fire and the gunfire rattled to a stop. Dayhuff barked a name Frank didn't catch, and a young man in black fatigues at the far right of the firing line turned and trotted toward them. Frank saw that the kid was carrying a CAR-18 assault rifle. The kid came to an abrupt halt in a stiff parade-ground position of attention.

"Patrolman Hernandez," Dayhuff said, "tell these gentlemen how you found the finger."

"Sir! Yes sir!" Hernandez barked. "At oh-one-thirty hours, Satur-day, twenty-one October, my teammate Murphy and I made a tactical entry at 4120 Kentucky Avenue, Southeast. Our point of entry was the rear door. Murphy took down the door. I went in over him into the kitchen. Nobody there." Hernandez's face darkened, remembering his disappointment.

"Busted play . . . place empty," Dayhuff said. "Shitbirds got tipped. Premises looked like a rabbit warren. Holes punched through the walls to the houses on both sides. You could run the whole block from house to house and stay under one roof."

"We searched the place," Hernandez continued. "A K-9 pooch sniffed out the finger in the disposal."

"You guys need any more from him?" Dayhuff said.

"No," Frank said, "that's all for now."

Hernandez double-timed back to the firing line.

"Who was there from Narcotics?" José asked Dayhuff.

✚ "Gory details all there. We didn't bring much home." Sellars said. Booth Sellars, Narcotics senior officer on the raid, handed Frank a copy of the after-action report.

"Who was supposed to be running the show?"

"Didn't have a name. Just there'd be three or four gunners. That's why we brought in Dayhuff."

"What'd you recover?" José asked.

Sellars had the sour look of a man getting his nose rubbed in his own screwup. "Four hundred grams of heroin. Stomped on so many times it was almost all sugar. A TV, two VCRs, six cell phones . . . and that fucking finger."

✚ Outside Sellars's office, the three men paused in the hallway.

"What next?" Janowitz asked.

"You go check Forensics. See what Calkins is up to," Frank said. "José and I will go commune with Emerson."

✚ "Oh my God." Randolph Emerson stared with morbid fascination at Susan Boukedes's finger. The finger, in the plastic evidence bag, lay in the middle of his desk. He kept staring, oblivious to Frank and José standing there. "Oh my God," he repeated.

"Saturday morning early," Frank began, "Booth and the tactical team tipped over a crack house on Kentucky Avenue."

"He found that finger," José said.

Emerson tore his eyes away from the finger. "The Greek in the Creek?"

José nodded. "Whoever took it also mummified it." José described Upton's analysis.

As if pulled by a magnetic force, Emerson's eyes went back to the finger. A silence developed that no one tried to end. It was finally broken when Emerson cleared his throat.

"It's a trophy," he said.

Frank shrugged.

"Have Eleanor run a check through NCIC. Homicide victims with missing fingers," Emerson said. "No, wait—make it homicide victims with a body part missing. This guy could be taking ears or anything else he could get to."

"Given the state of the finger," Frank said, "it's a good guess that it got to the crack house Friday night, October twentieth. Not much earlier or it would have picked up moisture and started to decay."

Emerson nodded. "So?"

"Well, Randolph," José said, "Susan Boukedes was killed August seventh up in Northwest. Her finger shows up over in Southeast almost two months later."

"So?"

"Don't you see? Somebody *had it* all that time. And it didn't get to Kentucky Avenue all by itself. Somebody had to bring it. And they had to have a reason."

"And?" Emerson asked.

"Frank and I are going to see an old family friend about some real estate."

Emerson looked at José and Frank. He almost asked the question: *Who?* But instead he picked up a pencil and poked Susan Boukedes's little finger across the desktop to Frank and Jose.

✛ Pennsylvania Avenue runs from Georgetown—just several blocks from Frank's home—all the way out to the District's southeast boundary with Maryland. Travel its length, and the avenue's personality changes.

Pennsylvania Avenue is a forgettable face in a crowd between Georgetown and the White House. There's Washington Circle at 23rd Street, the George Washington University Hospital, and blocks of anonymous low-rise apartment and office buildings.

Between the White House and the Capitol, Pennsylvania Avenue puts on Yankee Doodle and Battle Hymn of the Republic and struts its stuff as America's Main Street. It transforms itself into the majestic avenue seen on TV shots—an American president's parade ground. There is the Treasury, the Occidental restaurant, the magnificently ornate Willard Hotel, the Justice Department, the National Archives, the Navy Memorial, and finally, the proud dowager of Jenkins' Hill, the Capitol itself.

Frank and José drove southeast from the Capitol toward the Maryland boundary, where Pennsylvania Avenue undergoes its third metamorphosis and becomes a neighborhood street. Victorian rowhouses fill block after block. Those nearer the Capitol have been rescued and restored by gentrification; those further away still wait for the developer or the arsonist. Past Popeye's and the Tune Inn they turned off Pennsylvania and found a parking place on North Carolina Avenue. Frank fed the meter and they walked a block to Eastern Market.

Red bricked and red tile roofed, the market runs the length of the block between North Carolina and C Street. Inside, a labyrinth of stalls, counters, and display cases filled the cavernous interior. On Saturdays, market day, farmers and gardeners stake out spots on the sidewalk, beneath the corrugated metal porch along the front of the building.

Eastern Market is more than a historic building. It is a community. Generations of southeast Washington families have worked and shopped at the market. It has seen weddings and funerals. And like every community, the market looks to a handful of trusted members for news and advice, to settle arguments and mediate disputes. Gideon Weaver was one of these.

Gideon Weaver had been a market institution when Frank and

José came on the force. He was a round black Buddha, and his only concession to advancing age was his wheelchair. In 1986 the muscle-propelled chair gave way to electric power. Weaver consoled himself that the new chair gave him greater speed and range. This meant he could talk with more old friends and make more new friends. Gideon Weaver had friends on every block in Southeast.

Frequently, Gideon's friends had a word they wanted gotten to the police. They knew they could talk with Gideon without fear of something coming back and biting them. And Gideon would then call up and talk with Frank or José.

Gideon's stall at the north end of the market hall had a sign in Old English script that said BIBLES. Laid out on its broad counter for browsers, Bibles of all sorts: Revised Standard Version, King James, Catholic study editions. Bibles with and without the Apocrypha. Day Bibles, Year Bibles. Bibles in Korean, German, French, and Urdu.

"Franklin Delano Kearney and Josephus Adams Phelps." The voice rolled and rumbled. A basso profundo combination of strength and righteousness. Gideon Weaver tweaked his chair controls and turned to Frank and José, lighting them up with an incandescent smile.

"Maintain justice and do what is right?" Gideon challenged José.

"Isaiah." José got that out quickly, then started to flail. "Chapter . . . chapter . . ."

"Fifty-six," Gideon said, "verse one." He gave José a warning look. "You remember, now."

"Yes, sir." José nodded, uncharacteristically meek.

Gideon flashed a forgiving smile. "Your daddy taught you good, Josephus. And he's still saving the sinners of Bethel. But I haven't seen you in the congregation for some time."

Before José dredged up an excuse, Gideon turned his attention to Frank. "And your daddy, Franklin . . . I heard about the stroke . . . tell him he's in my prayers."

"I will, Gideon."

Gideon spread his arms to encompass the Bibles on display. "You're not here to buy a Bible."

José shook his head. "Not today."

"Then you're here to buy an old man a cup of coffee and a roll."

Gideon closed his stall the way he always did: he steered his chair out from behind the counter and left. Anybody needed a Bible bad enough to steal it was somebody who definitely needed a Bible. And anybody who definitely needed a Bible was welcome to it.

Five minutes later, the three men sat at one of the old soda-fountain marble-top tables at a coffee stand bearing the banner BEAN THERE.

"Good coffee," Gideon pronounced. He held his cup up, toasting Frank and José.

"We've had two women murdered, Gideon," José said.

Gideon swung his big head side to side in sorrowful acknowledgment. "Satan is on the loose. But up in Northwest . . . a world away from here."

"Satan's trail leads here, Gideon," José said.

"Where?"

"Narcotics raided a house," Frank said, "Saturday morning early."

"Yes," said Gideon, "the house over on Kentucky Avenue."

"No one was there. Narcotics found some street-quality heroin, some stolen electronics."

Gideon nodded and waited for more.

"They also found a finger, Gideon. It came from one of those women killed in Northwest."

Gideon's eyes registered the implications. He looked up, over Frank's head, shut his eyes, and passed his fingers over his eyelids. "God have mercy," he sighed. He opened his eyes. "You want to know who brought it there. To the house on Kentucky Avenue."

"Yes, sir," José said. "So the wicked will not go unpunished." He paused and gave Gideon a broad smile. "Proverbs, chapter eleven, verse twenty-one."

✚ Back in the car, Frank checked his phone messages.

"Renfro," he told José. He punched in Calkins's number. Calkins came on and Frank listened to the brief message.

"You're certain?" he asked Calkins. He listened to the even briefer reply, then hung up.

"Sounds like something certain." José said.

Frank pulled a U-turn and headed for Mass Avenue. "We got something certain we want to ask our friends at the Greek embassy."

FIFTEEN

✚ **A**re you here with answers?" Theodore Pappas asked. "Or more questions?"

Pappas sat at his desk, almost imperceptibly rocking back and forth. Irritation or nerves, Frank supposed. Probably both. Still the chiseled Omar Sharif good looks and the teeth. But the tan seemed to have a grayish undertone.

Frank shot Pappas a sunny smile. "Like you said, you work for the government, there're always more questions."

Pappas didn't smile. "I said that?"

"Just last Tuesday." Frank put his hand on the back of one of the chairs facing Pappas's desk. "Mind if we sit?"

Without waiting for an answer, Frank and José sat down.

José led off, going in strong, like kicking in a door. "You said you knew Ms. Boukedes socially."

Frank watched. *Your move, Pappas. Is it fight or flight?*

Pappas took a deep breath. He replied curtly, "*I said,* she came to the usual embassy functions."

Like, that's the way I talk to police, and particularly, to black cops. A mistake.

José threw another punch: "Were you ever in her home?"

Weigh that one carefully, Mister Diplomat Pappas. Very carefully.

Caution veiled Pappas's face. "Ah, yes, I think so."

José smiled, jabbing lightly. "You *think* so?"

Pappas cleared his throat. "What I *meant* to say . . . I *have* been in her home." The diplomat, having chosen his path, hurried down it, running his sentences together. "Of course, I've been in her home. Over the years we worked together, she had several cocktail parties—holiday parties—for her colleagues. My wife and I would drop by."

"You and your wife?"

Before Pappas could answer José, Frank came in with, "When was the last time you were in her home?"

Startled, Pappas's eyes shifted to Frank. "Exactly?"

Obviously feigning innocence, José asked, "Would your wife remember?"

"My *wife?*" Pappas looked back at José. The cross-punching left him bewildered, as if he'd lost all sense of direction back to his corner.

"Yeah," José said in a flurry. "Maybe she wrote it down on a calendar or something? Maybe you want to call her?" He pointed to the phone. "Go ahead. Call her. Don't mind us."

Behind Pappas's eyes, resistance died. Another deep breath, then, "Why this line of questioning?" His voice now flat and resentful.

"Our forensics technicians have identified some of the fingerprints in Ms. Boukedes's home." Frank said it almost in a tone of regret.

Pappas dropped his eyes to his desktop. "And you've found mine."

"Yes."

Pappas looked from Frank to José and back to Frank, searching for one last refuge. "They could have been there from one of the cocktail parties. What is the life expectancy of a fingerprint?" he asked. "Especially indoors?"

"We found these fingerprints, Mr. Pappas," José said, "in her bedroom."

"Bedroom." Pappas echoed hoarsely.

"On the bed's headboard," José said. Then he added, "And on a nightstand by the bed. And on a lamp on the nightstand by the bed."

Pappas drew himself up, sitting upright in his chair, throwing out his chest. "I have diplomatic immunity."

"You do," Frank agreed. "But do you think your government would extend immunity so far as to deny a request for a DNA sample?"

"What do you mean?"

"The DNA from the semen found in Ms. Boukedes's autopsy matches the DNA of semen stains in her bed. The bed," José added, "with the headboard, nightstand, and lamp with your fingerprints."

Pappas tossed in his cards. Both hands covered his face. He sat in a long and paralyzed silence. When he spoke, it was in a barely audible whisper. "My career, my God, my career . . ."

Frank pulled his chair closer. "We aren't interested in adultery," he said in an earnest voice. "We want her killer. You help us, we'll make every attempt to protect your privacy."

For a long moment, Frank wondered if what he'd said registered.

But finally Pappas dropped his hands. His Omar Sharif face melting in self-pity, Pappas looked up at Frank. "What do you want to know?"

"Let's start with Monday, August seventh. The day Ms. Boukedes was killed. She checked out early that day."

Pappas took several deep breaths, pulling himself together.

"Yes," he replied, strength returning, "I met her at her place."

"What time?"

"Just after five. Just after five o'clock."

"You met at her apartment. What then?"

Pappas paused, then swallowed. "We went to bed."

"The two of you had sex." Frank felt a flush of embarrassment at the question, then irritation at his embarrassment.

"We had sex." Pappas snapped it out angrily. "Does that satisfy your requirement for explicit clarity?"

"You ejaculate in her?" José asked.

Pappas's eyes closed as if in prayer. "Yes."

"Then?" Frank asked.

"Then we went to dinner."

"Where?"

"A restaurant on P Street. BeDuCi."

"How'd you get there?"

"Walked."

"What time was this?" José asked.

"Eight. About."

"You have a good memory."

"After . . . after it happened, I went over the timing. That day . . . I'll never forget it. How it turned out."

"Who paid?" Frank asked.

"She did."

"What time did you leave?"

"About nine-thirty or so."

"You leave together?" José asked.

"Yes."

"Then what?"

"We went home. That is, I went to my home. She . . ."

"She walked . . . by herself?"

Pappas scrubbed his forehead with a hand. "I assumed she would be safe."

"You *assumed,*" Frank repeated dryly. "Did you talk with her again that night? Any contact with her whatsoever?"

"No. I was home by nine forty-five. Ten at the latest."

"Who was there when you got home?" José asked.

"My wife was at the theater. With friends."

"Was anyone at your house when you got home?" José persisted.

"No," Pappas whispered.

"What time did your wife get home?" Frank asked.

"Just before eleven."

"When you heard of the death, did you immediately suspect anyone?"

"No."

Frank thought he detected the slightest tightening around the corners of Pappas's mouth, a shifting of the knees closer together. "Let's try that again," he said.

Pappas locked eyes with Frank. "I'm sorry?"

"Your 'no' sounded like you've got your fingers crossed behind your back."

The eye-contact duel continued. Somewhere outside the room a telephone rang, then rang again.

Pappas looked away. "Susan . . ." he hesitated, then plunged in. "Susan thought she was being stalked."

You turn a corner when you least expect it. "Why did she think that?" Frank asked.

"At first, phone calls. Music left on her answering machine."

"When was this?"

"She first mentioned it in early April."

"What'd she do?" José asked.

"She got an unlisted number."

"First the phone calls," Frank said. "Then what?"

"Then, in May, the books began arriving. She had an account with one of the Internet booksellers. She began getting books she had never ordered. They were charged to her account."

"What kind of books?"

Pappas shook his head and shrugged. "I didn't ask the titles. She only told me that she was getting books she hadn't ordered. She closed the account."

"What happened next?"

"She said she saw him."

"When?"

"The first time was in early July. She said a man had followed her onto the Metro at Farragut North station. He stared at her. She described the look as hypnotic, burning. She got off at Dupont Circle. So did he. He followed her up the escalator and walked behind her several blocks, almost to her street."

"A lot of people get off the Metro there and walk in that direction."

"That's what I told her."

"Did she describe this man?"

"White. She said he looked to be in his mid-thirties. Extremely clean-cut. Glasses. Short hair. Conservatively dressed."

"That it?" José asked.

Pappas nodded.

"Not much of a description," Frank said.

"It is what I remember." Pappas gnawed on his lower lip. "I . . . I did not press her for details." He raised his hands then dropped them helplessly in his lap. "I suppose I was so shocked . . . that suddenly our relationship had become threatening . . ."

"You said the first time she saw him was in July. She saw him again."

"Yes. At the grocery. Several weeks later."

"Grocery?"

"The Safeway on Wisconsin. She had been shopping. He was there. He had no cart, no basket. Walking the aisles behind her."

"He approach her? Say anything? Make any gestures?"

"No. She left. Left her cart and walked out. She got home . . . the answering machine had music on it. She was so upset, she dared to call me at home."

"Can you pin the date down?" José asked. "When she saw him at the Safeway?"

"All I can remember is that it must have been sometime in early August."

"Just before she was killed."

"Yes."

"And you?" Frank asked. "What did you do?"

Pappas's eyes widened. "Do? What *could* I do?"

"Urge her to report it, for one thing," José said, a tremor of anger in his voice.

Pappas's mouth worked silently. "Oh! But I did! I did!" He blurted out, looking first at Frank, then at José, scrambling around for a buyer. "But she said it wouldn't do any good."

"But I bet you sent flowers to her funeral," José said sarcastically.

Minutes later, in the car, José leaned back against the headrest and shut his eyes. "Lying sack of shit," he said. "If he urged her to report, I'm Michael Jordan."

"No such luck, Hoser."

. . .

✚ Randolph Emerson listened with rapt intensity during their summary of the Pappas interview. He said nothing, hands busy toying with a paperclip.

Straighten-bend, straighten-bend.

When they finished, he tilted back in his chair, gazed off into the distance, still toying with the paperclip.

"Access," Emerson said, dreamily, working on his mental checklist. "Pappas had access to the victim." He paused, then moved down his list. "Alibi . . . Pappas doesn't have one."

"Motive?" José asked.

Emerson shrugged. "His career. Maybe the affair turned shitty. Most do, given enough time. Maybe she was onto him about a divorce. Or maybe she was going to talk."

"If he killed the Boukedes woman," José asked, "what was he doing all this time with her finger? And how'd it end up over on Kentucky Avenue?"

Emerson's thin-lipped smile twisted itself into a smirk. "Very good questions. *Very* good questions. What are you and Detective Kearney doing to answer them?"

✚ Frank's voicemail light was blinking when he and José got back to their office. He picked up the phone, punched in his PIN, listened to the message, and hung up.

"If we got time tomorrow morning," he told José, "John Sheffield's available at nine-thirty."

José checked his calendar.

"We got time. Where?"

"Valley Green."

"I thought they tore that down."

"I did, too. But that's the address. Nine-thirty tomorrow morning."

SIXTEEN

John Sheffield was waiting on the sidewalk of the housing development the following morning.

"I remember both of you," he said, "from my father's trial."

Tension hardened his voice. He held a clipboard in his left hand. His right hand he kept jammed deep in the pocket of his faded jeans.

"My father said you were investigating Ms. Keegan's murder. He said I was to talk to you."

Sheffield wore a tan corduroy sport coat with the jeans. No tie with the pale blue button-down shirt. Eleanor's bio had given his age as thirty-eight. He looked ten years younger. Six feet, two inches, he'd kept the slender frame of the forward he'd been at Dartmouth.

"Can we talk in the car?" Frank asked, motioning down the block.

Without a word, the three men started for the car. Several yards along, José shook his head at the neat, freshly painted Georgian-style town homes.

"This used to be Indian country."

Sheffield nodded. "Five years ago. There were thirty-five housing project apartment buildings here. Only one was occupied. More rats than people. Elevators broken. Doors didn't lock. Plumbing? People defecated in the halls. Once you were here, wasn't any getting out. No public transportation, no taxi driver would stop here for any reason.

We open these"—he waved at the town homes—"next month. Mix of public housing renters and middle-class owners. Every one of them rented or sold. Waiting list a yard long."

"And your company did pretty well, too, didn't it?" Frank asked.

"Hired fifty former gang members. Trained and licensed them in the building trades. We all made money," Sheffield said. And then with emphasis he added, "Honest money."

At the car, Frank and José got in the front, Sheffield settled himself in the back. He patted the seat and looked around. "First time I've been in one of these . . . a real cop car." He locked eyes with Frank. "Just thought I'd let you know."

Frank smiled. "We appreciate your sharing that with us," he said.

"We really do," José added.

Frank put the smile away. "Mary Keegan was writing a book. You and your father were in it . . . were *going* to be in it."

Sheffield leaned back, his arms folded across his chest. "Yes."

"When'd you first meet her?" José asked.

Furrows between Sheffield's eyes. "Year," he finally said, "year and a half. Yes. Spring a year ago."

"Tell us about the meeting."

"My father and I met with her downtown for lunch. She explained what she wanted to do. I wasn't much for it. I didn't think my father would be, either . . . it'd be reopening a lot of things for him. We had lunch and after she left, my father and I talked about it. I was surprised. He was all for it. So we called her up and she started interviewing us."

"You said she explained what she wanted to do. What was that?" José asked.

"She wanted to do a book about fathers and sons. Said it'd be a book about values. That's why I was against it." Sheffield laughed softly. "And that's why the old man was for it."

"How's that?"

"Oh, I assumed she was going to contrast my father and me. The old man once the grand lord of D.C. crime. And here's his Ivy League kid, doing well by doing good."

"And never sitting in cop cars," Frank said.

"And never sitting in cop cars. I didn't need any attaboys from white lady writers."

"But your father saw it differently?" José guessed.

"Yeah. When I was a kid, I thought he was just stiff-necked. I didn't realize it, until I grew up some . . . it was a code he lived by. Fundamental code. Even when he was on the other side of the law. In his eyes, it was important that a leader took responsibility and kept his word. And he's proud he kept to it."

"And he should be," Frank said.

That got Frank a look of suspicion. "But you sent him to jail," Sheffield said.

"Your father did what he had to do," Frank said.

"And we did what we had to do," José added.

Sheffield looked hard at Frank and José for a long moment. "Okay," he said abruptly. "Mary Keegan's death."

"Let's start with the last time you saw her," Frank said.

Sheffield reached in his pocket and came up with a Palm Pilot. Several electronic bleets and he looked up. "September twenty-first. She was supposed to be here"—he gestured through the window to the town homes—"the day before . . . September twentieth. We were doing a ribbon cutting on the model home. She called and said she couldn't make it."

"She say why?" José asked.

"No."

"On the twenty-first, when you saw her . . . how was she?"

Sheffield shook his head. "Not good. I thought she'd been sick." He nodded, remembering more. "I kidded her about her looking like she'd seen a ghost."

"A ghost? What'd she say to that?" José asked.

"She said, 'I think I might have.' "

"She explain that?" Frank asked.

"No, she just apologized for missing the opening. Asked me to show her around. Took some pictures, I gave her some handouts . . . stats, sound bites, that kind of thing."

"That was it?" Frank asked.

"That was it."

"Any mention—any hint—that anybody had been following her?"
Sheffield's eyes narrowed. "A stalker . . . no."

"The ghost thing," Frank said. "When she said it, was it a come-
back to you? Or did she think about it before she said it?"

Sheffield pinched the bridge of his nose between thumb and forefinger. Then he shook his head and gave a helpless shrug. "I don't
recall. But she didn't smile when she said it."

"Let me ask you about her," José said. "Did she turn out to be a
white lady writer coming down to pat a nice African-American kid on
the head for not sitting in cop cars?"

"No. She turned out all right."

"How many times did you see her?"

"Total?" Sheffield thought. "Eight, nine times."

"You and your father?" Frank asked.

"Sometimes."

"Sometimes just the two of you," José asked, "you and her?"

Sheffield looked at José as if he knew where this was going. "Yeah,"
he said, drawing it out provocatively, "just the two of us."

"Where?"

"Lunch, dinner. Sometimes her place."

"When?"

"I don't remember."

José pointed to the Palm Pilot. "Why don't you ask your friend?"

"Look," Sheffield said, "I don't put everything in there. I had that
date in September because it was an appointment. I had some of my
people here. Other times, she'd call, we'd get together."

"Was it a personal relationship?" Frank asked.

"Sure," Sheffield said with a slight touch of sarcasm, "Somebody
digging into your life like that . . . you think it can stay impersonal?"

"I didn't mean it like that."

"Well," Sheffield asked archly, "how *did* you mean it?"

"Was there a romantic or sexual relationship?"

Sheffield folded his arms across his chest, keeping his face expressionless. Like a man teasing a dog, dangling a treat just out of reach. He finally tired of the game. "No," he said. "Wasn't about to be."

"Oh?" Frank said. "Why was that?"

"Personal preferences."

"Yours or hers?"

"I don't know about hers."

"You got something about white women?" José asked.

Sheffield shrugged. "Some of my best friends are white women," he said derisively, "I just don't want to marry one."

"I saw your father and mother at Mary Keegan's memorial service," Frank said. "I didn't see you."

"Came in late. Sat at the back."

José picked up. "Last question," he said. "Sunday night. The fifteenth. Where were you?"

The muscles at the corners of Sheffield's mouth tightened.

"It's a question we ask everybody," José said.

Sheffield gave him a squinty, challenging look. "Where I am most Sunday nights."

"And that's . . . ?"

Sheffield smiled. "That's church," he said.

✚ In the car, José watched Sheffield walk away while Frank flipped through his notebook.

"One tough fucker."

"Gets it honestly," Frank said absently. He found the page he was looking for. "He was going to meet her . . . when?"

"Twenty September, but that got canceled."

Frank wrote the date down, underscoring it twice and putting two question marks after it. "We get back, remind me to call her brother."

"Halligan? About?"

"About her book. See if we can get a copy of what she'd done."

"You think something's in there?"

"Beats me." Frank shrugged. "The people she was writing about all say there couldn't have been anything in it that could get her killed. But none of them knew for certain what she had."

José started the car. "So they say."

"So they say."

"And what about her ghost?" José asked. "The somebody she saw just before she met with Sheffield? If she was being stalked, it fits the same pattern as Boukedes."

"*If*'s a big word, Hoser."

But if it was the same guy, he's out there now, picking another victim. Watching her. Learning her daily comings and goings. This minute, he was out there, homing in on his target. And José and he were sitting here.

"Let's go," Frank said.

"Okay. Where?"

Frank shrugged impatiently. "Anywhere. As long as we're moving."

José drove in silence. It wasn't until they were on MLK Avenue, going past Saint Elizabeths, that he spoke. "We never had us a serial killer, Frank."

"We don't *know* that we have us one."

Another silence.

"What're you doing?" José asked.

Frank finished dialing the number on his cell phone.

"Bouchard. See if he can arrange a tutoring session for us."

✠ Later that afternoon, Special Agent Robin Bouchard checked them in through security at the J. Edgar Hoover Building's 10th Street entrance. From his father, the burly FBI agent had inherited his Mediterranean complexion, and from hustling his way through CCNY shooting pool, he'd developed a sharp eye for position.

"Not putting you out, Robin?" Frank asked as he and José shook hands with Bouchard.

"You're lucky," Bouchard said. "Haggerty's up from Quantico today."

"Haggerty?"

"Bill Haggerty. Supervisory Special Agent who runs the Behavioral Science Unit. After they caught Ted Bundy down in Florida, we had Haggerty study the guy to get a better understanding of serial killers. He spent four years wading through the sewers of Bundy's mind before the State of Florida finally fried his sorry ass."

"Hope we're not taking him away from anything."

"He'll thank you for getting him out of a budget review."

José needled Bouchard. "You do a lot of that, don't you, Robin?"

Bouchard laughed. "Seems like every time you guys show up, we're counting beans." He pointed to a bank of elevators. "I got us a conference room up on seven."

✠ "Tell me what you've got . . . what you *think* you've got."

Bill Haggerty looked youthful, Frank thought, until you saw the lines etched around the eyes and mouth, lines that came with an understanding of the human capacity for cruelty. Bouchard took notes, but Haggerty listened without comment or question as Frank and José described the murders of Susan Boukedes and Mary Keegan.

When they'd finished, he got up, walked to the window, then stared down on Pennsylvania Avenue for a long time. From the side, Frank glimpsed Haggerty's lips moving minutely. As if reaching back through shelves in his memory. *Or praying?*

Haggerty turned and came back to the table. "On the basis of what you have, I can't tell you that you *do* have a serial killer," he said. Then he leaned forward as if to make certain Frank and José understood what he was saying. *"On the basis of what you have,"* he repeated in emphasis.

"What should we look for," José said, "besides another dead woman?"

"Profiling has gotten a bad name," Haggerty said, "but there is a profile that might fit these two cases if—*if*—you've got a serial killer."

Haggerty got up and walked over to a large whiteboard. Uncapping a felt-tip marker, he drew a vertical line down the middle of the board.

"Serial killers come in two general flavors." He scrawled a large

"O" at the top of one column, and on the other, a large "D." "Organized and disorganized."

Haggerty leaned back against the whiteboard and folded his arms across his chest. "The organized offender can be compared to a person suffering from an antisocial personality disorder. The disorganized killer may behave in ways that indicate a psychosis such as schizophrenia and . . . or . . . paranoia.

"If you don't make me bet my mortgage, if you came to me with another case similar to the two you've described, I'd say you should look for an organized offender."

"Organized more difficult to spot?" José asked.

"Yes. The organized serial killer may well have an above-average intelligence, be socially competent, and work at a job requiring a high level of skill. He'll likely appear to be gregarious and outgoing. A good talker, he's very manipulative . . . and that was Bundy."

"Tell us about him," Frank asked.

Haggerty rested his elbows on the table in front of him, interlaced his fingers under his chin, and got the haunted, faraway look of people who have seen hell.

"Theodore Robert Bundy had already been sentenced to death when I met him. I told him I thought he deserved it for what he had done. After a few meetings, he came to realize I wasn't trying to judge him or get any new evidence on him. The only thing I wanted from him was to learn how serial killers thought.

"What was central to Bundy . . . what was at his core . . . was control and domination." For the next two hours, Haggerty described Bundy's growing monstrousness. The details of thirty killings. Eleven murders in Washington State. Eight in Utah. Eight in California, Oregon, Colorado, and Idaho. Then came Florida, and the animal-like rampage in a Florida sorority house, where he slashed two women to death and left three more to die. And two weeks later, Bundy's last killing, still in Florida, of a twelve-year-old girl.

Finally, Haggerty pushed back from the table, got up, and filled a paper cup from the water cooler in the corner. He took the cup to the window and drank while looking out on Pennsylvania Avenue.

Haggerty came back to the table and slumped into his chair, a man clearly exhausted. "If you've got a serial killer," he said to Frank and José, "know that he's out there planning another killing. If he's like Bundy, he fits his plans into some kind of sadistic fantasy. He'll stand down for a while . . . his cooling off phase . . . but he's going to do it again."

"Getting back to profiles," José said. "Do we have us a woman-killer?"

Haggerty sat back and thoughtfully rubbed his chin with his fingertips. "Most serial killers stay in their gender-ethnic 'specialties,' " he said. "With Bundy it was women. With Dahmer it was men." He fell silent then shrugged, "Maybe it'll turn out that way with you."

"But maybe not?" Frank asked.

"He'll stay in his 'specialty,' but that specialty is going to be shaped by his particular fantasy." Haggerty raised a cautionary finger. "And know, too, he's obsessed with what he's done . . . and with every detail of what *you're* doing. He already knows who you are, and he's made a meticulous search of the public records about you. What's there, he knows."

After departure handshakes and exchanges of cards, Bouchard turned to escort Frank and José toward the door to the hall.

"One last thing." Haggerty said it quietly. The men stopped and turned. Haggerty stood with his back to the window, his face obscured by shadow. "Don't get sucked into a swamp of root-cause psychobabble. Bundy wasn't sick. He was a serial killer because *that's what he was.*" Haggerty paused, then he said, sadly and as if to himself, "Bundy could never understand why people refused to accept the fact that he killed . . . *just because he wanted to kill.*"

✠ Janowitz met Frank and José in the corridor outside their office and followed them in.

"I got the books," he said, holding up a sheet of paper.

Preoccupied with Haggerty and Ted Bundy, Frank stared blankly at the young detective.

"The *books*," Janowitz repeated. "The ones Susan Boukedes got. The ones Pappas said she never ordered."

José pointed to the folding chair by his and Frank's desks. "Sit."

Frank rummaged around his desktop. As he did so, he saw that his voicemail light was blinking. Caller ID said Kate had called. Continuing his search, he found the folder he wanted and inside, the transcript of the Pappas interview. He took the transcript around to José so both of them could read it together.

> Kearney: First the phone calls. Then what?
> Pappas: Then, in May, the books began arriving. She had an account with one of the Internet booksellers. She began getting books she had never ordered. They were charged to her account.
> Kearney: What kind of books?
> Pappas: I didn't ask the titles. She only told me that she was getting books she hadn't ordered. She closed down the account.

Frank looked up from the transcript to Janowitz. "What kind of books?" he asked.

"Beats me." Janowitz laid the paper in front of Frank and José. *The Legends of Glastonbury* and *The Fisher King.*

Frank studied the titles. When he looked up, José was gazing at him with a question in his eyes. Frank shook his head.

"I think *The Fisher King* was a Robin Williams movie," Janowitz said helpfully.

✠ Frank settled back in his chair, called Kate, and watched José close up his desk.

"You and I are invited to dinner tonight," Kate said.

"Short notice. Any chance of begging off?"

"Pretty hard. It's at your place. Your dad's cooking. You pick me up?"

"Best offer I've had all day."

"Day's not over yet. Bye."

SEVENTEEN

✛ **S**plit pea soup started dinner, Virginia ham with cherry sauce followed, along with baked sweet potatoes and Brussels sprouts roasted in coarse kosher salt. A sinful tiramisù starred as dessert, accompanied by espresso.

Kate put her napkin down by her empty plate, applauded. "Chef, chef," she chanted.

"Cooked with these two hands." Tom Kearney held out his hands for inspection.

"Everything?" Kate asked.

"Well," he put on a face of mock guilt, "I *did* drop by Café Milano for the tiramisù. Franco insisted. What could I do?" He topped off Kate's glass with an old-vine Zinfandel. He pointed the bottle toward Frank.

Frank shook his head.

Tom Kearney poured the remainder into his own glass.

"So now *The Fisher King*," he said.

Dinner conversation had alternated between the Boukedes–Keegan case, the latest media storm over yet another gaffe in the Bush–Gore presidential campaign, and Tom's day of physical therapy and cooking. All in all, Frank was thinking, he'd rather have left the case at the office, but it stayed in the minds of all three around the table, and somebody invariably came back to it. It was like getting something caught between your teeth—you couldn't ignore it, but you couldn't work it out, either.

Kate skated her glass over the tabletop, causing the wine to swirl. "The titles strike me."

"How?" asked Frank.

She shook her head. "I don't know, exactly." She paused in thought, then shuddered as if suddenly chilled. "By itself, stalking is scary. Just knowing somebody's out there, waiting, watching, ready to follow you. But those titles . . . they add a dimension of . . . I know it sounds crazy . . ."

"Go on," Tom Kearney urged.

"They add a dimension of the unreal. Almost occult." She took a swallow of her wine. "They imply somebody smarter than what you think of as the ordinary demented killer. It's more eerie."

"He's not stupid." Frank said. "Somehow, he got into her Internet bookstore account."

Kate shuddered. "He learned her address, phone number—God knows what all."

"He had to know something else to order those books," Tom Kearney said.

Frank looked across the dinner table at his father.

"He had to have her credit card number, too," he explained. "Once he got that, he had a lot more than a way to order books. He had a window into the Boukedes woman's life . . . where she shopped, where she ate, where she filled up her car."

"The books," Kate said, "he was sending her a message. Telling her how powerful he was."

"How about Mary Keegan?" Tom Kearney asked.

"We know a lot less," Frank said, "a lot less. No books for her. At least none from the same outfit that sent them to Susan Boukedes."

"But something apparently upset her. It could have been the stalker," his father said.

"Yeah."

"You don't sound convinced."

"Could have been something else bothered her. Even if it was a stalker, we don't know it was the same one who was after Boukedes."

"Bureau doing anything?"

"We already had a query into the National Crime Information Center. Looking for any similar unsolved cases. Robin Bouchard said he'd make a few phone calls. Put a higher priority on the request."

Frank felt his mind rebelling. As if suddenly it had reached its day's fill of hunting and gathering pieces of Mary Keegan's and Susan Boukedes's lives and deaths. He reached over and squeezed Kate's hand.

"I'll take you home."

She squeezed back.

At the door, he turned to his father. "I'll be back in a few minutes."

His father raised an eyebrow.

Kate shook her head and smiled brightly. "No he won't," she told Tom Kearney.

EIGHTEEN

✠ **E**xposed *like ants on a plate, seven men work their way across the rice paddy. The dry-season sun has baked the gray crusty soil, cracking and heaving it up into rock-hard fists. The broken ground twists at the ankles and pulls at the balance. Booted feet stumble under a hundred pounds of weapons, ammunition, water, and body armor. Two hundred yards ahead, shimmering in the heat, the dark-shadowed greenness of the tree line. Thick underbrush fills the once neat lanes between the long-abandoned rubber trees. Eyes in the tree line watch each step. Death waits here, in the paddy. Death waits there, in the tree line.*

"No!"

Frank recognized the voice. It was his. But it was coming from far away.

"Frank?"

"No!" His voice came closer.

"Frank!"

He felt a hand on his shoulder. Kate's voice came from somewhere above and Frank felt himself lifted and drawn toward it.

She switched on her bedside lamp. "Frank. It's for you . . . phone."

Frank sat up. He shook his head clear as he took the phone from her.

"Hello."

"Frank."

"Who's this?"

"Hunter Elliott. I called your house. Your father said you were out. I figured you were with Ms. Dwyer."

The last of the rice paddy and the waiting tree line disappeared.

"What is it, Hunter?"

Elliott answered in a bored monotone, as if reporting that it was raining outside. "I just called to let you know I got into the Boukedes files."

"It's two-fifteen," Frank said, trying to keep irritation out of his voice.

"Yes . . ." Elliott sounded perplexed.

"In the morning."

"Oh."

Kate switched off her light and burrowed under her pillow.

"Well," Frank sighed, "what's there?"

"A whole bunch of cookies and a tracking program."

A moment of dead space.

Frank wondered if he'd jumped from one dream to another.

"*Cookies?* I'm afraid I don't understand."

"They're small text files sent by a website and left in a computer."

"Oh." Frank said, trying to make sense of the conversation.

His flailing must have been evident. "No big hurry," Elliott said.

I *am* still dreaming. I am now in the middle of an Abbott and Costello routine. "Well, Hunter, if there's no big hurry, why'd you call at two in the morning?"

"Why," Elliott said, walking through it patiently, as if to a slow child, "to let you know I got into the files."

"Thank you. A question?"

"Sure?"

"You ever sleep?"

"Sure."

"When?"

"Ah . . . well . . . whenever."

"Okay. See you in a couple hours?"

"Sure," Elliott said. "I'll be here."

"I don't think that was another woman," Kate murmured after Frank hung up. She rolled over to face him.

"Remember Hunter Elliott?"

"No."

"Hacker name of Orion?"

"Oh. The O'Brien case?"

"Yeah. Susan Boukedes had a password-protected segment on her computer."

"And he got by the password?"

"Cookies?" Frank said. "Tracking program." He punched up his pillow, lay back, and shut his eyes. "It'll wait."

He felt the pulsing of his blood. Somewhere in the dark, a click of a thermostat. The wind-up start of the furnace blower. A long silence. Down the street, a house door opened, closed. An indistinct voice. A woman's voice. Moments later, a car engine started. His eyes opened. Headlights from the car raced around the room.

"You're thinking about it," Kate said out of the darkness.

"Yeah." Frank lay looking at the ceiling.

"You're thinking you ought to go over there now."

"It's probably nothing . . ."

"You're thinking it could be something."

He thought some more about it. "Yeah."

Kate's light flicked on. She sat up and swung her feet to the floor. She stood, walked over to a chest of drawers, and pulled out a pair of jeans.

Frank got out of bed. "What's this?"

"This," said Kate, zipping up the jeans, "is a woman getting dressed. You owe me a breakfast. You aren't getting out of my sight until I collect."

Frank watched appreciatively as Kate, bare-breasted, shook the folds out of a sweatshirt.

"You're awfully tasty," he said.

Kate frowned and pulled down the sweatshirt. "And you're easily distracted." She brushed by him and as she did, swatted his bottom. "Let's go."

. . .

✝ Hunter Elliott didn't seem surprised to see Kate with Frank. He invited them into his apartment with a sweeping gesture of his hand.

"Welcome, Ms. Dwyer."

Surprise registered on Kate's face. "How'd you know my name?"

"That was your phone number I dialed."

Kate frowned. "But it's an unlisted number."

"Yes," said Elliott, with a small shrug, as though snaking an unlisted phone number out of Ma Bell was so elementary it didn't deserve explaining. Two chairs had been drawn up before a computer desk. Elliott wheeled a third over. A screensaver made whirlpools of light across a glowing screen.

"The Boukedes cookies," he said. He twitched the mouse. The screensaver disappeared. A window opened with a string of icons resembling tiny spiral-bound notebooks.

"Each time you go anyplace on the Internet," Elliott said, "your computer gets tagged with a small file—a cookie. You shut down your computer, the cookie stays with you. You go back on the Net, and that cookie identifies you and lets the various websites know where you're going and what you're doing."

"Everybody gets them?" Kate asked.

"Yes."

"Then what's unusual about these?" Frank asked.

"What's unusual is this." Elliott did something with the mouse and opened another window.

"This is a program that's like a phone tap—only this's a computer tap. It collects all the cookies—all the places you go on the Net—and transmits them over the Internet to a pickup computer."

Frank started getting it. "So someone at the pickup computer would know where you go, what you buy, what information you want—"

"And more," said Elliott. "This program copies your e-mail as well."

"How did this program get here? On her computer?"

Elliott gave another dismissive shrug. "Somebody like me put it there."

"A hacker?"

Elliott nodded. "A very good one."

"Someone sent her books from an online bookstore and used her Visa account. Could that"—Frank pointed to screen—"program let them do that?"

"That program," Elliott said, "could let somebody steal her entire identity. Social Security number, bank PINs, medical records—no end to it."

"Where does this connect?" Kate asked. "Who was collecting?"

"Can't tell. Whoever put this program on her computer also set up a website—a receiver—on the Net so the program could dump its take. That website has been shut down."

"When?"

"Her computer shows the last contact August seventh."

August seventh. Frank felt his pulse race. "The day she was murdered. Is there any way we can look at her Internet account? Who she e-mailed, who may have been contacting her?"

Elliott shook his head. "The service provider's computers have that." He got a thief's sly look. "You want me to," he said in a voice that was close to purring, "I can peek into . . ."

Kate got her lawyer's no-no look. She touched Frank's elbow.

Frank shook his head. "No. Maybe I just give them a call."

Disappointment flickered across Elliott's face. "That's not fun."

"No, I suppose not," Frank said. "Who do I contact?"

"An outfit on the Dulles tollroad. Lore dot com. Like America Online but smaller."

He flashed back to Mary Keegan's study. Monet's water lilies on her computer screen. He made a mental note to get a summons.

"You have time to look at another computer for me?"

Elliott pointed to Susan Boukedes's computer. "Does it have something to do with this?"

"Maybe," Frank answered, hoping it did.

· · ·

✝ Frank got in the car but made no motion to start it. He held the ignition key and looked at Kate.

"Well." He said. He said it again.

The first time he said it, it was a declaration. The second time, it was a question.

"High-tech stalking," Kate answered, "makes you think twice about sitting down at a computer."

He started the car. "Bed or breakfast?"

"Both's not an option?"

"I wish."

"Breakfast," Kate sighed. As Frank pulled away from the curb, she asked, "And what's next?"

"Next is finding the Fisher King."

"And how're you going to arrange that?"

"Call a tour guide."

✝ After bagels with Kate at Einstein Brothers, Frank called Nicholas Pasco's office at Georgetown University. Expecting to get the professor's secretary or the answering machine, he was surprised when Pasco himself answered.

"What's this, professor? At the office early, and answering your own phone?"

"Egalitarian Day at the department of economics and finance, Frank. Hannah's mother's sick and I have a seminar at ten with Greenspan." Pasco's voice got serious. "I see you and José are busy. I hope things are progressing."

"Not fast enough."

"I can help?"

"I want to know something about the Fisher King . . . besides that it was a Robin Williams flick."

"You peeked in my copy book. You tried the Internet?"

"With my skill, two hours on the Net will save me fifteen minutes with a real live person."

Pasco laughed. "Someone will call."

✝ That afternoon, Kaitlin McKirgan met Frank in the English Department lounge. McKirgan, a red-haired woman, wore rimless glasses and an expression of mild distraction as if she was listening to music no one else could hear.

"Nick Pasco said you were interested in the Fisher King," she said.

Frank nodded and McKirgan motioned to a cluster of chairs around a large bay window.

"First, Lieutenant Kearney, you must realize that this is legend. It is history only in the sense that it is an accounting of what others long ago have written and talked about." McKirgan paused. Apparently satisfied she had connected, she continued. "What do you know about the Holy Grail?" she asked.

Frank got the claustrophobic feeling when, unprepared, he'd been called on to recite in class. In what seemed to take forever, he snagged a scrap out of his memory.

"The cup at the last supper."

McKirgan gave him a charitable pass.

"You can't understand the Fisher King unless you first understand the myth surrounding the Grail. As you point out, the Grail was the cup at the last supper. Jesus supposedly drank from it, as did all his disciples. After the crucifixion, Joseph of Arimathea took Jesus' body to his own tomb for burial. Joseph also got possession of the cup, which, purportedly, had been used to gather some of Jesus' blood. Sometime later, Joseph carried the cup with him to what is now Great Britain."

A synapse made contact in Frank's memory bank. "The search . . ."

McKirgan rewarded Frank with a slight smile. "Yes. The search. In the time of King Arthur, the quest for the Grail was the highest spiritual pursuit of the knights of his Round Table. Chrétien de Troyes, a French poet, identified Percival as the knight sent to find the Grail.

Other authors, such as Malory, name Galahad as the chief Grail knight. If the Grail could be found, legend had it, humanity's sins would be washed away and the land would become fruitful."

"And the Fisher King?"

"The Fisher King is the guardian of the Grail. Some legends portray him as good, others as evil. The legends that regard him as evil cast him as the archetype of Satan."

"Where did the Fisher King live?"

McKirgan smiled and shrugged. "In a castle by a river. Like Brigadoon, the castle and the Fisher King can disappear into thin air."

"Besides being either good or evil, anything else about him?"

"Chrétien described him as handsome with graying hair, courteous and hospitable."

McKirgan's encyclopedic knowledge awed Frank. Pasco had described her as one of the world's authorities on Arthurian literature. Here was a sharp, intelligent woman on top of her game. She was the Sahara Desert and he needed only a grain of sand or two. She could go for days, weeks, nonstop. She seemed to sense his frustration.

"One thing you should keep in mind about the Fisher King, Lieutenant."

"Yes?"

"All the legends agree . . . the Fisher King is a man in perpetual torment. He has a grievous wound that affects his every action, that shapes his very life. And this wound will not heal."

NINETEEN

✠ José drained the last of his coffee, peered into the empty mug, then set it on his desk. "So Fisher King's more than a movie."

Frank nodded. Before him, in the Boukedes file, were the books she'd been sent in the weeks before her death. "Whoever sent those books . . . it wasn't a random choice of titles."

"A king in perpetual torment?" José asked rhetorically. "With a wound that won't heal?" He shook his head. "Not a good combination." José held up his empty mug. "You look like you could use another round?"

"I guess," Frank said.

He felt fuzzy, as though the morning's mental fog hadn't quite lifted. And the tightness in his thighs and lower back felt as if he'd been lifting weights all night.

José tossed the old filter and grounds into the wastebasket. "Got home last night, had a call on my answering machine."

"Lonely Ladies Society?"

"I wish. It was Gideon Weaver."

"Yeah?"

"Just said he'll be at the market by nine-thirty."

. . .

✠ By seven, all the market stalls have been spoken for. By eight, fruit and vegetables have been displayed, and catching up on the past week's gossip is well under way. Sundays are slower. The best produce is gone. Most of the farmers—the real farmers—are sitting in country churches in Virginia and Maryland.

Frank and José got to Gideon Weaver's stall as he closed a sale. An elderly woman tucked a white leather-bound New Testament in her shopping bag. She pressed a crumpled bill into Gideon's hand and teetered off into the market crowd. Without looking at the bill, Gideon stashed it in a cigar box.

"Bible business good, Gideon?"

Gideon smiled a benediction in the direction of the old woman. "Miss Effie is a regular. Ladies of that generation, they wear their Bibles out." His face shone with admiration. "Just . . . wear them out."

He tapped the joystick on his wheelchair, slewing it so he addressed Frank and José square on.

"Justice, justice shall you pursue."

He pinned down José for the answer. Then he gave Frank a quick glance. But that was as if it was out of courtesy, as he didn't expect much. He returned to José.

José lowered his eyes. Dry well.

Gideon shook his head, disappointed. "Deuteronomy. Chapter sixteen. Verse twenty." He gave both men a warning look—"And don't you forget." He waited until José and Frank nodded; then he said, "The house on Kentucky Avenue . . . Austell Lenwood."

"He brought the finger there?" José asked.

"I don't know *that*. I *do* know he was there when the finger was there."

"Any other names?" Frank asked.

"House on Kentucky Avenue . . . a finger . . . Austell Lenwood," Gideon recited. "That's all I know."

"I don't suppose you can tell us *how* you know," José said.

Gideon looked at him with all the expression of a snapping turtle.

José raised both hands in a surrender gesture. "Just thought I'd ask."

✠ Frank slipped the key into the ignition but didn't start the car. José flipped open his cell phone and dialed a number. Someone on the other end answered. José identified himself and gave Austell Lenwood's name. On hold, he looked at Frank. "Lenwood . . . how long's it been?"

"Couple years at least."

After he said it, Frank realized it'd been longer . . . five years. Ernestine Copley, seventy-three, killed in the crossfire between the Satin Satans and the Eighth Street Crew. She had been walking her great-granddaughter. Ballistics said the slugs had come from the Sig Sauer later taken from Austell Arthur Lenwood. But four relatives swore that Lenwood had been watching TV with them. Frank and José had two witnesses who put him at the scene; one died in a fire of suspicious origin, the other recanted his testimony. Lenwood walked.

Somebody came on José's line. He listened, hung up, and turned to Frank.

"Brother Lenwood"—José stretched out the word "brother," *brUH-thuh*—"has climbed the ladder in his chosen profession of low-life gang-banger. Narcotics now carries his worthless ass in the top ten dealers' club. Hanging out with the Jamaicans, the Sicilians, running the I-95 pipeline from New York. Four arrests for intent to distribute—zero convictions."

"They got a line on where he is?"

"Getting it."

Frank dropped the car into gear. "You ready for breakfast?"

"I'm always ready."

"You in the mood for sausage and hash browns today."

"I'm always . . ."

. . .

✠ Ruth slapped two sets of silverware on the table as Frank and José sat down.

"Hash browns, two over medium, double order sausage?"

"This woman knows us," Frank said to José.

"All too well." She poured two coffees. "You gonna catch this bastard or not?"

"Not's not an option," José said.

"People scared . . . angry," she said, writing up the order.

"Ought to be," Frank said to Ruth's departing backside.

✠ In the middle of coffee seconds, José's phone chirped.

"Records says he's still doing business outta the same old place," José said.

"I don't guess we need to make an appointment. We can just drop in."

José didn't answer, instead, both elbows on the counter, he hulked over his plate, intent on capturing the last of the egg yolk with the last of the toast. He ate the toast and then he just sat there, studying his empty plate.

And Frank just sat there, studying José.

Twenty-five years told him when to wait and when to break in. So he waited a few more moments until it felt right. "I smell brain cells burning."

"Lenwood." José said the name, his eyes still dreamylike. He nodded as if in agreement with a private thought, then asked Frank, "How we going to talk to him?"

Frank realized the simple question wasn't really simple. "Well . . ."

"Yeah?"

Frank exhaled loudly through his mouth. "Well, I thought we'd just grab him and ask him about the finger." As he said it, he felt the adrenals kicking in.

"And what if he gives us some shit? I mean, Frank, *if* he was there at that house with the finger . . ."

"If Gideon says he was there, he was there."

"Okay, so he was there," José conceded. "He *was* there. Now one of two things—one, he was there and he had something to do with the finger, or two, he was there and he had something to do with a deal. Either way, he was into something that could mean Lorton time. You think he's gonna say doodley-squat to us?" As if anticipating Frank's response: "And we squeeze him, we'll have the ACLU down on our asses."

Frank sipped his coffee. It had gotten cold. He forgot about the coffee and José sitting there looking at him. He started working options. You walked down a corridor. You tried each door. One after another would be locked. But if you tried enough, you'd find one that would open.

"Yeah?" he heard José asking.

"Let's have another cup of coffee and talk about an old friend," Frank said, and he felt the knob turn in his hand.

✠ "Apache Billiards," Frank said as he pulled up against the curb in front of the pool hall. "Used to be . . . be what?"

"Paradise Club," José said.

"Oh, yeah." Frank now remembered. "Fifteen fights to the pint."

"Word was," José said, "they'd search you for a weapon when you went in. You didn't have one, they'd give you one."

A black limo pulled up and parked across the street. José turned to Frank.

"Show time."

And Frank and José got out and walked in.

In front, Apache Billiards didn't look that much different from the Paradise Club: long bar on the left wall, tables in the middle, booths on the right wall.

What had changed was that pool tables now filled the large area in back where the band and dance floor used to be. Four rows of five tables each. Hooded lights hung low over each table made islands that glowed green against the gloom.

Frank counted six tables in play. Inky shadows surrounded the lighted tabletops, surreal arenas in which pairs of disembodied hands with pool cues suddenly materialized, made a shot or two, then disappeared back into the darkness.

Frank and José walked toward the rear, and play stopped as they passed each table. Frank saw the dim outlines of faceless players, standing still, watching.

Austell Lenwood's "office" hadn't changed—an antique shoeshine stand with a single elevated chair, all ornate cast iron and plush velvet. Lenwood, wired with headset and CD player, was a study in black: black lizard boots, black silk shirt, and black six-button suit. From his perch, he surveyed his realm through dark glasses.

Frank decided the glasses pulled together all Lenwood's stylistic elements. The brushed aerospace-aluminum frames held huge tear-shaped lenses tight against Lenwood's face. Add the round shaved head, and you've got one of those space creatures from the Roswell flying-saucer museum.

Lenwood ignored Frank and José standing below. The music escaping from around the headset earphones made a scratchy, irritating buzz, and Lenwood's fingers danced in time on the chair's armrests.

José reached up and unplugged the headset from the CD player.

Lenwood's fingers stopped. Like a swimmer clearing water from his ears, he shook his head and looked down.

"Morning, Mr. Lenwood," Frank said. "It's been a while."

Lenwood curled his lips in a theatrical sneer. "You here to shoot some pool?" he asked loud enough for his audience around the pool tables, "or shoot some bull?" A chorus of hees and haws rippled out from the tables.

José smiled. "Here just to talk with you, Lenwood."

"I suppose I should be flattered." He glanced at his watch, then sat back in his chair and clasped his hands together in his lap.

In the background, the rattling crash of a break as the pool playing started up again. Lenwood sat. More sounds, the muttering of the players, chalking of cues.

And still Lenwood sat.

And Frank and José stood motionless.

"Well?" Lenwood asked.

Frank smiled and looked up at Lenwood, sitting like a monarch on his shoeshine-stand throne. "Like José said, we'd like to talk with you."

"So talk."

Frank locked one hand around Lenwood's left wrist and the other around his ankle. At the same time, José grabbed the man's right leg and biceps. The two swung Lenwood out of his chair to stand between them, his back to the pool tables.

The lightning transition left Lenwood wobbling and disoriented, but not for long.

"Muthafuckers!" It came as a low, wheezing whisper. If the pool players had noticed, they weren't showing it. "What the fuck you think you're doing?"

With both hands, José pretended to straighten Lenwood's lapels, jerking the man's head back and forth. "Just helping you down, Your Majesty."

"Now we can have a talk about that house on Kentucky Avenue," Frank said.

Lenwood batted José's hands away, outrage exploding. "You muthafuckers fucked your chance to put me away once!" he screamed. "That's all you fuckin' get! We not talking 'bout *shit!*"

The pool playing had stopped and the silence stilled the air itself, but Lenwood didn't notice.

"I think you ought to reconsider that, Austell."

The voice behind Lenwood came soft and steely, like a razor cutting silk.

Lenwood turned around.

"Good morning, Austell," said Lamar Sheffield. His white shirt fluorescent against his black suit and dark-figured tie, Sheffield looked like a prosperous undertaker. Behind him, two men similarly dressed in black suits. Frank recognized them. John Galsworth and Martin Fleming. Old soldiers from Sheffield's campaigns. Men who'd taken their share of scalps. Old, but still very big, still very menacing.

Lenwood looked at the three men. Then he looked back at Frank and José, confused and stunned by the unlikely combination.

"My car's outside, Austell," Sheffield said. He took Lenwood by the elbow. "Let us go sit down and talk like gentlemen." With his other hand, he motioned to the two men beside him. "John and Martin here will make certain no one disturbs us."

"You comfortable, Austell?" Sheffield asked. He sat in the limo's front passenger seat, which had been unlatched and rotated so he faced Lenwood sitting in the back between Frank and José.

Lenwood muttered something unintelligible.

"Speak up," José said, with an accompanying elbow-dig into Lenwood's kidney.

"Yeah."

Frank put an elbow in Lenwood's other kidney. "Yes sir," he prompted.

Lenwood's eyes rolled right, then left.

"Yes sir."

"That's good," Sheffield smiled. "These gentlemen need some information, Austell. I hope you'll help them."

Frank felt Lenwood suck in a deep breath.

José started. "Last Saturday night you were in a house on Kentucky Avenue—"

"Wasn't." It came out sullen and defiant.

José tried again. "Last Saturday night you were in a house on Ken—"

"Wasn't."

Neither José nor Frank said anything, but sat quietly. Sheffield seemed frozen. Then, in a small, sad motion, he shook his head once.

"Will you gentlemen excuse us for a moment?" he asked José and Frank. "If you'd just step outside? . . . and ask John and Martin to join me?"

As he and José got out, Frank felt Lenwood stiffen.

Frank and José waited on the sidewalk as John and Martin got in. They stood outside for several minutes.

"What do you think's going on in there?" José asked.

"I really don't want to know," Frank said.

Just then, the back doors opened and Sheffield's two old soldiers got out and gestured to Frank and José to get in.

To Frank's surprise, Lenwood, very much more subdued, didn't seem to have been roughed up.

"Now, Austell"—Sheffield said it like a patient schoolteacher— "Mr. Phelps was asking you about Saturday night in the house on Kentucky Avenue."

"What you want to know?" Lenwood asked in a dutiful monotone.

José smiled and patted Lenwood's knee. "We found a finger in that house . . . how'd it get there?"

Silence.

"Austell?" Sheffield just whispered the name, but the message was there.

Lenwood swallowed. He took a breath and, exhaling loudly, seemed to deflate. "Eddie Jeter," he said, barely audible.

"Eddie Jeter?" José asked, "J-E-T-E-R?"

Lenwood nodded.

"What time was this?"

"Eleven. Eleven-thirty."

"You know where we can find him?"

Lenwood shook his head.

"Lenwood," José said, impatience edging his voice, "we gonna be here all day, the way you're dribbling this out."

Sheffield frowned and made an unhappy sound deep in his throat.

Lenwood's shoulders narrowed and his eyes dropped to his boots. "Eddie was wantin' to buy a quarter key. He was up his own self. Wild. Didn't want to go the tariff. Told him market was up. He gets crazier. Says he'll give me a little something extra. He reaches in this bag, pulls this . . . this *thing* out. Throws it on the table . . ." Lenwood raised both his hands and looked wide-eyed from Frank to José. "I mean, it was this *finger* . . ."

"Did he say how he got it?" Frank asked.

Lenwood shook his head.

"You didn't ask?"

"Ask?" Lenwood looked at Frank incredulously. "You doing a deal? . . . and your customer throws a *finger* on the fucking table? *Ask?* . . . man, I just about *shit!*"

✠ Frank and José stood with Lamar Sheffield and watched Austell Lenwood make his way across the street to Apache Billiards. He opened the door, looked over his shoulder at them, then scurried inside.

"Think we got everything?" Frank asked.

José checked his notebook, then closed it and put it away in his jacket. He nodded. "Enough."

"You need more, he'll cooperate," Sheffield said.

Frank smiled at the older man. "What'd you do? Make him an offer he couldn't refuse?"

Sheffield didn't smile back. If he recognized the line, he didn't show it. He shook his head. "I don't make *offers*," he said with disdain.

Lamar Sheffield turned and walked away to his waiting car.

✠ "Edward . . . Samuel . . . Jeter." Manny Dale rolled the names off the way a sommelier might announce a passably good—but not truly excellent—wine.

Back at his computer, José had come up with a first-entry hit on Jeter in WACIIS, the Washington Area Crime Intelligence and Information System. Jeter was a car thief. And Manny Dale was the department's authority on car thieves. Chubby, bald, and bifocaled, Manny Dale took pride in his collection of thieves and his encyclopedic knowledge of stealing and dealing in the hot-car market.

"The fellow could be world-class. His genius is handicapped by the regularity with which he snuffles his profits up his nose."

Frank shook his head. As long as he'd known the little man, he was always struck by the almost fatherly regard Manny had for the criminals he chased. Manny was a master at the game. But, thanks to the District's judges and sentencing guidelines, Manny could be assured that within months of going into the slammer, his thieves would be out on the streets and he could pick up his chase again.

"Manny," he asked, "you ever thought of putting your stars on bubble-gum trading cards? Maybe figure out some kind of statistical standing?"

José chimed in. "Maybe divide them into leagues?"

Manny laughed. His thick glasses glinted in the overhead lights. "A capital idea, fellows, but I'm afraid there aren't too many of us who recognize their talents. How'd my boy come to your attention?"

Frank and José outlined the Boukedes killing, how Dayhuff's SWAT people had found her finger in the house on Kentucky Avenue, how Lenwood had ratted out Jeter.

"The drug buying fits Eddie," Manny said. "The finger doesn't. He's rather bizarre, but he's not violent."

"He had to get it from someone," José said.

"Or somewhere," Manny amended. "Why not use your friend Mr. Sheffield to squeeze Eddie?"

"We can't use what we got from Lenwood as evidence. With Eddie, we're getting closer to the killing."

"And you want to be able to use what you get from Eddie in court."

"At least," Frank said, "we want the option."

" 'The option,' " Manny repeated. He sat a long time thinking. Hands clasped across his paunch, he set his eyes on an imaginary horizon and began humming to himself in a tuneless monotone.

He stopped the humming. "Give me some time?"

"How much?" Frank asked.

"A week, I should think," Manny said.

A moment of silence followed.

Manny's eyes darted between Frank and José, reading their expressions. "You're not happy with a week."

"We wouldn't be happy with yesterday," Frank said. "Why a week?"

"To set up our friend Eddie."

"Set up?" José asked.

Manny wrinkled his forehead, pretending dismay. "Did I say 'set up'?" He shook his head. "*Shame on me!* I should have said 'challenge.' " He got up. "I'll see what I can do. But Frank . . . ?"

"Yeah?"

"I can't do it yesterday."

José and Frank watched Manny shut the door.

"The grandmaster of auto theft," Frank said. And he thought, That's how Damon Runyon would have described Manny Dale.

TWENTY

✠ **R**ise and shine. Another day in which to excel."

"Hoser, what in the hell are you doing?"

"Right now, I'm holding a sunrise service at Hains Point for a busload of Japanese tourists. You better get down here."

Frank started to ask why, then realized José had called on his cell phone. "I've got time to brush my teeth?"

"Please."

✠ Frank found a pair of khakis, Topsiders, and a chambray shirt. Going out the door, he grabbed a windbreaker and dashed a note to his father and left it on the entry table. At that hour, no need for the siren. He drove down 30th Street to the waterfront, then south on the parkway past the Kennedy Center. At the Lincoln Memorial, he took Ohio Drive to East Potomac Park.

Hains Point is at the southernmost tip of the park. A little over a mile from the Jefferson Memorial and Tidal Basin, the Point overlooks the joining of the Washington Channel with the Potomac and Anacostia Rivers.

In the park, Frank drove along the channel harboring several king's ransoms' worth of sleek yachts. Near the golf clubhouse, a police cruiser blocked the drive. He stopped, showed his badge and credentials, and got waved on. Several hundred yards farther, as he approached Hains Point, he saw José's Mustang, two police cruisers, and a large red-and-white tour bus. He pulled in alongside José's car, found his camera in the glove compartment, and got out. A surreal row of disembodied Asian faces stared down at him from the bus's gray-tinted windows.

Rounding the bus, he saw *The Awakening,* one of Washington's tourist attractions. Set in a large circle of wood chips, the massive cast-aluminum sculpture featured a buried giant struggling to free himself. The head and portions of each naked limb had partially broken through the earth. A look of wild, demented rage twisted the bearded monster's face. His mouth opened in a frozen scream, while hands like claws tore at the sky.

José stood at the yellow police-line tape that staked out a perimeter around the statue. With him, two uniformed officers and a smaller man in a pale green sportjacket and darker green slacks. Fifty yards beyond the four men and the statue, the Potomac, and beyond the Potomac, Reagan National's minaret control tower. Frank heard popping from across the river as the propane cannons attempted to frighten the sea-gulls from the runways before the morning flights began.

José saw him and came to meet him, picking his way across the uneven ground.

"Brush your teeth?"

Frank nodded. Sleep's last remnants had finally drifted away and he lusted for coffee. "I guess, Lieutenant Phelps, sir, there's an explanation for all this."

"Japanese photographers," José nodded toward the tour bus, "came down here to catch the statue in the sunrise. Found a body. Called nine-one-one."

The two men walked toward the police line and the three men waiting for them.

Frank nodded to one of the uniformed officers, Emilio Sanchez, an old-timer. The other he didn't recognize. The man in the green sport jacket was a middle-aged Asian who had the watery-eyed look of a man who'd just been very sick.

"Officer Brittingham was first officer on the scene," José said.

"Nine-one-one came in at oh-five forty-five," Brittingham reported. "I arrived on the scene at oh-five fifty-five."

Frank turned and glanced at the tour bus. He turned back to Brittingham. "They came down here that early? Sun's just coming up now."

"I asked them, sir," Brittingham replied. "Mr. Nagata here"—he nodded to the sick-looking Asian man—"said it was SOP for sunrise shoots. Get set up and all."

"Was he first to find the body?" Frank asked.

"Yessir."

"And when you got here   what did you see?"

Brittingham frowned, pointed toward the bus. "All of them were taking pictures. I ran them back onto the bus, except for Mr. Nagata."

Mr. Nagata tried to smile.

"Names and addresses?" Frank asked.

Brittingham patted the notebook in his breast pocket. "Every one."

Frank looked back at the tour bus for a second or two, then turned and lifted the tape. "After you, Hoser."

José walked toward the back of the statue's left hand. Only the hand and wrist reached out from the earth.

"Not much chance of footprints," Frank said, unhappy with the thick layer of wood chips covering the ground.

"Here it is," José said as they rounded the hand.

A woman's nude body lay in the cupped palm. Spread-eagled on her back, her arms stretched out to the side, legs parted at a forty-five-degree angle.

"Jesus Christ," Frank breathed.

"He took a finger," José said.

As Frank stood there, the burnished-aluminum hand began to glow golden with the first direct rays of the sun, making the sight all the more starkly obscene. Frank felt a hot rush of anger mixed with revulsion.

"I already took the prints. No tattoos or distinguishing marks. At least, not that I could tell."

"Jesus," Frank repeated.

"Well," José said, "it's not another white woman."

"An equal-opportunity killer." Frank stepped closer to examine the body.

Multiple stab wounds of the breasts and abdomen. He stopped counting after ten. A loop of blue-and-green-brown intestine bubbled out from a slash just below the belly button.

"A dump job," Frank said, his eyes still fastened on the body. Somewhere there was a place where the killing had happened. A place with silent witnesses—blood, hair, fibers, prints. Someplace—but not here.

Watching where he placed his feet, he stepped closer and knelt inches from the corpse. The pectorals had stiffened. Postmortem blood had pooled in the dead woman's belly, breasts, and upper thighs, an undertone of bluish purple discoloring the milk-chocolate skin. Frank touched the abdomen, then pressed. The discoloration didn't change.

He recited the checklist from memory. "Cool to the touch. Rigor has set in. Victim was positioned facedown for some time after death. Lividity does not blanch."

"Yeah, I figure last night," José said, "sometime between ten and midnight."

"Age?"

"Twenties," José guessed, "early twenties."

After measuring and photographing the scene, Frank and José searched the ground, walking slowly, shoulder to shoulder, in ever larger circles around the hand with its corpse. A dime, part of a Snickers wrapper, a Gatorade bottle top, several cigarette butts. A lot of wood chips. Then a lot of grass. Nothing whispering a promise, *I'll tell you what you need to know.*

"Might as well have been dropped outta the sky," José said, frowning in disappointment.

"Maybe Calkins will find something," Frank said, but even as he said it, he didn't hold out much hope.

As if in unspoken agreement, the two men continued walking until they came to the railing of the retaining wall. They rested their forearms on the railing and looked across the narrow channel to Fort McNair, built on land set aside by George Washington to defend the new nation's capital.

Frank felt the rising sun's warmth and at the same time he felt the clean coolness of the morning air coming off the river. In the early light, the river was a sparkling and pristine blue. Later, with the sun overhead, the river would be a flat and dirty brown. The two men didn't say anything for a long time.

"Pretty out there," José said softly, not hurrying a reply.

"Yeah," Frank said after a moment or two. He continued gazing at the water and the fort. They'd hanged the people convicted of conspiring to kill Abraham Lincoln, over there at the fort. And they say the ghosts still wander the place, proclaiming their innocence.

José broke the silence with: "You know what pisses me off about this?"

"Three women getting hacked up?"

"Of course that. But you know what else?"

"No, Hoser, what?"

"What pisses me off is there's going to be people making money off this."

"Oh?"

"You know, if cops could copyright the stuff we handle, we'd make money, too." José nodded in agreement with himself. "This's gonna make it onto HBO—easy HBO. Maybe big screen."

"Who'd be you? Wesley Snipes? Denzel Washington?"

"Snipes, I think. Denzel's too good-looking."

"I'd sort of think about Jones."

"Quincy? Or James Earl?"

"James Earl."

"He's a little too chunky."

"Yeah, but good voice."

"I got a good voice?"

"Great voice, Hoser."

José frowned. "Shit, Frank. You shoulda told me that twenty-five years ago. Could have been selling Yellow Pages on TV—doing something besides policing."

Both men fell silent again. Frank tried to recapture the earlier feeling: clutch in, mind idling. Thinking about nothing. Especially not thinking about what lay in the statue's hand behind him. He fastened his gaze again on the water and Fort McNair. But it wasn't working. And he knew it wasn't working for José, either. Recess was over. Reluctantly, he let the dead woman on the statue come back into his head again.

"Three women," he said.

"Two white, one black," José said.

"Three knifed. Fingers taken from all three."

"Two he killed on the spot, one a dump job."

Frank felt good, leaning on the rail and looking out across the water with the morning sun in his face. He didn't want to think anymore, but something in him kept turning over. "There's something else," he said.

"What's that?"

"More'n a dump job, Hoser."

"Yeah?"

"Like a display. Naked, laid out like that in that hand."

Frank straightened up and took a last look across the water. Then both men turned back toward the statue and the flashing lights of the cars and the yellow tape fluttering in the growing breeze. The ME's ambulance had arrived. Tony Upton walked around the corpse, getting a three-sixty view of his latest client. Perched on the statue's head, a large raven, motionless, watched Upton. And waited.

TWENTY-ONE

Frank and José found parking places together in front of head-quarters.

"Eight o'clock," Jose yawned. "And end-of-the-day wearies already got me."

Frank rubbed the stubble on his chin and tried to remember if he had any throwaway razors in his lower-left desk drawer.

"A buck says Brother Emerson's already bouncing off the walls."

Frank shook his head. "Too early for Randolph."

In their office, both Frank and José's phone lines blinked an angry red. And there weren't any throwaway razors left in his lower desk drawer. Frank listened to his voicemail for a second, then hung up. From his wallet he pulled a dollar and slapped it on José's desk.

José pocketed the bill and started for the door with Frank. "Never too early for Randolph when his ass's in a sling."

Tina Barber's brown eyes strip-searched the three men.

"We're here to see the mayor," Randolph Emerson said, gesturing to Frank and José on either side.

Seth Tompkins had brought Barber in with him as he cleared the

District mayoral offices of Malcolm Burridge's toadies. She was a tall, well-proportioned woman who saw her job as Tompkins's main line of defense. As if everyone who wanted to see her mayor was either a felon or someone with intent to become one.

Malcolm Burridge had stepped down earlier in the year, before the scheduled election. Rumor had it that Janet Reno had called him over to Justice and hinted that a resignation—*Perhaps for reasons of health, Your Honor?*—and a long absence from the District of Columbia might be in Burridge's best interests. And so, in the summer's special election, in stepped Seth Tompkins, professional straight arrow. Party affiliation: Independent. Social liberal, fiscal conservative. Princeton, University of Virginia Law School. Former clerk to Thurgood Marshall on the Supreme Court, associate director at the Office of Management and Budget.

Frank had only seen newspaper photos and TV clips of Tompkins. A slight, precision-made man. A wearer of starched shirts and tie-them-yourself bow ties.

"And you're *who?*" asked Barber. The eyes seemed capable of penetrating granite.

"Commander Randolph Emerson, Detective Lieutenants Kearney and Phelps."

Barber glared at Emerson, then at Frank. She got to José and the gaze softened a fraction. Apparently concluding the three pitiful men in front of her posed no threat to her boss, she pushed away from her desk and led them to Tompkins's office.

Walking down a short hallway, Frank overheard Emerson try a scrap of suck-up conversation with Barber. But she wasn't having any. Frank smiled. Emerson wasn't doing very well. The meeting before they had rushed over to City Hall had been vintage Emerson. Hearing the Homicide commander's petulant hand-wringing rant, an outsider might assume that Frank, José, and the killer had conspired with the sole purpose of ruining Emerson's day.

Barber stopped at a polished walnut door, knocked, then opened it.

"The detectives," she announced. She gave Emerson a narrow-lidded warning look. She turned and left, brushing by José as she did so.

Seth Tompkins stood at the large window behind his desk, looking out on Pennsylvania and Constitution Avenues. A smaller, slighter man than Frank had imagined, Tompkins's dark slacks, pale blue shirt, and burgundy foulard bow tie accented his almost boyish physique. Noah Day, the department chief, bulky and glum, slumped wearily in an armchair facing Tompkins.

Day got to his feet. He nodded toward Emerson. "Randolph Emerson, Your Honor. Homicide Commander—"

"Pleased to meet you, Your Honor," Emerson said eagerly.

"Frank Kearney and Josephus Phelps," Day went on, "the detectives in charge."

Tompkins pointed to chairs by his desk. "Sit. What's the latest?"

"Your Honor," Emerson began, "we're going at this hammer and tong—"

Tompkins held up a belaying hand. "I'm certain you are, commander. Right now I would like to hear from the detectives in charge." He turned his attention to José and Frank. "I don't recall a serial-killer case here in the District."

"We may have had some passing through," José said, "but this's the first where it looks like we might have one taking up residence."

Tompkins aged as he took this on. "You've been with the department . . . how long, Josephus?"

"José, Your Honor. Twenty-five years. And a couple of days."

"And you . . . it *is* Frank?"

"Frank. Same twenty-five as José."

"Partners all that time?"

Frank and José nodded.

Tompkins looked at the two as if figuring out how they fit together. Finished, he asked briskly: "Okay—who, what, where, when, how?"

"We got a nine-one-one this morning," José began. "A bus of Japanese photographers . . ."

Tompkins listened intently as José, then Frank, walked him

through the investigation. Only his eyes moved between the two men. When they finished, he sat back in his chair, elbows on the armrests, head bowed as if in prayer. He looked up. "So your first task is to identify this woman."

Frank and José nodded.

"How long will that take?"

"If her prints are on file . . . today," Frank said.

Tompkins's face took on a hatchetlike sharpness. He pointed to Frank and José "The minute you find out, I want to know. From one of you. *Directly.*" He jabbed a finger. "You call Tina—tell her you want to talk with me. Anytime, anywhere."

He waited for an answering nod from the two men. He got up, and as he did he slapped both hands on his desk and looked at Day. "All right, chief, let's go."

"Go?" Startled, Day could only sit and stare at the mayor.

Tompkins was already getting his coat.

"This woman," he said, "I assume she's at the medical examiner's?"

Day and Emerson looked at Frank and José.

José nodded. "Yes."

"That's where we're going," Tompkins said, already halfway to the door.

"I'll call ahead," Emerson said.

"No." Tompkins shook his head. "They'll just waste time, trying to pick up and make pretty."

✠ "Well," José said, "a buck says we get there, we're gonna have to fight our way through the cameras."

Frank, driving, fell in behind the mayor's Cadillac. No flashing lights, no motorcycle escort.

"Think so?"

José yawned and stretched. "Comes in the politician's playbook. You think for a minute Malcolm Burridge would miss an opportunity like this for a photo op?"

"Maybe this guy's different."

"Well," José admitted, "he *does* have a fine-looking lady out front for him. I still say he'll play to the media. A buck?"

"Okay."

Five minutes later, José shifted in his seat. "Shit," he muttered as he dug out his wallet. No cameras, no print reporters on the sidewalk in front of the ME's.

"Double or nothing on when we come out?" Frank asked.

"I was born at night," José said, handing over the dollar bill, "but not last night."

✠ "Grace, Dr. Tony here?"

Grace, Tony Upton's receptionist, gave Frank and José a grandmother's smile. If the entourage impressed her, she didn't show it. She motioned toward the door leading back to the autopsy suite. "Back there," she said.

Cardboard cartons and a broken gurney lined the hallway. Ahead and off to the right, the autopsy suite. Suddenly, a high-pitched grinding sound filled the passage. It stopped as abruptly as it had begun. Frank pushed through the double doors and led the way into the autopsy suite.

Tony Upton and the diener were working from opposite sides of the dissection table. The body had been opened with a Y-shaped incision. Deep cuts began at each shoulder, joined below the breasts, and continued on to the pubic bone. The diener held an electric saw. Upton bent over the body on the table. Frank saw that the medical examiner was preparing to open the rib cage to expose the heart and lungs.

Upton looked up and nodded a greeting. "Your Honor." Upton said it matter-of-factly, as if mayors dropped in every day.

Frank did the introduction. "Dr. Tony Upton, Mayor Tompkins."

Upton raised his plastic face shield. "I'd shake hands but . . ." He raised both latex-gloved hands, both bloody, one holding a scalpel.

Tompkins, absorbed, ignored him and stepped closer to the table. "This . . . is the woman . . ."

"Jane Doe."

Tompkins stared in horrified fascination at the wounds. He ran his tongue over his lips and took several deep breaths.

"Oh . . . my . . . God."

Revulsion and anger coarsened Tompkins's delicate features.

"The *bastard!* The no-good bastard."

Upton dropped his professional detachment and he gave the distraught mayor a sympathetic look. He tried to reassure Tompkins. "The first wounds . . ." Upton trailed off, then picked up: "The first wounds probably killed her."

"How many . . . wounds?"

"Twenty-two. And there are rope marks around the ankles and wrists."

Sweat beaded on Tompkins's forehead. His breathing got deeper, taking on a desperate quality.

"He took a finger from the other women."

"He took one here, too." Upton lifted the corpse's right hand for inspection.

"Why?" Tompkins looked at Frank and José. "Why put her down at Hains Point? And nude?"

"One way to look at it is opportunity," José said. "He had her somewhere where he could . . . ah . . . do more."

"And another way?"

"He's getting more intense," Frank said. "Internal pressure's building inside him."

Tompkins winced. "Any sexual assault?"

"Nothing indicated. We won't have the lab analysis of vaginal swabs until this afternoon."

Tompkins took that in, then he turned to Frank and José. "I'm sure you have questions."

"We'll talk to Tony later," José said.

Tompkins looked relieved. "Thank you, Doctor," he said to Upton. He hesitated, and, bending over the corpse, said something in a low voice.

Following Tompkins out, Frank looked back. Upton and his diener had begun pulling back the chest plate.

In the reception area, Tompkins wiped his face with a handkerchief. "Bathroom?"

Grace pointed. "Over there."

The mayor made his wobbly way into the bathroom. A faint sound of retching came through the closed door, followed by the sound of running water. The four men stared at the floor, out the window, at the ceiling. Tompkins came out, wiping his mouth with a paper towel.

"Well," he said weakly, "good thing my mother and father didn't want me to be a doctor." He looked back in the direction of the autopsy suite. "Horrible, horrible," he said.

Chief Day nodded.

"Yes, yes it is," Emerson said all too quickly with an ass-kissing smoothness. As if the mayor had been inadvertently exposed to something beneath his dignity. Emerson touched Tompkins's elbow to escort him back to his car.

Tompkins stood fast.

"I want you," he said to the chief of police, "to bring me down here for every homicide."

Day, uncertain, took a second to respond. "Sir?"

"Remind us of our responsibilities. Mine is to make this city safe." Tompkins paused. Then he put his index finger in Day's chest, just below the chief's badge. "And *yours*, chief," he said in an steel-edged voice, "is to catch this son of a bitch."

✝ Frank and José stood on the sidewalk and watched as Tompkins's car pulled away.

"Little guy's not Malcolm Burridge," José said.

Frank nodded. The former mayor was a showman. And most grown-ups accepted that theater was part of politics. All the same, you felt better when a politician played human once in a while.

"What was it he said in there?" José asked.

"Catch this son of a bitch?"

"No. In the autopsy suite. Just before we left. It was like he was talking to Jane Doe."

"He was," Frank said. "He told her, 'I'm sorry.' "

✝ Frank's phone rang the moment he and José walked into their office. He wanted to ignore it but answered anyway.

"Lieutenant? This's Jessica Talbot . . . from the *Post*. Can we meet somewhere to talk?"

Frank had no sooner hung up than Hunter Elliott called.

"The Keegan computer?"

It took a moment for Frank to register.

"You wanted me to look at it?"

"Oh? Yeah?"

"Nothing there."

"Nothing?"

"No Internet connection. Clean as a whistle. Word processing, a calendar, and that's it."

"What was that about?" José asked when Frank hung up.

"Our boy Hunter. No tracking program on the Keegan computer."

"What's that mean?"

"Anything . . . or nothing. She didn't have an Internet connection, so even if the killer wanted to hack into her computer, he couldn't."

"So he couldn't stalk her on her computer," José said, "he does it the old-fashioned way."

"Yeah. If it was good enough for Jack the Ripper . . ."

TWENTY-TWO

✝ **A** few minutes before noon on the northwest corner of Lafayette Square, Frank found his favorite bench.

Across the path from him, an old man in a yarmulke and an olive-green army-surplus overcoat played chess with a young black kid with a nose ring. He couldn't make out the board, but from the way the old man was muttering and shaking his head, Frank knew that he was in trouble.

From his pocket he took a pack of crackers he'd bought from a street vendor. He broke the crackers and tossed the first crumb to the nearest pigeon. In seconds, a raucous mob of the birds surrounded him.

A few minutes later, he spotted Jessica Talbot crossing the street from the direction of Decatur House. Woman had a no-nonsense way of walking—chin up, shoulders square, someplace to go, something to do. She gave him a brief smile of recognition when she got closer. As the sea of pigeons parted for her, he realized suddenly how grubby he must look—unshaven, frayed windbreaker, faded khakis.

If Talbot noticed, she didn't let on. She sat down beside him. "A famous bench," she said.

"Yeah." Frank nodded. "Bernard Baruch used to sit here and feed the pigeons."

"How did you know?" she asked, astonished.

"My father used to take me for walks here when I was five or six. One day, he pointed to a silver-haired man in a vested suit, homburg hat, and rimless glasses. Dad said, 'There's a famous man.' He'd met Baruch several times, so he took me over and introduced me."

Fascinated, Talbot nodded. "And?"

"Baruch patted me on the head and asked if I wanted to help him feed the pigeons."

"Did he give you any inside tips on international financing?"

"No. Just how to feed pigeons." Frank looked around, thinking how little the square had changed, and yet how everything was so different. He patted the oak slats of the bench. "Ever since, I thought of this as mine."

"A legacy." Talbot smiled, then, social courtesies over, started fishing. "I hear you've had a very busy day already."

"Yeah," Frank ignored the bait. "I have."

"A black female. Very dead. Hains Point."

"You know as much as I do," Frank said. He tossed the last of the crumbs to the pigeons. "Maybe you know more?"

"Naked." Talbot added that in, watching him for a reaction.

Frank kept his eyes on the pigeons. "No comment."

"Off the record?"

"How'd you know?"

"So, yes?"

"Yeah. How'd you know?"

"I saw a photograph of her. In that statue's hand."

"Photograph?"

"Eight-by-ten glossy. Color." She opened her purse and found a pack of Camels. Shaking one out, she lit it with the steel Zippo. She inhaled deeply and exhaled with a sigh of satisfaction. "It's making the rounds. A guy came by a couple hours ago, wanting to sell it."

"Fast work."

"Wonders and glories of the digital age." Talbot took another deep drag.

"Did you buy it?"

"Was it real?" she asked.

"I haven't seen it. Probably was, though."

"We didn't buy it," Talbot said, "but he'll find somebody."

"Could you tell when it was taken?"

Talbot looked puzzled.

"Daylight? Dark?"

"Oh. Early morning."

The old man in the yarmulke sat transfixed. His chin had dropped to his chest. His thin shoulders sagged inside the long overcoat. It was as if he and the chessboard were locked together, opposite poles in a magnetic force field. The young black kid was sitting back and looking around the square.

Old guy's had it, Frank thought.

"You know this killing is going to make it pretty clear to us in the unwashed public that the same person killed Mary and the Boukedes woman, don't you?" Talbot asked.

"Yes," he said reluctantly.

"You guys have been pirouetting around the S-word. Now it looks like you're going to have to say it."

Neither spoke. Frank tried to play out how the rest of the day would go, when the photo inevitably surfaced and the details came out and the questions had to be answered. Talbot sat beside him, finishing her cigarette.

Her tone changed, signaling a change in subject. "What was your impression of Charles Trevor?"

Frank took a second to register. "That came in out of left field."

"Basic Interviewing 101: Come in out of left field when the detective's thinking about something else."

"How'd you know I saw him?"

"My job's knowing who's seeing who in this town. I'm good at it."

"But your grammar's lousy," Frank said. "He said you did the right thing, sending Mary Keegan to Moscow after her husband was killed."

"He said that?" Talbot dropped her eyes, and Frank thought he saw her blush ever so slightly.

"Modesty becomes you, Ms. Talbot."

"Oh, shit!" Talbot definitely blushed.

"He also confirmed her mood—Ms. Keegan's—the last time he saw her. Distracted. Disorganized. Something definitely bothering her."

"Nothing about a motive?"

"Except that he couldn't imagine one."

"Her book—have you found it?"

"Her brother FedEx'd me a copy of the manuscript. I'm going to try to get to it this weekend."

"When you do . . ." Talbot trailed off as if she'd thought better of what she was going to say.

"When I do . . . ?" Frank asked.

Talbot waved a hand. "It's nothing."

Frank shook his head. "No such thing as nothing."

Talbot got a guilty look. "I was starting to say, 'I'd like to see it.' Then I realized I had no right. It'd be like eavesdropping."

Frank searched Talbot's face. Her eyes brimmed with tears.

"The book," Frank said gently, "means something special."

Talbot nodded and took a deep breath. "Because it meant a lot to her. The way she talked about it . . . the book . . ."

Talbot lost her way for a moment, then looked at Frank as if imploring him to understand what she was trying to understand herself.

"I'm not a writer. Writing is a gift. A rare one. I don't have that gift. Mary did. But I *am* a damn good editor," she said fiercely. "And to a damn good editor, no book started by someone as talented as Mary should ever go unfinished. That book was her life. The book's unfinished. So's her life."

She sat for a long time, as if listening to what she'd said. Then she took a last, deep drag on her cigarette, leaned forward, stubbed it out, and got up. "Back to the fourth estate."

Frank got up with her and they walked toward H Street. Behind him, he heard the old man's voice, strong and triumphant: "Checkmate."

TWENTY-THREE

✠ The second meeting of the day with Emerson wasn't going any better than the first. The Homicide commander had a cornered, punchy look. As if he'd exceeded his limit of abuse for the day.

"She didn't say who was shopping the photo around?" Emerson asked.

"No."

"You didn't *ask?*"

"Randolph," Frank said patiently, "she's not going to name a source, even if she didn't buy what he was offering today. And even if she did, what can we do?"

Frank glanced over to José, sitting motionless, watching Emerson's growing irritation. His partner had the settled, complacent look of a big cat in the sun, with a faint curl of enjoyment playing at the corners of his mouth.

Emerson must have noticed, too, because he lashed out at José. "And I thought *you* had one of the uniforms collect the film from the Japs."

"I did, and the uniform did," José said.

"Then how come," Emerson asked, "a photograph's floating around looking for the highest bidder?"

José shrugged. "There were thirty-eight civilians of Japanese persuasion on the tour bus. There was one cop collecting the film. Obviously, somebody opened their camera, substituted a fresh roll of film and pocketed the one with the victim. Either that or it was one of those new cameras with a floppy disk. Switching that, no problem."

Emerson stared morosely at José, giving no sign he'd heard. He shook his head. "There's going to be hell to pay," he said, "hell to pay. The *Post* and *Times* are eating us alive." He clenched his teeth. "Goddamn Japs!" he exploded.

"Why not blame Seward Johnson, Randolph," Frank said.

Emerson's eyes widened. "Johnson? Johnson? Who's he?"

"He was the sculptor who did the *Awakening* statue," Frank shrugged. "Hadn't been for him, the statue wouldn't have been there, and nobody'd be taking pictures."

Emerson frowned. "Instead of making funny, gentlemen, how about a suggestion?"

José waved a hand like a school kid. "I suggest you call the chief," he said brightly. "Bad news doesn't get better with age."

✠ José opened his menu and shut it. "Reuben and slaw."

Frank didn't bother. "Pastrami on rye—no, make it corned beef on rye . . ."

Ruth held her pencil poised, waiting patiently.

"No," Frank frowned, finally handing her his menu, "pastrami."

Ruth wrote pastrami and disappeared.

"Good thing she's fast on the getaway," José said, "or you'd be back to corned beef."

Frank sat resting with his elbows on the table and let his mind drift. He played with the saltshaker, batting it gently back and forth between his palms, skating it across the scratched Formica.

After a moment or two, José reached over and rescued the saltshaker. "Anything going on between the ears?" he asked.

"Just thinking about Jane Doe. Wondering what she was doing this time yesterday."

"None of us got tomorrow guaranteed."

"No, we don't. But we don't see going out the way she did."

"She probably didn't, either."

"You're young, you don't see going out at all." Then, "We know what he did with Boukedes's finger," Frank said, thinking out loud, "you think he's done the same thing with Keegan and Jane Doe?"

"You mean, mummify their fingers?"

"Yeah. You think he's going to do that?"

José started rolling the saltshaker around in his hand. "Probably," he said slowly, feeling his way, "probably."

Frank felt as if he were running headfirst into a brick wall. And getting up and doing it all over again. Logic carried you in a straight line. At least most of the time. Sometimes logic turned elliptical. Or even circular. But generally, there were steps: Who says A must say B—like that. And you got to B and there was C. What if you had only an A and a Z? And nothing in between?

"Why?" Frank asked.

"The Shadow knows." José rolled it out dramatically, deep and serious.

"You know, Hoser, I should have never told you you sound like James Earl Jones."

José tried it again. "The Shadow knows."

Ruth showed up with their order.

Frank examined his sandwich, then gave José a mystified look.

"I ordered pastrami?"

The men ate without speaking until José, looking up from his plate, muttered, "It didn't take long."

Frank looked up. The TV behind the bar carried a newsbreak banner superimposed over a long shot of Hains Point and the *Awakening* statue.

"Hey, Ruth," José called. He pointed his sandwich at the TV. "Sound up."

The banner and long shot disappeared.

"Ah, pop goes the weasel," Frank sighed as Hugh Worsham appeared, sitting behind a news-anchor desk.

"Looks mighty grieved," José commented.

Worsham looked into the camera with a long, sad face.

"The serial killer stalking Washington's streets has claimed a third victim," Worsham intoned. "In a slaying that has authorities scrambling for clues, we learn that police have kept from the public the brutal nature of this killer."

"Guess what's coming next," Frank said.

Worsham put on the expression of a man about to do something he finds personally distasteful but something required by a higher calling to professional duty.

"I must warn our viewers. The following photograph contains graphic material that should not be viewed by children and may be disturbing to others in our audience." He put on an air of parental impatience as though waiting for the last of the children to be shooed out of the room. Then he turned to the screen on his right.

A repeat of the long shot of Hains Point and the statue. Then the camera closed in on the statue's left hand. Another shot—now a still.

"This is the gruesome sight that shocked visiting Japanese photographers this morning at one of Washington's popular landmarks."

"It's real," Frank said to himself. They'd airbrushed the breasts and pubis, but not the horrific injuries—the multiple stab wounds, even the loop of intestine obscenely hanging from the victim's abdomen.

"Should have known Worsham would buy the picture," José said.

The photo was still on.

"Okay, Hugh, we get the idea," Frank said to the TV.

As if defying Frank, the photo remained onscreen for another second or two, then Worsham returned.

"The body of an unidentified African-American woman in the hand of the famous *Awakening* statue. What does this mean? For some answers, we turn to Dr. Nels Pearson, an authority on serial killers."

The screen split. Worsham flicked over to the left, his guest appeared on the right with San Francisco's TransAmerica building in the background. Pearson was a study in academic credibility—tweed sport jacket, dark tie, long face with thinning hair, hornrim glasses, and a slightly scruffy mustache.

"Dr. Pearson, you've studied the reports of the murders of Susan Boukedes and Mary Keegan. With this latest killing, are you prepared to say that these women are the victims of a serial killer?"

Pearson nodded somberly. "Every bit of evidence available to me says yes."

"Nothing like a little distance to make a man more certain," José muttered.

"And the most recent killing," Worsham went on, "what might it tell us about the killer?"

"The injuries suffered by the third victim appear more severe. I believe it prudent to say that it is likely that this represents a progression in the killer's modus operandi."

"I understand the location is indicative of this . . . this progression," Worsham said.

Frank gave most TV "experts" little credence. Even so, he found himself listening intently to Pearson.

"Yes. The earlier victims were found where they were killed. This third victim tells us the killer did his work elsewhere. He then risked detection by carrying the body to a public place."

"Why?"

"For display."

"Display? Explain," Worsham said.

Studio lights glinted on Pearson's glasses. "Obviously, just the act of placing the body on the statue. But the killer went further. This victim was totally nude. And the killer posed the corpse in a position for maximum shock effect."

"Posed?" Worsham asked.

"Yes. Posed provocatively."

"Provocatively? You mean . . . ah . . . *sexually* provocative?" Worsham's voice had a veneer of clinical professionalism to it, but underneath, Frank thought he caught a slight tremor of lecherous excitement.

Pearson's eyes widened. "Oh," he said quickly, "there are all manners of provocation besides sexual."

"There are?" Worsham asked.

"The nudity—the posing could be a challenge."

"Challenge? To the police?"

José shook his head. "Here we go. Screw-the-cops time."

Almost in sync with José, Pearson shook his head, too. "Not just to the police. To society. I would say that this is a man who increasingly holds society not only in contempt, but harbors a hatred toward the world in which he lives."

"An example," Worsham prompted.

Pearson, obviously ready, nodded. "Edmund Kemper. Fourteen years old, he shot and killed his grandmother and grandfather. Seven years later, mental-health authorities released him to his mother's custody, provided that state psychiatrists conducted periodic evaluations. Within two years, he resumed killing. He picked up two coeds from Fresno State College. He stabbed them to death. He took them home. He took photographs of them. And then he dissected them and scattered their body parts in the Santa Cruz Mountains.

"Four months after these killings, he killed and decapitated a fifteen-year-old girl. The following morning, Kemper, as previously scheduled, drove to the clinic to meet with his evaluating psychiatrists."

Pearson hesitated and let the tension build.

"The interview went well," Pearson continued. "The board declared him no longer a threat to himself or others. The board also recommended that his juvenile record be sealed."

Pearson stopped, and Frank knew the man hadn't finished.

"The board gave Kemper a good bill of health," Pearson said, a tremor in his voice, "while the young girl's head lay in the trunk of his car in the clinic parking lot."

Worsham sat motionlessly for a moment. If he wasn't stunned, he faked it well. "Why?" he asked. "Why did he take her head with him to the interview?"

"To show his contempt for the system," Pearson said. "And his superiority to it."

Worsham nodded sagely, as if he'd take the rest of the day to think about that. "Dr. Pearson . . . a last question?"

"Yes?"

"Based on your knowledge, what's next here in this case?"

"Short answer?" Pearson asked.

Worsham nodded. "Short answer."

"More killing," Pearson said. "He will kill until he's stopped."

Worsham disappeared and the soaps returned. Ruth, who'd been standing to the side, watching, muted the TV.

Frank stared at the soap struggling along in pantomime. " '. . . the world in which he lives,' " he repeated to himself.

"What's that?" asked José.

"Something the shrink said. I wonder what world our man *does* live in?"

José's cell phone chirped. He answered it, listened, then turned to Frank.

"They've ID'd her."

TWENTY-FOUR

It's about Celeste, isn't it?" Rachel Matthews asked.

"Does Celeste Rochelle Foster work here?" José asked.

"Yes."

The chief nurses' station, a glass cubicle, provided a commanding view of the ER's treatment and operating rooms, a restless stage-set of beige tile, stainless steel, and green scrub suits.

"We've identified a body by its fingerprints," Frank said.

Matthews, a spare, sinewy woman with graying brown hair, stood for a moment, looking back and forth between Frank and José, then dropped into her chair. "Oh my God."

"Why'd you think we came about her?" Frank asked.

Cradling her face in her hands, Matthews didn't answer immediately, but shook her head in denial. Finally, she reached into a desk drawer for a tissue.

"Celeste didn't show up today," she said dully. "I called and got her answering machine. She's never been a no-show. In two years. *Never* a no-show. When did it . . ."

"We found her body this morning," José said.

Matthews paled and her eyes widened in horror. "The woman at Hains Point . . ."

Frank nodded.

Matthews shut her eyes and shivered as if caught in a cold draft. "When she didn't call, I *knew* . . ."

"You're her shift supervisor?" José asked.

She looked up at José. "Never a no-show." She said it with an urgency. As if it was important that José believe her.

"Never a no-show," José echoed. "She worked yesterday, did she?"

"Yes."

"When did she leave?"

Matthews worked on that for a moment. "Last night just after nine . . . shift change."

Frank glanced at the wall clock in the hallway. Just after eight. Twenty-four hours ago, Foster would have been getting ready to wrap up a long day's work. "Did you actually see her leave?" he asked.

"I saw . . . her . . . walk out," Matthews managed, face still pale.

"What was she wearing?"

"Her ski jacket, pale blue nylon. A thick wad of lift tickets on the zipper. Green hospital scrubs, white shoes."

"Where would she go from here?"

"To her car. In the garage. She had her car keys in her hand."

"Her parents," Frank said, "we have to notify them. Do you—"

"Oh, God." Another shadow passed over Matthews's face. "Yes, yes, of course." She got up and went to a small two drawer file cabinet in the corner. After unlocking it with a key from a chain around her neck, she walked her fingers to a file folder and pulled it out. From the folder she took a card and handed it to Frank.

Celeste Rochelle Foster. Father: Gerald Monroe Foster, advertising executive. Mother: Sylvia Simpson Foster.

"Her mother was a nurse, too," Matthews said.

A Pittsburgh address, a phone number. Celeste Foster had signed the card at the bottom. A bold, looping script. Below her signature, her address on Corcoran Street NW. Frank knew the neighborhood, nineteenth-century red-brick houses, just off Dupont Circle.

"I have two daughters of my own," Matthews said, "Cellie made a third."

"What was her mood like the past month or so?" José asked. "Happy? Sad? Frightened?"

Matthews paused, palms together, index fingers to her lower lip as if praying. "A month working here, you're all that and more."

"Any unwanted attention?"

"No."

"Did she ever mention being stalked?"

"No."

"Any male friends?"

"A boyfriend. It was an exclusive relationship."

"You know him?"

"Cellie brought him by last year. A solid young man. High school sweethearts. He still lives in Pittsburgh."

Frank finished copying the information from the notification card and handed it back to Matthews.

"Can you show us how she'd get from here to her car?"

"Let me get a substitute."

Matthews disappeared and came back shortly with a nurse in tow. On seeing Frank and José, she shot a sidelong glance at Matthews, then back to the two men, eager to make a connection but smart enough not to ask her grim boss. Matthews took a cardigan off a hook on the back of the door.

"Let's go, gentlemen."

As they walked down the passageway that led into the rest of the hospital, Frank looked back. The nurse was following them with unconcealed curiosity.

Matthews stopped in front of a door marked STAFF ONLY. "Here," she said, and pushed through to an indoor garage. "Our spaces are two levels down. The stairwell's over there."

"That closed at night?" José pointed to the vehicle entryway on the far side of the garage. Outside on 23rd Street, scattered evening traffic. Across the street, the Foggy Bottom Metro station. Two lanes led in and out of the garage. Spiral ramps led to floors above and below.

"No. Open day and night. All year."

Frank sketched the garage floorplan in his notebook, then followed Matthews as she led the way down the stairs.

"ER's got its own parking spaces?" he asked.

"Yes. A perk for working a fifty-hour week for a forty-hour salary."

Off the stairwell at the ground level, orange-yellow mercury vapor lamps provided light without ridding the garage of its gloom.

"This the way she'd have been walking to her car?" Frank asked.

"Yes." Matthews wended her way between the tightly packed cars. Frank noticed overhead signs designating parking lanes and rows. Five or six rows away, he saw the sign EMERGENCY ROOM STAFF.

"Cellie's slot is . . ." Matthews said as she rounded the back of a Land Rover, then stopped. "Oh," she said in a small voice, "she's . . . still here."

In the space beside the Land Rover, a shiny white Toyota Camry. Frank caught José's glance.

José shook his head. "If that's her car, she didn't make it this far."

The three stood for a moment, silently looking at the car. "It's like . . . it's waiting for her," Matthews said, her voice trembling.

José shot Frank an eye-message and took Matthews gently by the elbow. "I'll walk you back," he told her.

"I'll stay here," Frank said.

With his flashlight, Frank inspected the outside of the car, taking care not to touch it. A fine layer of dust coated the windshield. The car had been there, he figured, over thirty hours. He walked back the way he'd come, all the way up the stairs to the doorway into the hospital. As he got to the door, José came out.

"I called Renfro," he said.

Together the two men slowly walked back down the stairs, playing their flashlights on each step.

"Couple hundred people been down these stairs since she got off shift," José said.

Back at the ground level, they looked across the tops of the cars toward the bulk of the Land Rover.

"Matthews said she saw Foster with her car keys in her hand," Frank said.

"I'll work this side," José said, gesturing with his flashlight to the left of the path they'd taken with Matthews.

Frank nodded and broke off to the right. Slowly, he made his way toward Foster's car, searching beneath each parked vehicle. Two rows from the finish line, he knelt and played his light under a Saab convertible. A glitter of silver. A red leather key case.

"Bingo," Frank muttered.

"Got them?" José asked.

Frank pulled a handkerchief from his pocket and retrieved the keys. José came around the Saab and joined him.

"Toyota," José said.

Frank fitted the key to the doorlock of Foster's car and turned. The door unlocked. He locked the door again and took the key out. Wrapping the handkerchief around the key and key case, he put it away in his coat pocket.

"You think he grabbed her where we found the keys?" Frank asked.

José pointed to the doorway to the stairs. "We found them in line with the stairs and her car," José said. "She might of thrown them a short distance when he grabbed her. Or in a struggle, he might of kicked them. But I think he got her right around here someplace." He circled the area with his hand. "Someplace close."

"No blood on the floor."

"Way he cut her up, ought to be blood somewhere."

"He didn't cut her here, Hoser. Got her out of here and cut her somewhere else."

✠ Twenty-five minutes later, Renfro Calkins's Forensics van eased down the ramp, then made its way through the maze of lanes toward Frank and José. Calkins stopped the vehicle a short distance away, shut down the engine, and got out, leaving the lights on.

Eyes surveying the garage, Calkins listened intently as Frank and

José outlined what they thought had happened. When they had finished, he nodded.

"Okay," Calkins said, "I've got it. Where you going to be?"

"Doing some camera work," Frank said, pointing to the closed-circuit video recorder anchored to the ceiling several rows away.

✛ Marla Fernandez, the security director, sat between Frank and José at a conference table in the video surveillance center. Black-and-white monitors, like windows in a huge airliner, covered three walls of the room. She opened a large folder and found the schematics of the garage.

"The red squares are camera locations," she explained. "The blue fans mark the areas that each camera can see."

Frank oriented himself to the drawing. He found the cameras on the stairwell and on the bottom level of the garage that would have watched Celeste Foster as she made her way toward her death.

"These here." Frank pointed to the red squares on the schematic, then to the video screens around the room. "What monitors would cover them?"

Fernandez pointed to a bank of screens at the far end of the room. "Over there."

A young woman with a headset and lip microphone sat watching the screens. Frank counted four screens down, five across.

"She covers twenty cameras?" he asked.

"Forty." As Fernandez said it, Frank saw one screen flicker and the image switched from an exterior shot of the 23rd Street entrance to the garage to an interior view of the same entrance. "The cameras record full-time," she explained, "but the operator is here to scan for any real-time security problem."

"You say each screen covers two cameras," José said. "What's the cycle time?"

"Views switch every minute unless the operator spots something suspicious. Then the view can be locked in on that camera."

"Nothing unusual last night?" José asked.

"Sarah was on this position last night." Fernandez gripped the shoulder of the woman operator. "Sarah?"

Sarah shook her head. "Couple of maintenance glitches. Usual stuff. Otherwise, dull night."

"We'd like to see last night's tapes of the stairwell and ground-level cameras, starting last night at eight." Frank said. "Stairwell tapes first, then ground-level parking."

Fernandez nodded. "It'll take a few minutes to set up."

"We're going to need nurse Matthews," José said.

"Yeah," Frank said, "I'm afraid so."

"I'll call." Fernandez reached for the phone.

"No," said José, "I'll go get her."

✚ Fifteen minutes later, Rachel Matthews, Marla Fernandez, and Frank and José sat in a semicircle around a large console.

"Okay, Sarah," Fernandez said, "roll 'em."

The young operator flicked a switch and the garage stairwell filled the screen. Across the top, in white numerals, the date and time. The time, in day/date/twenty-four-hour format—hours, minutes, seconds, and tenths of seconds:

Thur/26–10–00/20:04:38.7.

For several frames, the only motion was the clock, and Frank came to think of it as Celeste Foster's clock, counting away the seconds of her life.

The door swung open. A young man, a thick shock of dark hair, a Boston Celtics jacket, obviously in a hurry.

"I don't know him," Fernandez said, barely audible.

Matthews shook her head.

"Rob Cunningham, Hematology," Sarah whispered. Something . . . an eagerness, a knowingness? . . . in the tone of her voice made Frank smile.

"We have offset shift changes," Fernandez explained, "spreads out the commuter traffic. What you're seeing are most of the lab people leaving."

Over the next fifteen minutes, the departures crested, then abated. Soon the door remained shut, the clock ticking off seconds, then minutes.

"Can we fast forward until something moves?" Frank asked.

On the screen, seconds and minutes blurred.

At 20:56:44.8, the door opened. Sarah slowed the action. Two women, one with a scarf, the other bare-headed, both with nylon jackets over hospital scrubs, ID cards on lanyards around their necks.

"Thurston and Bailey," Matthews said.

The door began opening more frequently. Groups, pairs, singles filing out at the end of a long day. All his life, faces had fascinated Frank. What did they say? What did they hide? Why did this person smile? Why—

"There she is!" Matthews said, voice hoarse and tight with tension. "There she is," she repeated.

Sarah did something with the controls. The frame froze at 21:09:27.7.

The camera caught Celeste Foster from an overhead angle. Frank made out a good-looking young woman. He willed her not to take the stairs. *Turn around. Go back. Find a friend for a few drinks.* He glanced at José and Matthews, both leaning toward the screen, faces tense.

He took a deep breath. "Okay," he said, "let it go."

And Sarah again worked the controls and Celeste Foster disappeared into the darkness at the bottom of the steps. Time: 21:09:38.2.

"I'm switching to the camera on her parking level," Sarah said. The video came up, a grainy panorama of the ground level. The on-screen digital clock showed 21:09:39.7.

"There's her car," José said.

Celeste Foster stepped through the doorway from the stairwell.

Sarah nodded. "I think this's where—"

The screen flickered. The garage image twisted and disappeared. The screen was black, a blackness broken only by the white digital clock. Time 21:09:44.6.

"You were starting to say something, Sarah?" Frank asked.

"I was starting to say this was where I called maintenance."

"What happened?"

"It turned out to be a circuit breaker problem."

Fernandez broke in. "It's not unusual. We draw enough power here to electrify a small town."

"Fast forward until we get video," Frank said.

The digital clock blurred.

At 21:25:17.1 it stopped. The garage image reappeared. Celeste Foster's car was there. But no Celeste Foster.

Frank stared at the screen, willing it to give up the smallest clue, the tiniest fragment of information. Then, turning to Fernandez, he asked, "How often do you lose video?"

"We can go a week, ten days with everything working. Other times . . . especially in the summer with the thunderstorms . . . a couple of times a day."

"It took over fifteen minutes to get the camera working again," José said. "That out of the ordinary?"

Fernandez, clearly uneasy, flushed and ran her tongue over her lips. "It's sometimes more, sometimes less."

"You know what the trouble was?"

"You'll have to ask maintenance."

✠ "Circuit breaker tripped, is all," Sandford Tyler said. "You get a surge, that happens."

Tyler, a gaunt, angular man in a stained blue jumpsuit, looked past Frank and José, attracted by Calkins's evidence techs dusting the circuit breaker panel box.

"A long time to reset it," José said.

Tyler shrugged, but kept his eyes on the activity around the panel box. "I was over to the other side of campus. You want faster service, you gotta hire more people. Simple as that."

Frank guessed that that was one of Tyler's stock answers from a shopworn two-answer arsenal, the other being "You want faster, you pay me more. Simple as that."

"When you got here, Mr. Tyler, did you see anything unusual?"

Tyler's eyes edged past Frank to the evidence techs then back to Frank. He got a wary, cunning look.

"No. I didn't see anything."

"The blown circuit breaker wasn't unusual?" José asked.

Tyler shrugged. "Happens all the time."

"You got a log?"

"I don't keep it. That's the clerk's job."

"And he's . . . where?"

"Off. Won't be in until Monday." Tyler looked at his watch. "It's my break time. You need me for anything more?"

Frank and José watched Tyler walk away.

"Killer knows what time Foster gets off shift," José said. "Knows her car. Knows where she parks. Knows which circuit breaker blanks the camera."

Tyler disappeared up the stairs.

"And," Frank said, "he's got a pretty good idea how long it takes brother Tyler to answer a call for a blown circuit."

Renfro Calkins came over to where Frank and José were waiting.

"You got all the prints?" José asked. "Car? Breaker panel?"

"We got the prints. There's something about the breaker panel— somebody picked the lock."

"Jimmied it?"

"No. Raked the pins. A sweet job. Hardly a scratch."

"But it was a pick?" Frank asked.

"Definitely."

"Can you say when?"

"No. Could have been last night, could have been a month ago. You want priority on the prints?"

Frank nodded.

Calkins waited only a second to see if there were any more questions, then hurried back to where his techs were packing up.

"Friday night," José said. "Everybody's got the get-outs."

Frank checked his watch. A quarter to nine. He was having trouble subtracting. The day had started—what?—fourteen hours before?

All of a sudden he was tired and hungry and felt greasy and he thought about a shower and a cold beer and a bowl of chili. If that wasn't paradise, it was pretty damn close. As he and José started up the stairs, he stopped to look back at Celeste Foster's car, still waiting under the orange-yellow mercury vapor lamps.

TWENTY-FIVE

✛ **S**aturday morning, Frank brought Mary Keegan's manuscript into the office, intending to start reading it. He got sidetracked when José held up an envelope. "Janowitz left us the warrant for Celeste Foster's apartment."

"Where is he?" Frank said.

"Janowitz? It's Saturday. I guess he's home with the wife and kids." A moment passed as José gave him a measuring look. "You don't like that?"

"There's time to be home with the wife and kids when we bag this bastard."

José dropped his chin and gave Frank a disapproving look from under his eyebrows. "There's always gonna be a bastard to bag, Frank. Wouldn't be anything for young Leon to do today except follow us around and get in the way."

He got up and slapped Frank's shoulder with the warrant. "Come on, let's go check out the Foster address. I already called Renfro."

Frank put the manuscript, still in its FedEx box, back into his briefcase and reached for his coat. "Okay. We finish up in time, we go to my place, and watch Maryland kick Duke's butt."

"Give me Duke and seven."

. . .

✛ Ten minutes later, Frank and José stood on the sidewalk on Corcoran Street looking up at a four-story Victorian-era apartment house, dark red brick with a slate-roofed turret. In the vestibule, a directory of apartment numbers. Frank found the manager's office listing and pressed the adjacent button.

✛ Dust motes danced in the sunlight streaming in the windows of the small living room. Under the windows, an antique camel-backed sofa, upholstered in a prim dark blue velvet, faced a low coffee table. Two platform rockers with needlepoint cushions had been drawn up on the other side of the table. Family photographs in assorted frames covered the table.

"Nice," José said.

And soon, Frank found himself thinking, *somebody will come and put all this in boxes and crates and take away the last of Celeste Foster.* A low divider with ferns set off the dining room where a door led, he guessed, back into the kitchen.

"Morning." The voice came from behind him. Frank turned. Renfro Calkins stood in the open door with one of his evidence techs.

Frank waved him in, then followed José into the bedroom. A four-poster double bed, matching marble-top bedside tables, and pickled pine wardrobe and chest of drawers.

"Certainly wasn't much for modern furniture," José said.

"Except that." A desk stood in an alcove adjacent to the bathroom, one of those compact matte black modular affairs that held computer, screen, and printer, with overhead bookshelves. Modern, but like the rest of the apartment, hospital-neat. Three-ring binders and file folders neatly labeled for bills, correspondence, recipes.

Frank turned on the computer. José stood beside him and the two men watched the screen bloom.

José pointed. "Seen that before."

"That" was a small icon—a pale blue box crossed by a lightning bolt, and beneath it the label LORE.COM.

"I think we need a little help," Frank said as he reached in a pocket for his cell phone.

✠ An hour later, Renfro Calkins and his tech had packed up and taken their collection of prints, swabs, and samples back to the lab. And Hunter Elliott was still at Celeste Foster's computer.

Elliott worked for another hour, locked in an eerie otherworld absorption, his hands moving as if independent of his immobile body. Frank and José watched as Elliott dug deeper, tracking over the fields and through the valleys of cyberspace. He finally dropped his hands to his lap, stared at the screen for another second or two, then swiveled to face Frank and José.

Elliott looked at Frank with an odd, penetrating expression. "She's got it," he said. "Somebody put the same program in this computer we saw in the Boukedes machine."

"So he was able to follow Foster?"

Elliott nodded. "Anything she did on that machine. And she was a very organized woman—daily calendar, to-do lists, bank account, investments."

"And all that went to an Internet address?" José asked.

"Yeah. Like the Boukedes address, this one closed down the day he made his kill."

"I think it's time, Hoser, we took a drive to the country."

✠ An hour later, Frank and José passed through a tollbooth exit in Fairfax County, Virginia.

"I remember when I thought Dulles was halfway to the Mississippi River," José said.

Frank nodded. Twenty years ago, this used to be a two-lane road that wound through miles of farmland and forests before ending at the scarcely used Dulles International Airport. Now IAD was handling more than fifty thousand passengers a day and the road was a multilane highway system to accommodate the lemminglike swarming of commuters living in suburbs around the airport. And the farms and forests had been bulldozed so Information Age America could build glittering chrome-and-glass incubators for its dot-com businesses.

A mile and a half after the tollbooth exit, José pointed ahead. "That must be it."

A low red-brick wall ran along the road for several hundred yards, rising to large pillars that framed a gateway. On both sides of the gateway, large bronze letters spelled out LORE.COM.

Drop gates blocked entry. A uniformed guard stepped out of the security post.

Frank rolled his window down and watched the guard approach. Young, neat, close haircut, flat-bellied. Clean, well-fitted uniform. Leather polished, and pistol, cuffs, and Mace carried firmly against the body. A quick but close check of credentials, a brief radio call for confirmation, and the guard handed Frank a laminated parking permit and waved the car in.

"Not your everyday rent-a-cop," José said.

The grounds resembled the campus of a small college. Autumn had turned the maples along the narrow roadway a lush red. Expanses of green lawn ran up to red-brick Federal-style buildings, each given woodsy names by gold-leaf-lettered signs on black wrought-iron posts. The road curved off to the right, through a grove of trees, and up a steep hill.

"Well, look at that," Frank murmured as they came out onto the open hilltop.

"I don't know architecture," José breathed, "but that damn sure isn't Colonial."

LORE.COM headquarters resembled an inverted L: a gray glass tower Frank estimated to be eight or so stories high with a horizontal leg protruding from the top floor.

"Must have cost the gross national product of Brazil," Frank said as he pulled into a parking spot marked for visitors.

José got out of his side of the car and looked up at the building. "And all that money came from stringing little bitty electrons together." He shrugged. "I still don't understand how you can make so much money on something you can't see."

Frank made an "After you" gesture. "Let's find out."

Several stories high and filled with a maze of giant abstract sculptures in stainless steel, the lobby made Frank feel as if he'd been shrunken to insignificance. Scale vanished as gray glass walls met a matching gray marble floor.

"This for real?" he heard José asking. It took him several seconds to locate the reception desk, a minimalist ledge of birch perched on a single leg of lacquered steel. The receptionist, a blond woman in a tailored gray suit, was talking animatedly with a man in jeans, black T-shirt, and black sport jacket. The man's attention riveted on Frank and José. As they got nearer, he walked to meet them.

"I'm Michael Lessner, corporate counsel." The tone was clipped and precise.

Frank guessed Lessner only a few years past thirty. A compact, wiry man with short, brush-cut black hair, Lessner moved with the fastidious attentiveness of a cat.

Frank motioned to José. "Lieutenant Phelps . . . I'm Lieutenant Kearney."

Lessner shook hands and gestured in a direction behind the receptionist. "Elevators this way. Norman Jonathan, our CEO, is waiting."

Frank held up a hand. "We only wanted to talk to somebody about a subscriber's account. We aren't negotiating a merger."

Lessner didn't laugh. "Norm's not doing mergers today. Any time the authorities are interested in LORE.COM, Norm takes a personal interest, too." Lessner led them around a surreal sculpture of a giant computer chip. Two parallel rows of large posters in clear plastic frames suspended by nearly invisible cables defined the path to the elevators.

"Some layout here," José said.

"Five years ago, this was a pasture. Norm and I were living off chutzpah and credit cards. Trying to put all this together."

A poster captured Frank's attention. He stopped. José and Lessner continued toward the elevators. A fist in medieval armor clutched a golden goblet. Another fist gripped a bloodied broadsword.

José and Lessner came back. "Frank?"

Frank nodded toward the poster. " 'The Search for the Grail,' " he said, reading the Old English text.

Lessner looked slightly impatient. "Our parade of games." He waved a hand that took in the colorful posters.

"Games?"

Lessner checked his watch. "Norm's waiting." He gestured toward the waiting elevator. "If you want, we can talk about it with him."

Seconds later, the elevator came to a smooth stop. The doors opened directly into Norman Jonathan's office.

Reflexively, Frank stepped out behind Lessner. Suddenly, his heart pounded as he seemed to be stepping out into thin air.

"It gets everybody," came a voice.

Frank's vertigo subsided. The floor was clear glass. So were the walls and ceiling. The voice was Norman Jonathan.

Jonathan's dark brown hair fell to his shoulders. A bright orange nylon jogging suit emphasized his tall, angular body.

"I had this office built out over thin air to constantly remind me how precarious this business is," Jonathan said, shaking hands with Frank and José.

Frank glanced at the ceiling. The sun blazed in a clear blue sky, yet no glare or heat penetrated the office.

Jonathan read Frank's mind. "Electronic pulses reorient the copper atoms in the glass to eliminate glare," he said, "at least that's how the engineers explain it to me. Do we want to sit over here?" He pointed to a sofa and cluster of chairs.

Frank and José gravitated to the sofa, Jonathan and Lessner took chairs facing them. To the west, in the near distance, Eero Saarinen's classic main concourse for Dulles International, still a model of sweeping futuristic grace after almost forty years. Farther out, the blue-green foothills of the Shenandoah Valley.

"Two homicide detectives want to know about one of our customer accounts?" Jonathan asked. "I've got to tell you, *that's* a new one."

"We're investigating the deaths of a Ms. Susan Boukedes and Ms. Celeste Foster. LORE.COM was their Internet provider."

Jonathan's quizzical look didn't go away.

Lessner spoke up. "Lieutenant, I don't see the relevance here. I don't want to sound flip, but those women probably shopped at the same supermarket chain. Maybe they bought gas from one of the big oil companies." His tone took on a courtroom combativeness. "Have you talked to Safeway? Or Exxon?"

Jonathan gave Lessner a "There, there" wave of his hand and flashed Frank an apologetic smile. "Tell us what you need, Lieutenant."

"We want to know about the Boukedes and Foster accounts," Frank said carefully, "because there's a possibility that someone had access to those accounts. And that someone may have used that access to stalk these women and kill them."

Lessner's eyes widened. "Our security is as good, if not better, than any other Internet provider."

Jonathan leaned back in his chair, stretched his arms out to the side, then clasped his hands behind his head. A confident man. "I'm sure you understand, officers, the subscriber has a role to play in his or her security. Every breach we've had sooner or later boils down to something the subscriber did, either carelessly or with intent, to give away their name, phone number, or address."

"We aren't pointing fingers, Mr. Jonathan. We just want to know about the accounts. Any evidence that could indicate illegal entry into the victims' computers through the Internet and access to their e-mail and any commercial transactions."

Lessner began to protest. Jonathan cut him off.

"Of course," he said. "You realize I can't get it just like that." He snapped his fingers. "My people are the best, but something like this will take time—"

"I told Lieutenant Kearney we'd explain our games," Lessner cut in. "We could kill two birds by getting Ballinger up here to take on the task of looking at these women's accounts and satisfying the lieutenant's curiosity about our games."

Jonathan nodded. "Ormond Ballinger is our vice-president for software research and development," he explained as he picked up the phone, "our resident creative artist."

A few minutes later, the elevator doors opened. Ballinger, rangy and boyish, stepped out. Dressed in khakis, MIT sweatshirt, and Nike running shoes, and with his wide smile and thatch of unruly brown hair, he reminded Frank of a *M*A*S*H*-era Alan Alda.

"Ormond Ballinger," Jonathan announced.

Ballinger shook hands with Frank and José. Jonathan gestured to a chair to his right for Ballinger.

"At your service, folks."

Ballinger was totally at ease with Jonathan and Lessner, Frank noted. A better indication of Ballinger's place in the corporate pecking order than a formal organization chart.

"Orr, we think we may have a security problem. And these gentlemen are also interested in our games."

Ballinger listened raptly. His smile disappeared as Frank detailed the finding of the tracking program on the Boukedes and Foster computers. He shook his head when Frank finished—a worried man. "We'll take the accounts apart," he promised.

Frank noticed that Ballinger didn't look to either Jonathan or Lessner for approval.

"Norm said you wanted to get smart on our games."

"I noticed a poster for one . . . The Search for the Grail."

Ballinger pulled what looked like a small TV remote from a pocket, aimed it at a nearby glass wall, and clicked. A patch of the glass, perhaps six feet wide and five feet high, clouded, then filled with a startlingly realistic image of a bucolic rural scene. A country road, the only sign of humanity, wound through sunlit meadows, along a stream, then into a forest, and, on the far horizon, toward a range of purple mountains.

"Impressive," said Frank.

"Take that glass wall home with me?" José asked.

"You'd have to take several hundred cubic feet of electronics down in the basement," Jonathan said.

"Grail, like all our games, is interactive," Ballinger said.

"Meaning?" Frank asked.

"Instead of playing the game against a score inside your computer, you play it on the Internet with other people."

"Real people?" José asked.

"Once people learn about Grail, LORE.COM will offer team membership on a monthly subscription basis. You pay and you join a team. We set up each player with a password, scoring rules, and the game history—the context in which the game's played. Then, at a certain time each week, or even more often, the players go online to play."

The graphics' reality fascinated Frank. "What's the objective?"

"To capture the Holy Grail," Ballinger said. "There are two parts to the game. Part one is getting to the Fisher King's castle. Part two is defeating the Fisher King within his castle and escaping with the Holy Grail. In both parts, you face various life-or-death challenges." He paused. "*Virtual* life-or-death challenges, of course. The game itself is simple. What gets complicated are the player relationships."

"Would you like to see a sample?" Jonathan asked.

Frank nodded. Ballinger pressed a button.

"In this one," Jonathan chin-pointed to the screen, "the weapons are from the medieval era. You start with a morning star. That's a club like a baseball bat, with a spiked steel ball hooked to the end with a length of chain. Watch."

Ballinger clicked his remote. At the bottom center of the screen, the wicked-looking morning star appeared.

Frank winced. "Ouch."

"Before you start competing," Jonathan said, his voice tightening with excitement, "you can practice with your weapon off-line."

Ballinger clicked again.

A man came striding up over a rise in the meadow. Highly detailed graphics made the virtual figure seem almost lifelike. As Frank's perspective adjusted, he realized this was a giant. Passing a large tree, the giant plucked it out of the ground like a weed. As he approached, sophisticated graphics created the impression of the earth trembling, and the computer speakers rattled with a blood-lust scream.

"Shit!" José muttered. And despite himself, Frank felt his adrenaline kick in.

"Easy target," Jonathan said.

Ballinger waved his remote. As he did, the morning star on the screen quivered slightly. The giant, now feet away, raised the tree like a huge club.

Another motion with the remote.

The morning star swung back and forth, picking up momentum. Soon it was circling overhead, the sound of it cutting through the virtual air, a whirring bass hum that filled the room.

The tree-club began its deadly descent.

Ballinger rolled his wrist slightly forward and to the right. The morning star split the giant's skull in a shower of brains and blood.

"Jesus Christ," Frank whispered.

The screen scenery shook as the giant crashed to the ground.

"So you have to get through uglies like that," Frank said. "To get where?"

Jonathan motioned to the mountains. "The castle's up there. And your uglies get uglier as you go along. But your weapons get more effective. After showing your prowess with the morning star, you get a battle-ax. Really do some creative chopping with that."

Jonathan held out his hand to Ballinger. "Let me, Orr." Ballinger handed over the remote.

"Okay," Jonathan said, "let's do the Red Swordsman scene."

On the screen, a long shot of a cavernous torch-lit room. Stone walls, high vaulted ceiling, and a long, massive wood table. A minstrel sat by the huge fireplace, strumming a lyre. Knights and their ladies in high-backed wooden chairs feasted greedily, eating with fingers from communal platters.

Suddenly, shouts and crashing of metal. A masked man in a red cloak bounded down a stone stairway into the banquet room.

"Watch this," Jonathan said, a tremor of excitement in his voice.

From the long shot, now a mid-view as might be seen from one sitting at the table.

"First-person shooter now," Jonathan said. "Notice the battle-ax."

In the middle of the screen at the bottom appeared a glittering quarter-moon of ax blade topped by a jagged spear point, allowing the user the choice of slicing or stabbing.

The Red Swordsman leaped from the stairway onto the table. With his broadsword, he began hacking his way down the table, lopping off arms, hands, heads. Fountains of blood blanketed the room. Frank sat hypnotized by the reality of the gore, the screams of the victims. He had to remind himself that computers were generating the startlingly realistic scene, shifting billions of tiny electronic pixels in fractions of a second across the huge screen.

Jonathan stood, body coiled, intent on the approaching Red Swordsman. As he waved the remote back and forth, the battle-ax followed.

Frank noticed that Jonathan had moved into a semicrouch, dropping his right shoulder, as a man would getting ready to swing a baseball bat. Or a battle-ax.

Jonathan, eyes wide, mouth pulled back in a savage grimace, dipped slightly and spun to his left. On the screen, the battle-ax sliced into the chainmail armor at the Red Swordsman's left knee.

The swordsman went down. As he did, Jonathan jabbed the battle-ax's spear point into the man's face. Blood interlaced with purplish eye fluid gushed from the fatal wound.

The picture faded. Jonathan stood for a moment, breathing heavily, staring at the glass wall where the screen was disappearing. He looked around, as if surprised to find himself in his office with visitors. He tossed the remote to Ballinger and sat down.

It was another moment as the five men reoriented themselves. In his chair, Jonathan sat, still hyped from his encounter.

"You said something about the player relationships getting complicated," José said to Ballinger.

Ballinger nodded. "In the first part, the search for the castle, individual players can team up to fight enemy knights, dragons, other monsters."

"Okay?"

"What makes it interesting is that in the second part, only one player can get into the castle to confront the Fisher King."

"So he or she has to be first to the castle?"

Ballinger nodded, then added, "Or the only player left alive."

"Sort of like that survivor TV show."

"Yes. And all players know this from the start. Players can e-mail each other privately to conspire against each other, establish secret alliances, trade insider information, set traps . . ."

Lessner's eyes glistened. "It is a game of intellect."

"Yeah," José said. "Sounds real intellectual to me."

"How many people play in a game?" Frank asked.

Jonathan, calm restored, answered. "It depends on our servers here at LORE.COM. We started the series with a limit of ten players. As we developed more computational power, we were able to get up to a hundred or so players per game." A flash of excitement crossed his face. "One of these days, we'll be able to re-create some really big stuff—a re-enactment of Agincourt, Gettysburg, or maybe even all of World War Two. And the special effects will be so real you'll swear you were there."

"Sounds like something I can wait for," said Frank. "The Fisher King . . . you say you now have a hundred players per game. How many games do you run?"

"Norm, I wouldn't . . ." Lessner jumped in, his concern evident.

Jonathan waved him off. "Just over four hundred."

"So forty thousand people have played the Grail game?"

Jonathan shook his head. "Oh no. Many more than that."

"You have an exact number?"

Again Jonathan shook his head. "Let me explain, Lieutenant. Every subscriber to our Internet service can play in the Grail game if he or she wants to."

"And how many subscribers do you have?"

"Latest count," Jonathan drawled, "just over two million."

"So you don't have any record of who's played in the game?"

"Not yet. As I said before, our plan is to offer Grail to all comers. Then, when we build a significantly large participant following, we'll offer the game on a monthly subscription basis. That, of course, will pare down the number of participants."

José frowned. "So once you get them hooked, you start charging."

Lessner got the startled-then-angry look of a man who's been jammed with a cattle prod. He came out of his chair. "I resent that, Mr. Phelps! You're making it sound like we're drug dealers."

"Well?" José asked, fists clenching.

Frank sensed José's tension. He put his hand on his partner's shoulder and turned to Jonathan in an attempt to get the interview back on track.

"About the Boukedes and Foster accounts, Mr. Jonathan. We would appreciate any information about attempts to break into their computers."

"Get a court order," Lessner said.

"I'd hoped that wouldn't be necessary," Frank said softly.

Before Lessner could reply, Jonathan shook his head. "It won't."

The color drained from Lessner's face. He started to say something then seemed to think better of it.

"It'll take a day or two," Jonathan said. "Although we won't insist on going through the courts to give this information to you, it *is* our right. As a compromise, I'm going to ask Michael and Orr to work up an agreement of confidentiality with the District's legal people."

Frank glanced at José and got an eyeball okay. "That's fine," said Frank.

Jonathan pointedly looked at his watch. "Is there anything else today?"

Frank and José exchanged glances, then stood. Ballinger stood with them. "I'll see you down."

As the elevator doors closed, Frank caught a last glimpse of Jonathan and Lessner standing as if they had other business, Lessner with a grim look on his face.

"I've got to tell you," Frank said to Ballinger, "I was impressed with the realism of that game."

Ballinger waved a hand in modest dismissal. "Thanks, but that's just the first step toward reality."

"Reality?" Frank asked, not certain he'd heard Ballinger right.

Ballinger nodded. "Archimedes said that if he had a place to stand, he could move the world. I believe that if we have enough computer power, we can create reality. Not just realism—a semblance of reality—but reality itself."

"So if a tree falls in the forest, there's a sound if a computer's there to hear it?"

The elevator sighed to a stop and the doors opened to the lobby.

Ballinger laughed as he touched Frank's elbow and the three men stepped out of the elevator. "Very good, Lieutenant. I'll remember that." He faced Frank, his eyes flashing with excitement. "If I can create a world in which you can see, smell, feel, taste, hear . . . isn't that reality? And isn't that ability to create reality a godlike ability?"

The three stopped in front of the sculpture of the computer chip.

"But you turn off the computer," Frank said, "and the reality goes away."

Instead of arguing, Ballinger smiled and nodded. "Precisely." He shook hands with Frank and José. "I'll look at those two accounts," he promised, "and have something to you the first of the week. Monday or Tuesday. Wednesday at the latest."

✠ Frank drove, both men absorbed and quiet. It wasn't until they got to I-66 that José broke the silence.

"Two million subscribers," he said. "If one of them's a Fisher King wannabe, we aren't gonna find out knocking on their doors."

"And that's just present LORE.COM subscribers. That doesn't include those who could have played the Grail game who've canceled the service."

"Did it surprise you, how realistic that stuff was?"

Frank nodded. "Yeah. I started thinking about those kind of games, I thought they were still like those space-invader games at the video arcades. You know, where you got rows of flying saucers coming down, trying to land on Earth?"

"That red guy with the sword came down those steps, I started feeling that cold steel in my guts."

The two men fell silent again. Then Frank asked, "Hoser, how much you think a human life's worth?"

"Where'd that come from?"

"Just sort of bubbled up."

"Multiple choice?"

"Just give me a number."

"Well," he said after a few moments, "it depends."

"*Depends*. Now *that*'s a real substantial answer."

"No, damnit," José said, "I got an answer for you if you cut me a little slack."

Frank waited another long break.

"Let's say you're driving in your brand-new Ford Explorer," José said, laying his groundwork, "when your brand-new Firestone tire blows out. Or you're one of those passengers on the Concorde when it crashes and burns in Paris. Your widow goes to a lawyer. How much do you think the lawyer's gonna go for?"

"Millions."

"Give me a number. Order of magnitude—two million? Twenty mil? Two hundred?"

"Let's say she's not greedy. Ten. Ten's a good number."

"Okay. Ten million." José moved on to build his case.

"Now, last month up in New York, five kids—youngest fourteen, oldest seventeen—ordered Chinese carryout. They beat the delivery guy to death with a brick so they wouldn't have to pay a sixty-dollar bill."

"Yeah?"

"Well, what does that make a life worth to those kids?"

"Sixty bucks," Frank said.

"Not even that. *Twelve*. Five kids, sixty bucks, that's twelve bucks each they thought this guy's life was worth."

"So now you got a range, Hoser. Between ten million bucks and twelve bucks. You think somewhere in the middle?"

José shook his head. "No. Right down next to the carryout food. More delivery guys getting whacked by kids with bricks than by Firestones or Concordes."

José took another tack while Frank was thinking about Concordes and Chinese carryout.

"That place back there," José said, "bothers me."

"How's that?"

José shrugged. "I don't know exactly. Maybe it was Ballinger and his reality crap, maybe Jonathan's enthusiasm . . ." He shook his head in frustration. "It's just something nagging at me."

"Bitchy nagging? Scary nagging?"

"Scary. It's like there's another world out there. Right alongside ours. But you and I don't see it . . . no . . ." José paused. "No, it's more like there's a world out there that you and I know is there but we don't understand it. People living in make-believe . . ."

"People have always had make-believe," Frank said, thinking about Kaitlin McKirgan and the medieval French poets.

"Yeah . . ." José shook his head as if worried by a persistent fly, then picked up on a further thought. "But now, with what Jonathan and his LORE.COM are doing, people are getting together in their make-believe. It's not just a mind game anymore. And it's not like sitting and watching a movie. *You* influence the action. *You* make things happen. And the computer makes it more real all the time. I mean, if you can live in a world where everything *seems* real, why can't it *become* real?"

"You're getting deep, Hoser."

"Can't have that."

"You ready for a little football?"

"And a few beers."

"How about Duke and three?"

"Three?" José made a face of mock outrage. "This morning it was seven! You been checking the line on me? Give me ten."

"Okay. I give you ten. A month's pay?"

"Let's split the difference . . . a six-pack of Miller Lite?"

TWENTY-SIX

✠ That evening, Tom Kearney barbecued ribs and Maryland beat Duke, 20–7. After finishing the ribs and the game, Frank passed his humidor around and the three men went out to the garden, José with the glasses and Tom Kearney with the bottle of port. Conversation turned from the game to the presidential campaign, then settled on the afternoon visit to LORE.COM.

Tom Kearney carefully worked the flame of the long cedar match across the tip of his cigar. After a moment or two, he puffed experimentally. Holding the cigar up in the dim light, he inspected his work. Finding it to his satisfaction, he puffed again. "It's natural that people like your Mr. Jonathan are skittish about the law nosing around." He waved the cigar at Frank and José.

"They're in a brand-new business. Uncharted territory. They know that the long arm of government's going to reach in and regulate it somehow. Democrat or Republican, socialist or monarchist, the government hasn't been made—hell, hasn't been *conceived*—that can leave a rich honeypot like the Internet alone. If Jonathan and his Internet colleagues are smart—and they are—they know they're going to have to put up with some degree of government involvement in their business. Why should they be any different than the airlines, food and chemical industries, radio and television?"

"So why," Frank asked, "were they so concerned about José and me?"

"What they're worried about is that they might get squashed by some crusader before they can find an accommodation with the politicians."

"They keep selling kiddie porn and 'Pipe Bombs for Dummies,' " José rumbled, "somebody ought to squash them."

"Yeah," Frank said, "and Norm Jonathan will have to go back to the pizza business."

José and Tom Kearney shot him looks of curiosity.

"Oh, yeah," Frank said. "Eight years ago, he was managing the Papa John's over here on Pennsylvania Avenue. Bald then. I guess he learned how to grow hair."

"He didn't recognize you," José said.

"We never met. I was in for pizza several times. Just another face in the crowd."

Tom Kearney yawned, then got up.

"You want to go to Clyde's for breakfast tomorrow?" Frank asked.

"Take a rain check," his father said.

"Oh," Frank said, not quite making it a question, but it was there, anyway, and he let it hang in the air between them.

"Judith Barnes and I are having brunch in Waterford. She wants to see the sawmill."

"Oh."

José got a wide smile.

Tom Kearney raised a warning finger. "She's interested in an armoire."

Frank nodded gravely. "I'm certain she is, Dad."

José's smile got even wider.

His father looked at the two men and shook his head. He tried a disapproving frown, but it didn't hold too well. He shook his head again, muttered something about no respect for elders, and went in.

Frank and José sat for a while without talking, Frank feeling mellow and relaxed. José stirred, finished his port, and got up. "I'm outta here. I got tickets for the game tomorrow. You interested?"

Frank waved him off. "Kate's coming over. We're going to read the Keegan manuscript."

José nodded and stood there, thinking. His face brightened as a thought struck him. "That Tina—the mayor's front lady. I hear she's single—"

"Oh? You checked her out?"

José got a sheepish grin. Another thought hit him and the grin went away. "It's sort of late. You think . . . ?"

"Never hurts to ask, Hoser. Who knows—she might be interested in an armoire, too."

TWENTY-SEVEN

✠ **A**t six-thirty A.M., Frank opened his eyes. He shut them, then opened them again and glanced at the clock. Light and time were out of sync. He stretched under the blanket. He realized that daylight savings had cut and run during the night.

"Spring forward, fall back," he muttered to himself as he pulled the blanket up around his neck. "Crime against nature. Felonious assault."

Next to the clock, the indoor-outdoor thermometer read 65°/38°, and from the sound of full-throttle jet engines overhead, Reagan National was launching the day's first flights into a north wind.

On the pillow beside him, Monty stirred. Frank turned to face him. He scratched the big cat between the ears. Looking deep into the large eyes, Frank thought, was like looking into another universe.

"You're really an extraterrestrial, aren't you? Galactic headquarters sent you cats here to watch us, didn't they?"

Monty regarded Frank with a stony gaze, like a banker considering a loan applicant.

"What do you report back?" Frank waited. "What do you tell them about us?"

But Monty didn't say anything, just kept his banker's stare.

Frank sat up and swung his feet to the floor.

Monty stood, arched his back, then stretched, reversing the arch.

He walked to the edge of the bed and looked dismissively back over his shoulder at Frank.

We shall let you know of our decision, Mr. Kearney.

Monty turned away, jumped off the bed, landed on the floor with a soft thump, and walked out into the hallway.

Frank kept his running gear on a peg rack in the bathroom: shorts, sweatpants, a ragged Bass Ale long-sleeved T-shirt, and sweatshirt and baseball cap courtesy the Maryland Terrapins.

Dressed, he drank a cup of coffee in the kitchen and scanned the *Post.* A color photo of a mother with a flag in a military cemetery—still burying the Navy's dead from the USS *Cole* explosion.

"Sorry, Mom," Frank said to the woman in the photo.

There had been the months in the Army, back in the States after Vietnam and before his discharge. The Army sent him out for what it called "notification next of kin," duty. A fine bureaucratic expression with all the emotion wrung out. What it was was knocking on a door and telling whoever answered that their son or husband or father was dead and would be coming home in a box. It was duty he hated so much he'd rather been back in-country getting shot at.

A nearby headline: "NEW GLOBAL ROLE PUTS THE FBI IN UNSAVORY COMPANY."

"What kind of company do you think the bureau kept before?" Frank asked the headline writer.

Celeste Foster, front page yesterday, was gone.

Just like that. Gone.

"And so we move on," Frank said.

He folded the paper and left it on the table for his father. The FedEx box with Mary Keegan's manuscript lay on the table where he'd left it last night. He picked up the box and considered opening it. Open it now, he thought, and you'll want to read a page or two. Then three or four. He put the box down.

Five minutes later, he jogged slowly across a deserted M Street to the Four Seasons Hotel, then down the steep hill to the Rock Creek path. He decided to run south. The morning sun in his face, the light wind at his back, he picked up his pace. By the time he reached the

Watergate, he felt the sweat gathering on his forehead, the cold air reaching deep into his lungs.

Here the path angled over and paralleled the Potomac. Under the Teddy Roosevelt Bridge, the path split. The left branch led to Hains Point and *The Awakening.* Straight ahead took him up hill to the Lincoln Memorial. The picture flashed in his mind of Celeste Foster's body in the giant hand. Without breaking pace, he took the uphill branch to the Lincoln Memorial.

From the Lincoln Memorial, he ran to the Washington Monument, north on 15th Street, then a left on Pennsylvania Avenue, past the Treasury and the White House. Fifteen minutes later, he turned off Pennsylvania Avenue onto 29th Street and then onto Olive and back home.

Two notes, both in his father's handwriting, hung from the kitchen bulletin board. "Gone armoiring," the first read. The second read, "Kate called."

✠ The Sunday-breakfast crowd, noisy and cheerful, filled Clyde's. Frank looked at the wreckage of his breakfast: two over easy, hash browns, sausage, toast. "I run ten miles and wipe out the gain in five minutes," he said.

"It took you at least half an hour," Kate said. "Besides, Sunday breakfasts get a special dispensation."

"From who?"

"Me." Kate was looking especially good. She was the kind of blonde who cold weather colored well. "You're quiet this morning."

He played with a scrap of toast, pushing a leftover of hash brown across his plate. "Been thinking. A real hodgepodge. Nothing really connected."

"About?"

"What it is you remember. What things stay with you. Not *the* things themselves . . . not the specifics of them. But what it is about some things that stay with you and others that don't. And there doesn't seem to be any rhyme or reason why some stay and why some don't."

"For example?"

"I see a picture this morning in the paper. It takes me back to two months before I get out of the Army. That's almost thirty years ago. I've got to go out to this farm and walk across a plowed field to tell an old man his only son is dead."

"And then?"

"And then it's like my mind skips a groove. I think about the guy at the *Post* who writes a stupid headline and I wonder what kind of world he thinks exists outside the Beltway.

"Next thing, I get to feeling like Celeste Foster's a disposable person. Yesterday's outrage. Today's ho-hum."

"And none of that's connected?" Kate's blue eyes had turned almost midnight, and they were looking into him and seeing something he couldn't see in himself.

Frank stopped skating the toast crumb and the hash brown around on his plate. "Yeah," he said, seeing some of it, but not all, not enough, "maybe it is connected." He watched Kate finish her coffee, then hefted the manuscript in its box. "Drop by Kinko's and run a duplicate—then you ready for some reading?"

✚ An hour later, Frank and Kate sat opposite each other at the kitchen table, the two copies of Mary Keegan's manuscript between them.

He riffled through his thick stack of double-spaced typescript. "Six hundred twenty pages." He pushed the manuscript across to Kate and got up. "You're the lawyer. Tell me how we ought to go about reading it. I'm putting on coffee and music. Bach, Mozart, Beethoven?"

"Mozart and Bach. Not my day for Beethoven."

Minutes later, CD player loaded, Frank brought the coffee to the table in an insulated carafe. He sat down opposite Kate. She had divided her copy of the manuscript into three stacks.

"Mary Keegan organized her book in sections," Kate explained. "A father-son section for the Sheffields, a similar section for the Trevors." She rested her hand on the third stack, a stack a quarter the size of the first two. "She started on her conclusions. Apparently that's where she was when she was killed. My suggestion is we read through separately, then discuss."

✠ Judith Barnes had been right, Frank thought. Mary Keegan wrote in simple declarative sentences that carried the reader along. By the second paragraph, the written words were coming to Frank in a clear voice, a crossing-over between prose and conversation. By the third paragraph, Mary Keegan had stepped aside and Lamar Sheffield, Charles Trevor, and their two sons had taken center stage.

For the next few hours, Frank read, totally absorbed in the trials and passions of two generations of Americans. A story of hardships and challenges met, of wars that changed the face of the world and a peace of sorts that was really war by other means. And above all, Keegan had written a captivating saga of two fathers and their sons' struggles to make their own lives on their own terms.

Finally, reluctantly, he read the last page. He turned it over and put it on the stack of manuscript pages to his left. He sat looking at the manuscript, not thinking about anything specific. He had an almost physical sensation of decelerating. As if he'd been speeding through a blurry kaleidoscope of images and emotions. Of private lives intertwined with a nation's history. The trip was over, and he was now rematerializing in the present. It was dark outside. On the stereo, Dennis Brain was playing a Mozart horn concerto. And Kate was looking at him from across the table, her eyes the midnight blue again.

"I just finished," she said. "If that was a first draft . . ." Kate shook her head in awe.

"I'm left hanging."

"Natural," Kate said.

Mary Keegan's concluding chapter—chapters?—seemed to be out

there somewhere beyond reach, the tantalizing conclusion to a fascinating story.

Frank started to check his watch.

"Almost seven," Kate said. "I'm hungry—no, I'm *starving*."

Frank got up and stretched. "How about La Brasserie? A cassoulet with a bottle of something red?"

Kate reached for her jacket. "Race you to the car."

✠ La Brasserie was not an American restaurant with a plastered-on French veneer. The small restaurant was European French to its core. Its sepia-toned atmosphere made it easy for Frank to imagine Edith Piaf sitting at the bar with Marcel Cerdan, and, at the table in the back, pre-*Casablanca* Bogart and Bergman, building the memories they would always have of Paris.

The cassoulet was well simmered, its white beans firm, not hard, the sausage tasting faintly of rosemary, and chunks of chicken and lamb tender and spicy. The bottle of something red turned out to be a slightly chilled Clos de la Roilette Beaujolais, rich with undertones of raspberries and blueberries.

Kate raised her glass. "To Mary Keegan."

She watched as Frank absentmindedly tilted his glass in acknowledgment.

"You're thinking about the manuscript," she said.

"An unfinished symphony."

"I thought it was spectacular writing. The Trevors and the Sheffields—the way she drew the characters of those four men—they were so three-dimensional. She was a sculptor who used words."

"Great writing. But there's something about the last chapters. A lot more penciled edits." Frank sipped his wine as he grappled with the thought. "They made her seem closer . . . more immediate. It was like she'd made a few corrections, notes to herself, and was just taking a break."

"We knew before we started that she didn't finish it."

Kate was right. He'd known before he started reading that there would be an abrupt drop-off. No tie-it-all-together ending where you could close the book, put it on the shelf, and walk away. Talbot had been right. Such a book shouldn't be left unfinished. He swirled the wine in his glass. "It was as if I heard her saying, 'And yet . . . ' "

"Was it worth reading?"

"Oh, yeah. I'm going to have to talk to David Trevor again. A note she made could fill in a blank in her time line. But something else hit me—nothing to do with the case.

"The part about Charles Trevor . . . how Kennedy asked him to leave the banking business and come to Washington. I realized while I was reading Keegan's account of the '61 inaugural, that Trevor and I were there. There at the same place, at the same time. Our sixth-grade class went to Kennedy's inaugural. I was there. So was Charles Trevor. We were both in that crowd. The way she described Trevor and the other Kennedy people . . . I made the connection for the first time between that day and the day seven years later I got wounded. I suddenly saw . . . how the men I saw that day when I was twelve made the decisions that took me to the war and to that rice paddy when I was nineteen. All those years since Vietnam, I'd always wondered how they could have done it . . . could have gotten us into such a goddamn mess. Now I think I understand."

"And?"

"They were people who had to do something. They did the best they could and hoped it would turn out all right."

"But it didn't."

"It didn't, and a lot of people died . . ." Frank trailed off and sat there with a distant look.

"And?" Kate asked softly.

"I know how Charles Trevor and those guys around Kennedy must have felt. It's like standing in the dark and knowing somewhere nearby is the edge of a cliff. And you can't just stand there. You've got to point the way for others who're also in the dark. I make the wrong decisions in this investigation, more people are going to die. As sure's the sun's coming up tomorrow, he's going to keep killing."

Kate reached across the table and closed her hand firmly over his wrist. "There's no way any human can know they're making the right decisions on something like this." She leaned toward him, looking deep into his eyes. "There are no guarantees—no matter how good you are, how smart you are, how hard you work—no guarantees that it's going to work out."

Frank got an ironic smile and put his free hand over hers. "That's supposed to make me feel better?"

She raised his hand and kissed the back of it. "No," she said, "just more human."

TWENTY-EIGHT

✚ The next morning, José pulled into the adjacent parking slot as Frank was locking his car. The old Mustang was ticking over smoothly, and its dark green paint glistened. José shut off the engine and got out smiling.

"Generator overhaul does wonders for you," Frank said.

"Unh-huh."

The wind gusted hard and cold out of the northwest and the two men walked shoulder to shoulder down the walk toward the headquarters building.

"How was the game?" Frank asked.

"Skins lost."

"I knew that last night. How about the rest? Did you call Tina . . . ?"

"Barber. Her last name's Barber."

"I guess you did."

"She was sort of put off, me calling late like that."

"Yeah. Women are like that. But . . . ?"

José did the little shrug and head roll he did when he was playing cutesy. "Aw, we talked some. I laid out Witty and Charming on her—"

"All of it?"

"Naw, just Part One. Yeah . . . we went to the game."

Frank opened the door for José.

"What I want to know is—"

"A gentleman doesn't talk about those things."

"You cut me off. I just want to know: Is it a one-time thing?"

José played cute again. "We'll see. How about your dad and the armoire lady?"

"He came home late. I was already asleep."

José shook his head. "Parents—what're you gonna do with them?"

✠ Manny Dale was waiting, slumped in a chair, still wearing his rain-coat and nursing a cup of coffee.

"Good morning, gentlemen. I trust *you* slept well last night."

"Meaning?" José asked.

Frank sat down. "Meaning our Manny didn't get his eight solid."

Manny rubbed an unshaven cheek and heaved a theatrical sigh. "The sacrifices one makes for one's friends."

"Eddie Jeter?" Frank asked.

Manny had the smug look of a man opening with a pair of aces.

"He is in a position where he may be convinced to talk frankly."

"Oh? And how'd he get that way?"

Manny's look escalated to that of a man who'd drawn to a full house.

"He was apprehended in the act of misappropriating an auto-mobile."

"And you just happened to be there."

"With several of my colleagues."

Frank sat for a few moments enjoying Manny. Real characters were an endangered species in the law-enforcement business, and Manny Dale was an original. Absolutely no doubt about it . . . straight out of Damon Runyon.

"Care to tell us how it happened?"

"Eddie is a specialist," Manny said. He set his coffee on Frank's desk and raised both hands, palms facing. "Eddie takes orders. If you want a silver Audi or a green Cadillac DeVille, see Eddie. It may take a day or two. Or even a few weeks. Never longer. Eddie has an impressive record at bat."

"So somebody we know put in an order to Eddie?" José asked.

A sly smile from Manny. "One of Eddie's associates who owes me a favor."

"Silver Audi?"

"Green Cadillac."

"He found it fast," Frank said.

Another sly smile. "He had some help," Manny said.

"Somebody else who owed you a favor?" Frank asked.

Manny didn't think that needed an answer. "Do you want me in when you talk with him?" he asked Frank.

"You know him," Frank said, "what do you think?"

"I think he'll expect me there."

"Okay." Frank nodded. "Bring him up in forty-five minutes?" Frank watched Manny shut the door, then he reached inside his jacket for his notebook. He scanned his to-do list for today. First item: Mary Keegan's penciled note to herself in the manuscript. He studied the note, debating whether it'd be worth the trouble to check. He decided it wouldn't. He drew a line through the entry and closed the notebook.

He didn't put the notebook away. He held it, looking at it and waiting. As he knew it would, his internal siren started wailing in self-recrimination.

Okay, okay.

Abruptly, he flipped open the notebook, found David Trevor's private number at State, and reached for his phone.

✝ An hour later, a uniformed officer brought Eddie Jeter up for questioning. Frank had asked for Interview Room D.

At first glance, IR-D was like the other six interview rooms: grubby institutional gray paint on the walls, a large one-way window, an unpainted wooden table bolted to the floor, a chair for the subject, and one or two chairs for the interviewers. The chairs weren't bolted to the floor, but it'd been years since a prisoner tried anything with a chair.

But IR-D was different. The differences, though subtle, were significant, intended to create a claustrophobic unease. The subject's chair, armless and lower than those of the interviewers, had had one leg cut three-quarters of an inch shorter. Circulation had been reduced and humidity increased to make the air close, almost suffocating. The paint, several shades darker than the other rooms, had been purposely applied more sloppily. Extra soundproofing ensured that no outside sound penetrated. Close the door and the sensation was one of total isolation. As though you'd been sealed in a submarine. Or a tomb.

From the observation gallery, Frank, José, and Manny Dale watched through the one-way window as the uniformed officer brought Eddie in, then left and shut the door.

A scrawny white man in his twenties, Eddie came over to the window. He thrust his face close to the glass. He smiled and waved. Then, as he walked back to the table, he stopped. In a quick motion, he dropped his trousers and bent over.

"Eddie, Eddie, Eddie," Manny said like a disappointed parent.

"Your boy's got bad manners," José said.

"Yeah," Frank said, picking up a McDonald's bag, "but he's a very expressive critic."

✠ Eddie Jeter was cocked back in his chair, feet on the table, when Frank came in.

"Who the fuck are you?"

Eddie's voice was deeper than Frank thought it would be. Frank didn't say anything. He put the bag on the table and sat down.

Over the tops of his shoes, Eddie stared at Frank. "I *said*, who the fuck are you?"

Frank reached across the table and grabbed one of Eddie's ankles. He jerked. Eddie's arms flew out. He fell backward and crashed to the floor. His cry of surprise disappeared into the thick walls.

Eddie got up. He stood in a defensive crouch, eyes wary, fixed on Frank.

"You can't—"

"I *did*. Now pick up your chair." Frank said it even and hard, as though he were talking to a dog that'd messed the carpet.

Eddie hesitated, then righted the chair.

"Sit."

Eddie sat.

"You don't make demands here," Frank said, still even and hard. "Not with me. Do you understand? Say yes or no."

"Yes," Eddie said.

"I am Detective Lieutenant Kearney."

Eddie looked like he'd been short-changed. "Where's Manny?"

Frank waited a beat, then answered, "Manny's Auto Theft. I'm Homicide."

It took a second to register. Eddie's mouth formed a silent O. Then, in a rush: "I didn't kill anybody."

Frank gave him his stone-face look.

"I *didn't*."

Frank reached into the McDonald's bag, pulled out Susan Boukedes's finger, and put it on the table.

Eddie froze, looking at the finger with undisguised horror.

"Remember this?"

Eddie shut his eyes, as if hoping he'd imagined the finger and it wouldn't be there when he looked again. He opened them.

"It's still here," Frank said. "You brought that finger into the house at 4120 Kentucky Avenue Southeast, Saturday night the twenty-first around eleven o'clock." He rapped it out like a judge pronouncing sentence.

"I—"

Frank cut him off. "You want me to tell you what you were wearing?"

Eddie gave up.

"I . . . found it."

"Sure," Frank said, "you *found* it. You were just walking down the street, minding your business, and you *found* it." He brought his face close to Eddie's. "Before you even *start* to give me some shit like that, let me tell you something, ass breath."

He reached across the table, grabbed a handful of Eddie's shirt, and pulled him even closer so their noses almost touched.

"Everybody in this town from Bill Clinton down wants to nail the bastard who's been killing these women—cutting them up! Now this"—Frank pointed to the finger—"this belonged to one of those women. And if you don't come up with a good story about how, where, and when you came up with this, *you're* going to be the bastard they nail."

Frank let go of the shirt and shoved Eddie back into his chair. Eddie looked as though he might cry. He searched the small room as if for some place to hide, some way out. He came back to Frank.

"I was set up on this, you know."

"Yeah. Sure. Somebody just put a gun to your head and made you steal that Caddy."

Eddie soldiered on, laying the foundation for a deal. "You're homicide."

"I already told you that." Keep marching, Frank was thinking.

"I help you with"—Eddie nodded at the finger—"with *that*, I don't want to get a rap for lifting a car."

"You help me, Eddie, I'll help you."

Eddie relaxed a fraction. "What's that mean?"

"It means," Frank said, now almost pleasant, "that you deal with Manny Dale and you don't see me again."

Eddie's eyes made darting sparrowlike motions as he worked on his future.

"You know Manny," Frank put in, "you don't know me."

Eddie's eyes settled on Frank. "I found it in a van."

"It was just there? Lying in the van?"

"No. It was in a plastic box with some white stuff around it. I thought it might have been coke."

"You were stealing the van?"

Eddie recoiled ever so slightly. "I was in the van."

God help me, Frank thought. Crooks are getting to be like lawyers, and the lawyers are turning into crooks. *Convergence?* "Let's put it this way, Eddie, where did you get into the van?"

Eddie turned the question over. Apparently he found it safe to answer. "Up near Dupont Circle."

"Get better, Eddie."

"Church Street. Sixteen-hundred block."

"When? Date, time?"

"Friday. It was almost midnight."

"Friday the twentieth?"

"Yeah."

"The vehicle—what was it?"

Eddie hesitated. "A telephone van."

Frank kept a straight face. *"Telephone?"*

"It was a '97 Ford Econoline."

"Oh. Customer demand?"

Eddie shrugged.

"What'd you do with it?"

"Look," Eddie began, "I can't—"

"Can't rat out who's got it now?" Frank finished for him. Frank leaned forward, the earnest mentor. "Manny says you're smart, Eddie. Answer me this: You know anybody who'll take a murder-one rap to keep from ratting on you?"

Eddie's eyes dropped.

"Franklin Motors."

"Where?"

"Arlington. Lee Highway."

"Resell? Chop shop?"

"Both. They'll chop that one."

"Why?"

"They didn't care it was a telephone truck." Eddie shrugged. "So I figure they were going to chop it for the parts. And then . . ." Eddie trailed off.

"Yeah?"

"And then there was the smell."

TWENTY-NINE

✝ "There it is," José pointed.

On the south side of Lee Highway, Franklin Motors was a flat-roofed one-story building of raw concrete. In front, an open-air lot filled with dusty used cars under strings of faded red, white, and blue plastic pennants. Posters on windshields promised easy credit in English and Spanish.

Frank drove several more blocks to an Amoco station at Military Road. He pulled in behind a tan Ford Taurus. The Ford had Virginia plates, and through the back window, he saw one person sitting behind the wheel.

"Must be him," José said.

Both men got out of the car and walked to the Ford. Frank tapped gently on the rear door as he approached the driver. The Ford's driver lowered the window.

"Yes?"

The driver, young, African-American, and decidedly pretty, had her purse beside her and her right hand in the purse.

"Uh . . . Detective Jones?" Frank glanced over the top of the car to José, who was standing there slackjawed.

"Credentials?"

Frank very deliberately reached into his jacket and came up with his badge and credentials case.

The young woman nodded, then pulled her own badge out of her purse. "I'm Liana Jones. Why don't you get in? We can talk."

Frank got in back, José in front.

Jones gave José an up-and-down.

"You're Josephus Phelps?"

"José."

She looked at José some more, then back at Frank. "You two seem surprised."

Frank and José exchanged glances. Frank broke eye contact. *Over to you, pal.*

"Well," José began, "Manny said he'd been working with you sometime . . ."

"But he didn't tell you I was a woman?"

José fumbled around and made it worse. "He . . . uh . . . didn't say you were . . . *pretty.*"

Jones's eyes widened and the muscles tightened along her jaw. "Just what does *that* have to do with stolen cars?"

José threw both hands up.

Jones didn't smile. "You've got a warrant?"

José pulled the document from an inner pocket of his jacket and handed it over. Jones read it, fingernail ticking off points on the warrant. Satisfied, she folded it and put it in her purse.

"Now, why Franklin?"

For the next five minutes Jones listened as José and Frank told her about finding Susan Boukedes finger and how that connected with Eddie Jeter and how the Eddie Jeter connection had led to their sitting here in her car in an Arlington Amoco station.

"When did Jeter bring in the van?"

"Saturday the twenty-first."

Jones shook her head. "They got a head start. They can chop a vehicle faster than my mother can throw out last night's garbage." She turned the ignition key. "We might's well see if there's any leftovers."

·   ·   ·

✠ Frank pulled out of the Amoco station, following Jones.

"Shee-ut," José breathed.

"Shee-ut what?"

José watched Jones's car turn down Lee Highway. He sighed. "I just don't know what this policin's coming to."

✠ Willis Thurman, owner and operator of Franklin Motors, sat behind a cluttered desk and squinted at the warrant with a mix of contempt and caution. A heavy-jowled man in garage-stained coveralls, Thurman seemed to radiate anger. The kind of guy, Frank thought, who came into the world pissed off at life itself.

Twenty or so cars filled the gloomy shop. Hoods, trunks, doors open. The sound of engines revving, the staccato hammer of impact wrenches on stubborn nuts, the smell of gas, oil, paint, and exhaust fumes.

Jones had handed Thurman the warrant, but Thurman had shifted so he was looking directly at Frank.

"Says here you're looking for a van." He held the warrant out to Frank. "We got some good ones on the lot outside."

Frank didn't say anything. Jones thrust her shoulder into the conversational space between Thurman and Frank. She snatched the warrant out of Thurman's hand with a quickness that snapped his wrist.

"We aren't looking to buy, Mr. Thurman," Jones said. "We are looking for a vehicle that was involved in a homicide. You want to assist us like a good citizen? Or do you want to play cute? Play cute and I'll have the DMV down here like flies on a manure pile. We'll run through every piece of paper here with a squinty-eyed squad of accountants. And then we'll bring the lawyers in and see about a charge of obstructing justice."

Thurman's small piggy eyes flashed. He started to say something, then thought better of it. He swallowed, then tried again. "Homicide?" He looked at Frank and José as if for confirmation.

Both stood expressionless. Thurman's attention switched back to Jones.

"What do you need?" The words came out tight, as José later put it, "like he was trying to shit a watermelon."

"We want to see your shop work order register for the last two weeks."

Thurman motioned across the shop floor to a glass cubicle. A stoop-shouldered man with a harried look perched on a stool and peered into a computer screen. Take away the computer, Frank thought, and you have a character out of Dickens.

✠ For the next twenty minutes, Frank and José watched Jones turn pages in an old-fashioned accountant's ledger as she traced each car entering and leaving Franklin Motors, stopping only to jot series of numbers in her notebook.

Thurman watched, too, trying to act unconcerned. He wasn't doing a good job of it.

Jones closed the ledger and smiled her thanks at the clerk, who by now Frank was thinking of as Bob Cratchit.

"Well?" Thurman asked.

Jones opened her eyes wide, playing the innocent child. "Well . . . *what?*"

"Well . . ." Thurman said, "did you find anything?"

"Did you think we might find something?" Jones asked, still the innocent child.

Thurman, eager to get the three detectives off his back and out of his garage, gestured toward the front, to the large drive-in door. Thurman started toward the door. Jones followed a few paces, Frank and José with her, when she stopped.

She jerked a thumb over her shoulder. "Let's look out back."

Thurman stopped and looked over his shoulder, mouth open in surprise and uncertainty. "What you want to do that for?"

Jones didn't answer and was already heading for the back door.

"Just junk and shit out there," Thurman called after her. Then, seeing Frank and José following her, he hurried to catch up.

"Junk and shit is right," José said, as he stepped through the back door with Jones. Truck and auto guts and carcasses covered a weed-grown acre lot behind the garage. "What're we looking for here?" he asked her.

Jones turned and gave José an exasperated look. "Why, a '97 Econoline van." She paused as Thurman joined them. "A word with my colleagues, Mr. Thurman?"

Thurman, unhappy, stepped a few paces away.

"If that van was chopped here," Jones said, "the only thing that'd be left would be the chassis. Everything smaller is probably on a freighter for South America as spare parts."

"What does a Ford Econoline chassis look like?" Frank asked.

Jones shrugged. "No idea." She saw the question coming and raised a hand. "What we want to do is find all the chassis on the lot." She looked at José, then Frank, as if making certain they were with her.

"Do you know what a VIN is?" she asked.

José rolled his eyes. "Vehicle identification number."

"Why, *very* good, Mr. Homicide Detective." Jones smiled. "American carmakers put the VIN on the dashboard of their cars and also engrave it on the frame."

"So what we're doing is collecting VINs, and then you . . ."

"Check them through DMV," Jones finished, "and come up with the last owner—the last *legal* owner."

With Thurman trailing them like an anxious puppy, the three found seven chassis over the next hour. Jones jotted down each VIN. As she did so, she had Thurman initial each entry. At the gate leading out of the yard, Jones turned to Thurman, tore out a page from her notebook, and handed it to him.

"A copy of the VINs we found," she explained. "Don't let those chassis disappear."

Thurman started to protest.

Jones turned death-ray eyes on him. He folded the paper and tucked it in his pocket.

At their cars, the three stopped.

Jones patted her purse. "I'll get back and run these."

"How long'll that take?" José asked.

"Priority—maybe today, maybe tomorrow."

✠ The phone was ringing when Frank and José walked into their office. Caller ID said it was FBI. Frank picked up.

"An update on the Boukedes and Keegan cases," Robin Bouchard said.

Frank reached for pad and pencil. "Yeah?"

"Damien Halligan?" Bouchard made it a halfway question with no preamble.

"Yeah?"

"He's IRA."

The letters took a second to register.

"Irish Republican Army?"

"He was their boy for the East Coast."

"Was?"

"We can't find him. He split sometime yesterday."

Feeling disoriented, as if he'd been suddenly dropped into another time and place, Frank struggled for a mental handhold. The conversation with Halligan outside the autopsy suite came back to him.

County Down?

Close. Armagh.

You must have been a kid when the bombing started.

Old enough to remember, never old enough to forget.

"Did he leave the country?"

"We don't know. He probably had a couple of sets of ID stashed away—just in case."

"Record?"

"Not here. He was careful about that. Has an impressive sheet with our British cousins. Five years in Long Kesh, before that, two years in Portlaoise."

"For . . . ?"

"There was suspicion of a couple of assassinations. Couldn't prove anything. They got him on bank robbery. I guess he showed a talent for fund-raising, so they sent him here to pick up a few bucks from old-sod sympathizers in the States."

"Anybody know why he split?"

"No," Robin said. "I thought you might run across something?"

"I do, I'll call."

Frank hung up and filled José in.

"I told you—guy was weird," José said.

Frank's phone rang again. He was going to let the answering machine take it until he saw it was Tim Haskill.

A retired D.C. detective, Timmy Haskill had worked with Frank and José in Homicide for almost ten years. Haskill now directed security for a branch of Verizon, which Frank still thought of as Ma Bell.

Frank hung up and turned to José. "Timmy checked the Verizon fleet. They haven't had a service van stolen in two years. And they use Dodges, not Fords." He tilted back in his chair and stared at the phone. A teasing thought played games with him. He'd almost catch it, only to have it disappear again. His mind skipped a groove to an image of a Verizon van.

He captured the thought. "Invisible," he said to himself. *Yes! Yes!*

"Invisible *what?*"

Excitement growing, he turned to José. "Nobody pays attention to a telephone van. You can drive it, park it, damn near anywhere."

"And nobody asks why it's there," José said.

Frank was already up, putting on his jacket. José was right behind him.

"Where we going?" José asked.

"See if we can find us a van."

THIRTY

✠ **R**erun the tapes?" Marla Fernandez asked. "Sure. Give us half an hour?"

"Where's the maintenance office?" Frank asked. "While you're doing that, José and I want to talk to somebody in records."

"Facilities Management building," Fernandez said, "at Twentieth and F."

✠ Colin Rule checked his computer screen once more. "Thursday, twenty-six October, outage on camera on Level C. Reported twenty-one ten." Rule interpreted for Frank and José: "That's nine-ten P.M."

"Thanks," José said. "Now when was it repaired?"

Rule highlighted the line entry. "At twenty-one twenty-five. That's—"

"Twenty-five after nine," Frank said. "Can you find the last time that particular camera went out?"

"Sure." Some mouse work and Rule leaned closer to the screen. "Ah . . . nineteen October. That's—"

"That's Thursday, the week before," José said. "What time?"

Rule's eyes narrowed. "At 21:04.4." He shook his head in wonderment. "I'll be damned! Now, *that's* a coincidence."

"No," Frank said, "*that's* a rehearsal."

✠ "I've had all the tapes for the night of the twenty-sixth cued up on these monitors." Marla Fernandez ran her hand down two columns of screens. She patted the console operator's shoulder. "You remember Sarah?"

"Last time," Frank said, "we looked at the tapes from the stairwell camera and the camera down on the ground level where Ms. Foster parked her car. Can you pull up the cameras at the garage entrance and exit?"

Sarah nodded and made quick keyboard entries. "Screens three, four, and five. We have two exits. Those are four and five. What time are you looking for?"

The two exits threw Frank. He'd been thinking about checking for vans leaving the garage after nine o'clock.

José had his notebook open. He checked an entry and pointed to screen three. "Why don't we start with the entry camera at nine-ten? That's just after the camera on the ground level crapped out. Then we run the tape backward until we spot a van?"

Frank nodded. "Why don't we?"

✠ At 20:57:29.7, a van appeared on screen three, comically seeming to rush in reverse out of the garage and into the traffic on 23rd Street outside. Sarah stopped action and reversed the tape. The van slowly drove into the garage, the driver reaching out the window to retrieve a ticket from the automatic dispenser. The camera, looking down on the van, captured a slant view of the vehicle.

"Can't see the license plates," José said.

"Some you can," Sarah said, "some you can't."

The van disappeared off the screen.

"Sarah," Frank asked, "can you track this van?"

"We'll have to check each up ramp," she replied.

Frank pictured the garage: two levels below the entry level, three above. Two ramp cameras on the entry level; one for the ramp going up, one for the ramp headed down. If the van were going up, three possible floors to park on; down, two possible floors. Five cameras.

The van appeared on the up ramp off the entry level. It showed up again on the up ramp off the first level. The screen covering the up ramp off the second level remained blank.

"He must have stayed on the second level," Sarah said. She rapped out a riff on her keyboard. Another screen bloomed. "Second level surveillance," she explained.

Headlights flared as the van made its way slowly down one aisle and another before it found a parking place. Lights turned off. The van's driver-side door opened, then closed.

"A woman," Frank said.

The woman walked to the stairwell. Sarah did some more keyboard work. The stairwell camera came on screen with a heavyset black woman carrying a shopping bag from which peeked a teddy bear. More manipulation of the keyboard brought in the camera on the next landing. The woman exited the stairwell on the entry level and walked out of the garage toward the hospital's main entrance. On screen, the digital clock showed 21:02:45.9.

"Okay," Frank said, "let's look some more."

Sarah switched to the entry camera and again, the tape ran backward. The next van entered the garage at 21:01:13.4. It parked on the third level up. Its occupants were a man, a woman, and a young child.

An hour later, Frank stood up and stretched and kneaded the back of his neck. "I didn't know there were so many vans in the world." They'd developed a process, Sarah and Frank and José: track each van to its parking place, then fast-forward until the driver got out. It worked smoothly, but it was taking more time than he had thought it would.

José, beside him, stretched, too. "And it looks like all of them have sick people in this hospital." He asked Sarah, "What are we back to?"

"Coming up on just before eight o'clock."

José and Frank sat back down.

"Okay, Sarah," Frank said as he settled in, "Turn on your magical time machine."

✛ Ten minutes later, a van entered the garage and disappeared. Cameras tracked it on the down ramps to the ground-level parking area. There, the surveillance camera caught the van coming off the ramp from above. The van approached the camera, then nothing. Time on screen read 19:55:25.

"Rewind," Frank said. He felt his heartbeat picking up. The screen blurred, stopped, and again the van came off the ramp directly toward the camera. The screen bloomed a bright silver then black.

"He's got his brights on," José said.

The screen cleared. As before, no van.

Marla Fernandez cursed softly. "He parked under the camera. There's an entire row of parking slots against that wall the camera can't cover."

"Let's look at him coming into the garage again," Frank said. "And slow the action down."

Again the van turned in off 23rd Street.

"Brights on there, too," Fernandez said.

The van pulled past the ticket dispenser. Frank, tense, waited to catch the best side view of the van.

"There!" Frank said. "Stop."

The grainy black-and-white image froze: a light-colored commercial van with roof racks for ladders and outsize cargo.

"There's some kind of logo," José said.

Frank shook his head. "Whatever it is, it isn't Verizon." He nodded to Sarah. "Okay, back to the ground level."

The van came down the ramp as it had before. And disappeared as it had before.

Frank stared at the screen. Straight ahead, Celeste Foster's Camry. Off to the left, the door she'd come out of little over an hour later. And beneath the screen, hidden under the camera's searching lens, was the van. And waiting in the van . . .

"If that was him," José said, "wouldn't he leave the garage before Tyler came down to check the circuit breaker?"

Fernandez saw where José was headed. "Bring up the exit cameras between . . . when'd this camera go out?" she asked José.

José checked his notebook. "Camera went out at twenty-one oh-nine, came back on at twenty-one twenty-five.

Sarah nodded. Two monitors fluttered, then settled on the garage exits.

At 21:22:37.9, the light-colored van with the roof racks showed up on one of the monitors.

Frank watched it wait, then merge into the night traffic.

THIRTY-ONE

✚ Let's run that again." Randolph Emerson flicked the remote.

The van enters the garage. The camera view shifts. The van leaves the garage.

"Let's see that again," said Randolph Emerson. He clicked the remote at the television set on his credenza. The scene repeated.

"We can't read the logo or license plate?" he asked Frank and José.

Frank shook his head.

"Surveillance took that video apart on their computers," José said. "Nothing."

"Well, he's partial to vans. A regular rolling slaughterhouse," Emerson said. "Anything else?"

"We might have the VIN for the van he used in the Boukedes killing."

"Might?" Emerson looked unhappy.

"We'll know maybe tomorrow."

"Maybe?"

Frank nodded. "Yes, maybe."

Emerson shook his head. "Not good enough. We've got to show we're getting somewhere. Mayor called the chief an hour ago. Chief called me. Tomorrow they're gonna have to go up to the Hill to testify."

"What?"

"The Senate Government Affairs Committee. Investigating law enforcement, or the lack of it, in the District of Columbia."

"I thought they were on recess for the election," José said.

"Think again."

"What's the Senate going to do?" José asked. "Mount up a posse to track this guy down?"

Emerson shot José a poisonous look. "What they're going to do, Detective Phelps, is authorize the budget for the District of Columbia. And in that budget is the money for your salary and retirement fund."

Frank got up and punched the eject button on Emerson's VCR and retrieved the surveillance tape. "That's what I like about you, Randolph," he told Emerson.

"What's that?"

"You're such a great morale-builder."

✝ Closing his desk, José tore a page off his desk calendar. "Don't forget," he told Frank, "tomorrow night's Halloween.

Frank glanced at his own desk calendar—October 28—two pages behind. "Damn," he muttered to himself, "some people run a few minutes slow, I'm off two days."

"Month's shot."

"A helluva month." Frank stared at the offending calendar, then ripped out Saturday and Sunday and pitched them in the wastebasket.

"You want to go for a beer?"

Frank shook his head. "David Trevor."

"I forgot. You want me along?"

"No need. I'm going to drop by his place on my way home."

✝ Just after seven, Frank showed his credentials to a uniformed Secret Service officer and pulled into the circular drive at David Trevor's home in Kalorama. Washington's communities, like tree's rings, mark the eras of the capital's growth. What Georgetown is to the eighteenth and early nineteenth centuries, Kalorama is to America's Gilded Age. Between the Civil War and World War I, Washington's wealthiest built magnificent mansions on the hill above Dupont Circle.

Frank surveyed the Italian Renaissance house. Five thousand square feet, minimum. And he didn't want to think about the utilities. Electricity alone probably triple the monthly mortgage payment on his Olive Street row house. Walking to the front door, he spotted the infrared motion detectors hiding in the manicured boxwoods and the shatterproof Kevlar panes in the windows facing the street. To his surprise, Trevor answered the door.

"Sorry to put you out like this," Trevor offered apologetically. "Impossible to get any time at the office. Monday . . ." He made a small gesture with his hands, letting Monday explain itself. A perfunctory handshake followed and Frank's equally perfunctory assurance that he hadn't been inconvenienced at all. Trevor escorted Frank to the library, crossing a large foyer with a huge crystal-and-gilt chandelier and a grand staircase that flowed from the upper floors like a white marble waterfall.

Trevor wore a conservative vested green tweed suit, ecru shirt, and regimental-striped tie. Standing in the library, with its dark paneled walls and bookcases, its genteelly worn green leather club chairs and Azerbaijan carpets, he looked every bit the English barrister or Whitehall diplomat.

"Drink?" Trevor asked, already halfway to a bar set into the wall. "I'm having scotch."

"Scotch is good, no water, no ice." Frank said. A nearby bookcase drew his attention. He was scanning the shelves when Trevor joined him.

"Scotch neat," Trevor said, handing Frank a glass.

Frank ran his fingertips across a row of leather-bound volumes. "Beautiful books."

"I started collecting when I was young."

Frank's fingers stopped on a title. Dos Passos's *Manhattan Transfer*. "You've read him?"

"Just this and *U.S.A.*"

"*U.S.A.* was the more popular. Mention Dos Passos and people automatically think *U.S.A.*"

"I liked *Manhattan Transfer* better."

Trevor cocked his head, dark eyes bright with curiosity. "Oh? Why?"

"The big-city setting. The interaction of a lot of very different characters. Some succeeding, some failing."

Trevor led the way to the green leather chairs. "Succeeding and failing. Pretty much a three-word picture of life." Trevor pointed to a chair and took his own. Settled, he crossed a leg and regarded Frank. "Speaking of success, my father told me he'd met you. What was your impression?"

"That's an intimidating question."

"Just curious," Trevor said, not too convincingly.

Buying time, Frank tasted his scotch. "I think he's a man who looks back over his life and sees his failures and successes."

Trevor laughed, a disagreeable guttural bark. "Now *that's* a non-answer."

"No," Frank disagreed. "He doesn't seem to be much for white-washing. I think he sees himself in a truer light than most of us do."

"A truer light." Injecting a trace of irony, Trevor turned the phrase over, poking at it like a boy with a stick might poke at a closed-up turtle, curious, but not malicious. He challenged Frank in an almost deadly playful manner. "And in this truer light of yours—his?—what would he see as his failures and successes?"

"I only spent a short time with him."

"Your intuition," Trevor pressed, eyes glittering. "Off the record."

"I think," Frank picked his way carefully, "I think the war hurt him badly . . . personally and professionally."

Trevor's face froze. "He lost a son and he lost his ideals," he said with surprising bitterness. "One hell of a price to pay for a small parcel of shitty Southeast Asian acreage."

Temporarily stunned by Trevor's outburst, Frank sat silent, casting about for safer ground. "He sees you as one of his successes. He's very proud of you."

Trevor's face softened. "That's important, isn't it? For your father to be proud of you?"

Frank waited and let the question drift away.

"As I said on the phone, I read Mary Keegan's manuscript yesterday."

Trevor got a sardonic smile. "Did she treat us well, my father and me?"

"I thought so. She hadn't finished. But she'd made a penciled note. That's why I called."

"Yes?"

"About seeing you on the twentieth of September. My partner and I checked our notes. We didn't have that meeting down. That day's a blank in her time line."

Trevor shut his eyes for a second or two, then opened them. "Let me check," he said. He got up and walked to a large oak partner's desk, where he picked up a leather-bound appointment book and brought it back to his chair. Settling in, he leafed through.

He found the page and ran his finger down it. "Yes," he said. "That was a Wednesday. My office. Three-fifteen P.M."

"Could you describe the meeting?"

Trevor took a sip of his scotch and smiled. "You'd better be more specific. You're asking that of a skilled diplomat. I could describe any given five-minute meeting for hours and end up not saying anything."

"What was the topic, then?"

"As I recall, it was basic fact-checking," Trevor replied. "Going over dates, places, people—that sort of thing."

"People?" Frank asked, "What about someone named Pulaski?"

"Pulaski?"

Frank opened his notebook to the page where he'd copied Mary Keegan's reminder. "Yes, her note reads: 'See David, September twentieth, re: Pulaski analysis.' "

Trevor looked thoughtful, then smiled. "Oh! Pulaski! Yes—that was what I meant earlier . . . fact-checking"—he waved a dismissive hand—"people, etcetera, etcetera, etcetera."

"So the meeting was just about getting the details straight about Pulaski?"

"Yes. A minor issue. But Mary was meticulous about such things."

"He—Pulaski was a he?—Pulaski was somebody in Moscow?"

"Joe Pulaski." Trevor nodded. "He and I worked together in the embassy. Killed in a horrible automobile accident."

"She didn't mention him in the manuscript except for that penciled note."

Trevor shrugged. "A good man, Joe. I accompanied his remains home. Tragic death, but a minor footnote, I should think, to the kind of story you say she was writing."

"This analysis of his—any idea what that might have been?"

"That was one of the main functions of the embassy—analysis. Finding out what was going on in a paranoid country spread across seven time zones. Then putting it in a context so Washington could blithely ignore it. Joe was always busy. We all were."

Frank shifted gears. "Do you recall her mood at the time? That Wednesday?"

Trevor massaged the back of his neck, then shrugged. "Not with any accuracy, I'm afraid. I do have an impression of fatigue—no, that's not it . . ." He thought for a moment, then, as though still not satisfied with his judgment, said, "Not fatigue, despondency."

"Despondent . . . in the sense of defeat?"

"No," Trevor shook his head. "More like sadness."

"And no guess as to why?"

Trevor threw his hands up in a gesture of futility. "The world has a complete catalog of sorrows, Lieutenant. Take your pick: Do you cry over AIDS in Africa? Or about an overdone egg at breakfast?" He shook his head. "I can't help you. But to fill in your . . . your time line, she was in my office that Wednesday. Now, do you mind a question?"

"Of course not."

"There's been another victim since Mary. The woman at Hains Point. Any leads?"

"We're working some."

"I suppose that's the book answer."

Frank closed his notebook and put it away. "I'm afraid so."

✝ No parking places open on Olive Street, so Frank drove until he found a place a block away on N Street, near the synagogue. Still rerunning the video in his mind, he parked and locked his car as though on autopilot. He snapped into now when a shaft of streetlight captured a wisp of cobweb weaving over the doorway of the nearest row house.

Tomorrow . . . Halloween, his organizer-voice came to him sounding like a long-suffering maiden aunt. Halloween always meant high-density kid traffic on Olive. He made his way home while the organizer-voice worked on the logistics: *Move the stoop planter inside, stock up on M&M's, bubble gum, miniature Hershey's and Snickers bars.*

Beethoven's *Pathetique* and the warming scent of garlic and olive oil met him at the door. Cooking noises drew him back to the kitchen, where his father stood at the big gas range, bustling a frying pan back and forth over a burner, sautéing crumbled sausage.

With his free hand, Tom Kearney thrust an empty wineglass at Frank. "Refill?"

Frank filled the glass and handed it back. "Sauce for the cook?"

"Liquid inspiration."

"Missed you when you came in last night."

"You were asleep. How you want the pasta?"

"Al dente. Ms. Barnes like the armoire?"

His father dropped his chin to his chest and gave Frank a menacing, squeezed-face look. "You better show more respect for the greatest generation, young man." He couldn't hold it long before a grin played at the corners of his mouth. "You'll have to ask her." He motioned with his head toward the counter nearest the door. "UPS for you."

Frank turned the heavy cardboard container over in his hands, looking for a pull tab. Finding none, he reached in his pocket and came out with the pimp's switchblade.

"Nasty-looking instrument," Tom Kearney said as the knife flicked open.

"Took it off a fella who did amateur surgery on one of his ladies' faces." Frank slipped the blade under a flap and ran it along a crease. He opened the box.

"Book," he said, puzzled.

"Something you ordered?"

"I don't remember."

Frank shook the book out of the package.

Somewhere a demon laughed. His father and the kitchen vanished. The book shimmered, then blossomed, filling the universe. Frank plunged into a dimension without dimension, a place without light or dark. He fell endlessly into a void without beginning or end.

"Jesus." He heard his own voice somewhere far outside himself, echoing as if coming back to him down an endless metal corridor.

"Frank?"

His father and the kitchen rematerialized around him. He stood with the book in his hand.

"What is it?" his father asked.

He held the book up so his father could see the cover. A dark reddish-brown smear that was blood underlined the title—*The Fisher King*.

THIRTY-TWO

✠ **A**s if he were handling a bomb, Janowitz put the book and UPS packaging on Frank's desk.

"It's her blood—Foster's."

Frank didn't say anything. He sat in his chair with his hands in his lap, looking at the book.

"Any prints?" José asked.

Janowitz, eyes fixed on Frank, shook his head.

"Fibers? Hair?"

Janowitz shook his head again. "Calkins said it was cleaner than Clinton's conscience."

"Except for the blood," Frank said.

Dark anger in Frank's voice caused Janowitz to shift uneasily from foot to foot. No one said anything. José said softly, "Thanks, Leon."

Still uncertain, Janowitz stood there. "I'm taking a couple of guys back to canvass Foster's neighborhood," he said, angling for an attaboy. "And I've got checks running on the UPS tracking number."

José nodded. "That's good, Leon," he said. "Do that. Good idea."

Janowitz looked for some kind of recognition from Frank, but Frank, slumped in his chair, continued staring holes in the book.

Janowitz clumsily aborted a good-bye, exchanged a worried glance with José, then turned and left.

Sounds of mid-morning traffic drifted up from Constitution Avenue, cut by the wailing of an ambulance siren.

"How you doing?" José asked in a quiet voice.

Frank pushed the book to the side. "Okay." It was his turn to search José's face. "We've been targets before."

"Yeah."

"What do you mean by that?"

"By what?"

"That 'I think you're bullshitting' tone," Frank said.

"Sometimes we bullshit ourselves."

Frank looked up. He and José locked eyes. Two lives times twenty-five years of sharing made for a lot of sharing. And not just the on-duty stuff. José had pulled Frank out of the bottle after the divorce, and Frank had lived with José, twenty-four hours a day for weeks, keeping him on an even keel after the grade-school hostage situation had gone terribly wrong.

"I had a dream last night," Frank began. As soon as he said the words, he felt like he could start breathing again. "Took me back to where I never wanted to go to again."

"Yeah?"

"We had a sniper tracking our outfit . . ."

The office and the present faded as time reversed. Fragments of the once-whole appeared, shimmering and transient. Vivid seconds out of countless days of a war. A war that seemed then to last forever, but was now a thing that never quite was.

". . . he'd wait . . . the sniper . . . for a sure-kill shot. We'd go days, sometimes weeks. Think he was gone. Then one shot . . . it was always a head shot. And he always went for the guy up front . . . the guy walking point. He killed four guys in our squad. It got so all we thought about was him."

Two kilometers east of the village of Ben Cat. Where French plantation owners had grown rubber for Michelin. And where French legionnaires had died in ambushes sprung from among the rubber trees. A stone obelisk stood outside the American army brigade head-quarters—À LA MÉMOIRE DES OFFICIERS GRADES ET SPAHIS DU 2ᵉ R.S.M.—and below it, MORTS POUR LA FRANCE. The Viet Cong left the marker standing as a warning to the Americans. But the Americans, confident because they weren't French, paid no attention to the inscription.

"We set a trap. We had our own snipers covering a tree line where we thought he was. My squad crossed the rice paddy toward the tree line."

"And you walked point," José said, guessing.

Again the sun and the paddy and the tree line, dark and waiting. "You think," Frank said in a whisper, "you think, every step you take, he's watching you. Waiting for you to come into range."

"You got him."

"He was a sixteen-year-old kid. Kept a diary. He'd killed twenty-three people. He'd gotten so he'd liked it—liked the killing."

Silence drifted down into the office like a feather.

After a while, José pointed to the book. "You talk with your father about this?"

✠ "Well?" Tom Kearney asked.

Father and son faced each other across the kitchen table. The book lay between them.

"Well," Frank said, "he's sending a message. I'm his target."

"Why would you be?"

Frank felt a stabbing burn of impatience. "You're asking for logic, Dad. We're dealing with a crazy man."

"I'm not denying that you're his target." Tom Kearney raised a calming hand. "But crazies *can* be logical. The trick is to get inside *their* logic." He leaned forward for emphasis. "I *am* saying that it's important to think about *why.*"

. . . the world in which he lives.

His father raised his eyebrows. "Pardon?"

Frank realized he must have said the words out loud. "Something a shrink on TV said," he explained. "That the killer . . . how'd he put it?" The words he was looking for came back to Frank: " 'He harbors a hatred toward the world in which he lives.' "

"Go on," his father prompted.

"Boukedes and Keegan . . . he killed both of them where he caught them. He could have taken them somewhere. The way he did with Foster."

"But he didn't."

"No," Frank said, feeling his way to the next thought. "He *used* Foster. He killed because he wanted to kill, the same as the others. But Foster, he used. He posed her on that statue to show us how powerful he is."

"And that leads to this," Tom Kearney said, pointing to the book.

"A cop's a symbol of authority. To make his next kill a cop . . . he's spreading his wings."

Tom Kearney somberly appraised his son. "And what do you think you ought to do about it?"

"Take him out."

"No. I mean, about your safety."

"Same answer, Dad. Take him out."

"How about a safe haven as an option?"

"You mean a protection program? Retire? Change my identity? Hide somewhere?"

"It's an option."

Frank looked across the table at Tom Kearney the judge. The judge, impersonal professional. Weighing alternatives. Deliberating.

"Would you support me if I did . . . get out of this?"

"You know I would," his father answered.

"And you know I can't."

His father and the judge both smiled.

"But I want you out of here," Frank said. "I don't want you in this."

His father's smile vanished. "I'm here." He rapped a knuckle on the table. "I'm staying."

. . .

✠ "You didn't really think he'd leave, did you?" José asked.

"No. He's too damn stubborn."

José started to say something when his phone rang. He answered, scribbled a line or two on his scratch pad, then hung up.

"Manny," he said, getting up and reaching for his jacket. "We got us an address on the VIN. Four-thousand block of New York Avenue Northeast."

✠ "Royal Communications," José read off the scratch pad.

Frank looked across New York Avenue. A trash-filled vacant lot next to a boarded up Jiffy Lube.

"I knew this was too easy," José said.

Frank shrugged. "Why should this be easy? Nothing else has been."

He watched the traffic. Who were the people in all those cars and trucks? He'd had a conversation once with a Virginia highway trooper. *If you knew what was going on behind those steering wheels,* the trooper had said, *you'd never drive again.* He found himself wondering if he and José had passed the killer . . . passed *who*? For the first time in the case, he felt the need to name the killer. More cars passed. And the sniper's name came back to him.

We called you Charlie, didn't we? he asked the North Vietnamese. He remembered the days and weeks of hunting, the fear. How, in the minds of the targeted Americans, the sniper had become an evil spirit—every-where, all-knowing, immortal. And he also remembered how the lifeless sniper sprawled at the base of the rubber tree with the heavy-barreled Dragunov rifle still clutched in his hands—a sixteen-year-old boy.

"I'm thinking we ought to be looking somewhere else."

"Yeah?"

"Where Charlie bought the van."

"Who the hell's Charlie?"

"Charlie . . . whoever . . . is Royal Communications," Frank said, thumb-pointing across New York Avenue. He flipped open his cell phone and dialed Manny Dale. Moments later, he hung up.

"Manny says maybe an hour, maybe two. How about lunch?"

"Ben's?"

"Chili? I'm out of Maalox."

José shrugged. "Fight fire with fire."

THIRTY-THREE

✛ **B**en's lunch crowd had thinned out. At a table in the backroom, Frank and José were finishing apple pie and coffee when Manny called back.

Frank answered, listened to Manny's brief message, and jotted an address in his notebook.

"Hector Ramos owns Ramos Painting and Decorating in Silver Spring. He sold the van to Royal Communications a year ago," Frank said to José.

✛ "Yes," Hector Ramos said. "I sold it."

They had found Ramos just after three. His wife had given them an address in Rockville. But through gritted teeth, an unhappy home-owner there said Ramos hadn't shown as promised. Frank had called back, and Señora Ramos had put them on hold. Frank had been ready to hang up and dial her back when she came on with another address in Takoma Park.

At this second address, they'd found Hector Ramos in the front yard of a bungalow, shouting instructions to three men on ladders as they burned and scraped layers of white paint from the trim along the roof.

"Who'd you sell it to?" Frank asked.

"The guy who answered the ad," Ramos said.

"What was his name?"

Ramos studied the tops of his work shoes a long time. "Gaston," he said at last, and not sounding certain at that.

"Can you give us a description?" José asked.

"For certain." Ramos smiled, showing good white teeth. "A white man. Dark hair. Not fat. Not thin. Very polite." Ramos stopped and looked as if he expected a passing grade.

José shook his head. "Age?"

Ramos frowned. "Hard to say."

"Older than you? Younger?"

"Younger, I think."

"Five years? Fifteen years?"

"Maybe five."

"Was he taller than you, Mr. Ramos?"

"About my height."

"Did he wear glasses?"

"No."

"Eye color? You remember his eye color?"

"I only saw him once." Ramos got a defensive, crowded look. "For a few minutes. When he buys the van."

Frank eased off. "Your words, Mr. Ramos. Tell us how you put the van up for sale and how this guy bought it."

"It is a good van," Ramos said. "I would not sell it, but my wife . . . my wife says this thing about a professional appearance. I do not know where she gets professional appearance, but once she begins, it is all I hear. Professional appearance. It is only three years old—the van. No dents. A good engine. I do not abuse machinery." Ramos's eyes darted between the two detectives and he added for emphasis, "Nor do I abuse people."

"Of course not," José said.

Ramos nodded in relief. "But I put the ad in. I get three calls. Two of them are merely people with telephones who look to make money from others' misfortune. This man—Gaston—calls. He asks the price, the mileage, and says he will come look. He comes to my shop promptly. He looks at the van. I tell him about my wife. He smiles. He says that it is indeed a splendid van. He says that he will meet my price. I sign the title over with the notary and the man drives away."

Ramos looked at Frank. Then looked at José. The story was short. It had a beginning, a middle, and an end. It was a well-told story.

Frank rewarded Ramos with a smile. "It is clear, Mr. Ramos. Thank you."

"You are welcome, Lieutenant."

"Can you help us further?"

Ramos cocked his head.

"How did he pay you?"

"Ah, yes," Ramos smiled, remembering the transaction. "He paid with cash. He insisted I count it."

"He left no address?"

"There was no need. We signed the papers with the notary. I gave him the keys. He gave me the money."

Frank imagined he heard a mocking laugh. *Charlie you sonofabitch.*

Frank went into neutral. He shut out Ramos and José and replayed Ramos's story. He replayed it again. He brought his eyes back into focus and realized he'd been staring at Ramos—looking through the man—and Ramos was staring back, eyes widening.

"You put the ad in the paper? The *Post*?"

"Yes," Ramos whispered.

"And he called you?"

"Yes."

"Where?"

"Excuse?"

"Did he call you at your shop?"

"That was the number in the ad."

"What day was this?"

"That I sold the van?"

"That Mr. Gaston called."

"It was the day of the ad."

"What day was that?"

Ramos plunged a hand into the depths of his coveralls. "I run the ad over the weekend . . ." He came up with a small wire-bound appointment book. He leafed back, squinting and holding the book at arm's length.

José reached into his coat pocket and came out with his reading glasses. He handed them to Ramos.

"*Gracias.*"

"*De nada.*"

Ramos resumed his search and finally stabbed a finger into a page and looked up. "July the ninth," he said, triumphantly. "A Sunday."

✠ In the car, Frank made a call.

"Timmy, a favor."

"I'm holding a lot of your IOUs, Frank." Tim Haskill sounded annoyed.

"All for the public good, Timmy."

"Yeah, yeah. What do you need?"

"Hector Ramos owns Ramos Painting and Decorating in Silver Spring." Frank read off Ramos's phone number. "On Sunday, nine July, Ramos got a call from somebody wanting to buy his van. We need to find that somebody."

"And so you want a record of who called Ramos on nine July," Haskill said.

"That's it."

"And you want it yesterday," Haskill continued, a reluctant drag in his voice.

"That'd be nice."

"And you don't want to bother Ma Bell with a warrant."

"I'd rather not have to."

A silence, then Haskill asked, "This to do with those women, Frank? The statue . . . ?"

"Yeah."

Haskill's reluctance vanished. "I'll get back to you."

✠ "Remember when coffee was a nickel a cup?" José asked.

Afternoon-coffee-break regulars crowded the Starbucks. Frank and José sat side by side at a counter, looking out on New Hampshire Avenue.

"I remember when it was either black or cream-and-sugar."

José looked at his decaf skim-milk latte, then at the crowd. "Shows you what a rich country we are—Mr. Starbuck making millions selling coffee at five bucks a cup."

Frank finished his cappuccino and spooned out the remaining foam. "You think there's a connection with coffee and crime?"

"Connection?"

"Yeah," Frank said, playing with it, "you plot the crime rate since the fifties, then, alongside that, you plot the increase in coffee prices—coffee's up, crime's up—and you got a coffee crime crisis."

"And put out a press release," José grinned, joining in, "next thing we know, we got coffee-crime-crisis centers all over the country."

Frank added a manic layer. "And Ph.D.'s offering coffee-counseling services."

José raised with: "And Congress passes a law for blood coffee level tests for drivers."

"Don't forget coffee-buying licenses."

Frank's phone chirped, and the tower of absurdities toppled.

"Hector Ramos got three phone calls at that number on nine July," Tim Haskill said. Haskill gave three numbers. "First two are still active accounts—a used-car dealership in Gaithersburg, second's a guy named John Saunders in north Arlington."

Frank copied the addresses.

"The third account's closed out. A cell phone account. Royal Communications."

"Closed out?"

"Yeah."

Frank felt his throat tighten in disappointment.

"But," Haskill added, "there's a billing address: Royal Communications, 4301 Connecticut Avenue."

✠ "I remember . . . Royal Communications . . ." Alexander Paulson, the manager-owner of the Mail Boxes Etc. on Connecticut Avenue. Paulson, a thin man with a faintly European accent who looked to be in his upper sixties, tapped the computer keyboard. He searched the monitor, then shook his head. "Not here." He rattled the keyboard again and waited as another screen came up. "Ah, yes," he said. "Inactive account."

José leaned forward, his elbows on the counter. "When'd they close it out?" he asked.

"Saturday the twenty-first."

"How?" Frank asked. "Somebody come in here?"

Paulson shook his head. "Computer. The Internet." He gestured toward his machine. "Open accounts, close them. Never see a human face."

"You must have had a name . . . a credit card number?"

Paulson dropped his hands into his lap and walk-rolled his chair back from the computer. "You have a warrant?" His eyes darted between Frank and José. "I don't want to cause you trouble, but . . ." He rolled both hands palm up in a gesture of helplessness.

"We'll be back," said José.

"Lawsuits . . . lawyers . . . I am a small business here. I cannot afford—"

Frank sighed. "I know," he said. He told himself he understood, but the burn began, a low, volcanic bubbling in his gut. The burn got worse, and, on the way back to the car, he had to stop in a CVS for Maalox.

. . .

✠ It took two and a half hours and three more Maalox tablets to drive back downtown, get the warrant request through the U.S. Attorney's Office, and then to the judge.

It was just after six when Frank pulled up in front of the Mail Boxes Etc. on Connecticut Avenue.

"Thought of something, Hoser."

"Yeah?"

"We got the warrant, what do you think we're going to find? This guy's been two moves ahead of us all the way."

José got a furrow of exasperation between his eyes. "How long we been doing this, Frank?"

"Twenty-five years."

"An' every time we go for a warrant, don't we find something we didn't expect to find?"

"I guess."

"Guess, my ass," José said, as if he'd made his point. "We're gonna find something we didn't expect to find, that's what."

✠ Paulson bent over his desk and held the warrant under an old-fashioned goose-neck lamp. Twice he went over the document, top to bottom, tracing his path with a palsied finger. Finally, he straightened.

"It seems in order." He glanced warily at the warrant one more time, as if a legal tiger still crouched somewhere in the fine print. "What do you want?"

"Like the paper says," Frank tapped the warrant, "everything you've got on Royal Communications."

Paulson sat in front of his computer and worked the keyboard and mouse. Windows on the screen opened and shut. He clicked the mouse, and, after a few seconds, the printer began disgorging a document.

"The account," Paulson explained, as he handed the single sheet to Frank.

Royal Communications' business address was the vacant lot on New York Avenue. There was an account number, presumably belonging to Mail Boxes Etc., and a box marked "Funding" with a sixteen-digit Visa credit card number. And a name.

Frank handed the account to José and pointed to the name.

"L. Glastonbury," José read.

"Yeah. Hector Ramos's Mr. Gaston."

José held out the account to Paulson. "Says here, Royal Communications had box number 326."

Paulson craned his neck to verify the number. "Yes. But we closed the box with the account. On the twenty-first." He tapped the last entry with his index finger.

"Yeah, but what happened to any mail in the box?"

Paulson's lips made a small O. "We hold any mail for two weeks, then return it to the post office." He looked from José to Frank. "It's in the contract!" he said anxiously.

"I'm sure it is," Frank said in his best bedside manner. Then, "Are you holding any mail for Royal Communications?"

Another O from Paulson. "We can check." Without enthusiasm, he waved weakly, gesturing toward a door at the back.

"Let's do," said Frank.

Paulson led the way through a clutter of cartons, stationery supplies, and a bicycle with a flat tire to a nest of pigeon-hole boxes. He searched the boxes and from 326 pulled four envelopes. He held them protectively against his chest.

"This is *mail*," he said, "I'm not certain that the warrant—"

"Withholding evidence in a homicide is a felony," José intoned.

Paulson took a breath, held it, then handed the envelopes over to Frank.

Frank shuffled through the envelopes. "Junk, junk, junk," he said, tossing the first three envelopes down on a carton. " 'Office of Tax and Revenue,' " he read the return address from the fourth envelope.

Paulson tried again. "You shouldn't open that."

"I beg your pardon?" Frank asked. He pulled the pimp's switchblade from his pocket, flicked it open, and slit the envelope. He fingered out the folded document and smiled. "Gotta hand it to the tax collectors," he said. "Greedy bastards will track you to the end of the earth." He passed the statement to José. "Royal Communications owes three thousand, one-hundred and eighty-four bucks on a property on Galena Place, Northwest."

THIRTY-FOUR

✠ **G**alena Place runs four short blocks through the Palisades, a northwest Washington neighborhood along the Potomac River.

"There it is." José pointed ahead to a mailbox at the foot of a steep hill.

Frank pulled over to the curb and shut off the engine and headlights. He found his flashlight under the seat and opened his door. At the top of the hill, a nineteenth-century three-story Victorian stood dark against the night sky.

"Steps over there." José's flashlight revealed a stone stairway cut into the hill.

At the top of the stairway, the house's isolation became apparent. It looked out over an old-growth forest along the C&O Canal and, a bit farther, the Potomac. Across the river, the sheer rock face of Arlington Ridge. A dense stand of evergreens to the north blocked any view of the neighborhood.

"We could be out in the country," José said.

"In a castle by a river," Frank said softly, recalling Kaitlin McKirgan.

"What's that?"

"Where the Fisher King's castle is."

They mounted the steps to a wraparound porch. A wicker sofa and several chairs faced an old-fashioned porch swing suspended by chains from the ceiling.

Frank twisted a bell-key set into the middle of the front door. Inside, an old-fashioned bell shattered the silence with a whirring clatter. He waited. Silence returned, smothering the last echoes inside the house. He tried again. Nothing.

"Let's check out back." José suggested.

As they walked around the house, Frank played his flashlight over peeling paint and sagging shutters.

"Spooky," José said. "Bates Motel—all we need is Tony Perkins in a dress."

"He's dead."

They came around the house. A building stood some twenty feet or so from the house, big, bulking, and black in the night.

"Barn," said José.

"Must have had horses once," Frank said.

One of the large doors at the end of the structure stood partially open. Above it, a window opened into the loft. Above the window, a beam and pulley for hoisting hay bales.

Through the open door came a sweetish, almost floral chemical odor mixed with a fainter scent of ammonia left by generations of animal inhabitants.

"What was it, Hoser, you supposed to close the door after? The horses run away? Or is it cows?"

"Horses. You wait for cows to come home."

Frank swept his light inside. The barn's central area between the stalls had been paved. An oil stain marked the center of the rough concrete floor. The flashlight beam crossed a machine partially hidden by a drop cloth.

Frank brought the beam back.

"What do you think?" asked Frank.

"Think we need a closer look."

Frank pushed the door wider and entered.

Inside, the chemical smell got stronger. Crossing to the machine, Frank pulled away the drop cloth.

"Paint sprayer," José said. He ran a finger over the spray gun nozzle and came away with a smear of dark blue.

Frank played his flashlight into an open drum beside the sprayer. A crumpled ball of heavy-weight paper had been sprayed with the same dark blue paint. Frank pulled it out and tugged it open.

"Looks like Charlie's in the utility business."

The stencil carried the legend and logo of Pepco—the Potomac Electrical Power Company.

José pointed his flashlight to the floor. A misted border of cream-colored paint outlined a large rectangle on the concrete. Two blotches of dark blue paint marked where the Pepco stencil had been put on.

"Got himself a new van, painted it here," he said.

"Where is it now?" Frank asked. He searched the floor around the sprayer. No footprints, no pocket trash, and, probably, no fingerprints. Charlie was—

"Frank."

It was almost a whisper. Abrupt. Filled with caution. Reflexively, Frank slipped his hand toward his shoulder holster.

José, transfixed, stood looking into a horse stall. Frank came up beside him.

The dagger lay across the massive butchering bench. Blood, now dry and brownish black, stained the bench's scarred surface. José swung his light upward. Above the table, a rope ran to a block and tackle bolted to a rafter.

Frank felt a wash of anger. He looked back at where the van would have been parked, two, three feet away, and put the dynamics together.

"Charlie kidnaps her in the hospital garage and brings her here . . ."

Did she die quickly? Die like Upton said she had?

"He pulls her out of the van, ties her, lays her out on the butcher's bench . . ."

What did he do then? Bundy sometimes masturbated over his victims . . .

"He uses the dagger. He stabs her. He cuts her throat. He hauls her up . . ."

After draining the blood, Charlie lowers her corpse . . . maybe onto a plastic sheet . . . puts her back in the van . . .

José had been piecing together the same gruesome sequence. His eyes darkened with pain and anger. When he spoke, the words came tense and brittle.

"What'd he do with her finger?"

In unison, both men started toward the unexplored darkness at the back of the barn.

Household junk—an old ironing board, a Philco television set, a bicycle frame, several lengths of garden hose, two automobile tires, a soiled mattress—lay strewn in the next three stalls. In the last stall, four large boxes of heavy-duty cardboard stacked on a wood pallet. Frank bent to examine the shipping label on the nearest box.

"Sodium carbonate, USP," he read.

"The stuff Upton found on Boukedes's finger," José said. "For making mummies."

The remainder of the barn yielded nothing. Outside, Frank pulled in the night air with its scent of apples and fallen leaves. He looked at the old house thoughtfully. Then, as if drawn by a compelling force, the two men walked to the back door. The door was solid wood, heavily built with a sturdy dead bolt.

"Emerson'll say we should get a warrant," José said, reading Frank's mind.

"Unh-huh," Frank agreed, reading José's mind.

"That'd take time."

"Yeah. Meanwhile . . ."

"Meanwhile," José finished, "Charlie's out there in his Pepco van."

The two men looked at each other for a moment. José spoke first. "I'll work on the lock."

"And I'll work on Emerson."

José produced a small flat leather case of picks and bent closer to inspect the lock. Frank punched in Emerson's cell phone number.

Emerson answered on the second ring.

"Randolph?"

"Frank? That you? What—"

"Randolph, our boy may be in a van with Pepco markings—"

"How do you know?"

"No time for that now, Randolph. You got to lean on Pepco."

"Pepco?" Emerson's voice rose. "Goddamnit, what are you doing? What's happening? Where are—"

"Randolph!" Frank snapped. "You want a play-by-play, you're gonna get another hacked-up body. You want to help? Or you want to fuck this up?"

Silence.

Emerson surrendered. "Pepco?"

"Call John McDonnell at Pepco. The security guy. Have him bring all his vans home. Then put out an APB for anybody driving a Pepco van."

Silence.

"Okay. Now, where the hell are you?"

"What'd you say, Randolph?"

"I said—"

"Randolph? You there?"

Frank hung up.

José was struggling with the back door lock, trying to manipulate the pick with one hand, the tension tool with the other, while gripping his flashlight in his armpit. Frank took the light. José grunted something in thanks and his movements evened out. For a man as big as he was, José was startlingly dexterous. His boxer's broken-knuckled hands felt the minute vibrations of the dropping of the dead bolt pins.

"Think he's got the house wired?" José asked.

"Wouldn't think so . . . alarms bring neighbors. Or cops. Or both. Don't think Charlie wants that."

Then, in a silence broken only by tiny metallic nickings, José worked the lock. Seconds later, he whispered, "Got three of the pins, two to go."

With the pick, he continued probing in small, deliberate motions. "Four . . . yes, ah, come on, five . . . always one that's a holdout . . .

yes, gotcha, you little bastard." Under the constant pressure of the tension tool, the lock cylinder rotated with a crisp click.

He slipped the pick and tension tool back into the leather case. With his free hand he turned the knob. "Trick or treat," he whispered, edging the door open.

The air had a lifeless, damp-earth, old-house smell to it.

"Empty," José said, shining his light around the kitchen. More than empty—totally devoid of any sign of human presence. No plates, no glasses or cups. A dust veneer coated the countertops and windowsills.

Three doors led into the rest of the house. One to a hallway and another to a large dining room. Frank opened the third door to a stairway landing. Stairs led up, a servant's access to the living quarters, stairs led down into the darkness of the basement.

"Upstairs first?" Before you go down into a basement, you want to clear the upper floors first. It was the kind of thing that didn't need asking, but you asked it anyway to hear your own voice.

"Yeah." José's whispered, his voice tight.

Stairs: stairs up, stairs down. He and José had acquired a certain respect for stairs. They had stood at stairs like these hundreds of times. Not knowing where they led. Or what they led to. He'd learned early that if there was trouble, it was better to be going down stairs than up stairs. There'd been a couple of times when up or down hadn't made any difference—it'd been bad both ways.

He slipped his pistol out of his shoulder holster and flicked the safety off.

"Okay," José said, close behind him.

Fingers over his flashlight lens so only a sliver of light escaped, Frank swept the stairs going up. Fourteen steps to a landing. A door to the right, a door to the left.

He flicked the flashlight off and started up the stairs.

Each step you take—you plant the ball of your foot on the side of the stair close to the wall. Now, shift your weight forward . . . slowly . . . slowly.

Feel for the loose tread before it gives you away. Anticipate a door slamming open up above you. Wait for a shotgun blast to boom down the stairwell toward you—each step you take.

If somebody burst out of one of those doors at the top of the stairs with a shotgun, and if he, Frank, was lucky enough and fast enough, he'd drop to the right and fire. And just behind him, José would drop down, firing on the left. He didn't like this at all. He would have liked it a lot less if anybody but José had been at his back. He realized his lungs were screaming for air and he made a conscious effort to relax his chest enough to breathe.

Two steps to go.

A frantic, clawing blow just above his ear.

. . . blood explodes . . . a whispering flutter . . . the world disappears . . . heart hammers . . . lungs gasp . . . nerves scream . . .

And inside a voice shouts . . . *Death . . . Danger . . . Kill . . . Kill . . . Kill!*

He doesn't feel the impact of hitting the stairs. Or hear José drop behind him. He has his pistol in a two-handed grip. Muzzle points up to the top of the stairs. His finger's squeezing down on the trigger.

And the screeching and fluttering disappears down the stairway behind the two men.

"Fucking bats." A hoarse whisper. *Had he said it? Or José?*

The two men lie motionless. And the hearts slow and the trigger fingers relax and the rest of the world reconnects to the stairway.

✦ Ten minutes later, Frank and José stood in a dormer on the third floor. The big room could have been used once as a kid's playroom. High above the trees, the window offered a view of the Potomac, silver-plated under the new moon.

The top floors had been as empty as the kitchen. Dust everywhere. Water-stained wallpaper had peeled away in strips from the walls and fallen plaster had left ribbed wounds in the ceilings.

"Nobody up here in a hundred years," José said, his voice hollow and echoing. "Ready to check out the basement?"

. . .

✠ At the first-floor landing, José flicked his light down the basement stairway long enough to count the steps and see they were clear. Snapping the light off, he whispered to Frank. "Twelve steps. Concrete."

Frank started toward the first step, but José gripped his elbow.

"My turn."

Frank felt José take the first step down. The big man moved quietly. Frank had to strain to hear the slight rasping sound as José planted his foot on the first, then second step. Frank followed, pistol in one hand, flashlight in the other. With every step the smell of damp earth grew stronger, reminding Frank of the clutching odor of a grave.

Reaching the bottom, the two men stood frozen, listening. Nothing but an empty old house whispering and creaking in the night. They turned on their flashlights.

"Engine room of the *Titanic*," José said.

To their front, a tangle of plumbing connected a large boiler to a furnace. Behind the boiler and furnace, a tank ran the length of the wall. The slick odor of fuel oil mixed with that of the basement dirt. More plumbing carried the heated water to radiators in the upper stories of the house.

Frank glanced around. On his left, a row of floor-to-ceiling storage bins formed a passage to the far wall. The first two bins held wiring, rags, odds and ends of pipe, scraps of lumber. The other four, like the rest of the house, were empty.

Frank had walked back to the stairwell when he realized José wasn't with him. He turned to see his partner studying the floor toward the end of the row of bins. He rejoined José.

"Look here," José said. He played his flashlight over the concrete floor. Two faint parallel scratches about three feet apart ran from under the storage bin to the center of the passageway.

José angled his light upward. Two similar scratches furrowed the plaster ceiling. He put his light on the floor.

"Cover me," José said.

Frank, flashlight in one hand, pistol in the other, stepped aside to give José room. The big man's back muscles bunched and strained. The heavy wood bin grated in protest as José dragged it away from the wall.

"Now, *that's* a door," Frank muttered.

The door, at least eight feet high, consisted of six teak timbers bound together by three thick wrought-iron bands, top, bottom, and middle. A heavy ring hung in the door's center. The iron and wood bore the staining of age and weather. Old as the house was, the door was far older and its workmanship spoke of another civilization entirely.

José had picked up his flashlight and had his pistol in his other hand. Frank exchanged a glance with his partner, then reached for the door's iron ring.

He twisted. The ring turned smoothly. He pushed. The door swung open.

The door probably triggered the lighting. A soft glow, at first a pinpoint, blossomed rapidly in the center of the pitch-dark room. Hypnotically, a shape took form within the misty globe of light as Frank and José stood entranced. Within seconds, the shape was complete . . . gold and jewels glowed with an unearthly luminescence.

"A cup," said José.

"The Grail," Frank whispered.

For a moment the Grail seemed suspended in midair. Then, as hidden lamps brought on an artificial dawn, Frank saw that the cup actually rested on a high glass pedestal surrounded by a lower semicircular counter. The light grew brighter and irregular shadows on the counter wavered as darkness fled.

"God have mercy," José breathed.

Neatly laid out to either side of the Grail . . . fingers . . . hands . . . something that could have been an arm.

At the far end of the counter at one end of the grisly exhibit, a small framed photograph, like a place-holder for a museum's coming exhibition. José reached up and took the photograph down.

Like a dark, evil cloud, Frank's horror billowed and grew. What had gone into this exhibit . . . no . . . this devil's altar? The ghoulish care . . . the *planning* . . . the twisted insanity . . .

The explosion came, not cracking and sharp, like a plastic charge.

But a soft, almost cushiony blossom of heat and light behind Frank and José.

"Furnace!" José shouted.

Through the doorway, Frank saw a waterfall of flame pouring from the ruptured fuel tank and spreading across the basement floor.

"Let's go!" José was now yelling.

Halfway to the door, Frank turned back, entranced by the sight of the Grail.

"Frank! My God, Frank! Let's *go!*"

Waist-high flames covered the ten yards to the stairway. The two men hesitated for a fraction of a second.

Frank pounded José on the back. *"Go! Go! Go!"* he yelled, as much for himself as José.

✠ Outside, the air still smelled like apples and fallen leaves. Frank and José, bent doubled over, coughed and retched, trying to clear their lungs of the oily smoke.

"The empty space at the end," José got out, "had a picture in front of it."

"Mine?" Frank guessed.

"No. Your father's."

THIRTY-FIVE

✚ **F**loorboarding the car, Frank fishtailed the Crown Vic onto MacArthur Boulevard. The speedometer hit fifty and kept climbing. Traffic ahead parted for his siren and lights. Dispatch was sending two cars, one from Dupont Circle, one from Second District headquarters. Two officers on foot were making it over from Wisconsin and M.

"Hoser . . . call the house again."

José caught the tight anxiety in Frank's voice. He punched in Frank's home number. He listened as the phone rang and willed Tom Kearney to pick up, then hung up. "Same-old, Frank," he said, shaking his head in frustration. "Answering machine."

Frank turned off on Reservoir Road.

"Why my father, Hoser? Why not me?"

Headlights of oncoming cars streaked across José's face.

"You said Charlie was escalating . . . showing his contempt for society."

Frank thought about it. "So, why not kill a cop's father—"

"—and especially since the father's a judge," José finished.

The radio squawked. The two officers on foot were at Frank's door. No answer inside.

"Tell them to break in," Frank said.

Seconds later, the radio came to life again.

"This's Officer Gold," a filtered voice said. "Nobody here."

They were now passing Georgetown Hospital.

"Ask him—"

"Any sign of violence?" José asked Gold before Frank could finish.

"No," Gold answered. "A note. Says 'At Café Milano. Dad.' "

"Get over there," José told the officer. "On Prospect, next to Morton's. Look for Thomas Kearney. Sit on him." José stashed the microphone. "Thirty-fourth coming up," he said, eyes on the street signs flashing by.

At 34th, Frank took a hard, high-speed right. The big car handled the turn badly, its rear end whipping out in a gut-wrenching skid.

Frank twisted the wheel to the left, jamming the accelerator to the floor.

Smoking and screeching in protest, the tires grabbed traction. The car, weaving and jouncing, straightened, then sped through four-way stop signs at P, then O Streets.

"Kid, Frank!" José shouted.

Frank saw the child at the same time: A darting figure in the street ahead . . . a flutter of white . . . a Frankenstein mask. No way the brakes would stop the hurtling car.

"Damn!"

Frank slammed on the brakes and spun the steering wheel hard left. Rending sounds of breaking glass, grinding metal. Airbags boomed open. Plowing along the cars parked by the curb, he brought the car to a stop.

A sudden silence. Frank felt his pulse pounding.

"The kid . . . ?" Frank gasped.

José unsnapped his seat belt. "Probably home changing his underwear."

"You okay?"

José pushed aside a collapsed airbag. "Yeah."

Frank tried his door. Jammed. He hit it with his shoulder. Nothing. José, already out on the street, rounded the front of the car. Frank hit the door again. Dented sheet metal popped and his door gave way.

Homeowners poured into the street, at first stunned, then outraged as they realized their cars now inhabited an instant junkyard along the length of the block.

Frank and José started out at a run toward Café Milano, three blocks away. José fell behind as the two sprinted down 34th and left onto Prospect.

More costumed Halloween partygoers jammed the sidewalk as Frank neared the restaurant. José, even though running full-tilt, had fallen half a block behind him.

Café Milano was packed. Making his way to the bar, Frank scanned the tables in the main room. He felt a touch at his elbow.

"Mr. Kearney."

He turned. "Franco," he said to the dapper man standing beside him, "my father here?"

"He was," Franco answered, eyes working, on the lookout for the slightest misstep in the restaurant's bustling choreography. "They left . . . oh"—he checked his watch—"a half hour . . . maybe forty-five minutes ago."

"They?"

"Your father and the Signora Barnes. They make a handsome couple."

"Do you know where . . . where they were going?"

"Sixteen hundred something, Thirty-second."

"How do you know?"

"They asked that I call a cab"—Franco shrugged—"so I call. But the cab company calls back. The crowds . . . the traffic"—another shrug—"so they decided to walk."

Frank squeezed Franco's biceps. As he turned to leave José pushed through the doors.

"Her place." Frank pulled out his phone and dialed 411. Directory assistance—*when did they stop calling it "Information"?*—came on with its recorded query, then dumped Frank into isolation. He was about to give up when a different recorded voice came on with Judith Barnes's number and offered to dial it for thirty cents.

"Hello?"

"Mrs. Barnes? This's Frank Kearney. Is my father there?"

Silence, then a slightly flustered Judith Barnes came back on. "Frank? Oh . . . *Frank* . . . yes. I mean—no. Your father *was* here. He left . . . to go home . . . I mean . . . to your house—"

Frank was already outside, heading toward Wisconsin Avenue, José beside him.

"How long ago?"

"Several minutes. Four, five or so. Do you want me—"

"No, no thanks, Judith." Frank pocketed the phone. "He left her house," he told José, "he's walking."

"He's walking, he's coming down Thirty-second to P, then down P to Thirtieth," José said.

Frank thought, then decided. "See if we can catch him at P."

The two men fought against a mighty river flowing down Wisconsin Avenue—a veritable Amazon—of costumed men, women, and children, all heading to the M Street intersection, Georgetown's equivalent of a town square. Witches, leprechauns, devils, angels, Darth Vaders. Boom boxes blared a demented mix of rap, country, and rock and roll.

A massively built man wearing high heels, a thick pelt of body hair, and a woman's fluorescent orange bikini teetered into Frank, nearly knocking him over. Desperation clawed at Frank's throat. The crowd . . . grotesque masks . . . noise . . . shoving and pushing bodies . . . As they made their way north, the crowd thinned.

"Look!" José pointed up the avenue.

Half a block away, at the intersection of Wisconsin and P, a van pulled away from the curb and disappeared down P Street—a cream-colored van with a dark blue Pepco logo.

Frank ran into the street, dodging between cars congealed in the thickening gridlock. He vaulted over the hood of a BMW. Ignoring the driver's howling protest, he sprinted to the corner and turned down P Street.

There, half way up the first block, the tail lights and dim outline of the van. Frank snatched his pistol out of his shoulder holster. It wouldn't be an easy shot, but he could put a round or two through the back of the van . . . and possibly kill an innocent Pepco worker getting in overtime with three kids at home.

Pistol in hand, he chased down P Street after the van, which had now passed 32nd Street and was some fifty yards away. The van's headlights picked up a man in a trench coat. The man was making his way down the brick sidewalk using a cane.

"Dad!"

At the same time, brake lights flashed. Frank heard the van screech to a halt.

Through the headlight beams, a man darted toward the sidewalk and Tom Kearney. He wore dark clothes and a ski mask. Metal glinted in his hand.

Waves of adrenaline flooded every nerve and reflex. The world around Frank slowed, then warped inward on itself. Susan Boukedes . . . Mary Keegan . . . Celeste Foster . . . their images faded, replaced by those of a grinning young paratrooper . . . an old man in a hospital room . . .

Again Frank saw a flash of metal swinging up, then starting down. The masked man and his father, gladiators in a dimly lit arena, too close to each other to risk a shot.

"Dad!"

He ran, his whole body pounding with the beating of his heart. But he knew he was already seconds too late.

In slow motion, he saw Tom Kearney block the thrust with a forearm, saw the blade rise again, saw his father crouch, then thrust his cane upward toward the blade arcing toward his chest.

And suddenly, Frank knelt over his father on the sidewalk.

"Dad!"

"I pinked him." Tom Kearney waved the sword-cane, thirteen inches of Solingen steel courtesy of a now dead SS colonel. "I'm okay!" Tom Kearney shouted. "Get the bastard!"

Behind him, Frank heard the van transmission shift out of neutral. Down the block, some twenty yards away, José was rounding the corner.

Frank looked around. The van began pulling away. Scrambling to his feet, he sprinted, then lunged toward the accelerating vehicle. His left hand found the short ladder on the side of the van that led to the roof rack.

He felt a hot, tearing pain in his shoulder and began losing his grip. Almost without thinking, he dropped the pistol, freeing his right hand to find an adjoining rung, fingertips grazing the rough metal. Willing himself, Frank strained forward.

Fingers, then his hand got a firm grasp.

The van rocketed east on P Street. Frank pulled himself up on the ladder, scrambling to lift his feet onto the lowest rung. Hooking his right arm through a rung, he flattened himself, hugging the passenger side of the van.

In the side-view mirror, Frank caught a glimpse of the ski-masked face, lips pulled back across clenched teeth. Their eyes met.

Hello, Charlie. Hello again.

The violent, looping swerve caught him by surprise. The van veered into the left lane. Like a powerful hand, centrifugal force tried to peel him from the ladder.

Bobbing lights and a blaring horn. An oncoming car weaved frantically right, then left, then right again. At the last second, the driver took to the sidewalk, bouncing over the curb to avoid a head-on with the van.

The four-way stop at 31st swept by. The van swung back into the right lane, headed directly for a row of parked cars. A fraction of a second before impact, the van edged left.

The crash came as a glancing blow. The van's bumper and right side creased the cars with a half-block-long shower of side-view mirrors, door handles, and metal-on-metal sparks. Frank felt his trouser legs catch and tear. Closer, and he'd be hamburger.

Charlie you sonofabitch.

Clutching the ladder with his right hand, Frank angled for a better hold. He got his left hand chest-high. The shoulder refused to work and a wave of liquid pain rolled down his arm, threatening to black him out. His left hand scarcely closed itself around the ladder.

The van hurtled through the traffic light at 30th. Two more blocks, the traffic light at 28th. An Uptown Bakery truck pulled out from the right, completely blocking the intersection.

Frank braced for the collision. Brakes screeched and the van bucketed as it heeled over in a skidding hard right turn. Charlie was steering toward the rear of the truck to avoid a head-on. The van's right rear tire blew out with an explosive gust as it slammed into the curb, clearing the bakery truck by a fraction of an inch. Frank felt the rush of a wall of steel flashing by inches from his face.

Now headed down 28th, hobbled by the blown tire, the van lurched crazily, its bare steel wheel rim ripping huge asphalt chunks out of the street, its rocking getting worse as they passed Dumbarton.

Just past N Street, the front suspension struts exploded in a cloud of hydraulic fluid. The front bumper dropped, hitting the pavement. The rear end, driven by the van's momentum, jackknifed upward, throwing Frank onto a parked car and into the street.

The van, balanced on its crushed front end and now totally perpendicular, paused, then tilted on over, crashing onto its back like a beached turtle.

Stunned, Frank staggered to his feet. He limped unsteadily, around the overturned van. The driver's door hung open. The van was empty. Blood smeared the door handle and pooled on the pavement marked where Charlie had climbed out of the van. More blood several feet away led back toward N Street.

Ignoring the pain in his shoulder, Frank ran to the intersection. N Street here was only a block long, ending at a park. If Charlie got to the park, he could go north or south along the bike path. North would take him into the thicker woods of Rock Creek. South, he'd be headed for the open spaces along the river.

He doesn't have that much of a head start.

On Frank's left, an uninterrupted stretch of row houses ran down N Street toward the park. On his right, a long-empty public school being converted to expensive condos.

N Street was empty. The park beyond was empty.

Charlie, you're around here somewhere.

Frank walked slowly toward the school, checking the street. Halfway down the block, he found it—a small splash of blood, dark and wet on the stone curbing in front of the hulking skeleton of the school.

Pallets of new brick, stacks of concrete block, piles of sand and odds and ends of construction debris surrounded a rough wood ramp leading into the school. Frank heard the sound of sirens in the far distance.

Wait here?

He patted his pockets. No cell phone.

Wait here and Charlie goes out the back.

And your pistol is somewhere up on P Street.

Frank thrust his hand into his right trouser pocket, fingers closing around the pimp's switchblade. The sirens didn't seem any closer.

He took off his jacket and wound it around his left forearm. Reaching back into his pocket, he pulled the switchblade out and pressed the release, the knife kicking in his hand as it flicked open. Walking up the ramp into the school, he stooped to pick up a scrap of PVC pipe about the size of a billy club, wincing with the effort.

Just inside the entry, Frank peered into the darkness.

Where are you, Charlie?

You watching me now?

Sizing me up?

You don't know that I don't have a pistol, do you, Charlie?

But you know you have to get out of here before those sirens close in, don't you, Charlie?

Frank made his way into the school, shoulder brushing the right-hand corridor wall. His jacket-wrapped left arm he held out waist-high, using the length of plastic piping to probe the darkness ahead of him.

His eyes began adjusting. Ahead, some twenty feet, the darker shadows of an intersecting corridor. Further on, slivers of light cut across the floor, angling down through cracks in the boarded-off back entrance.

He held his breath, straining to hear . . . breathing . . . a foot shifting. Nothing.

Nothing . . . yet something.

Something indefinable. Silent yet palpable.

A kind of pressure in the still air.

A presence in the darkness.

You are here, Charlie. I feel you.

And I'm blocking you.

And the picture flashed of the kid with the nose ring and the old man in the yarmulke and green army overcoat bent over their chess game.

Check?

And when it came, it didn't come the way Frank thought it might.

No furtive attempt to slip away in the dark. No sudden rush for the open entry.

Instead, six feet away, a shadow stepped out from the deeper shadows.

Hello, Charlie.

Charlie stood in the center of the corridor, the angled bands of light cutting across his chest. And Frank saw the ski mask and the sword.

Frank moved to his left, out into the corridor. He kept his right hand with the switchblade down by the side of his leg. He waved the silly length of PVC pipe in his left hand, pointing it toward Charlie's waist.

There was procedure: He should announce that he was police, he should tell Charlie to put down the sword. But Charlie wasn't going to put down the sword. And whatever he said—however he said it— would shatter his own concentration. And his concentration on the next fraction of second and the next fraction of second after that was what would get him out of here alive.

This was no longer policing. Or enforcing laws. This was something more basic. More fundamental. Something that existed before police. Before laws.

Frank shifted, turning slightly to his right, keeping his knife hand hidden. At the same time, he angled his left foot so it pointed to Charlie.

Charlie faced him square on. He held the sword in both hands, like a Japanese samurai, the sword point leveled at Frank's gut.

No lunges or thrusts.

Charlie's into chopping tonight.

Frank searched for Charlie's eyes. But all he saw was the dark featureless ski mask. He caught Charlie's first move—a slight back tilt of the head. A split second later, the sword point rose as Charlie swung his hands over his head.

Frank stepped in closer, keeping his left foot forward. He raised the PVC pipe to eye level, slightly to his left. At the same time, he pivoted, shifting his weight to his right foot.

The distracting motion broke the flow of Charlie's downward swing. The heavy blade, deflected by the plastic pipe, missed Frank's left hand by inches.

Before Charlie could recover, Frank smashed his left foot into Charlie's left knee.

Charlie managed to stay up even as his leg partially buckled. He brought the sword around as if he were swinging a baseball bat. The blade made an ominous whirring sound as it cut through the air.

Stepping so close his face almost touched Charlie's, Frank threw his forearm up, blocking the stroke. Despite the padding of his jacket, a bolt of pain shot through his body from his injured shoulder, almost blinding him.

Charlie was now off balance, and his momentum carried him past Frank.

Frank swiveled and plunged the switchblade into Charlie's ribcage, burying it blade-deep under his upraised left arm, then twisted it a quarter turn and wrenched it free.

Charlie gave a surprised, high-pitched sigh. He dropped to his knees, sword still in his hands. For a moment, he seemed to be praying. Then slowly he dropped the sword and crumpled to the floor.

Frank looked at him for a moment, watching for any sign of life. He kicked the sword away and turned Charlie over.

He pulled the ski mask off.

He had found the castle. He had fought the Fisher King and he'd won. And that was a reality that all the computers in the world couldn't create.

"Checkmate, Charlie," Frank said to Ormond Ballinger.

THIRTY-SIX

✛ Frank and José had Ben's Scrapple Breakfast. For $4.95, you got biscuits, two eggs to order, an Everest mound of home fries, and a slice of scrapple the size of an aircraft carrier. Tom Kearney had coffee and the $2.65 BLT.

". . . man was sliding in and out of his craziness," José said, cutting into his scrapple.

Frank and José had cleared Ballinger's body out of the school by midnight. They had spent the rest of the night going through his home. Two miles upriver from the house on Galena Place, it was six thousand square feet of glass, stone, and stainless steel on a bluff near Great Falls.

"And each swing seemed to carry him further into the Fisher King fantasy," Frank said.

Video cassettes bore witness to Ballinger's progressively malignant imagination. Cassettes neatly labeled with mythic names connected to the Grail legend: Galahad, Lancelot, Percival, Merlin, Arthur, Joseph of Arimathea. But the videos themselves were of real people. Ballinger had filmed it all—torture, death, dismemberment. The exquisite care Ballinger had taken to ensure the camera caught each stroke. Bloody work with an armory of medieval weapons—daggers, swords, morning star, battle-ax.

"He was in his forties," José said, "he'd lived in Silicon Valley, Seattle, and Boulder before coming here."

And police departments in California, Washington, and Colorado would be sorting through their files, hoping they could use Ormond Ballinger's trail of death to close cases that had stayed open far too long. Robin Bouchard's people would match the faces from the videos to those in the cold case files.

"FBI's already come up with two possibles in San Francisco," Frank said.

"He used some of his victims as models for his computer games," José said.

"His dress rehearsals," Frank said.

Each of the cassettes had been cross referenced with computer games Ballinger had developed for LORE.COM. The morning star Frank had seen crushing the imaginary giant's head had a counterpart in real-life video: a middle-aged man, tied upright to a stake in the ground, a masked figure swinging the heavy spiked ball . . .

"Reality shifted," Frank said. "What he created on the computer became more real as the world around him became less real. If he could kill on the computer, why couldn't he kill in Rock Creek Park?"

And Ballinger could stalk his victims with impunity. A white male or an Asian female? A couple in their forties? Red hair? Thin? Hunt them down with LORE.COM's subscriber profiles. And if he wanted more detail, use the LORE.COM network to infect subscriber computers with a tracking program.

Something signaled Frank from the back of his mind. He leafed through his notebook until he found the entry from his interview with Kaitlin McKirgan, the expert on medieval literature.

" 'The Fisher King is a man in perpetual torment,' " Frank read. " 'He has a grievous wound that affects his every action, that shapes his very life. And this wound will not heal.' " He put the notebook away. "The wound got worse."

"What now?" Tom Kearney asked.

"Press conference in"—Frank checked his watch—"an hour and a half. Mayor, the chief, Emerson are going to get up and officially mark the cases closed. Tell the citizens they can rest easy."

"And Hollywood's gonna do a slasher movie and LORE.COM is gonna make a zillion dollars off their Grail game," José added.

Tom Kearney pushed the uneaten half of his BLT away, finished his coffee, and left a five on the table for the busboy. He got up and put his hand on his son's shoulder. "You going home with me?" he asked. "Get some sleep?"

✝ At four-thirty that afternoon, Channel Eight rebroadcast Mayor Seth Tompkins's morning press conference. Frank and his father sat in the kitchen to watch, Frank working on his second mug of coffee. He was still groggy. He'd always had trouble sleeping during the day, the pain in his shoulder didn't make it easier.

Tompkins stepped forward to the lectern. Behind him on the stage stood Chief Day and Randolph Emerson. The camera panned the press room. Frank spotted Hugh Worsham in the second row. He pushed his coffee away and stood.

His father gave him a questioning look.

"Oh . . . I don't know." Frank shrugged. He made a vague wave-off gesture toward the TV. "That . . . I suddenly don't give a damn . . . what they're going to say." He got a closed-in feeling. "I don't want to hear it."

He pulled his jacket off the back of his chair.

"Going out?"

"Yeah. Take a walk. Want to go with me?"

Tom Kearney looked at his son for a second or two, then shook his head. "I think it's better you go alone."

Frank was at the front door when his father called him.

"Yes?"

His father came from the kitchen. He put his arm around Frank and kissed him on the cheek. He hadn't done that since Frank was a

kid—their good-bye ritual before Frank set out for school or the play-
ground.

"Love you, son," his father said.

"Love you too, Dad," Frank came back with their countersign.

As he stepped out on the sidewalk, he thought his father had for-
gotten the closer for the three-part ritual. Then, he heard the parental
warning: "And look both ways before you cross the street."

✝ At 30th Street, Frank turned right and walked up the hill to R
Street. Oak Hill Cemetery's gates were still open. He paused, then
continued along R Street. No cemetery today. In Montrose Park, a
handful of dog owners clustered together talking while their dogs
ripped and tore through the park in a noisy but fruitless pursuit of a
squirrel.

Nearing Dumbarton Oaks, he heard a car approaching from his
rear. When the car didn't pass, he stopped at the mansion's drive, as if
looking up at the majestic house. Casually glancing around, he saw that
a dark green Mercedes had pulled over to the curb in front of a house
with a For Sale sign. The afternoon light silhouetted two people sitting
in front.

At Wisconsin Avenue, he started downhill, putting a chill north
wind at his back. He stopped in Olsson's for ten or so minutes. In used
books, he found a first edition of Lartéguy's *The Praetorians*—tight
binding, good dust jacket. He paid and continued down Wisconsin to
the waterfront.

At the river, he walked to Harbour Place, where benches faced a
bend in the Potomac. The river came in from the west, to his right,
under the Art Deco arches of the Key Bridge. To his front, the river ran
on to the south, past the Kennedy Center, beneath the Roosevelt and
Memorial bridges, toward Reagan National. The sky was a deep blue
with scattered mare's-tail clouds; the wind had died, and the afternoon
sun was taking most of the chill out of the air.

He found a bench and opened *The Praetorians.* He'd read Lartéguy's *The Centurions* in Vietnam, but that'd been more than thirty
years and several lifetimes ago. *The Centurions* had been about the dis-
illusionment of the French Army, defeated in Vietnam. *The Praetorians* was the sequel. He'd never had a chance to read it. Maybe now he'd
have the time to find out what had happened to the soldiers he'd met so
long before.

He had gotten through the front material—Lartéguy's dedication,
and the James Joyce epigraph, "History is a nightmare from which I am
trying to awake"—and was reading the opening paragraph:

> Two weeks before being promoted to the rank of major and
> receiving the ribbon of a commander of the Légion d'Hon-
> neur, Captain Philippe Esclavier, of the 10th Colonial Para-
> chute Regiment, handed in his resignation. He was still under
> treatment at the Val-de-Grâce for the wound he had received
> in the—

"Good afternoon, Frank."

Damien Halligan stood off to his left front, several feet away. He
carried an attaché case in his left hand; his right was jammed deep in the
pockets of a dark wool overcoat. Fifty yards away, a dark green Mercedes
had pulled in by the boathouse. Someone sat at the wheel, waiting.

Halligan nodded toward the bench.

"Do you mind?"

Frank closed the book and moved over to give Halligan room.

Halligan sat. He put the attaché case on the ground by his side of
the bench and, hands on his knees, looked downriver toward the Roosevelt and Memorial bridges.

"A beautiful city, this." Halligan sounded like a carefree tourist.

"Better than Long Kesh?"

Halligan smiled. "A very tough school. I'm proud to be an
alumnus."

"You're on the run."

"I got the word the English are asking your government to extra-dite me."

"Any grounds?"

"If the English want you badly enough, there're always grounds."

"Why'd you risk coming here?"

Halligan hoisted the attaché case up and into his lap. "Your friends at the FBI have already been looking for me. Once extra-dition papers are signed, you'll have to cooperate with them. This's the last chance I had to make certain you got this." He patted the attaché case.

"And that's . . ."

"This is Mary's last chapter. The last chapter and the supporting materials. I think you'll find them interesting."

"Why now?"

"What do you mean?"

"I mean, if this's something relevant—"

"I think you'll find it interesting."

"Then why didn't you give it to me before?"

"It was in her safe-deposit box. The box was sealed on her death. Her lawyers sent it to me two days ago. I didn't open it until last night."

"Bottom line?"

Halligan got up. "I'm leaving bottom lines to you. If you'd go after that fellow with just a knife, you'll know what to do with this," he said, gesturing to the attaché case.

✝ Frank settled back in the wing chair. "It's a copy of the last chapter of her book."

The chapter, a manuscript of some thirty pages, lay in the center of David Trevor's desk where Frank had put it.

Trevor, hands folded in his lap, gave no sign of interest. Instead, almost catatonic, he looked steadily at Frank.

"It's interesting reading," Frank said into the silence.

His voice as flat and expressionless as his eyes, Trevor finally spoke. "Why don't you tell me what it says?"

"It says that you plagiarized the article that launched your career."

Trevor showed no emotion. "I suppose there's more."

"Mary Keegan says that the article was actually written by Joseph Pulaski. The two of you were close friends in our embassy in Moscow. Pulaski was killed in an accident. In gathering Pulaski's effects, you came across Pulaski's analysis of the failing Soviet economy. You submitted Pulaski's work for publication under your name."

Pain crossed Trevor's face. He shut his eyes for a moment, then opened them. "She had proof?"

Frank regarded Trevor sadly. "You know she did."

"How so?"

"That's what she came here to see you about on September twentieth. The penciled notation . . . 'See David September twentieth, re: Pulaski analysis.' She confronted you that day, didn't she?"

Trevor's hands came up from his lap and covered his face. He slumped forward, elbows on his desk.

Frank heard the vague sounds of people elsewhere in the house. Wife, three children, Eleanor's bio had said. Trevor had to be thinking about them now. Frank recalled Trevor's wife from the memorial service, coming down the aisle between her husband and Charles Trevor, her father-in-law. And then, unbidden, came the image of Mary Keegan's ruined face and the blood-soaked leaves in the park.

Trevor dropped his hands and sat back in his chair.

"Do you know what it's like . . . to be a prisoner?"

Trevor wasn't talking to him. Not with that trancelike voice. Almost imperceptibly, Frank shook his head.

"That's what it was like . . . all my life . . . a prison. They worshiped my father's greatness . . . they sentenced me to stay inside his shadow all my life. 'You're Charles Trevor's son,' they'd say. 'There goes Charles Trevor's son,' they'd say. I'd meet people, 'He's Charles Trevor's son,' they'd say."

A lifetime of banked anger tightened Trevor's mouth. "It was never David Trevor—*just* David Trevor. It was always David-Trevor-

Charles-Trevor's-Son." Trevor paused. Then, in a child's singsong taunting voice he repeated the name: "David-Trevor-Charles-Trevor's-Son . . . David-Trevor-Charles-Trevor's-Son."

His eyes locked in a thousand-yard stare, Trevor's lips worked silently, and he rocked in a slight metronome motion as though "David-Trevor-Charles-Trevor's-Son" was still beating on inside him.

"And I paid . . . every day I paid." Trevor's voice came so softly Frank had to strain to hear him. "I paid with every door that opened, every handshake, every goddamned smile. I paid because I knew none of it was for me." Trevor's lips trembled. "David-Trevor-Charles-Trevor's-Son," he whispered.

"Then *she* comes here!" Trevor's voice rose. "She comes here . . . she shows me this"—Trevor pounded the manuscript with his fist—"this . . . this *shit!* This *filthy* shit." Eyes bulging, he picked up the manuscript and hurled it backhanded across the library.

Frank watched as pages fluttered and whispered to the floor.

Like a burst soap bubble, the angry and self-pitying Trevor vanished. On stage stepped a buoyant, cheerful Trevor.

"I worked with Joe Pulaski on that analysis, you know," he said brightly.

The sudden transformation ran a chill down Frank's spine.

"As a matter of fact, *I* did most of the work." Trevor paused and looked at Frank as if he wanted—*needed*—Frank to agree. "I *told* her that. I *told* her I could prove it. I asked for time . . ."

Frank sat quietly.

The besieged expression left Trevor's eyes. The metronome started ticking again. He rocked and his face hardened in anger.

"And so you killed her," he said to Trevor in the silence that followed.

Trevor froze. Then a small, snakelike smile played at the corners of his mouth. His eyes shifted off into the distance. "They would have loved it . . . the fall . . . watching me slink off . . . I'd have had no place to hide . . . because of *him.*"

He raised his chin slightly to look past Frank. His expression was that of welcoming someone into the room.

Frank glanced in the same direction. The oil portrait of Charles Trevor stared down from the wall at the two men.

As he turned back, it took Frank a moment to realize that Trevor now held a pistol—a service Colt. And that moment was all it took for Trevor to put the muzzle in his mouth.

✠ Jessica Talbot shifted on the bench, pulling her coat closer around herself. Lafayette Square was practically empty under a slate-gray sky that said that autumn was nearly over and that it would be a cold winter.

"So you were just there at Trevor's house, wrapping up details of the case. Trevor, distraught, lost it and committed suicide." She searched Frank's face. "You really expect that to fly?"

"There's testimony from his wife about depression, pressures at work."

"My bullshit detector's overloading, Lieutenant."

Ten or so feet away, a flock of pigeons grazed, filling the walkway. Frank looked at the bench opposite and wondered where the old man in the yarmulke and the black kid were today. He looked at Talbot. "I'll tell you why it's going to fly. It's going to fly because it's convenient. The mayor closed the case on Boukedes, Keegan, and Foster. Officially, Ballinger did all three. Plus a lot more. The Trevor family's devastated by the suicide. Nobody in Washington's got balls enough to open that case in order to prove David Trevor, deputy secretary of state, son of Charles Trevor, was a murderer."

"And you could prove it?"

"I think so."

Talbot, eyes still locked on Frank's face, didn't say anything. Finally, she nodded and broke eye contact. She dug in her bag and came up with the Zippo and the unfiltered Camels. Lighting up, she drew the smoke deep, held it, then exhaled.

"I don't understand how he worked the timing."

"Trevor?"

"At the restaurant."

"I don't know exactly. I can give you an educated guess."

Talbot nodded.

"A call from David Trevor's number at State came into her house around six-fifteen. We don't know what he said. My guess is he told her something had come up, could they push dinner back to eight, eight-thirty."

Talbot took another deep drag on the cigarette, eyes following the smoke. "She wouldn't bother changing the entry she'd made earlier in her calendar."

"Trevor shows up at the restaurant a few minutes before seven, waits, leaves. He knows there's only one logical route for her to take. He waits in the park . . ."

Talbot shook her head in disbelief.

"Where's truth in all this?"

"Are you talking about truth? Or what you print?"

"What do you mean?"

"Just because you don't print a story doesn't mean truth's been trampled to the ground. Every day, you make decisions about what's going to be in your paper, and what isn't. The truth is that Ormond Ballinger killed a lot of people. Another truth is that David Trevor has paid for what he's done—whatever that was."

"And so justice's been done?"

"It may not have been *done*. But it has *happened*. Not in the courts. Not in your paper. But it's happened." He reached down beside the bench and came up with Damien Halligan's attaché case. He stood and handed it to Talbot.

"What's this?"

"It's Mary Keegan's manuscript. The part about Lamar and John Sheffield. She finished that. It's a good story. And you're a good editor. I thought you might see that it gets told."

Frank left. The pigeons on the walk fluttered and took noisy flight, wheeling and making a dark comma against the gray sky.

XXXXX FINANCE JOURNAL BULLETIN XXXXX

FRI DECEMBER 1, 2000 12:08:39 ET XXXXX

REVIVAL OF DOT COMS?

Norman Jonathan, Chief Executive Officer of LORE.COM, stunned industry financial analysts when he announced today a 27 percent increase in projected earnings over the next year for the embattled Internet company.

More

Jonathan, interviewed today by Tony Snow on Fox News, credited the startling financial upturn to development of a series of interactive computer games. "We're reinventing our-selves," Jonathan said. "There's a tremendous market out there for games of unmatched realism, and we're at the leading edge in providing our customers with what they want and are willing to pay for."

LORE.COM (NASDAQ:LORE) shares closed at $47.23 today, up $9.72 from this morning's opening. . . .

———————————

Last modified 1:37 a.m., Wednesday, June 13, 2001
© 2001 The Lubbock Avalanche-Journal

Boy kills playmate in backyard game

FORT WORTH (AP)—A twelve-year-old Fort Worth boy killed his playmate yesterday in a tragic reenactment of a medieval legend.

The boy, whose name has not been released, struck and killed his eleven-year-old friend with a crudely fashioned club. The club, a baseball bat to which a heavy stone had been tied with a length of rope, crushed the younger child's skull, resulting in instant death.

Friends said that the two had been constant companions and were devoted partners in an online computer game involving knights of the Round Table and their search for the Holy Grail. Authorities today . . .

ABOUT THE AUTHOR

A Murder of Promise follows *A Murder of Honor* as Robert Andrews's second novel of crime, punishment, and politics in the nation's capital. Four previous thrillers drew on his experiences as a Green Beret, a CIA officer and senior liaison with the White House, and a national security advisor to a senior U.S. senator. An expert on intelligence and defense matters, Andrews is the principal Deputy Assistant Secretary of Defense for Special Operations. He and his wife, B.J., live in Washington, D.C.